Denise Crittendon

WHERE IT RAINS IN COLOR

ANGRY
ROBOT

ANGRY ROBOT
An imprint of Watkins Media Ltd

Unit 11, Shepperton House
89 Shepperton Road
London N1 3DF
UK

angryrobotbooks.com
twitter.com/angryrobotbooks
Be Who You Are

An Angry Robot paperback original, 2022

Cover by Morgane Magloire
Edited by Eleanor Teasdale and Gemma Creffield
Map by Glen Wiklins
Set in Meridien

ISBN 978 1 91520 212 3
Ebook ISBN 978 1 91520 213 0

Printed and bound in the United Kingdom by TJ Books Ltd.

9 8 7 6 5 4 3 2 1

To my mother, Nellie Mae Crittendon, the embodiment of inner and outer beauty.

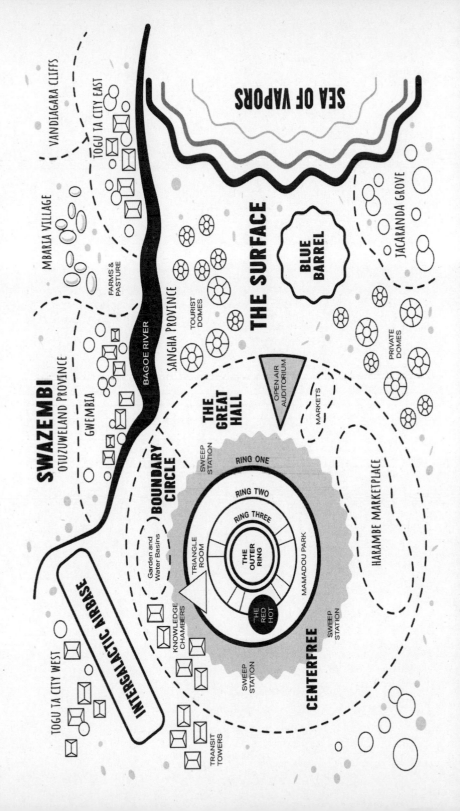

PROLOGUE

She had the witchery of fire in her eyes and her skin twinkled as she traipsed about the village, her ebony arms bare, her face black as a moonless sky. Such skin, it was said, must have had stars rubbed into it. With one breath, Ahonotay could make it flicker. With another, she could enchant anyone who came near.

Elders, overcome by her elegance, insisted that she had been anointed by the ancestors. They proclaimed she possessed the gift of Shimmer – an unnatural glow said to creep through the veins of the darkest of women and flash on and off like fractured light. At their prodding, Ahonotay agreed to leave her rural community for what they called "a more fitting status" in Swazembi's glittering capital city, Boundary Circle.

Unaware of what the elder women had already prophesized, it wasn't long before Ahonotay was lured into an elite cadre of glorious Aspirants and honored with their most prestigious title – the Rare Indigo. But the privilege didn't sit well in Ahonotay's spirit. On the day she was chosen, she fled into the wild mists that floated across the Surface of the planet. Crouched in a grove of jacaranda trees, she hid for nearly an hour. Fretting. She peered through gaps between spindly branches, watching rainbows melt on the horizon like waves on a gentle sea. Wondering what to do, how to proceed.

At a distance, she spotted two minor-children exploring the drifting colors, and in their wandering eyes, she detected mischief.

"Why do we live underground?" one girl asked her friend. "It's so much... *prettier* up here."

1

"It's… it's hypnotic," the friend said. She twirled one of her braids and grinned.

"Yes, that's it!" the second girl shot back. "You're real smart. I wish I could think of things like you."

"No, no. If you're real smart, you have to meet with the Mhondora. He sees things, and hears things, and then you might too. Do you want that to happen?"

"No! Not me! I never want that to happen."

Her friend laughed and swung her hands over her head, swatting at a thick spiral of pink and green flitting through the air.

Ahonotay sat watching amid the lilac flowers of the jacaranda grove, smiling as the girls skipped away. Then came a shrill voice. Without warning, it burst inside of her head, screeching and buzzing, filling it with gibberish.

Task, horrors, Task. Do. We must break. Destroy.

She held her breath against the onslaught, numb to any other sensation, convinced the warm winds had stopped blowing.

Your task your task your task.

"Who is that?" she asked out loud. Her heartbeat quickened.

Tasktasktask

Ahonotay jumped up and dashed out of the grove. "Either tell me who you are now or I'm going to the Sonaguard!" she said.

Task, the voice repeated. *Pick it up. Task. Task.*

Ahonotay waited. The scattered whispers grew louder. She pressed both hands over her ears.

Go. Dome. To the dome. Go.

Trembling, Ahonotay dropped her hands and obeyed, teetering toward a cluster of twenty-five-by-twenty-five-meter domes. Her eyes skirted the brass tiles on the ground and landed on a clump of sand stuck in a crack along the dome's edge.

The sand had hardened and formed a three-inch crust. Ahonotay checked to see if anyone was watching, then following the direction of the invader in her head, yanked on the crust. It didn't budge. Her hands shook as she gathered up red rocks and shattered limestone pieces that were scattered along the periphery of the dome. With a rock in each hand and her fingers still trembling, she chiseled the clump free and dug out a wedge of burlap cloth that was buried inside it.

The cloth was bound tightly and tied in a strip of crumbling ribbon. She tried to steady her hands as she unwrapped it slowly, carefully. Inside was a scrap of crude bark paper that had been rolled into a tiny scroll. She opened it and felt a sudden jolt.

The words *"I loathe you"* were scrawled on the scroll. Ahonotay clenched her fists, afraid to read more. What was this sinister scribble? She inhaled and forced herself to take in the rest of the note, all the while struggling to comprehend what it meant. The ramblings were vile, and she couldn't fathom why she had been led to them. She shoved the scroll into her pocket and ran. The winds were lifting higher, and the abundant rains were turning into deep swarms of color that tenderly caressed her cheeks. She blinked and brushed a flutter of orange away from her eyes. Suddenly, her legs weakened, and she recalled the two playful girls, strutting arm in arm across the sand.

"The Mhondora sees things, and hears things, and then you might too."

The idea made her shiver even more. Had she tapped into something supernatural? Was the scroll a threat? Who could she tell? Certainly not her parents. They would send word to the Mhondora himself, and he was known for his intolerance. What would he think of a Rare Indigo who delivered him such a wicked message? Would he accuse her of being cursed, of spreading evil?

No, she could never reveal her discovery to him. The thought of destroying it popped into her mind, but she feared the consequences. If she got rid of it, would the whispers return? Would they nag her until her death?

Ahonotay resolved never to show the scroll to anyone. She would hide what she'd found and, if need be, deny that she'd ever heard that caustic voice. She would seal it all in her mind. Swear herself to total silence.

Ahonotay didn't say another word for forty-one years.

PART I
Rare Indigo

1

The dance of water had ended. The swirls of purple, the swishes of yellow and green, spilled over Swazembi's upper Sangha province and dissolved into vapors. Lileala wasn't physically there, witnessing the spectacle, but she could feel it, nonetheless. Her intuition always peaked during the summer rains, and she had a way of sensing their patterns, the way they swarmed, swelled and spiraled.

When the rains finished, she knew. She saw the signs. Above her in The Outer Ring, the planet's tourist center, the jacaranda trees unfolded, and scraps of violet petals trickled through the air shafts into the underground city of Boundary Circle. The petals were strewn along the private outdoor track where Lileala was stretching and running. The sparse petals were a distraction, disturbing her focus as she ran past. She hadn't seen the Surface since she was an elder-child of twenty-six, but she could recall it clear as water; the flowers thrusting into the warm winds, the tree branches whipped into a long frenzy.

She slowed her pace to a trot and thought hard about stealing a glimpse. If only she could come up with a way to sneak out. She glanced over her shoulder, then searched both ends of the track. There was no trace of her trainer. Good.

Slipping a finger through the small, glowing halo above

her wrist, she whispered, "Otto? Otto, are you there? Otto?"

The halo shimmied in rapid circles, but it didn't produce an image, not even a foggy one.

She hurried past the five-kilometer marker.

"Otto," she whispered again. "I'm on track level Y, but I'm sneaking off. Be there in a few minutes."

Lileala darted toward the end of the track, ignoring the colors that suddenly began flickering beneath her feet. The colors chased her, brushing against her shoes the way water folds around the heels of a swimmer. The faster she moved, the faster they came. They raced up her shoelaces, then billowed and foamed just above her ankles.

"That's it, I give up," she said, sighing. She wanted to laugh, and maybe she would have, if the situation hadn't been so annoying.

"Okay!" she yelled out again. "Baba Malik, I know you can hear me! The Drifts. Call off the drifting colors, will you? Please?"

The colors withered. Then Malik turned the corner wearing the expression he always did when he accused her of being lazy. "Lileala Walata Sundiata! I take one short break and you're giving up already? You've been training for a mere thirty minutes."

"Is it your dial?" Lileala asked, scanning his wrist. "Is that how you knew?"

"No, Miss Rare Indigo." He pointed to a clear cord that was clamped to his collar and draped over his left shoulder. Colors were fluttering from a rear opening of the device and onto the floor of the track. "I had this made just for sly ones like you. If the heart rate slows or you get too far out of my range, it syncs with the Sea of Vapors. Then –" he made a sucking noise, "– swish! It suctions drifts right out of the Surface."

Disgust disguised itself as a smile on Lileala's face, but she knew it lacked the sweetness of her real smile. It felt rigid, and the dimples that normally pinched her cheeks were absent.

"Clever. But I don't like that thing; it's tacky." She wiped her hands on the sides of her leggings and ran them through the coils of her hair. They spilled around her temples in scattered clusters. "How does it work, anyway? What is it? I mean, what's it called?"

Malik gave her another disapproving glance. "Doesn't matter. If you'd stop slipping off, I wouldn't need it. Honestly, I didn't have these problems with your predecessor."

"That's not what I heard."

"What?"

"Nothing."

"I heard you," Malik scoffed. "And just so you know, Ahonotay may have been silent, but she was not uncooperative."

"But Ataba Malik, I'm tired of exercising. And I need to see someone."

"Is that so?" he asked. "Rushing off to see Otto again?"

"Is it okay?"

"Sure, if you want to contend with this!" Malik waved his fingers around his device and laughed as skinny streaks of red drizzled down his back and formed webs around Lileala's feet.

"Ataba!" she yelled. "Stop doing that!"

"Just having a little fun with you." He sighed, "Go on then, but be back in Point Two Hours; and if you're not, you're going to run even harder."

"Okay, okay." Lileala glanced at her dial. The halo in the center of the dial device was spiraling and taking on the outline of a face. "Otto, finally. I'm leaving, but I'm stopping by The Ring first. Be there shortly."

"What?" Otto whispered. "Lileala, it's midday. You can't –"

With a shake of her wrist, he vanished. Lileala concentrated and blocked out his attempts to reappear. She wanted to stroll through The Outer Ring on her way to see him. If she didn't avoid him, he'd try to talk her out of it. Diving into her satchel, she pulled out a string of amber beads and a yard of patterned cloth that she wrapped around her lower body. Her fitted leg liners weren't suitable for public appearance, but the woven textile would hide them.

After tying a knot at her waist, she tossed the beads around her hips and bolted down the track, her pulse skipping. She could almost see the Surface, the fresh storm of colors spreading before her in a bouquet of drifts and hills.

At the exit, a limestone path forked east and west. Lileala headed west, took a lift to the nearest Sweep Station and hurried. Passengers were in line on a platform facing a vast span of airspace and were already preparing to board. She panted and ran. But just as she stepped onto the ramp of the platform, a cloud of energy funneled upwards and sped off. She had missed the Point Two Sweep.

"No, no!" she shouted, despite knowing that no one was there to hear her or care. She sulked and continued up the sixteen-meter ramp to the boarding area. The station was more of an atrium, open-roofed with iridescent floors and high walls shrouded in green ivy. In contrast, a fusion of cranberry and yellow stones brightened the ramp and all four platforms.

Rather than take a seat, Lileala stood near the edge and leaned against a steel railing. Out of habit, she yanked a palm-sized mirror from her satchel and toyed with the tight coils of her hair, watching as each strand pooled into a teeny loop and bounced back in place. She loved her hair's buoyancy, though it was her complexion that was most celebrated. It was the height of Indigo: a shimmering blue-blackness that Indigo Host, Mama Xhosi, described as coal kissed by the sun.

Lileala looked skyward, wondering how long she'd have to wait. She inched away from the railing and paced, hands on her hips. A family of locals joined her, but the man, woman and minor-child were so busy fussing over an infant curled in the woman's arm, it took a few minutes for them to glance at Lileala and gasp. She heard the woman whisper, "Is that her? Is it really her?"

Mirror in hand, Lileala checked her appearance again and flashed the family a smile. Their adoration reminded her that before long she'd be an actual showpiece. At her Eclipse Ceremony, set to happen in just three months, she would be ushered into The Nobility's palatial headquarters, The Grand Rising, and declared the first Rare Indigo in four decades. She would be the only woman in Boundary Circle's cloistered society allowed to escort visiting dignitaries on guided tours, and she would stand beside The Nobility during their bi-annual speeches or when they attended interplanetary functions within The Outer Rings. She would be the ultimate idol. One of Swazembi's main attractions.

While Lileala was still doting on herself, The Sweep barreled into the station. Raising both arms, she surrendered to the suction of the cloud, letting it pull her inside. The family followed and along with Lileala settled in a short distance from three female passengers who were already on board. One was local, swaddled in a body wrap of gold fabric. The others were dressed tourist-style in body-hugging trousers that no local woman would ever consider wearing.

Lileala always considered their undignified attire strange, but deep down she admired it, just because it was disrespectful. She wondered what it would feel like to be as free of oaths and codes as they were. The two tourists floated upright, wobbling and giggling, and she tried to guess where they originated – from Jemti? No. Not with faces the color of clouds and chins that narrowed to a sharp point. Lileala figured them to be residents of Toth, Swazembi's ally world.

Positioning herself flat on her belly, she allowed The Sweep's magnetic winds to propel her forward. Sweep energy was like a friendly storm swooshing through an invisible tunnel, just below the upper circumference of the underground. Lileala swam through the moving currents until she was adjacent to the Swazembian woman who lay flat just like her while the force transported them to the next station. They arrived at an atrium and The Sweep dipped without jerking and deposited all of the passengers on a platform ramp just above The Outer Ring.

At the end of the ramp, everyone but Lileala boarded a moving skywalk and rode it down to Ring Two, Concourse

B30. Lileala stopped at the entrance to the concourse and tried to unlock her stubborn lips. The best she could do was a half-smile. She was still aggravated about Baba Malik's peculiar device and had to fight to stomp it out of her mind. That was the only way she'd be able to summon a hint of Shimmer.

She pushed air through one nostril, releasing gently. After the second breath, she wore wisps of pale light, almost imperceptible. The very first stage of Shimmer. A tourist was loitering and staring at her. She was obliged to act cheerful and demonstrate a shine, however frail. "Waves of joy," she said, letting a full smile replace the half one.

"My stars, you're lovely," the man answered. He was stout, dressed in rumpled trousers and a crude, rubbery jacket made of animal skin, probably a relic from Earth.

"Thank you," she said and gave him a gracious nod. The man continued, "Are all the women of Swazembi like you?"

"All of us are dark, if that's what you mean?"

He gawked and extended a hand. "Dalton, from West Neptune. My first time here. It took a while for me to finally get acceptance stamps." He bared both wrists to reveal two glowing green lines, then he gazed over her head and down a busy aisle of pedestrians. "I just love it here."

"Grace to you," Lileala said, fake smile still in place. She wished he would hurry up and be on his way.

"And, bless the stars, you have the best music chips here too. I understand all of it's from Earth," he went on. "Too bad, don't you think, that those people were so reckless."

"Yes, too bad," Lileala shrugged. She wasn't nearly as intrigued by Earth history as the tourists were. She always wondered why some locals believed that Earth was part of Swazembian history. She found the idea ridiculous.

Dalton kept rambling: "It's been thousands of years, and no one's been able to figure out how they destroyed themselves. Sometimes, I think there might be clues in the music. What do you think?"

"I don't know," Lileala said. "Maybe you should visit the tourist knowledge haven. It has information about the whole galaxy." She took a slow sidestep toward the concourse.

"But listen," Dalton stood in place. "I hear your people are planning more visits to Earth's ruins and are digging up more music. Do you get to go?"

"No. Never been." Lileala answered in a tone that no longer hid her lack of interest. She was fighting the urge to reach for her compact and check the tidiness of the scarlet paint she had smeared onto her lips.

Dalton's eyes were a blizzard of questions. Lileala could see them examining her and she noted that at least he was careful not to intrude her personal space.

"I think I saw a report on the viewerstream about ladies who glitter like you," he said. "You're one of those Indigo Aspirants, aren't you?"

"I'm no longer an Aspirant. I'm the Rare Indigo."

He stared.

"But, well, I guess I misunderstood. Doesn't the Rare One have to be at least fifty?"

"I am. We live till we're nearly five hundred here."

For a moment, Dalton didn't react.

"Um, you look n-nineteen, miss," he stuttered. He walked away wagging his head.

The Outer Ring was a jumble of chatter and the wails of reconstructed Earth horns. Lileala flowed with the melody and waded into the crowd nearly unnoticed. Most of the tourists were distracted by the gliding crystal floors they were riding on and by gift havens that hung from the ceiling in ten-foot glass globes. The globes were stationary boutiques among a banquet of jewels that shimmied, flickered and opened and closed like hundreds of sparkling eyes. Gusts of pink sugar swarmed from the windows of confection stores. Rock songs blasted from octagon dance havens.

Oval hotels, encrusted with amber and opal, spun in place like stranded planets. Tourists looked up, then down, their heads twisting, their senses competing to take it all in.

Lileala scuttled past them all and entered one of the smaller, slower-moving orbs for a twist of sweet cassava and a few chunks of hard molasses. Right away, she flinched. The interior of the confection haven wasn't misted with colored sugar like most and, judging from the empty shelves, the majority of the inventory had been cleared out long ago. She approached the counter that was being tended by a man with a bewildered stare. He might have been handsome, she thought, if not for the confusion on his face.

"You are the rare girl, no?" the merchant said. It sounded more like an accusation than a question.

"Yes, I am," she said. She looked around and nodded. The haven was plain, but one showcase near the counter was packed with cocoa-sprinkled pine nuts. She stepped beside it and peeked inside.

"I recognized you soon as you walked in," the merchant continued. "But I don't understand. Rare One, why are you here?"

"For this," Lileala pointed to a square of molasses next to the pine nuts. "And for..."

He spoke over her. "That is not for sale. Not to you."

"What? Did you say...?"

"I said no sale," he said. "The sweets cannot go to you."

"Pardon me?" Her voice shook.

"I know who you are, and I have made my decision," he said.

In defiance, Lileala showed him a sheer marble the width of a thumbnail. The marbles in her allotment were larger than most, fashioned from pure, sand-blown glass and laced with colors from the Surface, colors that were fresh and still in motion.

"There's no need to offer payment," he said. He flattened the palms of his hands on the glass countertop.

To calm herself, Lileala bit down on her lip and glared. He watched her with an equal amount of indignation.

"I'm told that as the Rare Indigo you are not to have sweets," he said after a pause. "Be on your way."

"No," Lileala said. She held up her marble and waited. "I would like four chunks of molasses, please. I'm not leaving without them."

The merchant scowled. Reaching for a gauze sack from beneath the counter, he filled it so fast a couple of pieces toppled onto the floor.

"Here, take it." He thrust the sack in front of her. "And keep your payment."

She fiddled with the marble and shoved it at him. "You can't tell me what to do."

"Young one, you are not yet official," he said. "I suggest humility."

"I suggest you leave me alone," Lileala said in between breaths. She was trying to maintain her glow and add more firmness to her voice. "I'll complete my Eclipse ceremony three months from now. Until then, I don't have to stick to restrictions. And I don't have to listen to you."

A group of tourists wandered into the haven and the man fell silent while Lileala dropped the marble on the counter and moved back, her smile gone.

The merchant looked her directly in the eye. "I meant no harm, but you must be mindful. You are the first Rare One in a long while. That means you…"

"That means I listen only to The Nobility and to The Uluri," Lileala said, then breathed deep. Dim twinkles seeped from the pores of her skin then flit across her forehead. She pulled in her ribcage and the twinkles became a soft blue spritz.

"I'm the Rare Indigo, yes," she added. "But I'm still a person."

The merchant said nothing, and she knew she had made her point. She snatched her sweets and hurried off.

Outside the haven, his insults clung like tar. Was he

suggesting that she had dishonored The Grace of the Ancestors? With what? A sack of molasses? Lileala bristled. She knew it was unorthodox for a Rare Indigo to yield to useless desire, particularly for a thing so common among the villagers. But The Nobility had not granted merchants the right to chastise her. Had they?

While the merchant gawked through the window, Lileala tucked a music chip in her ear and poured herself back into the highway of pedestrians. They swept around then past her, moving like a single organism. She shuffled through them, again unnoticed. Onlookers were drawn by the noisy aroma of spiced chickpeas, the knit caps with "The Sweep" emblazoned on the front, and stretchy shirts labeled "EarthWear".

Content, she moved on, undisturbed, and took an automated walkway to a spot that offered a panoramic view of the grounds below. At a drop of one hundred and twenty meters was Mamadou Park, the only region in The Outer Ring with enough gum trees to make up a small forest. Lulled by the view, Lileala lingered. The guard rails around the area were sturdy, easy to prop her back against while she peeked at her dial. She'd wasted too much time in the confection haven, she knew she needed to get moving. She didn't care. At the moment, she wanted to do what she felt like doing. And she felt like lounging in the park overlook before visiting Otto.

2

*"Your mind should always sync with the proper channeling of mela-
nin and the drapery of Shimmer. Anything else is a predator thought.
Eradicate it immediately."*
— Indigo Aspirant Code A, Provision Xiiz

Lileala lazed around much longer than she should have. After
taking in one last whiff of the bitter fragrance of the gum leaf
trees below, she decided to take the scenic route through the
park to Otto's.

The Sonaguard stationed nearby stopped her. "Lileala? Are
you allowed to be out and about at this hour?"

"Waves of joy," she said, trying to sound upbeat. "It's okay.
I'm no longer an Aspirant."

"I know you're the Rare Indigo, but you're not permitted to
wander either. Sorry. I can't let you pass."

"Come on. Please." She smiled at him shyly. "I'm not trying
to be pushy, but I am in sort of a hurry."

He tightened his shoulders and Lileala had the brief thought
of inhaling through her nose and going from a quiet shine
to a heightened Shimmer. Before taking the first breath,
she changed her mind. It was wrong to exploit her Aspirant
training. She doubted she could persuade him anyway, even in
the advanced glow of Shimmer. The young man was standing
as if his silver uniform was made of armor. Clearly, he was far
too disciplined to respond to charms.

"I'm just doing my job," he said. "And I'm not supposed to let any of the Aspirants gallivant around The Ring in the middle of the day."

"Oh, but I've been excused," Lileala explained. "I just left the track a few minutes ago and came up here for a quick break. You can check with my trainer, Ataba Malik. He gave me permission to visit Aswaka."

"You know Aswaka is the other direction." The Sonaguard pointed to a lift to his right. Then he stuck out his hand to stop a wandering traveler who tried to come close.

"That leads to Boundary Circle. Only locals are allowed."

The man staggered closer. "Special treatment," he sneered.

"She's Swazembian," the Sonaguard snapped. "She lives in Boundary Circle."

He directed Lileala to move on. "Ignore him. I've been dealing with this pest all day." He shook his head. "I can't wait for tourist season to end."

The man brandished his fist while swerving back and forth, making a clumsy attempt to walk.

"He's under the influence," Lileala said to the guard. "They must be making that Mirth ale more potent." She stirred her index finger above her wrist and waited for the time to appear. It was Point Three. "Listen," she added. "I'm thinking of taking a different route. Through Mamadou Park, maybe?"

He held up his hand to block her. "I already told you. Not allowed."

A slow heat warmed Lileala's face. "It's on the First Ring. That's considered part of Boundary Circle."

"But tourists have access to the south side of that ring," he said. "My afternoon instructions are to deny Aspirants access to the park and all three rings. That includes Ring One."

"Okay, fine," Lileala blurted. She hurried off, not wanting to hear another word about restrictions, about what Rare Indigos could and couldn't do. An aisle of lifts was up ahead, and one already was waiting. She took it down to a network of corridors that streamed into Boundary Circle's Great Hall. Someone, Lileala wasn't sure who, shouted hello as she passed. She did a quick wave and rounded the corner toward the lavish dwellings of the Aswaka Community. Aswaka was a generous spread of oblong towers and two-story homes shaped like baubles and spheres. She stopped in front of one that was green and black and glowing.

"Otto," she said aloud into her halo. "I'm here."

"Here? Why, yes you are. Lileala, my dearest Lileala."

Lileala whipped around and faced a lanky woman with a copper complexion and tufts of unruly bangs. Wooly locks tumbled down her back.

"Zizi! You're home!" Lileala squealed with joy.

"Why are you so surprised? Otuzuweland's not that far away."

They hugged. "Those two years seemed like ten," Lileala said. "When did you get back?"

"Couple of days ago," Zizi said. "Haven't even found my own sphere yet. I'm here in Aswaka with my forebears. And you?"

"With my elder Ma and Baba where we've always been," Lileala answered. "Still down on Mampong Ave."

Zizi nodded. "I never understood why someone as important as Baba Kwesi lives on Mampong. I mean he's Scientific Pineal Crew chief."

"I know, strange huh?" Lileala said. "But he says it's nice enough. Anyway, I'm here to see Otto."

"Otto? The Otto next door to me?"

"Yes, that Otto," Lileala replied, taken aback. "Don't act so surprised. He'll be my devoted in a few months."

"You and Otto are getting joined?" Zizi faked a cough. "Never imagined the two of you."

"Why?" Lileala rolled her eyes. "We were always friendly."

"Friends, yes, but devoteds? Isn't he kind of serious for you?"

"Zizi Anwi Mdonzo! What does that mean?"

"You're reckless and you know that. You act quiet sometimes, but you can't trick me. On the inside, you're as wild as a runaway Sweep."

Lileala laughed. A billowing Sweep cloud had lost its way one time and run amok. Frightened tourists were spinning in a loop for three and a half hours before Sonaguards were able to rescue them. She and Zizi were only thirteen years-old then, still in minor school, but since they had been among the few who actually witnessed it, they had made it their private joke.

"Not that chaos!" Lileala squealed. "I'm never going to forget that."

Zizi chuckled. "No more adventures like that for you, not if you're getting joined. And no more sneaking to The Ring, either."

"For Grace's sake," Lileala protested. "I haven't been in a night dance haven in so long it's not even worth bringing up."

"You're forbidden, that's why," Zizi said.

"And you're a tease," Lileala said. She checked her mirror and glanced over her shoulder. Otto was walking toward the ladies, whistling.

"Come on, join us for a cup of fig tea?" Lileala asked. "Otto has some fresh from Togu Ta City."

"No, no. I'll move along. Waves, Otto!" Zizi nodded and walked off just as he sidled up next to Lileala. He was out of uniform, dressed in an oversized sweater and trousers with sloppy creases. A light smattering of freckles dotted his long, boyishly handsome face.

"Hi, my love," he said. He hugged Lileala with one arm. In his other, he held a metal disc that was chunky and about a meter thick. "Let's take our tea near the garden."

At the end of the nearest passageway was a crystal path that cut through Aswaka and winded through the Mampong neighborhood. They followed the path to a stone oasis that had nothing but wide basins filled with clear water. Otto led

Lileala to the rim of one basin flanked by a tangle of plants with awkward limbs. They were leafless and as transparent as the water. Tiny silver beads flowed through the plants' clear veins.

Still clutching the disc, Otto began to unfold it. He rattled it hard until it sprouted legs and turned into a stand. While Lileala settled on an iron bench facing the oasis, a decanter and cups popped up from a portal in its center. He reached for the decanter, and she stroked the fuzz around his chin.

"Perfect look for a Pineal officer, don't you think?" He smirked. "The crew was supposed to give The Nobility an update on the Earth excavations today, but the meeting was cancelled, and we took a leave. So, I figured why bother with razors."

"A leave? I'm jealous." Lileala's tone dripped with sarcasm. "What did you do with your free time?"

Otto poured himself a cup of tea and waited for it to cool. "Mamadou Park. I didn't mention it because I knew you couldn't join me."

"My devoted, The Eclipse isn't happening for months. I could've figured out a way to be there."

"Don't you always," he laughed.

"Well," Lileala hesitated, "this time I... um... used you as my excuse. I'm going to sneak to the Surface, and don't try to talk me out of it."

"What are you saying? When?"

"Now." Her head dropped.

"And keep Ataba Malik waiting?"

Lileala clutched her thumb and let it go before Otto noticed her nervous habit. "Are you more worried about Malik than me?" she asked. "I'm the one in prison."

"My love, it's called training," he said.

"It's all the time, that's what it is," Lileala whined. "Why do I have to stay in Boundary Circle so much while everyone else goes off to do whatever they want?"

"Put in for a respite or something," Otto's voice was brittle. "But don't go getting in trouble with Mama Xhosi. Or The Uluri."

"You mean The Nobility."

"It's the other way around," Otto said, softening his tone. "The Nobility only get final say. You know that. But they rely on the judgement of The Uluri." Otto sighed and Lileala kept talking.

"Otto, you're teasing, right? I probably know more about The Nobility than anyone, and The Uluri too, all thirteen of them. But we're talking about Ataba Malik, not The Uluri. I need you to cover for me. Tell Ataba I was feeling faint and went home to rest."

"Come on," Otto said. "You know I can't do that."

Her shoulders drooped and Otto knelt next to her and pulled her to his chest. "Listen to me. You have to stop disobeying your oath. Just ask for a break."

Lileala fell silent and fumbled in her satchel for the molasses. She took a delicate bite.

"So," she said. "If I get this respite, are you coming with me?"

"I can't. The Pineal Crew has another big Earth excavation, and then there's the Coalition Summit on Toth."

"Light stealer," she quipped, smothering a laugh.

Otto responded with a peck on her cheek.

"Never mind," Lileala said. She gulped down her tea and smoothed both hands over the beads around her hips. "Zizi's just back from Otuzuweland. She should be able to go."

Another kiss and a quick squeeze from Otto, and she was circling the water basins alone. Her wrist tingled again, and she shook it vigorously. Ataba Malik was trying to force his way onto her dial, and she had to focus really hard to block his signal. She knew she was in trouble. Again. Mama Xhosi had already given her a stern warning. Would Malik tell Mama Xhosi about today, that she left and stayed too long?

It was Point Four exactly. The evening light pods were already hovering, casting a glow onto triple tier fruit stands and lanes of garment havens, all crammed with textiles so bright they seemed to be shouting. While the pods roved from one side of the cavernous hall to another, a soft haze of purple and orange from the Surface poured through open spaces in the ceiling. Lileala wrestled again with the idea of sneaking a glimpse. But the central location of The Great Hall meant she'd have to take a lift that was due west of the headquarters and dwelling spheres of The Uluri and The Nobility.

Although locals would recognize The Nobility anywhere, The Uluri operated in secret. Their nosiness was one of Lileala's biggest frustrations. Whoever they were, they were nearly always poking about, and she despised them for it. They avoided appearances on the viewerstream so they could fit in and observe the behavior of Circle residents. Their edicts and their annoying, self-righteous principles were constant shadows. Still, she figured there was a chance they might not spot her sneaking onto the western rim lift if she was lucky...

One quick check in her mirror and Lileala was boarding another Sweep. She found a cozy corner spot and stretched out, letting her arms and legs dance in the currents. Torrents of wind sailed around her shoulders, and she turned her face to the left, giving her a full view of The Outer Ring's wildest night haven – The Red Hot on Ring Two.

The Sweep stopped abruptly and dumped her at the next station, Concourse B30, leaving her confused. The currents followed gestures and strong movements. A heavy lean forward was an indication the rider was ready to disembark. She hadn't done that, at least not deliberately. Or maybe she had? As she oozed out of the clouds, Lileala giggled at the notion. She couldn't believe she was back on the Ring. Feeling freer than she'd felt all day, she practically skipped through the concourse.

A popular Earth hymn was playing somewhere, and she could hear a stampede of dancing feet.

"Ya'll gonna make me lose my mind."

Lileala followed the music past a shining lane of gift havens and toward the night danceries. They were in orbit faster than she remembered, and something she couldn't explain made her want to steal a peek inside. She was no more than a couple hundred meters away. Who would know?

The floor slid along, and with each glide she was hit with chatter, laughter, howls. Before reaching the vicinity of The Red Hot, she had a strange premonition and thought she saw glints of a silver uniform. Was a Sonaguard nearby? How many Ring guards were stationed near the dance havens? She wondered if she should leave. Maybe they were everywhere and all of them had been given specific orders to zero in on her? She mustered up the confidence to move forward anyway. So what if a guard was around. She could handle him.

The Sonaguard who had redirected her earlier was off duty. In his place was a silver-haired man with a muted, walnut-brown skin tone. He glanced at Lileala and grinned. She grinned back slyly. This one wasn't nearly as disciplined.

"You look so strong," she said in a soft, coy voice. Then she took a slow breath.

He stared, captivated while she took another breath, then another.

At the end of her breath cycle, Lileala had bloomed from an intense black to a glossy midnight swathed in intermittent speckles of blue. Her skin winked and bled a field of soft starlight. It was as if the light was pulsating. Alive.

"Rare Indigo?" the guard gushed.

"Yes," Lileala said. "Are there others around? Other guards on duty?"

"Two or three, but not here on Ring Two," he said. "They'll only come here if I summon them."

"Good, that's so good." Lileala beamed. "Listen, I'm touring The Ring. Please give me your promise that you won't alert the others."

He nodded yes, but seemed unable to say much more.

"If need be, send them signals to go elsewhere, please?" Lileala said.

Again, another nod.

Leaving the guard in a stupor, Lileala dashed off, feeling guilty but pleased that her ploy had worked. He was too dazed to report her or care. Lileala headed straight to the Red Hot. The shiny lane ahead was a Silverstone gray slate that meandered past the skywalk overlooking Mamadou park. At the intersection between the skywalk and the concourses, she followed the path that flowed toward a big twirling ruby. Fierce beats greeted her. The thrums of a sweet, ancient melody. In between the beats, the dance haven slowed its orbit just enough for Lileala to bounce up an incline and through the crescent entrance. The music wrapped around her, making her lightheaded.

"Up in here. Up in here."

Lileala swooned into the rhythm and prepared to swing herself onto a dance aisle that zigzagged down the center of the haven. But her feet didn't sync with it. They were heavy and the moving walls were triggering a wooziness she'd never experienced. The purple ceiling pumped up and down, and the scarlet floor looked bloody. The hazy outline of someone she could barely see bounded through the darkness and reached for her hand.

Lileala recoiled. The stranger reeked of Mirth, and she couldn't understand his garbled speech. A fuzzy embarrassment swaggered around her brain, making her feel sick. Was this guilt?

She held her stomach and reversed her steps. She wasn't mad at the tourist. She was mad at herself. Just because that Sonaguard was foolish was no reason to take advantage of him. Shame gripped her and kicked down the wall that had been blocking her common sense. She clasped the corner of her thumb and tugged harder than ever. Without looking back, Lileala ran out of the haven and down the automatic walkway. She didn't stop until she was on her way back to the track.

3

"There is a magical zing to Shimmer. At its height, it can skim light from flames and leave observers spellbound. Do not abuse this talent. Shimmer misuse is an abomination. Violaters will be suspended."
– Indigo Aspirant Code B, Provision Xiipm

By the time she reached the track, Malik was standing near the entrance with his arms looped together and pressed firmly against his chest. A bright field of vapors circulated beneath his feet. They lunged at Lileala's ankles and shot up her calves. She jumped and tried brushing them away, but the more she struggled, the more aggressively they attacked.

Malik watched. "You address me as Ataba and yet you disrespect my rules," he said.

"Sorry, Ataba."

"Too late!" He snapped his fingers. "I'm calling off the neon pests, but I'm adding an extra two hours of stretching."

"Nooo! Ataba, two whole hours!" Lileala shrieked.

"Two hours late. Two hours of added training."

"But Ataba..."

He frowned. "You do realize, don't you, that you're making me work longer too?"

Lileala moved closer to him, thinking he resembled a stone statue that had taken years to chisel. His jaw was an inverted pyramid, and he had the toned physique of a dancer.

While the colors evaporated, she tried to charm him with

trinity breath – she pulled air through her nose for three seconds and envisioned a flame until she felt a soft sting ripple through her cheeks. Within ten seconds, her skin was in hyper glow, and she had gone into full-blown Shimmer.

"Exploitation of Shimmer talents is one of the worst violations of the Indigo Aspirant Code," Malik said, indignant. "You know this."

"I'm sorry." Lileala looked away, embarrassed. Though she and other Aspirants sometimes broke the rules and got away with it, he was right. Shimmer abuse was a serious offense. While the sparks subsided, she hung her head. "I'm sorry, Ataba. But I'm always in the knowledge chamber or I'm wave dancing or I'm on one of these tracks."

"I don't feel your pain, only my own pain right now," Malik countered. "Now get to work, so we can finish before it gets too dark."

Lileala's thumb ached from all of her pulling and squeezing. Her upper lip trembled. "Ataba Malik, I'm not a minor-child. All day everyone's been treating me like one just because I want a little freedom."

"For Grace's sake," Malik said. "What about me? Don't you think I'm tired too?"

"Ataba, I'm not tired. I'm *exhausted*. I have refinement sessions, melanin upkeep, stretch and run discipline, dance rehearsals, Shimmer practice. It's on and on with no break."

Malik softened. "Mercy of the Grace," he said. "I understand. You feel like a captive. But it takes work to be the Rare Indigo. You knew that when you started."

"I was only twenty-two, just an elder-child."

"The perfect age." He smiled. "That makes this your life, Rare One. Your whole life."

"But I'm so weary, Ataba. It was okay when I first started. I could still go places. But the Aspirant training feels like a locked cage."

"This was your choice," he said.

"More my elder Ma's, and Mama Xhosi. She handpicked me. What was I supposed to say?"

Malik held no expression. "What do you want me to do?"

"Waves of nothing." She sulked.

"Young one, I asked you, what do you want me to do?" Malik repeated.

"You don't want to hear it."

"Try me."

Lileala perked up. "The Surface. I want to go there more than anything! Just for three days. For one day. For one hour. Can I? Please."

His face was grim.

"Ataba?"

"I'm thinking, I'm thinking." He relaxed his arms and sighed. "It's just that you're going to be the first Rare Indigo in years who actually speaks and –"

Lileala gasped.

"What was that about?" He tensed up and pulled his arms back to his chest.

"I'm amused, that's all. You've never told me I can do something that Ahonotay couldn't do."

"Come on, Lileala. I wasn't making a comparison. I was proud of her, and I'm proud of you. But her muteness, that was tough on everyone. No one, not even the Mhondora, could figure out what caused it or why she moved away so soon after her reign began. I hear she's living all alone in a village now, somewhere in Otuzuweland."

"Doesn't sound like she was such a model-Aspirant to me," Lileala said.

"Be nice. I'm just trying to make a point that we haven't had a sitting Rare Indigo in decades. We waited far too long, thinking she'd return. But she didn't and now we're under pressure, I guess. There's a lot resting on you."

"I know. But it bothers me. Day after day after day…"

"And what about your skin?" he asked. "Up on the Surface,

you're going to have to protect it. The color drifts help trigger melanin healing properties, but they still tend to dull the skin."

"I know," Lileala answered. "I'll sprinkle Euc powders on my face and I'll make sure not to walk through the drifts for more than thirty minutes at a time. I'll do anything!"

"My, my. Waves, listen to you." Malik smiled. "I had no idea you knew so much."

"Indigo training isn't all I do. I'm in the knowledge chamber four times a week, just like all the regular students. I know the radiation from the colors on the Surface make it unlivable. And that the color drifts can either regenerate your limbs or leave you scorched."

"And you still want to go?"

"With all my heart. Please. Please."

"I'll tell you what," he said. "I'll talk to Mama Xhosi. She's been asking about you anyway. Thinks you're getting restless. But..." He stroked his chin. "I'll go easy on you. I won't tell her about today. I'll just see if she can get you some time off."

"Really, Ataba? Do you think she'll listen?"

"I'll check with her early tomorrow morning while she's fresh. I'll let you know as soon as I get an answer," he said.

A surprise grimace registered on Ataba Malik's face, almost as if he had overstepped his authority. Immediately, he shut up, and Lileala feared he had changed his mind. Instead, he gave her a swift nod.

"You're lucky, you know that. Mama Xhosi's manual has a respite code. I'm sure you know it, too. It states that while we discuss you, you are to be free that morning, free to do what you want. Do you hear me?" He chuckled.

Lileala frowned.

"My dear young one," he clarified, "until you hear from me or Mama Xhosi, you are released from your duties."

Daybreak came and went without Lileala hearing a word about

her request. By Point Nine she was starting to get excited. She
took Ataba Malik's tardiness as a sign that she'd have spare
time for herself, a whole morning to do whatever she pleased.
She scarfed down her breakfast, the usual bowl of mango with
almonds, and rushed to the nearest Sweep station.

A mild breeze made her shiver. Hunching her shoulders, she
pulled her thin shawl tightly around her, wishing she hadn't
forgotten her music chip. An Earth hymn might ease her tension
now as she waited alone in the quiet. She fidgeted. Funny, how
empty the station was during the early hour.

The currents came within a few minutes and had a more
aggressive undertow. In the morning hours of the day, The
Sweep transport clouds always flowed with more urgency.
Lileala kind of preferred it that way. She yielded and let them
pull her in. Then she settled into smooth bundles of wind and
wondered how long Ataba Malik and Mama Xhosi would meet.

Difficult as she thought the codes usually were, she
considered her waves of luck. The High Host, Mama Xhosi,
had spent the latter half of her two hundred and fifty years of
life adjusting the provisions, but Lileala never expected to gain
any special freedom because of them. The idea made her giddy.

She burrowed deeper into the currents. They were soothing,
and she never tired of riding them. She'd been told there was
nothing close to it on other planets along the Milky Way Border
– not even Toth, with its advanced architecture and spacious
transport ships, had whirling clouds carting passengers from
place to place.

She snuggled against the blankets of energy and let them
lather her skin. If she could, she'd never bother riding a wall
shuttle or a lift. She used them only to get to Sweep stations
and through the far lower regions of Boundary Circle. The
Circle bored her, though she'd never admit it. She liked being
up high, where she could observe the tourists. She didn't talk
to them much, but the swift hustle of their walk and their mad
obsession with old Earth lore amused her. Just thinking about

their fascination with a dead planet made her want to laugh out loud and, since she was alone, she didn't bother to stop it. Rare Indigo or not, she enjoyed silliness, even if only inside the privacy of The Sweep. Here, she could peep at The Outer Ring below, but no one could see her inside, behaving improperly. She plopped a piece of molasses in her mouth and savored it.

The Sweep plowed through the upper air space above all three of the rings – the two Outer Rings were mainly for the tourists, but the lower Ring One, just above Boundary Circle, included private regions just for The Nobility and Uluri. The Sweep lurched forward. Rolling and undulating, it spun in a loop, passing a tall cluster of spheres before crossing over a city park dotted with black walnut trees.

A few minutes later, it released Lileala onto the platform of an open-air pavilion. She had escaped. Almost. Her dial activated and someone angry was forcing their image to appear above her wrist. Lileala concentrated and tried to block it, but it was too late. The Aspirant High Host, Mama Xhosi, burst through. Her image was vague, but it was clear that she was distraught.

"Lileala, come quick. That's an order!"

Her face vanished.

Lileala shook her wrist and waited. Mama Xhosi reappeared, clear this time. And she was more furious than ever.

"We're on the Triangle, waiting for you."

"But, Mama Xhosi, I thought I wasn't supposed to be there this morning? Not while you and my Ataba were talking."

"Malik and I finished a half hour ago. Get in here. Now."

"No, no. I'm confused," she said, but not loud enough for Mama Xhosi to hear. She couldn't talk back without offering a prolonged confession. She'd have to admit that she was on the circumference of the Surface, preparing to get drenched in the drifts. Ataba Malik was supposed to be explaining that. All she was supposed to do was wait.

But she had no choice now. She'd been summoned and

had to do what she was told. Glad that she was dressed in the proper attire – the flowing half-pants-half-skirt often worn during Shimmer practice – she boarded another Sweep and rode to the Glass Triangle on the southwest rim of Ring One.

To her relief, Mama Xhosi grunted hello but said nothing else. She found her place and focused.

Beware... Stone... Stone

Chills raced up Lileala's arms. The strange murmur made no sense. She tapped her ear, assuming she'd embedded an Earth music chip and forgotten it was there. She breathed deep and brushed the unsettling feeling aside.

She crisscrossed her legs and closed her eyes. The open triangular corner was bathed in color from floor to ceiling and she was seated with seventeen other Indigos, upright, directly on the unforgiving glass. They were expected to transcend discomfort and maintain an elegant posture no matter what. The glass was smooth, though it had a shattered appearance. It pressed against her thighs and made them sweat. She continued sitting anyway, in the harsh silence, visualizing a flame and stealing its light to make her flesh glisten.

To hold Shimmer, she had to call on all of her willpower. She relaxed, allowing a slow burn to stir in her fingertips and rise until the temperature was almost too much to bear. She sealed her lips to suppress a cough, then she touched her brow. It was damp. She was ready now. She could do it. She could call the flame.

With both of her palms upturned, Lileala crinkled the corners of her eyes, and visualized herself stationed beneath an arch of fire. She exhaled. Her lips moistened and the trickles of perspiration on her neck felt as stony as the amber beads looped around her hips.

When Lileala couldn't stand it any longer, she opened her eyes and let them land on Mama Xhosi's folded arms. The other ladies were whispering now, and she wondered if Mama Xhosi was expecting her to speak. But judging from her scowl, she wanted silence. Her face was full of consternation, as if contemplating some deep disappointment. Lileala took that as a sign she had to go another round.

She pushed herself back into her own mind. Posture erect. In position on the floor. Slowing the scamper of her heart. But when her eyes reopened, everyone on the triangle still had theirs fixed on her. They were all waiting.

Her session ended after another five minutes. Lileala's head throbbed, and a cramp squeezed and pinched its way through her left foot, while Mama Xhosi, her round figure draped in sheaths of green and blue silk, moved to her side of the room. Mama Xhosi was attractive in a calculated sort of way. Her head was always wrapped in smooth fabric and her lightly bronzed skin, known among locals as Tawny Dramatic, was powdered to perfection. She looked aloof to Lileala, like someone who didn't know how to smile.

"One beat, one accord, one protection," Lileala prayed.

"Stand, please," Mama Xhosi said.

"Me?"

"You," she said. "My dear, you were glowing like a pod of light. If there was ever a doubt, it has been removed. You will be the one."

"Was there a doubt, Mama Xhosi?"

"No, but as stated in the manual, Code H, Provision Xiivii, the selection must be made with complete certainty." Mama Xhosi cleared her throat. "We have never revoked a title and had no desire to do so now. But Malik and The Uluri wondered if you had the discipline. They worried about your stubborn streak. Despite their reservations, I believe your willfulness adds fuel to your Shimmer. You will still be the one to succeed Ahonotay."

For a few seconds, Lileala was convinced the fire was still dancing around her and it was turning her numb.

"I didn't realize I was being questioned... But thank you," she said.

"I will submit the final determination to The Nobility tonight. You proved yourself and you did it quickly."

Mama Xhosi gathered up the corner of her garment and took a cautious step backward. The slowness in her gait made Lileala think she was stalling. Rigid as she was, maybe Mama Xhosi wasn't truly convinced of her decision. But then Lileala noticed that the river of ruffles flowing behind her no longer dragged the floor. The High Host was taking her time and clutching the ruffles so she wouldn't trip.

"It is official," she announced, making sure everyone could hear. "Lileala Walata Sundiata has been reconfirmed as our new Rare Indigo."

She turned to look at Lileala, and in her glare, Lileala saw pride. "I know The Uluri's edicts annoy you," Mama Xhosi warned. "And I know you haven't always followed the Aspirant codes. But your Shimmer is exquisite. And you hold it with such permanence."

The room rustled with murmurs. One young woman, against all training, rolled her eyes.

"Stop it, Issa," Mama Xhosi ordered. Immediately, the Aspirant softened her expression. No one defied Mama Xhosi in her presence or dared to ignore her commands.

"You all trained very well and have earned your place in Lileala's court," she said. "You will be expected to support her throughout her fifty-year reign."

Most of the ladies approached Lileala and gave her a courtesy hug. The Aspirant, Issa, took her time. She walked up to her, lifted both hands and moved them in a slow, silent clap.

"Thank you, Issa," Lileala said. But she could tell Issa wasn't genuine. The whispers of blue streaking her cheeks had a dull quality and her voice was unusually tart.

"Waves of joy," she said. "I'm glad you were able to reclaim the lost honor."

Lileala stiffened. *Reclaim the lost honor?* Nodding her thanks, Lileala prepared to exit the Triangle, ignoring the twirling and rattling of her beads.

"Once more, I must thank all of you beautiful young ladies

for your years of dedication," Mama Xhosi added. She gestured toward Lileala and waited, lips parted, as if she was about to say something difficult.

"Now go, all of you."

The Aspirants started their chattering, and two heavy brass discs in the Triangle's courtyard clapped together and made a sharp clang. Mama Xhosi turned her focus back to Lileala. "I will consider your respite request later. Give me a bit more time."

"But Mama —" Lileala began, but she had already turned to walk away and probably couldn't hear amidst the clamor.

It was Point Two of the afternoon hours. All Aspirants were free to take a lift to The Circle Marketplace and no longer worry about rushing home to practice Shimmer. They could listen to lots of crazy Earth hymns now and eat handfuls of sweet, spicy cassava cakes. But Lileala wasn't sure what to do or think. The announcement was good – part of it. She was disturbed by the rest of it and by Issa's comment: *Reclaim the lost honor.*

She took a lift down to the markets, chastising herself the entire time, kicking herself for such awful judgement. Did someone see her last night and decide to give her a break anyway? She had entered The Red Hot, of all places. Her chest tightened and she couldn't stop the inner scolding. *How could I have been so stupid?*

At the entrance to The Great Hall, a few locals congregated, and she nearly collided with a vendor who was tending a floating cart of figs. Thinking maybe she'd be better off at home, Lileala headed toward Mampong Avenue just as Zizi was running toward her. Zizi threw up her hands and grinned.

"Don't tell me they've announced it twice?" Lileala said. Her voice was flat.

"It's all over the viewerstream!" Zizi couldn't seem to contain her excitement. "Congratulations, my friend. A second congratulations!"

"Thanks."

Zizi looked startled. "What's wrong? Aren't you happy?"

"Real happy... But..."

"Lileala, don't you dare complain. Sing praises to The Grace. Don't complain."

"Zizi, I'm nervous," Lileala said. "I just found out they were thinking of revoking my title."

"But they didn't," Zizi said. "So why do you care?"

"Because I might make a mistake," Lileala said. "I'm not disciplined. You told me that. Now *they've* told me that too. It's just my Shimmer Mama Xhosi likes. That's all. What if that's not enough?"

"Shhh," Zizi whispered. "Be careful what you fear, or you might attract it." When Lileala didn't respond, she continued: "You're worried about disappointing your elder Ma, aren't you?"

"Maybe," said Lileala. "She's wanted this for me for a long time."

"What matters to you, though? Your elder Ma isn't going to live your life." Zizi's voice was laced with annoyance. "You know what? Everyone admires you, but sometimes..." She searched for the right words. "Sometimes, I wonder if you even admire yourself. The real you, I mean, not just your looks."

Lileala didn't speak. She stood still, staring at her feet.

"Well, put it out of your mind right now," Zizi said. "Come on. Let's go buy some old Earth hymns."

The markets were scattered in haphazard loops, some dead center in the hall and some on the fringes, no more than a ten-minute sprint from Aswaka. Lileala and Zizi wandered through a figure eight of booths loaded with sandals and ear baubles, before heading to the popular textile galleries. Arched over limestone floors, yards of iron-coated cloth served as a shining canopy for a couple dozen vendors. Stone walls and pillars separated the havens packed with shoppers, leaving the ladies little space to move. They sorted through a few items and left.

Po Tolo has answers.

"Oh no," Lileala said out loud.

"What?" Zizi asked. "What's wrong?"

"Waves of nothing," Lileala said. She tapped her ear. Maybe the chip tucked inside had gotten stuck.

They proceeded around another figure-eight lane that took them through Centerfree, an art and residential district for locals who depended on meager marble allotments. A couple of strangers approached.

"Would you mind taking an optic with my son?" asked one of the men, short statured with a graying mustache. Lileala wedged herself between the men and the three posed in front of a star-shaped structure that was sixty meters high, twenty meters wide.

"The last time we had a reigning Rare Indigo, my son hadn't been born," the man said, waving a sliver of metal before their faces. "He's on his way to Toth now to take some courses he needs for the Scientific Pineal Crew training. This is going to be a great memory to take with him."

Lileala observed the son's apparel – a collarless multicolored shirt and primitive pendants affixed to gaudy, bronze bracelets.

"Do you hope to visit the ruins and do excavations?" she asked.

"Most definitely," the young man answered. "I'm a huge fan of Earth culture. I don't care what The Nobility and the scholars say; I think we originated in the Earth land, Africa."

Zizi gave the guy a thumbs up and Lileala offered a quiet smile. When they were out of earshot of the two locals, she murmured, "It figures. From that guy's jewelry and the way he was dressed, I knew he was of those types. Always linking us to Earth."

"Let him," Zizi said. "I'm tired of everyone being so divided. Some people say yes, some no. But when you really think about it, where else could we have come from?"

They wandered on and Lileala considered Zizi's comment. She didn't want to admit it, but Swazembian history was pretty vague, and no one had either proven or disproven their link to Earth's melanin bearers. Lileala mulled it over for a minute and let it go.

Centerfree's most popular structure, a royal-blue tin cup

trimmed in yellow, was a few paces ahead and she found that far more interesting. The art piece was nearly eighty meters tall and a doorway in the cup's handle opened into a hollow interior that spread out into dozens of galleries and living quarters.

Hoping to avoid a crowd that was gathering out front, Zizi and Lileala bought new music chips from a shop inside the cup and sneaked out through the staff's private side exit. Wrong move. The limited space along the side was jammed with spectators, watching and listening to a strange woman with a piercing, staccato voice.

"Ye, waves of joy to all!" she was saying to the crowd. A straw basket of fruit dangled from one hand, and while she talked, she passed each person a peach. "Today, they do not cost," she said, swinging her arms in time with her words. There was a playful rhythm in her dialect, and she swayed as she spoke, laughing at the same time.

"You come now to hear the words of Cherry, no?" she asked. "Cherry has the new story, ye." The crowd expanded and Cherry, known as the marketplace clairvoyant, continued speaking.

Lileala and Zizi edged closer and peered through a throng of onlookers huddled in one spot as if the woman was holding them captive. There was a defiance to Cherry. The Otuzuweland fruit seller was nearing three hundred years, but, contrary to custom, she wasn't wearing an elegant skyrise headwrap. The tall, layered headwraps were favored by notable women of middle-age, but Cherry's was a dainty, brownish-purple swath of cloth that hugged her forehead and meshed with her berry and cocoa complexion.

"Today, Cherry will tell of the clam giants, ye. They are so sad, these clams and all the time, they hum and moan." Cherry talked fast, then slow, then fast again. The cadence gave her story a musical quality. "They disturb the morning sleep, they do."

A solemn hush overtook the crowd, and no one said a word.

"These wide beings of the great river, they are of the high

waters of Earth," Cherry went on, increasing the volume of her sing-songy pitch. "And the shells are ever big for even the human to dwell."

Cherry gestured toward the avenues of The Great Hall and along the First Ring immediately above Boundary Circle. "Here, in the Sangha Province, beneath the ground, no ears are touched by the noises," she said. "But in the lowlands of Otuzuweland, their hum flies above the corn fields."

She wet her lips and adjusted the brim of her headwrap. "Oh, the people there they did believe the beasts warned of danger, ye. But no danger ever has come, just the moans. And so in the Mbaria village, they make a name for them, no. They call them *ite*, their way to say crazy, and *irhe* for music. They make the crazy music."

Cherry slowed her cadence and closed her eyes.

A blurred face fluttered on Lileala's dial, and she turned to leave. "I need to go, Zizi. Please tell Cherry I said hello. I'd tell her myself but she's longwinded, you know, and I don't want to be out too late. Otto invited me to a special meeting with him on The Ring in the morning."

"What?" Zizi shot her a doubtful stare. "A meeting on The Ring?"

"He just summoned me. Says it's a big, big surprise."

4

"A rare gift it is. Use it well and melanin will help you conquer hard and fast the scientific laws."
— The Creed of The Nobility

"Almost ready, Otto! Just give me a minute." Lileala flipped through her satchel and pretended to hunt for her mirror. She had accidentally dropped it that morning and stuffed the broken pieces in a trash evaporator in the Mampong community courtyard. But she didn't want Otto to know that. He'd given it to her as a gift for her forty-ninth birth year, and had a habit of reminding her it was an Earth artifact. Once it was cleaned and the gold clasp was repaired, it had quickly become her favorite trinket.

She kept fumbling through her bag, not bothering to rush. Otto hadn't ever gone out of his way to surprise her. She didn't want to appear too anxious.

"You look like you were sent by The Grace itself," he said. "Come on, beautiful, let's go."

"Waves of joy," she said. They stepped outside her living quarters, and she used her dial to close the door in slow motion. "It's okay, but you do realize you were kind of late, don't you?"

"Had a quick chat with the Pineal chief." Otto moved closer and brushed one hand across her cheek. "You know how exact your Baba is; it's so hard to steal time away from him. The Coalition's not meeting till next week and he's already on Toth, dialing everyone, wondering when the rest of us will arrive."

"I know," Lileala said. "My elder Ma's there with my Baba now."

She walked ahead a few paces, allowing Otto to steal a peek at her legs. She turned and caught his smile, but tried to pretend she didn't notice. She had risen earlier than usual and fussed over what to wear before finally settling on an empire waist gown with elaborate designs on the sleeves and a tall slit just below her knees.

"Gorgeous," he said, looking her over again.

Lileala took in a slight breath and let herself glow as they walked arm in arm past the hub and onto a waiting lift. "So what made you plan a surprise?" she asked.

"Just concerned about you, especially after the other day," Otto said. "Thought this might help." The lift spiraled up to Ring One, right above Boundary Circle, but Otto and Lileala stayed put. They exited at Ring Two and headed down a concourse. "You're just in time!" one of the locals shouted. He was an elder, draped in a gray, hooded cloak. "To the left of here, a good imageflow is showing on viewerstream number nine. It's a new film from the Earth ruins."

He addressed Otto: "Take the lady to see this imageflow, why don't you? Only two marbles?"

"No, thanks," Otto said.

The man stood in his way. "Then let me direct you to the Old Earth Eatery. We serve all Earth delicacies, even the hamburgers."

Otto maneuvered around him and signaled for Lileala to ignore the merchant.

"I know he's not affiliated with that eatery – I don't know what he hopes to gain," he said. "A special compensation, maybe. He's probably from Centerfree, and those people don't own businesses."

"Otto, that's not nice and not true. One of the Aspirants is from there. I don't like her much, but please don't say that!"

"Issa, right? She's very beautiful." Otto whispered, as if she was nearby. "She was next in line, wasn't she? I mean if you hadn't been named Rare Indigo, wouldn't she have been picked?"

Lileala bit her lip. "I don't want to discuss her. I was just saying that people who live in Centerfree aren't bad just because their allotments are smaller."

"You're right," Otto said. "They're not bad." He glanced across the concourse. "And they're good at my favorite game. That's one nice thing I can say. They make good TET players."

"So, you like them when they're throwing those tin tops around, huh?" Lileala laughed.

They were riding past a portable TET station where a male elder-child sat with a young tourist under a stained-glass awning, tossing electronic tops. A patch of onlookers stood on the sidelines, but the young gamers were oblivious. Both were staring at the vertical rays of white light that striped the narrow panel hanging in front of them. One at a time, they tossed small silver discs. Most of the discs crashed into the light rays which turned solid temporarily as the discs fell into a magnetic tray on the floor.

One of the men playing furrowed his brow and tossed with more precision. The disc slid through the narrow cracks in between the lights.

"That's Lekan Odetin," Otto said with pride. "He's one of the best. I believe he's ranked high enough for the next Coalition TET tournament. Not small-scale stuff like this. He'll be throwing cylinders in one of the huge fields on Toth."

"Quite impressive." Lileala watched Lekan and snuggled close to Otto, wrapping both hands around his right arm. It felt so good to tour The Ring without having to worry about being judged. No one would criticize her now, not while she was accompanied by a Pineal Crew officer. But her guilt from the night before lingered, and when they glided past The Red Hot, her hands trembled.

"My stars! Are you okay?" Otto asked. "You seem nervous."

"I'm fine," she mumbled under her breath. She inhaled the cinnamon aroma of a nearby sweets haven and relaxed.

Let's go crazy. Let's get nuts!" burst through the door of the haven.

"Not again," Lileala blurted out.

"What's wrong?" Otto grinned. "Isn't that one of your favorite hymns?"

"No, I mean, yes, I –" she stalled. "But… Otto, I need to tell you something."

"I'm all ears."

"Well." She paused. "I did something… something kind of bad."

The silence between them lasted longer than Lileala could bear. She tore into it.

"I came here last night to a dance haven, but I left like straightaway," she blurted.

There was a moment of disappointment and Otto's eyes went dead. "Why? What if you'd been caught?"

"No, Otto, it's not like you think. I stepped in and I left. The guilt hit me. I thought of Mama Xhosi, and I thought of you too."

When Otto's shoulders relaxed, she leaned against him and held back the tears welling in her eyes. "I don't understand it myself. I don't know why I keep violating the Aspirant codes."

"You're headstrong, that's why."

"I know, but I don't want that to cost me my title," Lileala said and cleared her throat. The dreaded drops of tears escaped and wet her cheeks.

"Maybe you need more discipline training," Otto said.

"That's the last thing I want."

He didn't answer, and again the silence became a river between them.

"No tears," he said, crushing her against his chest. "And no guilt either. It's done. We move on." He wiped her tears and continued: "Maybe we've been too hard on you. The Nobility,

Ataba Malik, even me, working all the time. You're human, that's all."

"I-I don't know what to say." Lileala was stunned. "You're not worried someone will find out?"

"Come on," he said. "I think I know what will take your mind off all of this."

The couple turned right, and Otto led Lileala down a concourse that was noisier and had at least six lanes, all of them automated and packed with pedestrians. They found a less congested lane and rode along beside two men Lileala recognized as Boundary Circle merchants. One tapped the other's shoulder and spoke under his breath: "Rare Indigo on your left."

By the time he dug in his pocket and pulled out an optic strip, Lileala and Otto had already hopped onto an adjoining lane that was busier but faster. Within two minutes, it had wound through another concourse and rolled under a sign that read, "*Screeners*". When Lileala noticed the sign, she gushed.

"I can't believe it!" She smiled and squeezed Otto's hand. "You're the best!"

Once inside, the walkway halted, and tourists spilled in all directions. Walls of the Screeners room were one hundred and twenty meters high and more than seven times as wide. From ceiling to floor, interactive images pulsated. A sparkly-clothed performer, with the name "J. Monae" emblazoned on her back, pranced and danced sideways, undulating like water tumbling over a cliff. Daredevils in dark goggles rode two-wheeled electric vehicles. A man and woman with narrow panels beneath their feet slid down mountains buried in snow.

"Ready for some action?" Otto asked.

"Ready!" Lileala shouted.

At the entrance gate, he bought a small cup of liquid tickets and smeared them on their wrists until their palms began to emit pink and gold beams.

"Let's go!" he yelled. "Pick one."

Lileala held her hand in front of the Screener of the mountain peak and both she and Otto, their palms upright, jumped inside. The Screener yielded and swerved around them, fully immersing their bodies into the scene. Immediately, they were bundled in thick, foamy snowsuits while hard boots with long skis zipped onto their feet. The two screamed and charged down a two-thousand-meter slope.

"That was amazing," Lileala said, still huffing as they coasted to the base of the ski-route. "Want to go again?"

"We can't, we'll be late for lunch," Otto said. Shifting his hand to her shoulder, he guided her out past a tumble of gift shops.

"Do you realize how high that altitude was?" he asked. "That adventure should take your mind off dance havens for quite a while."

Winding past a blur of blinking globes, Lileala and Otto navigated their way to the sign, *Concourse 57, HOVEL OF THE TREEGREENS*. Treegreens were eateries for those who preferred meals that hadn't been culled from Otuzuweland creatures – mostly locals but some visitors.

They chose a gazebo at Treegreen Number Six, an octagon enclosure of seats and tables made of mirrors and firm banana leaves.

"I'm not very hungry but I'll ask the table for a menu," Lileala said. A mist of words rose up from a leaf and streamed in front of her. But Otto stopped her.

"Wait," he said. "The surprise, remember? We're having guests."

She was looking at her reflection in the tabletop when a woman walked in. A big Grand Rising S pendant dangled from her neck and her mane of curls jutted toward the ceiling. The curls were dense and cut like the razor-sharp angles of a tall cube.

"Pathem Nomsa Ju?" Lileala jumped out of her seat.

"No, please." The woman waved with the back of her hand. "Please, sit."

"Otto," Lileala said. "The Nobility? Otto, I can't believe you."

"The pleasure is mine," Pathem said. "My other half will be here shortly."

She seated herself and Lileala tried to soften her stare. Although not dark enough to be called High Indigo, instead Pathem was considered Tawny Dramatic, a hue that mirrored the first stage of dusk shaded with dabs of golden sunset.

"You are as lovely in person as you are on the viewerstream," Pathem said. "And I see you're wearing an Otuzuwe gown. Did you purchase it in Gwembia, young one?" She turned toward Otto. "Or did you buy it for her, my dear?"

Lileala cut in before Otto could answer. "Cherry Willems gave it to me. She comes to Boundary Circle a lot, and one day she just handed it to me. Wouldn't take a single marble for it."

Pathem smiled and inclined her head.

"She makes beautiful garments," Lileala went on. "And she always sews Otuzuwe patterns on them." Lileala brushed her hand over her favorite, a string of bells. "The bells are Cherry's most popular because they show timeliness. And her fabrics, you should see them. They're lush, just like yours."

Lileala realized she was rambling and paused, unsure if it was proper to compliment a woman who represented half of The Nobility. "She never uses the S design though. Only symbols that are proverbs or parables."

Pathem faked a laugh. "Ah, Cherry. She tries so hard, that one. Always creating or entertaining and even trying to imitate the Inekoteth, or so I'm told." Pathem's mouth took on the shape of a smirk. "I'm pleased that she avoids the wave letter," she said. She touched her S pendant and gave Lileala a slight nod. "Thank you, young one for sharing that. But knowing when not to use it and when not to speak it, that's for us, ye, The Uluri, The Nobility, the Mhondora."

Lileala hid both hands beneath a shroud of leaves and picked at her thumb. She liked Pathem, but she didn't understand her criticism of Cherry. "She's a clairvoyant too," Lileala volunteered more quietly. She waited, careful not to go too far.

"Oye, she tries." Pathem tossed her head back, her laugh too quiet to hear. "But she'll never be a seer like the Mhondora," she said. "Her Inekoteth trances are weak, and her speech is so peculiar. Don't you think?"

Before she could respond, Lileala felt Otto kick her foot.

"She knows a lot," she said, ignoring Otto.

"But she's still learning, too." Otto looked at Lileala. "Isn't that what you were trying to say, my love? That Cherry is interesting but still has a long way to go?"

The laugh from Pathem was real this time. She leaned forward.

"Young ones, both of you," she said. "I know Cherry has followers. You don't have to try and hide it. My devoted and I might live cloistered lives, but we know that people gather around to hear her tales. But understand, there is only one Mhondora in the entire galaxy, and that is Mhondora Chinbedza. He is the only one who can truly tap into the Inekoteth tongue of our ancestors and look ahead.

"It is remarkable that Cherry uses the ye, as well," Pathem continued. "Ye, she understands the power of the sacred wave, and that it should not be used by dignitaries when creating an affirmative word. But that is all she shares in common with the Mhondora or with my devoted and I."

"But you are The Nobility," Lileala said. "Maybe you have never interacted with her, I mean not in the way we have."

"We don't need time with her," Pathem continued. "Our Uluri have studied her and given us a full report. They say Cherry has gone into maybe three or four trances. Just four trances! That's not close to being Mhondora. And that devoted of hers, Fodjour. He is an insult to The Grace. That's why he was asked to leave the capital."

Her voice rose an octave but didn't stay there. While Otto and Lileala sat quietly, she relaxed and slowed her speech. "But enough, ye," she said. "We didn't come here to talk about Cherry."

The second half of The Nobility, Oluntungi Methap Ju,

approached behind them with both of his arms outstretched. As he walked, a pendant bearing the S symbol slid along the chain around his neck and slapped his chin.

"Ah, my devoted," he said, kissing Pathem's forehead. He nodded at Otto. "Waves of joy, officer," he said, then straightened his coarse ivory vest and acknowledged Lileala with a subtle bow of his head.

"I've heard so much about you," he said. "Oye, and we have studied you from afar. Even when you didn't know it, The Nobility and Uluri were watching."

His stare deepened. "I'm pleased that you haven't strayed too far from your oaths," he went on. "You're quite the mischief maker, I'm told."

"Not anymore," Otto said in her defense. "You know, of course, that she passed another advanced Shimmer test."

"And came through with the elegance of The Grace." Oluntungi laughed. "You don't have to convince me of anything, young man. That's why we're here." He faced Lileala. "We were tired of distance observing. We needed to see this young beauty up close."

He slid into a seat and continued: "So, what were you talking about when I arrived? Did I walk into the heat of a debate? Sounds like someone was being surly." His gaze fell on Pathem.

"Not at all, love," she said. "We're about to order food so we can chat with the Rare Indigo." Mist seeped from the leaves and formed a banner of swerving words.

"The roasted breadfruit sounds delicious," she said. "What about you, my devoted?"

When everyone had ordered and the mist had cleared, Lileala wondered if she'd be able to eat. She didn't have an appetite for the stewed grains she'd requested. She was too nervous and annoyed with Otto. This was some surprise. He should have at least hinted that The Nobility were coming so she could have practiced what to say.

"So, this is what we want to explain," Pathem said. "My

devoted and I have realized it must be a heavy burden to be the Rare Indigo." She waited while a waiter in a black and brown shawl approached. Two covered platters floated in front of him then hovered just long enough for the waiter to manually place them on top of the table's crest of leaves.

Pathem went on: "We may have overdone the training and restrictions because, you see, it has been so long and, in that time, we've been deprived. We've had no Rare Indigo to greet special visitors, to lead tours or to present the first cylinder at TET games."

"We value you," said Oluntungi. "That is what my better half is trying to tell you. When dignitaries come here, particularly those from Toth, there are three things they want to see most: the Surface, The Sweep and the Rare Indigo. It's all they talk about, right Otto?"

Otto bowed his head in a Nobility salute, but Lileala couldn't bring herself to join him. Her stomach was a soup of emotions and she still worried how she would eat.

"Toth has its attractions," Otto said. "But they're manmade. Ours are unique because they're natural."

"Your point is appreciated, young man." Oluntungi directed his attention toward Pathem. "I've known this young Pineal Crew officer since his university days on Toth. My Baba was still The Nobility then, but he said it too, that this young man would go far."

"I am sorry about the honorable Akunna Ju," Otto said. "He was the finest."

"Waves of thanks," said Oluntungi. "He was in the range of five hundred and fifty years, and he lived well, but, ye, it is hard to lose a forebear. I hope I inherited his strength as much as I inherited his power." He turned to Lileala again. "But as I was saying to the Rare One, we are an admired people and it is okay, the vanity." He suppressed a laugh. "We're an insular society, but we do enjoy the accolades from abroad."

"He likes the attention," Pathem said. She chuckled and

pinched his left cheek. "He's kind of a glutton for praise about Swazembi."

"Tours fuel our economy," he said.

"And ego," Pathem added.

"True." Oluntungi winked at his devoted. "We have quite the legacy. We're the darkest bearers of melanin who have ever existed in the galaxy."

Pathem sat up straight. "I don't think so. What about the work of the Melanin Commission and the Scientific Pineal Crew?" she asked. "Haven't some Coalition members studied their results and learned how to self-melinate or whatever they call –"

"The mental self-tan?" Otto asked. "It's called M-S-T and it's going well... but." He paused to consider his next comment. "I'm not sure if you're totally correct about our legacy, Noble Oluntungi. There's Earth. Approve of them or not, we have to share credit with their melanin bearers."

Oluntungi thought for a moment. "There is little proof, young man, that our kind has any connection to whatever went on before those ruins, but you're right, I suppose. They were the original melanin bearers." He turned to Lileala. "Have you studied the Earth theories yet? You know the theory that we descended from the melanin bearers from a forested Earth land, Africa?" He ate a spoonful of breadfruit and watched for Lileala's reaction.

"I'm conflicted about that," Lileala answered. "I just met a couple of Centerfree residents who were trying to convince me."

"They're bored," Otto said. Lileala reached beneath the tabletop of leaves and squeezed his hand. He never missed a chance to criticize the Centerfree residents.

He kept going anyway: "They have it so easy and live so well, but they're complacent."

"Ye, have you seen their new wing?" Pathem asked. "We're so proud of it. Oye. We built a north end lane of artwork dwellings. Grand sculptures of Swazembian women have been hollowed and filled with furnishings. These homes are even bigger than the first ones."

"What about the young man, Lekan?" Lileala spoke louder than normal, hoping she could change the subject. "Otto didn't you say he was amazing?"

"Oh, yes." Otto lit up. "Noble Oluntungi, do you like TET? I play a little myself but nothing like this new champion."

Otto, Pathem and Oluntungi swapped TET opinions, debating one tactic after another, discussing the signature maneuvers created by Lekan. After nearly ten minutes of banter, they switched back to Lileala.

"Why so quiet, Lileala? You've shared very little about yourself," Oluntungi teased. "Don't tell us we have another Ahonotay on our hands."

Both of The Nobility laughed and Lileala struggled to come up with something interesting to say.

"Well, I'm honored, first of all," she said. "I've been preparing to be an Indigo Aspirant since I was only twenty-two. I never expected to come this far. My elder Ma still can't get over it."

"We took to you immediately," said Pathem.

Oluntungi butt in. "We found you beautiful but erratic. I'm even told that you have a fondness for danceries and music havens on The Outer Ring."

Lileala froze. Did he know about last night? She tried to appear nonchalant. "No, no. I used to do that but no more. I still love Earth music though, but I usually buy it in Centerfree. I have friends there because the minor school I attended isn't far from the art dwellings. I grew up in the Mampong community."

"Mampong is nice. Do you think you'll miss it?" Pathem asked.

"No, my elder Ma, my Baba and me, we still live there. It's not all that elegant, but we like it. They're in one huge bauble, and I live in the smaller one that's attached. I plan to stay there until I join Otto in Aswaka."

The Nobility grew quiet. They focused on Otto.

"You didn't tell her," Oluntungi said. "Why haven't you told her?"

"Told me what?" Lileala sat very still. "What didn't he tell me?"

"After we're joined, we're moving," Otto said. "You know you're the first Rare Indigo in years, and that means extra honors. You and I will be expected to live in The Grand Rising."

Lileala didn't feel her spoon slipping from her hand, but she heard a chime, like the sound of a bell hitting the floor. "Sorry," she said, but she didn't look down or pick it up.

"Isn't that wonderful news?" Otto asked. "I was saving it for last."

"Wonderful, yes," she stammered. "Wonderful... and frightening, I guess. I don't know."

"You'll be fine, dear," Pathem said. "Oh, and before we forget, the answer is Ye."

"Ye? You mean ye as in yes?" Lileala asked.

"Ye," Pathem confirmed. She dropped several marbles within the cushion of table leaves.

"Yes to what?" Lileala asked.

"The respite you requested, my dear one. You did ask if you could spend a few days on the Surface. Correct? Well, it has been approved." Both of The Nobility stood, and Pathem patted the top of her tower of hair. It remained in place like a hat, but strong as a concrete building.

"Oluntungi and I have to leave now," she said. "I have a coif appointment."

5

"Breezes are lost memories trying to find their way home."
     – Swazembian superstition

"One of my teachers used to call them electromagnetic puffs," Zizi said. "He had all sorts of theories about…"

"NO!" Lileala shouted and kicked off her sandals. "This isn't science class. I'm up here for fun."

She squinted. Plumes of red, green and yellow were percolating on the Surface. Lileala plunged into them, then ran barefoot through the colored sand while drifts swept over her head and made a soft landing on her back. They swam around her, helter-skelter, throbbing and twirling. She stopped running and twirled with them.

"This is like a dream, Zizi. Don't you love it?"

Zizi threw up her hands and playfully brushed the colors through her hair. "It's not new to me; I was just here last week." She giggled. "Sorry, but I couldn't resist."

"Light stealer!" Lileala laughed. "Watch this!" With her arms arched and her wrists limp, she lifted one limb at a time. In slow silence, one arm rose, the other inched downward. A thin breeze blew jacaranda petals around her nose and inside her ears. Lileala kept her control, pushing her torso against gravity, holding herself in place. Her knees relaxed, and with her right foot resting on her left knee, she twirled.

"Wow, I've never seen anyone wave dance on the Surface,"

Zizi said. She watched as Lileala lifted to her toes and stayed there on bent knees.

"Very impressive, my Rare friend. But enough. Time to go inside."

Lileala's eyes still weren't open; she planned to keep dancing. Her body seesawed and she spun. Zizi stepped in front of her and pushed.

"Hey! What are you doing?" Lileala squealed.

Zizi pushed harder, knocking them both into a mound of pink sand. "Who's the light stealer now!" Zizi said, laughing.

All Lileala could do was laugh with her. "Me! But you started it!"

"Okay, enough." Zizi stood and brushed off her skirt. "You can prance around in your dome. Let's go."

Lileala resisted. She sat in the spot where she had landed and watched the colors leap. They spooled around her forehead and dribbled down her cheeks, tickling. Most people said they couldn't feel the drifts, and when she claimed she could, everyone around always blamed her imagination. That never stopped her. Ever since minor school, she swore the color splotches were like tiny ghosts and that she could feel them in a way that was different from an actual touch. She tried grabbing a handful out of the air. They traveled between her fingertips and filled her hands with a fistful of vibrant nothing. She tossed the nothing at Zizi.

"Okay, we're out of time," Zizi said. "We've been out here for nearly forty minutes. That's ten minutes too long."

"Not the dome again," Lileala said. She steadied herself in place, positioned to run.

"Lileala!" Zizi's tone was almost hostile. "You! You! You're making me so mad."

"Stop calling me 'you'!" Lileala shouted. "You're making a scene."

A passing man and woman stared a minute and kept walking. More interested in the drifts than the quarrel of two locals, the young tourists moved toward the shore of the vast sea of vapors. The vapors were broad shafts of color, rising from a deep pit of candy bright mist and fusing with a color-blazed sky. While the endless hues clashed, the tourists stood before them, waving a sliver of metal no larger than the palms of their hands. Their cotton hats flopped over their slightly tanned faces, but Lileala could still see their reaction. With the sea in the background, their images froze on the optic square. The tourists grinned.

"They're young and newly joined," Zizi said. "They don't care about what's going on with us. But I care. Let's go." She gazed at the magnetic colors and winced.

The Surface stretched for several hundred kilometers, farther than The Great Hall and more than twice the width of all three Outer Rings combined. There were only a few vendors on it most days and they sold only image squares for optics and straw cups filled with sliced mango or fig. Paraphernalia was limited due to time restrictions placed on the tours through the drifts.

"Okay, your time's up," Zizi continued. "Ataba Malik asked me to make sure you don't linger among the vapors too long. He's your trainer. You ought to listen to him sometimes."

Lileala turned and followed her.

"Don't worry, Zizi. I don't want overexposure any more than he does."

"And?"

"And I'll go inside now and come back out when the sun drops." She pointed herself toward a trail of brass domes.

Zizi paused a second. "I forgot to tell you. I have to go back to The Circle to finish some studies in the chamber. I'll be back this evening." She waved. "Be good, Lileala."

"I'm not a child. What is wrong with everyone?"

Lileala watched her walk away. Then she waited. The Surface was warm, the colors hypnotic, and she couldn't pull herself away. She was riveted by the bevy of sand hills, red at the bottom but with tips capped in blue. Otto appeared on her dial.

"My devoted. How does it feel?"

"Amazing." She spun in a circle. "That's how I feel. I've been deprived for so long."

"Not deprived, prepared," Otto said. "Look at it that way, my love. You have many, many years of life to enjoy the colors. But," he paused, "right now, you have to think about your complexion."

"I know. I need to get to my quarters." She glanced at the nine conspicuous domes to her far right, the only tourist structures on the southern corner of the Surface. Hers was on the opposite end, among the nineteen reserved for dignitaries, but none were permanent dwellings. Too much time in the drifts wasn't considered safe, and no one, no matter their status, was permitted to live among them.

"Zizi had to go to the knowledge chamber but I'm fine alone," she said. "The vapors' currents are getting to me though. I'd say I've had enough."

"That's what electromagnetism does. Get out of it now, Lileala."

"I am. What about you? Shouldn't you be on Toth?"

"I'm at Togu Ta City Port now, waiting for space transit. The meeting's been pushed back, but I need to stop through and help with planning. Should be back before you return. Waves!"

"Waves!" Lileala said. She jogged all the way to her dome and darted inside, barely taking time to glance in the mirror. She figured she was a mess, but was too tired to care. The drifts had drained her some. She chastised herself and made an internal vow to be more careful, maybe make her next visits at night.

Rest summoned, but instead of heeding it she stood by the bed, still as a rock. She had to push herself to move. Slipping out of her gown was the easy part. But it pained her to pick it up off the floor and pull a night frock out of the corner cabinet. The door, not used by a Rare Indigo in years, squeaked and scraped like a roomful of chatter. Lileala blinked. She thought she heard a human voice. "Is someone here?" she shouted. "Hello?"

Silence.

The room was empty. After landing on her bed, she stroked her earlobe to turn on her music chip. *"Uptown funk you up,"* barreled through her ears. But that's all she heard. She fell asleep immediately and dreamt she was sitting alone on a ledge, overlooking a blazing red canyon.

A feathered creature dipped from the sky and flew over her head, causing Lileala to slip and nearly tumble down the side of Blue Barrell, a turquoise sandhill that loomed seventy-six meters above the shore. It was given the name hundreds of years ago by a couple of young tourists who had too much to drink and sneaked on to the Surface after hours. In complete disregard of Swazembian policies, they had a reckless night sliding down the hill and rolling into the sea's churning vapors. On the first few tries, they managed to climb out, but on their last free fall they got caught in a riptide and were sucked under. A Sonaguard found them the next morning, washed up on the shore, unconscious, with purple lesions all over their arms, their faces scorched. When they recovered, they were kicked off Swazembi and told never to return. But the incident, dubbed the Blue Barrell Scandal, became a Surface legend.

Everyone had heard about it at least once, and the Sonaguard started late hour weekend patrols just to watch out for stragglers. Worried that she might be spotted, Lileala looked around, then steadied herself and pulled her body upright into a high boa position.

"That's it, that's it," she whispered. Under Zizi's watchful eye, she'd been climbing Blue Barrell for the last two nights and sitting on its peak, close as she could to the winged being that flew about in the dark. She didn't know where it had come from, but she marveled at its fluid motions. "It's called a twilight," she yelled down to Zizi. "The last time I talked to Otto, I asked about it and he said they've been around for thousands of sun years, but they're rarely seen on the Surface."

Zizi laughed. "Those? They're just scuffs."

"What?"

"Scuffs," Zizi said. "Those little square-eyed fuzzy things running through the park."

"Right, *those* are scuffs. But these are...?"

"Scuffs," Zizi repeated. "Otto was just indulging you. Tourists sometimes catch scuffs and sneak them up here. Once the drifts hit them, they transform. It takes a day or two, but the drifts vaporize their fur. Then they change colors and two of their legs sprout wings."

Lileala tugged on her thumbnail. "No one ever told me about this."

"Because it hardly ever happens and they don't live long anyway, not in that state," Zizi said. "Up here, they flap around and look pretty but they only last about five days."

Zizi watched it. One of its wings was switching from purple to pink. "I come up here a lot and I've only seen one, besides this one. Sonaguards check tourists' satchels all the time. But they sneak them in some way. Don't know how they do it."

It sailed past again and Lileala leaned back, disappointed. She had romanticized the being and pretended it had descended from an ancient pet that, maybe, the great ancestor Tnomo had brought with him. She didn't know which star he came from but figured twilights must have been smeared with some of its dust. Now, Zizi had destroyed the fantasy.

"Light stealer!" She yelled down at her and made a face. Zizi was checking her dial. She had refused to climb the hill with her and, for reasons Lileala didn't understand, had remained at the foot, complaining.

She's gotten so serious, Lileala said to herself, remembering how hard it had been to talk her into relaxing in the darkness while she watched the winged creature fly past. She finally said yes, but kept her eye on her wrist, not giving Lileala sufficient time to enjoy the twilight or whatever it was, its feathers shining, its sharp beak stabbing the black and red sky. Lileala was so captivated she had no problem blocking out her friend's pleas for her to climb down.

"We've lingered long enough," Zizi coaxed. "It's time to get back inside."

Lileala pretended not to hear her.

"Okay, I know you don't think I'll do it, but I'm going to call the Sonaguard." Zizi stuck out her wrist and displayed a pinwheel of light. "Don't believe me? Just watch." She lifted her arm.

"Alright, alright," Lileala said, dragging her voice. After a final wave to the twilight, she curved her body into one of Blue Barrell's wide crevices and used her hands to guide her as she scooted to the ground.

"I feel so comfortable up there," she said. "It feels natural." She wiped the sleeves of her linen gown and planted the bare bottoms of her feet onto a carpet of crimson sand. The sand swirled.

"Waves of joy! Nighttime on the Surface is amazing," Lileala said. "You must have really missed all this when you were in Gwembia."

"Not really," said Zizi. "It's different, but I loved Otuzuweland, the villages, all of it."

"But it's so, so, rural. Isn't it all fields or something?"

"You have it all wrong," Zizi replied. "It's beautiful. There are no color vapors, but I could smell the grass and watch the stars at night. I even saw the ite irhe up close."

"You mean those big clam things Cherry was talking about?"

"They're more than clams, Lileala. They're ancient and they really do whistle light from their shells. Dr Fodjour thinks they're originally from Earth."

"Right," Lileala scoffed. "From a planet that destroyed itself? Who's Dr Fodjour, anyway?"

"The one who told us all those old Earth tales, remember? In minor school. You used to call him Mr Crop."

"Oh, him!" Lileala smiled. She remembered him well. He was one of the younger teachers back then, only in his seventies and so gangly he reminded her of a tall weed, especially when his beard was growing out of control. It seemed that no matter how often he shaved, the unruly coils would reappear and spread along his jawline like a vine of wild ivy.

She thought about him while she and Zizi pushed their feet through the heavy sands. "He's Cherry's devoted one," Lileala said. "I was disappointed when he and Cherry moved so far from Boundary Circle."

"The Nobility forced him to leave," said Zizi.

Lileala remembered Pathem's comments. "That's right. I did hear that. It's too bad. What's there for him to do in Otuzuweland, out there with nothing but trees?"

"Teach at the university, farm, research," said Zizi. "That's what he does mostly. While I was there, he taught our class about the spontaneous seeds."

"Spontaneous what?"

"Seeds," Zizi repeated. "They're still in the experimental stage, but when these seeds are perfected, all you'll have to do is toss them on the soil. In less than thirty seconds, the crops sprout."

Even though she could tell Zizi wanted a reaction, Lileala sank her toes into the sand and watched it crowd about her sandals and pour beneath the soles of her feet.

"You're quiet all of a sudden," Zizi said. "Why?"

"No reason."

"Don't you think the seeds sound fascinating?"

"No, they sound silly to me. Anyway, who would want to be on a farm?"

Both ladies shut down for a while and Lileala could tell Zizi was irritated. "You know," Lileala said quietly, "you've changed so much I feel I barely know you anymore. What happened to you?"

"I learned to be productive. What happened to *you*?"

Lileala didn't feel she was any different, but she felt her friend slipping away from her. Zizi didn't look at her, and when Lileala tried to hug her she pulled back.

"Don't," she said. "We need to get inside."

With their heads draped in silk scarves and bursts of color dusting the hems of their gowns, they headed toward a golden dome that had a large L-shape, Lileala's first initial, atop a keystone attached to an arch above the door. Zizi opened the door to the dome next to Lileala's and hurried inside without a word.

"Waves of joy to you, too," Lileala mumbled. She stomped into her dome, fell across an oval bed and moped. The walls of the room were a maze of colors but not much of a mood booster. She picked up her satchel and plucked out her favorite music chip, a delirious hymn by an ancient musician. *"Just go wild,"* she sang and closed her eyes. *"If your life's too crazy, just go wild."*

Lash is a–

Lileala sat upright with a jerk. She didn't remember that line in the song. She tugged her ear lobe and the tune continued.

"Let's go wild..."

Then that word again.

Lash.

"Who is it?" she shouted. "Where are you?" She pressed behind her ear and released the music chip.

Link. Link. Link. The voice reverberated.

Grabbing her bed cover, she dived under and peeked at her dial, hoping the voice she heard was a signal from the Sonaguard. She waited.

Lash. Link.

"What is this?" Her fingers stiffened and she tapped her ear harder. She'd once placed two chips in her ear accidentally and heard double sounds.

It. Link.

The cover bunched around Lileala's face, and she yanked it out of the way.

"Whoever you are, come out now!" she said. "I'm calling the Sonaguard."

She waited.

Five minutes passed.

Nothing.

Still shaking, she focused her mind on Otto and watched the energy spirals light up her dial, connecting her to him. "Otto," she said. "When you get this message, contact me." A few minutes later, she got out of bed and searched the floor to see if there was another discarded music chip.

She'd been told that the same dome had served as a Rare Indigo respite site for more than a century. She wondered if any of them listened to Earth hymns and, possibly, had left a couple behind. Lileala went to her vanity and pulled out the center drawer and rummaged through it. She found a stick pen with a blue diamond on top and a necklace of garnet and amber beads. In the next drawer, there was a shiny metal image of Ahonotay wearing a pink and yellow gown that cinched her waist, then ballooned around her lean form. Her complexion was darker, even more sensuous than Lileala's, and her eyes had a distant quality that made it seem as if she was shying away from the optic strip. Lileala compared Ahonotay's cheeks to her own and traced the sharp points of each eyebrow arch. She was stunning, no doubt. But why, Lileala wondered, did she look so frightened?

Of course, Lileala thought, annoyed that she was struggling with such an obvious question. Ahonotay had buckled under the pressure. Maybe being Rare Indigo wasn't even her choice. A breeze of compassion felt its way to Lileala and any resentment she had for her predecessor vanished, replaced by understanding and warmth. For years, she had competed with this woman she'd never met. She had been a heroine Lileala had admired as a minor-child. Later, she'd become a phantom to live up to, be compared to – a vague persona she was supposed to emulate. The idea was nothing but foolishness, she realized now. Ahonotay was just as vulnerable as she was.

She tucked the optic back in the drawer and touched something scratchy. Several crushed music chips had rotted into one ball and left a crumbled mess. Lileala laughed like she had uncovered a treasure. The mystery of the sounds that had been nagging her was now solved. No voices. Just residual murmurs from old, withered chips.

She reached for it as a keepsake and a reminder. For the first time, she felt a sisterhood with the former Rare Indigo. They were different, yes, but the same.

"Of one beat, one accord, one protection," she whispered. "Not such opposites, after all."

Lileala turned off the pod of light floating above her nightstand and climbed back into bed, reflecting on the strangeness of her day.

She pulled the covers over her chest and made a vow. The joy that lay ahead would be a victory for both of them.

"I promise you that, Ahonotay," she murmured. "I'll make you, and every Rare Indigo before you, proud."

6

"Never ignore footprints left by pioneers."
– Swazembian Proverb

Lileala crawled out of bed and ventured through Aswaka, past the water basins and toward a pebbled cabin that resembled a large-mouthed barrel lazing on its side. Behind a door made of shells from various mollusks, walls were splashed with colors from the entrance and along a dim passageway which twisted and meandered into a training chamber of glass floors and pale green walls of rock. A tiny white bulb in the far corner of the ceiling provided the only artificial light in the room.

When Lileala walked in, a group of minor-girls were waiting. Clutching the hands of their elder Mas, some of them were wiggling and wiping sleepy eyes.

"You can find a seat in a room in the back chamber," Lileala told their elder Mas. "There's fig tea and cassava there. Don't worry. I'll take good care of the girls."

The women filed out and Lileala studied the eager little faces. Ever since her trip to the Surface, she'd been unusually cooperative, trying on gowns with Mama Xhosi, participating in extra-credit wave dance rehearsals and agreeing to help with the girls' bi-weekly Black Glass rituals. The practices lasted a couple of hours and she had complained in the past that she didn't have space in her schedule, that they would rob her of the only free time she had. Her vow to the former Rare Indigo

64

had changed all that. Just because she had never walked the Black Glass herself, didn't mean she couldn't offer a few crumbs of guidance. Hand-picked and pushed by Mama Xhosi, Lileala had skipped that early stage of Aspirant development but thought it only proper now that she forgo a bit of sleep and lead a few young ones onto the path.

She stood before them and allowed herself to softly shine. They watched her and squealed.

"I'm Miss Sundiata, your new teacher," she explained. "I'm going to prepare you as best I can. The glow you manufacture will be your navigator. To get it, you'll need to rely on lots of breathing inside you."

She sized up each child individually. Nine minor-girls between the ages of eight and eleven teetered on a floor that was a slick glass blackened by smoke and constructed as a training ground for would-be Aspirants.

Just looking at them made Lileala tingle inside and want to inspire them as much as she could.

"Not all of you will become Rare Indigos," she said in her sweetest voice. "Some of you won't even be Aspirants. But what you will learn on the Black Glass is the Swazembian woman's art of grace, of walking and that special way some of us reflect light. Once you learn that, it will stay with you forever."

"What if I don't learn how?" a girl sputtered. Her eyes had a natural slant and her tiny round lips pursed while she spoke.

"Don't fret. You're all pretty," Lileala said, "and, waves of joy, you have that special wink-wink in your faces already. You will learn what you need to learn."

"This floor tickles," one of the youngest participants announced. "And it's so black I can't see my feet."

"It's not a mirror," Lileala told her. "It's glass. And just like the sacrosanct Black Glass in The Grand Rising it can sparkle and show off your sparkle too. The Uluri designed it that way, just for little curious ones like you. The more you sparkle, the more you'll reflect in the glass."

At that, the girls puffed out their cheeks, trying to force a sheen on their faces, and Lileala had to suppress a giggle.

One day, she thought, one of those girls will stand before Mama Xhosi, glowing. Who would it be?

From her seat in the TET field, the sacred 'S' hovering over The Grand Rising didn't seem quite so daunting. Lileala fixed her gaze on it and held it there, as if seeing it for the first time. While Otto cheered the TET team, she tried to figure out how she'd keep up with the demands of the new assignment she had taken on.

She couldn't wait to meet with the girls again, and already she was pondering various ways to offer instruction. The more she thought about all the fun she'd had, the less she focused on the game. Instead of paying attention to the TET players, she studied The Grand Rising emblem again and sorted through ideas about how she would introduce her young charges to Trinity Breath.

Otto was glued to the field, but she couldn't hide her lack of enthusiasm. "If only you could imagine how I feel right now," she whispered, then leaned in closer to make herself heard over the clamor. A player had just swung an eighteen-pound cylinder and the chime reverberated so loudly her comment was lost.

"What, hon?" Otto said, not bothering to turn his head.

"I said I'm thrilled. There's so much going on, the girls, the Black Glass walk..."

Otto caught the last few words and smiled.

"The Black Glass? You? You're doing that?"

Lileala grinned. "I tried it this morning for the first time. Mama Xhosi doesn't train them that young, you know. She asks Aspirants to prepare new potentials and I volunteered."

A loud crash sent Otto to his feet, shouting and proclaiming another ten points. He sat down and pinched Lileala's right cheek. "I've never seen anyone change so rapidly," he said. As he turned back to the game, Lileala corrected her posture, remembering that she was slumping. A couple of TET fans had recognized her, and their shouts of Rare Indigo had somehow penetrated the noise.

Shimmer big, she told herself. *Give it your all.*

"Waves of joy!" she suddenly announced. "Waves!" Letting her skin gleam, Lileala showcased her excitement and flaunted her stature. She was the pride of Swazembi, Rare High Indigo Native of the Sangha Province, the Most Revered of All Women on the Milky Way Border. The lavish title no longer awed her. She owned it, flaunted it. The respite and its tiny dash of escape had given her an attitude boost.

"Twenty-two to fifteen!" a TET referee shouted. He stood centerfield flapping an Otuzuwe cloth banner that was frayed around the edges. It bore an S and the sun life symbol.

"The Swazembi Waves are too far ahead to be beat now," Otto said.

The referee hoisted the flag higher while men and women on the opposing team gathered on the sidelines and huddled.

"It's nearly over; Lekan's winning this game for us." Otto glanced at Lileala and grinned. "Just so you know, you're the only real star on this field."

Her lips moved before she spoke. "We're both stars."

He kissed her cheek. "I love that you're so happy."

"I don't think I've ever been happier," Lileala said.

Sealing his eyes on Lekan, Otto blinked as the player tossed a cylinder toward a ray of light.

"One more shot. Come on, Lekan!"

The cylinder brushed against the strip of light, turning it solid. It made a screeching noise then landed with a heavy thud onto the ground.

"Cheers! The Waves are the victors!" The declaration sounded throughout the field. Lileala sprung up beside Otto who was already standing and screaming.

"Get him, Lekan!" he yelled. His voice was hoarse.

"That's Centerfree for you," Lileala said. "They produce the best players."

"What about Togu Ta?" Otto asked.

"Which one, East or West?"

"West, obviously."

"Of course, let's not forget your hometown," Lileala teased.

"I'll never let it happen," Otto said. He reached into a sack beside him and pulled out a small gauze bag.

"What's this?" Lileala asked.

Before he could answer, she loosened the string tied around the top.

"Molasses? That's hilarious, Otto! I thought you didn't approve."

He shrugged. "All your hard work should be rewarded."

"Thanks, sweetie." She ripped the wrapping off a molasses chunk. "And, yes, I'm working hard and enjoying every minute."

"So, tell me more about your Surface visit."

"Oh, now you want to hear it? Now that the game is over."

"And?"

"Not much to say. I ran through drifts and felt their tingle on my cheeks, the same stuff the rest of you do all the time."

"What else?"

"Nothing major, just looking forward to the pre-Eclipse tomorrow. You know I have three more before the real Eclipse ceremony. And I'm still thinking about what I found, you know, that optic of Ahonotay I told you about? Seeing that inspired me. I can't get over how much she reminded me of me. She seemed worried though. Maybe she couldn't handle all the demands. Do you think that's why she stopped talking?"

"Maybe. Or maybe it was the Inekoteth," Otto said. "Someone told me once that she heard ancestral voices."

Lileala pushed a chunk of molasses behind her tongue, held it a minute then swallowed it whole. *Is that what she had been hearing too?* She dismissed the idea and kept talking.

"You never told me that," she said. "What else haven't you told me? About Toth? About the ancestors? You probably know more about them too. More than you're willing to admit."

"No, just Tnomo."

"Oh, the star man from nowhere." She thought about their lunch with The Nobility. "There's some pretty big secrets being hidden around here. One day, I'm going to figure out what they are."

7

"A burning stone can damage the fingers, but a burning memory can destroy the heart. The wise will release them both."
–From The Sacred Doctrines of The Uluri

The Mhondora Chinbedza Zi Abebe was nothing like Lileala expected. She had always envisioned him as skinny, with casual attire and a sagging grin. She'd assumed he laughed all the time and never stopped adjusting the inflections in his voice, just like Cherry. Instead, he was bundled in heavy layers of roughly hewn cloth and had a frown that appeared to be permanent. His thick body might as well have been a sealed box. He was wrapped up like a package and stood at arm's length from everyone, as if it was a crime to let guests get too close. When she and Otto walked into the Grace Chapel, he nodded a hasty greeting and stayed clear of pleasantries.

"Sit where you please, but hurry," he said, as if they were late. "The proceedings will begin at Point Two exactly."

She and Otto were followed by Mama Xhosi, Ataba Malik and two female members of The Uluri who were Tawny Dramatic, like Mama Xhosi and Pathem. They wore gold and black headwraps covered with Otuzuwe designs and bowed their heads slightly toward Lileala. She bowed in return, careful not to act too friendly or too aloof. She avoided smiling in case it was disrespectful.

As soon as The Nobility were present, the Mhondora walked

in front of the room and began to pace. The remaining Uluri, cloaked in gold-streaked Otuzuwe garments similar to the Mhondora's, were still entering and he couldn't begin until they finished their parade into the temple. Eight men and three additional women bowed their heads, shared brief apologies and directed their gaze at Lileala. She nearly gasped.

Among them stood a man Lileala guessed to be around two hundred and fifty years of age, but with a round, somber face she would never forget. He was the merchant from The Outer Ring who had grudgingly sold her the molasses. She hung her head.

"Otto," she tried to whisper.

"Shhh. Respect the silence," he murmured, so low she could barely hear him.

She trembled. The disgruntled merchant was watching her, and she didn't want to make eye contact. Instead, she deliberately fussed with the puffed sleeves of her pre-Eclipse garment, wondering if she should have requested another fitting. The sleeves were a bit too inflated, and the hemline, which stopped just below her ankles, should have been only a half inch above the floor.

After trying and failing another attempt to get Otto's attention, she debated taking a side aisle and sneaking out of the room. Why was this happening now? Finally, she was content, ready to celebrate and now, this. Could she be on the verge of losing her title for a second time?

The Mhondora ceased pacing and addressed the crowd.

"Welcome to the Eclipse preview. "His voice was gravelly but the expression on his face had a vaguely pleasant quality. The Mhondora's elbows were on the podium, and he was twisting his mouth into something that resembled a smile.

"The long-awaited Rare Indigo is here," he said. "I understand the Noble Pathem and Oluntungi made personal acquaintance with her recently due to the courtesy of Pineal Crew Officer, Otto Keita Gonga. But for the rest of us, this is our first official encounter. As well it should be. No one but her direct supervisors, The High Host Xhosi Sekou and Ataba Malik Osei, should have had managerial contact with her before the pre-Eclipse rituals."

Beneath the surface of her skin, subdued sparks were waiting to be released, but Lileala wasn't sure if she should Shimmer or honor her desire to flee. This couldn't turn out well, no matter what she did. She tried again to get Otto to face her, but his eyes were cemented to the Mhondora, who began pacing again. Several appointed minor-children stood about three meters behind him, holding lit candles and assembling into a choir.

"Iiet Kyree Ilettisone," they sang in fluent Otuzuwe, a village-tongue Lileala studied in minor school.

"Rise and be grand. Iiet Kyree illetis ke Tinonehh. Rise and be of the Grace.

Ase' From the rumbling straits of the Bagoe River
Ase' From the forests to the drifts
Ase' From here, we deliver
Ase' From here, the High Grace lifts
Et Cem Tiris Totwo ke Tinonehh. It is grand to be of the Grace.
Et Cem Tiris Totwo. It is grand."

Two choruses later, all the minor-children but one girl, the lead candle lighter, filed out of the temple. Like the others, she wore a decorative grass vest that could have been mistaken for painted burlap. Her two braids were askew, and she stood far behind the altar, watching the Mhondora with great interest, her head tilted to one side. The Mhondora bowed his head and continued.

"Of one beat, one accord, one protection."

The congregation repeated: "Of one beat, one accord, one protection."

"High honors to The Grace." He spoke with a calculated slowness and each word seemed like a drip of thick syrup. Lileala picked at her thumb and tried to force out a strong breath. Doubt and worry were all she could entertain at the moment. Her mind was under siege. Would there be another announcement? Would her title be torn away for good?

"We are ready," the Mhondora said to the merchant. "Come up to the front please."

The Uluri merchant rose and Lileala buried her head in her hands.

She felt Otto glaring at her in disbelief. He kicked her heel, but she refused to respond.

"And now, the incoming Rare Indigo, please come forward for the pre-Eclipse introduction."

The Mhondora's command felt like a death sentence. She remembered all the times she had foolishly abused Shimmer. What if the sneaky merchant had seen that too? Or seen her at the Red Hot? Is it possible that he infiltrated the dance haven the evening she broke her oath? The torment was too much. Pushing herself to her feet, she clutched Otto's shoulder and walked. Each step was a journey through anguish.

A man in sacred cloth was waiting up front, possibly, to condemn her. She didn't stand a prayer.

The gravelly voice of the Mhondora was the next sound she heard.

"Rare High Indigo Lileala Sundiata Walata: we will be ready to present you to the public within the next forty-seven days. It is official. Will you accept the call?"

Her response was a question.

"Did you say 'accept'?"

There were loud murmurs, then silence.

"Will you accept?" Mhondora Chinbedza repeated.

"Yes?" Lileala said, wondering if her shock was apparent.

"Of one beat, one accord, one protection," the Mhondora rasped.

"In honor of the Grace, Chief Akin Rilem Yakeni will make a presentation to the Rare Indigo."

Confusion flooded Lileala's mind. *The merchant was The Uluri chief?*

"Young Rare One," he said, flipping a sash of Otuzuwe cloth behind his back. He held a black velvet box in his hand

and thrust it toward her. "I have been part of The Uluri for centuries, but never have I met an Aspirant as strong-willed as you."

He turned to the audience.

"My good people, did you know my son owns a haven on The Outer Ring?"

Oh no oh no oh no oh no.

"Well, I was there a few weeks ago, substituting for him while he and his devoted visited Toth, and I did not expect to see..." He pointed. "*Her.*"

Lileala's stomach dropped, and she struggled to breathe without shaking.

"She was conflicted," he continued, "but also arrogant. A bold risk taker. Pretending to know it all but possessing an... interesting will."

He turned to look at her and a small smile appeared on his face. Lileala held her breath.

"She showed me that the true Rare Indigo does not have to be a total follower. She should adhere to the codes, ye, but not to the point of sacrificing the soul of her ye. In this case, the ye is her inner truth."

Lileala clasped her hands in front of her, trying to keep them still.

"I was not in a place where I typically spend time," he went on. "But, ye, I was there. And I observed this one before me, wrestling with decisions on how to control a whim."

The wrinkles on his forehead came to a point and his countenance changed. "I believe there is something deep in our history that fights for life in this Rare Indigo," he said. "That something is powerful and should not be extinguished. It is for the good of the soul of this land."

His stare turned back and rested on Lileala.

"Young one, before the Eclipse, fig cones, sweets and wanderings are allowed. Outer Ring dance havens, however, are not."

He saw me!

"Yet, I watched you venture into a night haven. But I also watched you pull yourself away. Another Uluri also informed me that she had seen you at the early hour hurrying toward the chambers of the Black Glass. And knowing that you, with so little free space in your duties, took the time to guide minor-children, made all of us take note."

With a slight bow of his head, he hesitated before continuing. "Ye, it was me who made the report on your brazen ways," he said. "And it was still me who decided to let it rest."

Tears welled in Lileala's eyes as he handed her the velvet box. She was afraid to open it until he nudged her. Then with her fingers shaking, she clumsily pried it apart and stared at a skinny black rod, about two inches long, with a glistening aqua green tip.

"The key?" she said. "The Grand Rising key?"

"Ye, the key carved from moldavite crystal. It is yours now, to keep."

"But I thought…"

The Uluri chief hushed her. "Ye, I know what you are thinking. Normally, the key is given to the Rare Indigo after The Eclipse. But you are the long awaited one. And –" He glanced at the other Uluri and appeared unsure if what he was about to say was their consensus. "You are different, young one, an explorer like no other. You go against tradition, ye, and for that reason I fought with The Uluri. I convinced them to see reason and not trample upon the imaginings that make you who you are. We must become accustomed to Indigos with strong minds that challenge and inspire us."

Lileala nearly gasped again. A strong mind? Since when? "Th-Thank you," she stuttered.

"Why do you thank me?" he asked. "I did not bend tradition and I did not skirt it. Now, this key is made from particles of a meteorite that struck the Earth countless years ago. Receiving it is a great honor that has been passed along for centuries.

Giving it is an honor and, in my lifetime, this honor has only occurred on a few occasions because, as most of you know, I am still a very young man of two hundred and fifty."

The Uluri and Nobility laughed gently.

"Youth is relative," The Uluri chief told them. "Our pigment ensures that ours is lasting, and it heals our injuries, does it not?" He turned back to Lileala. "Melanin is your birthright, but you inherited the exquisite loveliness and, I might add, inquisitive spirit." He waited a minute and poked his index finger at the black box in her hand. "You have earned your place as our Rare Indigo. But it is up to you to do this title justice. Go to your own knowledge chamber, and also visit the chambers in The Grand Rising. Search more, obstinate, curious one, but –" he shot her a stern glance, "– be careful how deep you dig."

8

*"Anger is not an aspect of civility. Dispel it quickly, lest it sprout
thorns in the spirit and erase the gloss from your character."*
– Indigo Aspirant Code D, Provision Xiim

The woman evaporated, then returned. She had a pompous
air and a harshness in her demeanor that bothered Lileala. She
wondered if the woman was overwhelmed by the hoop of jewels
jutting from the band around her neck. The ornament was
striking, but it looked cumbersome. Lileala figured the spokes
surrounding it gave a circumference of at least two meters.

"Show me something else," she asked. The woman flowing
from the knowledge stream was interesting and an essential
part of her daily lesson, but ever since the Eclipse preview,
Lileala had been yearning for more.

Nothing more appeared. The woman's image remained in
front of her, and an explanation floated next to it: "Sadi Aja
Daouda, the Rare Indigo of Swazembi, three hundred and
sixty sun years past."

Lileala sighed. Sadi had blue-black skin and eyes that seemed as
if they weren't looking at anything. She was burdened with neck
gear that made Lileala nervous. Lileala wasn't sure she wanted to
wear one of those things. It reminded her of those old-fashioned
wagon wheels she'd once seen in an imageflow of Earth artifacts.

"Come on," Lileala said loudly. "Can I get a stream about
Toth?"

A streak of words wavered in place: *Not part of your scheduled lessons.*

"So, what?" Lileala mumbled. She gazed out at the marketplace. Her bubble in the knowledge chamber provided a full view of the comings and goings, but the sun had barely risen and not much was happening. No one was playing the drums and there wasn't a single trace of minor-children buying fig cones.

She turned back and continued reading the stream. It was filling up with miscellaneous information about Swazembi.

"Sheesh," Lileala said. "If you can't show me Toth, then show me another world. I want to dig deeper."

A ghost of a being fluttered in front of her and was joined by another and another until there were ten of them, humanoid and bald, with skin that was waxy and transparent enough for Lileala to see outlines of opaque, throbbing organs. The odd creatures appeared to be squabbling over a black stone. Lileala let out a laugh that rattled through the chamber.

"What, under the stars, is so funny?" Zizi was close by, seated in an adjacent bubble.

"Here, look. These are the strangest jokesters I've ever seen," Lileala said.

The crepe-like bubble of glass around Zizi disintegrated and she scooted her seat closer.

Lileala laughed louder and pointed at the floating words: *They are prone to outbursts, provoked by the excess of adrenalin periodically surging through their blood.*

"Those aren't jokesters, they're Kclabs," Zizi said. "I didn't believe in them either, until some of my Sonaguard friends told me they were real. I don't get it though. How did they leak into your stream?"

"Maybe the knowledge loop felt my impatience," Lileala kidded. "'Even it knows that Aspirants need to be entertained sometimes too."

They giggled together and Lileala felt encouraged.

"Zizi," she asked. "Are you still angry at me?"

"About what? That encounter on the Surface?" Zizi made a dismissive motion with her right hand. "I've forgotten it."

"Waves of joy!" Lileala paused for few seconds then, before Zizi could reactivate her bubble, she blurted: "I think they liked me."

"Who?"

"The Uluri, The Nobility, all of them."

"I know. I heard they gave you a key to The Grand Rising."

Satisfaction swelled inside of Lileala, and she pointed to the silver chain around her neck. The moldavite key hung from the chain, but it was hidden behind her blouse's ruffled collar. She wondered if she should show it off, but wouldn't that make her a light stealer?

"They did, yes," she said. "I thank the Grace of the Ancestors! I'm humbled."

"I'm surprised," Zizi studied her. "I believe you. I can see it all over your face."

"Does it show that much?"

When Zizi nodded, Lileala went into a Shimmer, releasing scatters of bluish light across her cheeks. "Sometimes, I wish you could do this too, with me," she added.

Zizi scrunched her nose and chuckled.

"Don't laugh," Lileala said. "We could be a Rare Indigo duo."

"There can't be more than one Rare One, silly. And, you know I don't know how to Shimmer."

"Then what's next for you?" Lileala asked. "Are you still thinking of joining the Sonaguard?"

"Yes, but not here. I want to be stationed on Toth." Zizi spoke fast, as if leaking a secret.

"On Toth! You!" Lileala clapped. "Waves of joy!"

"I'll just be a guard, okay?"

"And what's wrong with that? Think of all those worlds you'll get to visit."

"I agree about that part." Zizi shifted in her seat. "In Gwembia, I was studying agriculture, but I decided I wanted to do something that would get me all the way out of Swazembi for a while. It feels so insular sometimes."

"But shouldn't you be doing Sonaguard training?" Lileala asked. "Why are you here?"

"Same reason you are," Zizi said. "Chamber lessons seem to be a requirement before you can do or study anything."

Lash. Lash. Lash.

The words buzzed in Lileala's ear. She swirled her finger inside it, though she knew there was nothing there. She'd taken Ahonotay's rotted music chips to her compartment. She didn't know why she'd kept them but realized now that she should throw them away. She blocked the intruding voice by focusing on the knowledge stream in front of her. It had moved past Kclabs and on to information about the revered ancestor, Tnomo. A story that still puzzled Lileala. How was he proclaimed as Swazembi founder, yet there were so few personal details about him? He traveled to the planet from his native star more than five thousand sun years ago. But what star and where was it located? Nothing had ever given these details.

She focused again on Zizi.

"Sometimes Swazembi makes me feel trapped," Zizi was saying. "I love it here, but I want to explore."

"I understand. But..." Lileala paused. "Just think if you were me and couldn't leave at all. Not grumbling, though! Not anymore. I'm finally ready. I'm not worried and I'm not confused about my destiny. But you – you'll be on Toth! And I'll get to see you here when you're on duty."

"Sure. We can meet up at The Zambezi. Have you been yet? It's Boundary Circle's newest raids."

Lileala made a face. "I really miss sneaking to The Outer Ring, just you and me. We're the only ones who had the nerve. You called the rest of them Boundary Girls? Remember?"

"Ironic, huh?" Zizi said. "Now look at us; *we're* the Boundary Girls." She shrugged. "You think you might be able to break tradition? Maybe set some new social rules?"

"Rules? The Rare Indigo?" Lileala scoffed. "If I'm lucky I might just get to weigh in on a tourist dispute now and then." "Doesn't matter." Zizi laughed. "All those parties, and dinners. I think I'd be having so much fun I wouldn't care about much else."

"You think that now, but…" Lileala sighed. "I don't know, it's not for everyone. Now, you get to sleep all you want and eat whatever you want. Women without Shimmer don't have nearly as many demands and –"

"And??" Zizi said, aghast.

The hurt on her face was Lileala's cue to shut up. But it was too late. Zizi was escaping into the privacy of her chamber bubble. With one swoop of her hand, the bubble had solidified, forming a sheer film around her study cubicle.

Lileala knew there was no use in trying to choke out an apology. The damage was already done.

9

"As we take one step, oh Grace of the Ancestors, please help us take two more."
– Otuzuwe prayer

Flee you must. Cry and flee.

A tingle crept through Lileala's ears, trailed by a jumble of confusing words. The little nagging voice had turned into a symphony overnight and it was finally clear to her. This was not Earth music, and these messages were not coming from chips.

Precepts. Precepts.

As discretely as possible, she wiggled her head, hoping to shake off the taunts. Mama Xhosi had set aside one hour as a preview for Swazembians who wanted to get an early peek at the new Rare Indigo. Perched on a crystal stool, Lileala was expected to be a living centerpiece, casting sparkles over the triangular glass on Ring One and holding an exquisite state of Shimmer. She couldn't afford to so much as flinch.

She swallowed and breathed in so deeply she worried that she might choke. Letting her neck relax, she used her palms to make soothing circular motions around her throat.

Cry. Your go way is tears to cry. The voices came like irritating little bells ringing in unison. *Cry and flee. Flee.*

Flee? Lileala's entire body tightened, and she desperately tried to reclaim her peace. But she wanted to shout back at the

82

voices that she wished she could flee their nagging, that she was preparing for one of the greatest Swazembi honors and didn't have time for strange games and cruel gibberish.

A cluster of viewers assembled around the Triangle. For the showing, Mama Xhosi had the area encased in a colorless vapor that ebbed and flowed. She could also solidify it into an impenetrable bubble with one press on Lileala's dial. She said it was to protect Lileala from the threat of errant wanderers, but Lileala knew she only did it for effect.

"Hi there, wonderful Rare lady!" one of viewers yelled. He was young and hyper and thin as a nail. He was disrupting her concentration and she had been promised that rowdiness would not be allowed here. Although annoyed, she saw no need to press the bubble signal. She took a wait-and-see approach. The Triangle was located on the south end of Ring One, in an area that tourists easily could access, especially if they had just attended a TET game. Maybe, this tourist was lost. The TET field was less than one thousand two hundred meters away, a distance that could be traveled quickly on an automated floor path.

"Hey there, sexy lady Indee Gooo!" he yelled, waving an optic square.

She remained poised and told herself that after her Eclipse, she'd ask The Sonaguard to do a better job pre-screening anyone attending TET games, maybe place special restrictions on their tickets. Her head turned toward the other visitors, and she deliberately avoided the one who was misbehaving. He'd get no image of her today.

"Oh, rare lady," he said in a tone that made her queasy. She breathed out, hoping her frustration wasn't affecting her Shimmer.

She waved at a little one who was clutching a molasses chunk and batting his hands at the mist. His elder Ma laughed and held him up so they could both get a closer look. "You're stunning," the woman said. The toddler took the seat in her arms as an opportunity to yank at her headwrap. "No, no, sweetie," she said. "I want to look nice like the Indigo lady. Look. Isn't she pretty?"

The male tourist proceeded past the woman and child and into the vapor barrier, but by then a Sonaguard had spotted him and ordered him to leave. He resisted and Lileala realized he was drunk. The guard brandished a blinking, fist-sized orb of color and light.

"No, you don't, Mr Sonaguard man," the tourist said. "You're not going to spray..." The guard aimed it at the drunken heckler, letting the colors flow from his fingers. His target dropped to the floor, sound asleep with perfect, round circles of color orbiting his forehead.

"Send me backup," the guard announced in his dial. "I just color sprayed a visitor with nap pellets."

Several Sonaguards arrived at once and Lileala used the commotion as a chance to take a quick break. Children were scampering about, delighted by the chaos. An audience gathered and a local middle-aged couple in floor-sweeping Otuzuwe garments snapped an image of themselves posing in front of the tourist while he was carted away on a floating stretcher.

Before Lileala could wonder what was next, a couple of Aspirants rushed up to her with powders, a mirror and a comb. Mama Xhosi couldn't be there, so it was up to them to freshen the Rare Indigo's make-up, tidy her hair, give her whatever she wanted. *Some of that tourist's drink,* Lileala thought, then laughed inside at the shallowness of her wish.

"Hurry now and return to your post," one of them said. Lileala went without an argument.

Flee, flee. The voice was back, along with the tingling sensation. She winced, trying to ignore it, and not worry about the diminished size of her smile.

Several local minor-schoolboys chased one another along the perimeter of the Triangle while their elder-child chaperone waved an optic square and captured an image of Lileala. "The Rare Indigo statue," he announced.

"She's the most resplendent in the galaxy, not a statue," a woman in a sheer blouse and red, body-hugging trousers – clearly a tourist – reprimanded the young chaperone. "Be respectful."

Lileala smiled graciously, hoping her eyes didn't announce her worry.

Flee, flee, the voice continued.

She grasped a clump of hair and let it bounce through her fingers to soothe her. Then someone tall and dark with heaps of coarse curls appeared in the crowd. The hazy film around the Triangle was blinking in and out intermittently. The minute it slowed, Lileala got a better look. It was Issa, her night-black skin saturated in an even darker liquid make-up. Instead of smiling, she wore the bruised smirk of someone who had been snubbed. Lileala beamed. She couldn't let Issa know anything was wrong.

The ear-tingling and the taunts dissipated and Lileala breathed through her nose, relieved. Issa hurried away as a dozen more strangers paused to observe Lileala in silence, then moved along, trailed by a trio of women who had been selling goods in The Great Hall. They were conspicuous, balancing braided breads and baskets of wildflowers on their heads and toting the plumpest, ripest of berries. The bread and flowers were their own gifts, but Lileala was certain the oversize fruit was from Cherry – she was the only farmer from the valley who could grow produce as large as it once grew on Earth. The farm women sat the baskets on the ledge surrounding the Triangle. They waved and shouted out Cherry's regards.

"This is from us and the head grower herself," said one of the women. She and the friends accompanying her appeared to be of the same age status, though Lileala couldn't tell from their faces exactly what those ages were. Together, they were a black and brown sea without waves or ripples. Yet, they had a mature presence, wide and searching eyes and voices with depth and confidence. Lileala guessed them to be two hundred and fifty, even three hundred sun years, perhaps.

"Cherry will visit later, when she's finished selling her fruit," another one of the women called out. "I have come in her place," she added. "I am Yewande."

She ended her greeting by softly ululating, a celebratory series of yelps that were Otuzuwe tradition. She topped it off with a slight curtsy and a sassy little dance. Yewande was the most outgoing and flamboyant of the trio, decked in a green headwrap and a red and pink octagon-patterned dress that swept the floor, swinging as she spoke and rhythmically swayed her hips.

"Waves of joy," Lileala said, tightening her jaws. She hadn't expected any of her visitors to be so talkative. If she had known that she wouldn't have stuffed a square of molasses in her mouth during her break.

Yewande's brows raised, and her eyes caught Lileala's. "Self-control is a virtue, young Indigo and it's something we all need to learn," she said in a tone that sounded, to Lileala, like she was being scolded.

"An old habit," Lileala explained. "I was trying to hide it but, honestly, it's not off limits yet, not until after my Eclipse."

"You're human," said Yewande, suddenly amused. She twisted her mouth to hide her grin. "Well, enjoy. We have to return to the valley, back to our mates. We don't want to face the backlash of their tongues."

The women with Yewande laughed, but Lileala grimaced. It was that word the women used that bothered her. Backlash. It troubled her. But why?

Then a sudden piercing sensation raced through her ears and began slow laps around her neck.

"For Grace's sake, why such a sad face?" Yewande asked. "Is something wrong?"

"Waves of nothing," Lileala lied. But while she spoke, she played with the springs of her hair and let her mind drift.

"Please excuse me," she said. "And please tell Cherry I might not be here when she arrives, but I hope to stop by another one of her talks soon. She's a wandering light, that one."

At that, the ladies were able to laugh again. "Now, get back to your duties," said Yewande. "Shimmer."

"Waves of thanks!" Lileala stood up then, brooding and watching until they became dots in the crowd. She checked her dial. Showtime was over. Time to get back to the knowledge chamber.

Her return was yet another disappointment. There was only one other student in the chamber, and he was an elder-child whose stream displayed a sequence of numerical equations which then switched to images of a battlefield exploding on the Earth. Lileala became distracted and tried to peek, but he shrunk the space in his bubble and somehow managed to make it roll a few meters away. Insulted, Lileala tried but failed to get her bubble to move in another direction.

How did he do that? She pondered a minute and let it go. She knew there was a reason she didn't like science students. She went back to her own boring lessons and tried to dredge up something new.

"Lash," she said out loud, still troubled by the village women's usage of the term. A hologram of a woman appeared in the empty space before her. The woman's skin shimmered around a tiny smile and small, slanted eyes. She wore a gown lined with strips of gold and red jewels.

"Lash," Lileala said again. "I'd like to see this item, please. What is a lash?"

A procession of facts streamed in front of her like a river in a storm, but the information was the same unexciting drivel:

"Tnomo is the founder of Swazembi. He came from a star and is credited with establishing scientific formulas that created an energy transport system known as The Sweep."

"I know. I know," Lileala said, exasperated. The tingle at the nape of her neck had come and gone and come back again. She stroked the skin beneath her curls and found a pimple, teenier than a crumb of bread. *Is that all?* she thought. Let it go. It's almost nothing. But she knew better. Her pores were always clean and clear.

She let out a sigh first, then a long, tired yawn. The Euc, she thought, that's what she'll do. The blend of eucalyptus and cypress oils and powders was her favorite Shimmer rinse, but she hadn't been using it as much as she should lately. Too busy. Too exhausted. And now, this. She caressed her neck again, chastising herself for being so neglectful and fretting over how long it would take for the Euc to do its job.

The worries hung on to her and she couldn't resist making one last swipe with the back of her hand beneath her chin.

The blemish was a wee bit larger.

"How did I let this happen?" Disgusted, Lileala made her way to the door and headed home. On the shuttle ride, she considered asking for another break, but dismissed the idea. She'd found such good favor with The Nobility and The Uluri. Besides, the Eclipse was only five weeks away.

"A Euc bath, please," she announced as soon as she walked into her sphere. Bubbled water gushed from spigots in the amber-studded wall of her grooming studio and into the shallow tub below. She threw her satchel to the side and slid out of her clothes and into the hot bubbles, letting the cypress oils soak her skin.

After a long soak, she stepped out of her bath and reached for her robe. She stuck an arm through the left sleeve and accidentally nudged a stack of items piled high on the counter. They tumbled to the floor and Ahonotay's crumpled ball of Earth chips rolled down with them.

Tired of looking at it, she grabbed the ball and threw it toward a compact trash evaporator but missed. It hit the floor and she cringed, expecting it to explode with musical voices. But it simply cracked into pieces. Within one of the pieces was a ragged scrap of bark paper with a decaying chunk of molasses stuck to its side.

Lileala walked over and picked it up. Evidently, her predecessor enjoyed sweets as much as she did. The idea made her smile. She flattened out the ripped corner of the paper, careful not to tear it any further. After smoothing its fragile edges, she noticed some handwritten words, barely legible.

"I loathe you. Whoever you are you make me want to vomit."

"What?" she said out loud. "Ahonotay?"

She couldn't stop looking at it. Why would the former Rare Indigo leave behind such a horrid note? Was she furious because she couldn't speak? Was she jealous of the next Aspirant to follow her? Lileala read it over and over, trying to find some meaning, but she couldn't. None of it made sense. In a fit of frustration, she ripped the wad of paper in half.

Maybe she and Ahonotay were not alike at all. If this note was any indication, maybe she was mean and resentful. But why? Lileala dropped the note in the evaporator and pushed it out of her mind. She didn't have time to deal with nonsense. She had ceremonies to prepare for, more wave dance rehearsals coming up and a stupid blemish to heal in a hurry. Hoping that, maybe, it had shrunk, she sat in front of her vanity table and took another hard glance. She spotted it instantly and gasped. The pimple or whatever it was had grown as big as a grain of rice.

Her face twitched. She considered contacting Otto, then decided not to trouble him. There was no need to mess up his evening with something that might be gone in a day or so. The same with Mama Xhosi. She'd only tell her to bathe in Euc again. What else could she instruct her to do? She thought about Zizi. She really missed her friend and at times like this needed to talk to her more than ever. Zizi could be unpredictable, but Lileala had a strong hunch that she'd make her laugh right now. Probably, she'd tease her, force her to see how silly she was acting over a flaw that was scarcely noticeable. Lileala called herself childish, assuming that would be the other comment Zizi would make. They might even argue, call one another light stealers. She didn't mind.

She prepared to reach out to her, despite their recent spat. A slight tickle on her forehead and a second peek in the mirror stopped her. There was a new scar forming and it was as large as the tip of her finger.

A sudden reflex made her gasp again. How could a scar form so fast? What triggered it? Lileala breathed in and out until she had summoned a thin flame in the back of her mind. But it was dim and its power so weak. When she went into Trinity Breath, a mild warmth always seemed to sway along her arms and around the circumference of her neck. She usually felt it, the little flicks of glitter that were as gentle as the Surface rain. This time, there was nothing. No fuzzy feeling. No Shimmer. Instead, there was a thicket of heat, a discomfort that caused beads of perspiration to line her forehead and soak her cheeks. She wanted to wipe the sweat away, but her hands were shaking too much. When she tried to lift them, her whole body tensed. She gasped once more and whispered under her breath. Stay calm. It will go away.

But it didn't go away, and each time Lileala tried to Shimmer her breaths became increasingly shallow and her body felt parched. Confused and miserable, she slowly made her way to the bedroom and slid between the sheets.

Several hours passed and she lay wide awake. For the first time in her pampered life, Lileala Walata Sundiata was too upset to sleep.

PART II
Trieca's Reckoning

1

"If worlds with suns exist, why do we cling to a leftover fragment of the Earth, hurtling nowhere?"
– Weekly scroll message, Trieca Menton

Outside Roloc's window, a night work crew was quietly installing a row of peculiar lamp posts. Twisting and slithering, the posts moved about like serpents curling toward the sky. Above each post, a pod of light hovered. Then it free-floated.

Each pod left its base and fluttered along dark, snow-covered roads. Flickering, they shone through flimsy dormitory curtains, penetrated crude ice shelters, and lit up the tin shacks hidden within snowy valleys. By the time the pods floated back to their posts, every dwelling was left with traces of bright, golden light.

In his sleep, Roloc could feel it. He stirred and a half smile inched up one side of his hollow face. He had been dreaming about basking in the heat and had seen himself swimming in a sea of flowing sun rays. He awoke, looked around, and trembled. Fingers of light lay across his blanket and rested on his shoulders. But where had they come from? He shook himself free of his cover, pushed aside the window curtain, and peered out at the winking pods.

Roloc sucked in his cheeks. Had the Sector accepted a gift from Swazembi? Without telling security? He blinked, glanced again at the procession of lights and reached for the cracked hand mirror on top of his dresser. Gazing into it wasn't easy.

His own appearance offended him; he detested those pebbles he called eyes. They were too small for his round face and conspicuously uneven. He was still cursing them and balking at the sheerness of his flesh when his door rattled. Someone was banging and speaking in a muffled tone.

"Open up now. Right now! We have to talk."

"Who is it, damn it?"

"You know who. Haliton. Open up."

Roloc shifted all his weight to the left side of his body and limped toward the door. He had aggravated his right knee during a recent scuffle, and it had become hard to walk. "I didn't recognize your voice. Hold on, hold on."

Before Roloc had even opened the door all the way, Haliton hurried inside. He yanked the corner of Roloc's curtain, and pointed. "This! This can't be. I said no. The entire Sector said no. We're the dammed security and they got this past us."

A beam of light pierced the curtains and flitted across the room. Roloc grinned. He was in a foul mood too, but it made him feel better to know that Haliton was just as upset as he was. "Nothing we can do now," he said.

"There's plenty we can do!" Haliton said. "We can have them taken down."

"Not a good idea. You know how long it's been since our orbit shifted. Kclaben is farther from the sun than we've ever been. There's a full generation here that's never known this much light."

Haliton cackled, then opened a rusted folding chair and cringed at the sound of its legs scraping the floor. The dingy concrete was standard in quarters provided to the security team. They were at the bottom rung of the Sector, with few privileges and even fewer furnishings – just a cot, a small nook for eating, a wood-burning stove, and a flannel drape that hid the metal tub used for bodily hygiene.

"Why aren't you as mad as I am?" Haliton buried his face in both hands.

"I am, but I know we can't deprive the unders," Roloc said.

"Now that they've experienced light, they're not going to let it go."

"The lights will be removed even if I have to do it myself!" Haliton declared.

"You saw those things. The lamp stands move like they're alive or something. I wouldn't touch them if I were you."

"They stopped."

"Stopped what? Moving?" Roloc asked.

"Yeah, they're stiff as nails. Maybe it was the cold air, or maybe that's just how these Swazembi gadgets work."

"But how?" Roloc glanced outside and looked back at Haliton.

"I don't know," Haliton said. "But they're solid. They should be easy to grab and dispose of."

"Just try it. There will be an uprising." Roloc plopped down on his cot and smiled as he spoke. He was proud of himself for keeping his wits about him.

Haliton glared at his security partner and raised his voice. "You know what the worst part is? The unders are going to be looking up to Swazembians now like they're gods."

"Let them look where they want. They're unders."

"What about their young ones? Do you want them to become full grown, still believing Kclaben is inferior to Swazembi?"

Roloc stood and searched until he found a small wedge of black ore crystal that he'd left on top of his nightstand. He put it in his mouth and crushed it with his back teeth, chewing hastily. Once the intoxicant melted into his saliva, he relaxed just enough to avoid acting like Haliton. He could see clear veins bulging on his temples.

"I'm thinking more about how the unders must be feeling," Roloc said. "They're happy, I'm sure. They can get around now and can probably find their way without holding those heavy lanterns. The stupid things are always running out of fuel, and when we actually have fuel, there's not enough lanterns to go around. They have to pass them from one dwelling to the next."

"I don't care," Haliton said.

"But that's what we must learn. To care, right? Here, we already have some light spurts and there's even more in some of the other halls. The unders have done without. So, just contain yourself, why don't you?"

"Contain myself?" A colorless vein in Haliton's forehead throbbed dangerously. He pressed on it with his left palm and headed toward the door, wagging a finger at Roloc.

"I'm going to find out who allowed this and have him punished. There's a gathering at Point Three. Chief Hardy wants us all there – overseers, scribes, security, damned near everyone in the Sector. We're meeting in Principal Hall."

The lights in Principal Hall were sporadic, trickling like water from a broken shower head. Roloc limped in wearing loose white trousers and a white calf-length tunic with a wide collar that left a lot of room for his scrawny neck.

"I hope this session doesn't end up like the last one," he griped to himself. "My knee is still aching from that brawl."

He found a seat and waited as the fifty-one other Sector members filed into the hall. Among them were eleven bald women wearing white smocks that hung to the floor and eyes that sat lopsided in faces that were as translucent as molten wax. But one stood out: Trieca Menton. A series of white birthmarks coated her lower left cheek, the tip of her nose and the bottom half of her forehead and chin. The milky patterns made her more appealing than most women on Kclaben. That, and the fact that her eyes were symmetrical, helped her become the first of her gender allowed into the Sector. The others were appointed soon after, but none held as high a role as Trieca, overseer and scribe.

Haliton rose from his seat, turned to the crowd and made a cackling noise as he cleared his throat.

"Well, I guess we can all agree there's nothing like the flashing new light pods that have suddenly popped up over the icy roads and hills. Splendid, aren't they?"

There was a murmur.

"I said, splendid, don't you agree?" he asked.

Bertram, second in command to Haliton, stood up and pointed. "So, you're the one who accepted charity from Swazembi?"

Haliton shot him a mean glance. "Bertram, you report to me, correct? Then you already know my position on this. Shut up, will you?"

Then he waited for someone else to take the bait.

There was no answer. Even the murmuring in the back of the room quieted.

"I'll get to the point then," Haliton continued. "Someone in here is happy about those pods and I assure you it's not me. I don't condone gifts from Swazembi, or any part of the Coalition for that matter. But someone else in here does, someone who isn't speaking up." He paused again, waiting for a response.

"This is a disgrace!" he shouted. "Until they admit us onto Swazembi, let us visit like everyone else, we are to *shun* them. Do you understand?!" He looked to Roloc in the seat beside him for help, but Roloc's ore crystal had left him dizzy. He swayed and tipped forward, trying not to lose his balance.

"Ore," Roloc whispered. He was staring at Haliton and shrugging his shoulders. Stumbling to his feet. He tried to speak into Haliton's left ear. "Take a wedge of black ore. Like I did." Roloc slumped back into his seat and promptly slid onto the floor. The room thundered with laughter.

"Now you see why I don't depend on those damn things?" Haliton mumbled. But Roloc's head was spinning so fast he couldn't answer. He lay on the floor, staring at the fractured spurts of light and waiting for the laughs to subside. When they did, they were replaced with more accusations and the rumble of low voices.

But one voice rang louder. It penetrated the storm in the room and silenced it. "I did it! Yes, I did it." The voice was gruff but with a high-pitched lilt. Trieca Menton stood. The room was a den of mad shouts and threats. "Listen, hear me out!" she said above them all. "I did it, and after I say what I have to say, I defy any of you to disagree."

"You're out of line!" Bertram shouted. "You should be jailed for insubordination."

"Let go of your damn pride!" she shouted back. "How much longer do you think our fuel will last? Our wells have been coming up dry for days!"

Three overseer security officers escorted her to the front of the hall. Trieca's face went cold. With a dare in her eyes, she lifted her chin as if her birthmarks offered her protection. Chief Hardy jumped to her defense. He was a primary overseer, taller than most on Kclaben, with a longer neck and a higher bridged nose.

"Leave her alone and let her talk," he said, standing up from his seat in the front row. "She and the other women have some sort of plan and I want to hear it."

Trieca nodded a thank you at Hardy, walked to the podium facing the crowd and continued. "All of you, listen. You let me in this Sector so females could have a say. Well, I had my say and, as an overseer, I think I had every right to accept those lights."

"We voted against them!" Bertram shouted. "You can't shut out the entire Sector." Bertram waved at the chief. "Why are you allowing this anarchy? Arrest her."

At Chief Hardy's urging, several officers shunned Bertram. Along with the female Sector members, they formed a human chain in front of Trieca in a show of support.

"If you take her, then you might as well take every woman here," the chief said. "Then what will we say to the unders? We promised their young ones that there would be women among us, that those who join us will not do so as concubines. Make the women leave and they'll never trust us again. You say you don't want them to see Swazembians as superior; well, they will. Just keep doing what you're doing now. And they will."

A wave of groans rolled through the room and Bertram grudgingly conceded. "Yes fine," he said finally. "The chief is right."

"We need this lighting," Trieca said. She looked in Bertram's direction, making sure he saw the grin curling up the corners of her cheeks. "With these pods, the unders will be able to find their footpaths through the alleys. And they will be able to see so they can wash their bodies in the communal basins. Is this not good? Is it not a way to halt disease, a way to boost their production in the salt mines and our failing oil wells?"

Haliton helped Roloc up from the floor, and Roloc managed to pull up to a seated position and listen. His stupor was fading just enough for him to take in Trieca's words. "Listen to her," Haliton whispered to him. "She's crafty. That's why she dared such an abomination as this. She and her birthmarks and her poetic way of talking, they help her get away with a lot."

Bertram was seated close enough to Haliton to hear his whispers. In what he thought was a quiet tone, he murmured: "She's a disgrace." But Trieca was within earshot and the remark made her gloat more.

"The energy emitted by these lights will help us extract heat from salt," she added. "So, what does it matter if they're a contribution from Swazembi? That doesn't mean we're kowtowing to them. And I'll be damned if I think of them as better or allow them to continue banning Kclaben from the Coalition. I'll let Mernestyle explain the next step. Where is she? Chief, with your permission, my chemist, Mernestyle, is ready to step to the podium."

Mernestyle was rounder than Trieca and didn't have her air of superiority. She stood next to Trieca before the group with her head bowed, as if awaiting instructions. When Trieca nodded, Mernestyle held up a rolled scroll. She unfurled it and read. "Please do not overreact to what you are about to see. The female portion of the Sector has established a worthy contact inside the Coalition. He was instrumental not only in securing the pod lights from Swazembi; he also is the one who supported our efforts to develop a groundbreaking product. We feel confident that you will approve of what we are doing."

Trieca looked behind her and waved her left hand at one of the overseers. "Lorrence, please bring out the Wilfins."

There was another loud outburst, but she didn't react to it. While she motioned, Lorrence, who was top overseer strategist, began leading eight beings that were gasping and shaking as they wobbled into the room.

"We've invited them to be our guests," Lorrence announced. He stopped and clutched his stomach, trying to hide his disgust. One at a time, the Wilfins rolled and lurched forward, allowing their sloppy underbellies to rub against the floor. With each wriggle, their speed increased, and they soon settled beside one another and clucked in unison.

"We are not accustomed to being out in such wide, open spaces," one of them announced, gazing around and squinting under the light. "This makes us glad. We were not able to move about before. But now that the confinement has ended, we can relearn the joy of movement. It feels good. We will catch on to it quickly."

After the beast quieted, Trieca nodded and signaled for the creatures to begin a round of introductions.

"I am Egna 7," said the second beast from the end. It was oblong and bulbous, with one stubby leg protruding from its neck.

"Welcome, we're glad you're here. In fact, we're honored to have the venerable Wilfins share this auspicious occasion," Trieca said. She turned back to the crowd. "And I am the one to congratulate for their appearance here," she said. "As you know, these Wilfins have spent a lifetime locked in our prisons. They're the only members of their species left on Kclaben. And today, we're showing them mercy."

The Wilfins clucked in appreciation, irritating Bertram further. "And for this, we let women into the Sector!" he complained loudly. "First, they accept presents from our enemies, then they haul out these horrible beasts."

"Shut up!" Chief Hardy shouted. "I'm sick of looking at them too, but at least I'm giving her a chance to explain."

Trieca continued, "Here, right before our eyes, we have beasts with glands that secrete a powerful substance. I call it Mecca. Do you get it? It's a term I heard in a viewer show about Earth. It means the promise of something good. We've been keeping Wilfins in cages, flogging them, not knowing they held promise."

"No, I don't get it," Bertram called out. "They only secrete that substance when they're scared. What kind of promise is that?"

Chief Hardy walked up to the podium and glared down at Bertram. "I don't care about you being security, I'll have you thrown out if you don't quiet down."

"Listen, here it is," Trieca said, motioning to Mernestyle, who held up a tube of gray liquid.

She held the tube higher. "With this Wilfin substance, we believe we will eventually have the means to help the Coalition. Us, the ones they look down on, us, the mere Kclabs, can make a contribution now. We're not sure yet what this Mecca can do but I'm convinced it's our answer."

A calm hung over the crowd and Trieca spoke again. "I thought you were tired of being pushed around by the Coalition?" she asked. "That's the point we're making here. This Mecca might seem like just a serum, but it could change the way the entire galaxy sees us."

"But what does it do?" Haliton asked. "You haven't explained that yet."

There was a brief silence and Trieca stood still, her hands tucked behind her back.

"That's because we don't know yet," she admitted after a pause. "So far, we've been using it as a cleaning product."

The crowd groaned and Trieca turned to face Mernestyle.

"It's a cleaner for now, but that's temporary," added Mernestyle. "Mecca's potency is unbelievable, and we're convinced that once we add one more ingredient, it will be able to do so much more. We're still working on it, but I can tell you, just like Trieca said, it will be the answer. I'm not making any grandiose claims, but just wait. Everyone's going to want this stuff. Everyone's going to need us."

"Oh, I get it," Haliton said, smothering a laugh. "We'll tidy up homes all over the galaxy and then go from scum to heroes? Like one of those advertisements from an old Earth film."

Laughter exploded through the room. When it subsided, Trieca continued.

"You can laugh now, but you'll see," she said. "The Coalition will turn to us for help. Do you understand what that means? It means respect and more authority than we've ever known. You just have to be patient with the process."

The sneering stopped and the crowd seemed ready to listen, everyone but Bertram who was strumming his fingers on the wooden rim of his seat. "You can humor her all you want," he spat, looking at the other Sector members. "I think it's stupid. In fact, I'd like to personally eject Trieca from this meeting."

Bertram bolted from his seat.

"That's enough!" Chief Hardy shouted. "Someone, anyone, stop him!"

Roloc stumbled toward Bertram, but Lorrence beat him to it. He raced to Trieca's side and grasped Bertram's sleeves, blocking him from apprehending her. Bertram fought back, and Dlareg, a new security member who had rushed from the back of the room, howled and cheered. Everyone else scattered, adding to the mounting chaos. The crowd shoved and kicked as they scrambled in all directions, arguing with everyone and trying to find the exit.

In an effort to free himself, Bertram slung Lorrence against the wall.

"Be seated! Please be seated!" Chief Hardy yelled. He snatched the microphone from Trieca and tried to proceed with the meeting. But the melee continued.

Lorrence slid from the wall down to the floor, screaming, complaining of a twisted wrist and ankle. Two female Sector members bent over him, spraying a salt solution on his joints.

"It will be okay, this will help," one of them said. "It soothes."

"Trieca!" the other called. "Come help."

Trieca took two steps toward Lorrence and suddenly came to complete halt. She turned to the crowd clambering over the seats. "Stop it, all of you!" she yelled. "Stop it now!"

The crowd silenced. An instant calm fell over the entire Sector, including overseers and security. Even Trieca couldn't believe it. *Was it her tone?* She turned and smiled at Chief Hardy. "You may continue," she said.

Chief Hardy breathed in and out like a sputtering fire. He had almost been trampled while trying to control the scuffle. He glanced at Trieca and gave her a wink of appreciation before hopping back onto the podium and continuing.

"Well done, Trieca," he said. "So where were we? Let me see – yes – on this, our auspicious occasion, we must, all of us, behave. So please, please return to your seats."

But it was too late. Those who remained of the crowd had completely lost interest and were streaming out of the room. "Where are you going?" the chief asked. "Come back."

Trieca stood beside him, wearing a withering stare. "It's no use," she said. "This meeting might as well be over."

"What do you mean? Trieca, speak to them."

Her eyes widened, and she pointed at the front door. "What for? Can't you see? They're gone."

"Who's gone?"

"The Wilfins. They've escaped."

2

*"My deceased forebear, Una, was the first female Kclab to repudiate
the spartan mantle of the concubine. I am here to invoke her power
and wield it with even more ferocity."*
– Trieca Menton's scroll of acceptance into the Sector

Frost Season on Kclaben was far from over, and in the dull
communes of the unders, its wrath was nearly intolerable.
Their shelters, made of rusted sheets of metal, leaked and
sagged under the weight of mammoth snowpiles. If the roofs
crumbled, which they sometimes did, unders coped by building
pit fires and sitting around them, singing *Raindrops Keep Fallin'
on My Head*, some crazy Earth song that had passed among
them for generations.

Roloc always sang the loudest. No one from the Sector
knew it, but the security officer sneaked out of the compound
and mingled with the unders at times. On one special night,
(at least he said it was special) the sun peeked out for a day
and, though it vanished all too quickly, Roloc insisted on a cold
weather feast. He appeared with a tin bowl of wilted carrots,
hidden in his knapsack along with a sparse bundle of leeks
from his own personal rations. Five families of unders milled
around him and, at his insistence, sang and ate until the fire
petered out and the tips of their toes had reddened from the
deep freeze.

After an hour of plain tomfoolery, Roloc hurried back to

his quarters, lifted by the idea that he'd actually helped someone and not been chastised for it. But, even in his rush, he couldn't avoid seeing the conditions he hated most – the lingering residue of frost. During the fleeting emergence of the sun, slabs of ice that had sealed themselves to the shacks were now a barely visible moss – a slickness that had softened but didn't melt. The entire grassless valley had become a sunken mud hole and icicles were dripping into puddles of slush. The minute Roloc arrived in his room, he pulled his curtain over the window so he wouldn't have to look at it. He had been in a foul mood ever since the Principal Hall meeting two weeks earlier. Bertram was blamed for the fight, but the entire security team was blamed for losing the Wilfins.

Ore crystals were banned after that, and for Roloc, that had been the worst part. The withdrawal was more agonizing than the thought that he and the rest of the security team might be thrown in a filthy Kclaben prison cell. He finished adjusting his curtains and headed back out, trudging over to the hall for a session he didn't feel like attending. After the disaster at the last meeting, Trieca and Mernestyle began working around the clock and making threats to Security about shake ups in the Sector. Roloc had run into them during one of their desperate vigils. Both women were bleary-eyed and unkempt but still raving about the powers of Mecca. Now, they were summoning security again and claiming they had some big announcement. No one knew what to expect. Roloc pouted and wished he could get his hands on something to steady his nerves. Bertram and Haliton met up with him outside and they seemed just as shaken.

"You better come up with something good to say," said Bertram. "If we don't give the chief an explanation for what happened two weeks ago, we're doomed."

"We?" Roloc said. He rubbed his sore knee and tried as best he could to keep up with his partners.

"Yes, *we*," Bertram whispered. "You're as low ranking as we are. Trieca's the one with all the damn power. Ever since this Mecca business."

The three of them shuffled into the hall and followed the small crowd heading towards a separate room on the left. It was much smaller and neater than the last one. It was a fully functional laboratory, well-lit because of an oil-fueled generator that supplied electricity to three of the Sector's main buildings. Roloc noted that the laboratory had become a big priority lately. The site was new, yet already equipped with wooden chairs that swiveled without squeaking and a viewer screen that nearly covered the wall.

"This is our updated viewer system," Trieca said. She seated herself at the front and prepared to give a short presentation. "But just so we're clear on this, I want you to know that you're not out of trouble. I'm showing this to you so that you understand the importance of what we're doing. And to make you understand that Mecca works."

Haliton almost gagged. He was controlling his anger by rolling his tongue and holding it on the roof of his mouth.

"Luckily for everyone, I have more than enough Mecca to last," she went on. "I stored a lot of it in metal vials and had most of it frozen for later use. The source that I mentioned in our last meeting is from Toth. Around twelve days ago, he picked up some of the unfrozen Mecca in exchange for wood and a few other essentials."

"Splendid," said Chief Hardy. "Now, let's see those images."

Trieca clicked a hand projector and began showing images, first of Wilfins, then of a jade green hand that was covered with lumpy scar tissue."

"Watch closely, because you're not going to believe what happens next," she said. She flipped to a slide that revealed close ups of the same hand being doused with a sticky serum. In the next slide, Trieca showed the hand once again, this time clear and free of blemishes of any sort. "The important thing to remember is that the subject must not be distracted with too many other concerns. I don't know why, but since it's a Wilfin extract, maybe it exhibits their outlook. They're passive and have a single-minded, almost obsessive, focus."

"I'm not sure I understand," the chief said. "What does all this mean?"

Lights from the projector flitted across Trieca's face, and Roloc couldn't help but admire her conspicuous patches. She was striking, but not a single male had been able to couple with her.

"Good question, Chief," she said. "Just so you know, Mernestyle didn't know Mecca had this curative property. We stumbled upon this when we were using it to clean a winter berry stain from her blouse. We added a pinch of granulated black ore, just as an activator. It's not totally perfected, but we're really confident in it. Look at this." Trieca placed two images on the screen of a female elder wearing a see-through nylon veil over her violet face. Beneath the veil, lumps dotted her nose and cheeks. "And now…" Trieca switched to a slide of the same woman with her face exposed. "Here she is only six hours later with radiantly clear skin.

"I don't know what this ailment is, but it seems to be going around right now, and here we are with something that heals it," Trieca added. "And here's the fascinating part. The subject must have skin color. Our Toth guy tried it and it doesn't work on him. But on skin of various hues, it doesn't matter how bad the condition; Mecca can heal it. This subject is from a non-Coalition planet. I was able to visit her homeworld two days ago and conduct this healing myself."

"Excuse me," Roloc said. "But how'd you get there? In that old, rusted heap parked behind Principal Hall?"

"I thought the Wilfins stole that one?" Bertram said. "Didn't they use it to escape?"

The chief nodded. "Apparently. They can move fast when they want to."

"They won't make it far in that thing," Trieca said. "But

to answer your question Roloc, I went in a transport rocket supplied by my Toth connection. He's the same person who made the arrangement with Swazembi for the light pods."

"He gave us a vessel? Where is it?" Bertram asked, his voice cracking.

"It's near the Mealing Center, inside that old shed."

"But that doesn't make sense. How could you get a whole vessel here without anyone knowing it?"

"Who says no one knew? Mernestyle knew. So did the chief." Trieca turned toward Bertram, disgust plain on her face. "If you must know, it was delivered deep into the late hour when nearly everyone was asleep. I had to fly the guy back to Toth and then fly myself back immediately. I was so tired I had to chew on some of his dry coffee beans just to stay awake."

She lifted her chin and continued. "And, another thing, Bertram, the vessel wasn't a *gift*. I gave him a substantial supply of Mecca."

"The Wilfin secretions?" Roloc asked. "A whole space rocket for that?"

Trieca shrugged. "We're not the only ones benefitting. This Toth guy is getting something out of it, too. I don't know what it is, but he can't seem to thank me – I mean, us – enough."

"Well done," said Chief Hardy. He smiled, then scowled at Haliton and Bertram. "And all of you thought it was women who were the problem. From the looks of it, we're damned lucky to have them. You know," he went on, "if this works on Swazembi, maybe you two will have to step aside. Maybe we'll have a couple of women take your place in security. What do you think, Trieca?"

She chuckled and raised her chin again. "I have a better idea," she said. "Lock them up."

Chief Hardy laughed. "By the way," he added, "did you hear that the Coalition can't find one of their planets? That's the strangest thing. Wonder what happened to it?"

"Who knows?" Trieca answered.

"Maybe you can help with that too," he joked. "With all the

breakthroughs you and Mernestyle are making, I wouldn't be surprised."

Chief Hardy slapped his knee and laughed even harder. But Trieca didn't seem to hear him. While he was talking, she had discovered a stray image that hadn't appeared in the slide show. "Who is this?" Her voice quivered. "Is this one of those rare girls the Coalition is always raving about? Is it?"

"Yes, I suppose," said Hardy. "What's the problem?"

She paused.

"Nothing," she said. "The meeting's over." But she was still clutching the Rare Indigo's image and, when no one was looking, she slipped it into the pocket in the front of her gown.

3

"They have moving gems, for my grand-forebears saw them, crafted in the steamy skies of a world where we are not allowed."
– Trieca's weekly scroll, Midfrost, 5051

Roloc thought he stood a chance. In fact, he knew he did. He saw the way Trieca was eyeing him in that last meeting. Sure, she snarled a lot, but that was directed at Bertram. She hated him, and so be it – he deserved it for trying to have her arrested.

In revenge, she had insisted that Chief Hardy throw Bertram in jail. Meanwhile, Roloc had been summoned to a personal dinner with her, just the two of them, all alone. Roloc closed the door to his quarters and hurried toward the Mealing Center, a squat stone structure about ninety paces from the security housing. He slid into a seat behind a concrete table under the faint lights and waited for his date.

She didn't disappoint. Trieca walked in wearing a white terry cloth gown and beige powder that accented the markings on her face. "I'm glad you could do this," she said. "We need to talk."

"You look lovely tonight," Roloc said.

She ignored him. "I brought a scroll with me," she went on. "I wrote it so I can alert the unders that I have big plans. I'm not ready to reveal them, not most of them anyway, but I want them to know that we've actually created something that can elevate our status."

"Very nice," Roloc said. But, in secret, he no longer cared. He was sitting alone with the most coveted woman on Kclaben, and she had promised to treat him to the entrée of his choice. At the top of the menu, he had already noticed a dried, double roasted worm casserole with boiled white potatoes and lightly steamed carrot tops seasoned with stewed garlic.

"So, I'm wondering something," Trieca continued. "You've heard of a Rare Indigo, right? She's a big attraction on Swazembi; the whole galaxy is always raving about her."

Roloc continued studying the menu, oblivious.

"I have an image of the current rare one and I believe the unders should see her, just in case," Trieca went on.

"In case of what?" Roloc asked.

"You already know what!" Trieca answered. "That damn skin disorder that's going around. The Toth guy's heard of it but says he doesn't think anyone in the Coalition has it. At least not yet. I'm thinking ahead. What if she gets it? Or what if she just decides to use something to protect herself from it. What I'm saying is that once she finds out about it, she'll be concerned."

"There's no reason she would," Roloc said. "You know, I think I'm going to follow my first mind and get the casserole."

"Fine," Trieca snapped. "Now, put the menu down and listen. I want to showcase her anyway. I want to tell the unders of our friendship."

"You're friends?"

"Don't be silly. Of course not. I just want the unders to think so. They won't know the difference. And when word gets out about that skin ailment, I can take credit for having a cure that can help protect the most admired woman in the galaxy. If I use the right wording, the unders will look up to me, don't you think?"

"Yeah but..." Roloc shuffled his feet nervously beneath the table. "I'm confused. It just doesn't seem important."

Trieca grinned slyly. "That's because you don't know my goal. I want a stronger position in the Sector, and one way to get it is through more support from the unders. They already like me because of those pod lights. And now, I – or rather, we – have Mecca to promote."

"You sure you're not getting ahead of yourself? I thought you said the rare person or whoever she is isn't even ill."

"And she may never be," Trieca said. "I'm just trying to convince the unders that I have influence everywhere, even on Swazembi."

She held up the scroll. "I'm going to hang this outside the viewer room. Should I include the rare one's image?"

Roloc stalled, wondering why he should care. "You'll have to excuse me," he said. "I can't really concentrate until after I've eaten. This will be the first good meal I've had in a while."

"But you didn't answer me. Should I hang the image or not?"

"Um, I don't know. Why are you asking me instead of the chief?"

"The chief said no already. He doesn't like for the unders to know much about other worlds. He thinks it makes them restless."

"True," Roloc mumbled. His food had arrived, and within moments his mouth was too stuffed for him to talk.

"I didn't show it to Mernestyle, or any of the other women, or even the other overseers for that matter. You and Hardy are the only ones who have seen it. I need one more opinion. So, what do you say? Should I do it?"

"But the chief said no."

"The chief listens to me. I can bring him around."

Roloc shrugged. "So, it just depends. You brought in a Swazembian gift against his wishes. How much of a rebel do you want to be?"

"I'm not trying to commit mutiny," Trieca said. "I just want to do things my way." She pushed her plate to the side and looked him up and down. "You think I'm pretty, don't you?"

Roloc dropped his fork and coughed. "Pretty? Of course." A

flash of jitters raced through his heart. It had been a long time since he had coupled.

"Good," she said. She put her hand under the table on his bad knee. "Finish your food and come with me."

Trieca led Roloc outdoors, across a mud bank and into the Old-World Earth Corner, a bell-shaped structure made from plaster and concrete bricks. They removed their galoshes by the door and stood near a back row, sorting through a pile of moving films from Earth.

"I would like to watch this one," Trieca said, holding up a large disc. "It's about those lawless ones, you know, with those smoking weapons."

"We need a viewer system. Are we taking it back to your laboratory?" Roloc asked. "Or should we stay here and watch?"

"No, I don't mean tonight," she said. "It's Unders' Night."

"Oh, yes, Salt Night," said Roloc.

She gritted her teeth. "I have no idea what that means."

"I'm from a family of unders," Roloc explained. "My male forebear used to work in the mines. On the days when he and the other miners were rationed their share of the salt chunks, he saved just enough to buy viewer entries for me and my brothers. We looked forward to it every month."

Trieca only half listened. "Salt Night, Unders' Night, I don't care what you call it – a crowd is coming. After they find their seats, we're leaving."

Roloc and Trieca watched as dozens of unders shuffled inside, their burlap robes draped over opaque flesh. The robes smelled of salt and were marred by scattered holes and gashes. Long, filthy strings dangled from hems that had dragged across the mud. They each grasped a fistful of burlap, raising their robes a bit to keep from stumbling as they climbed up to the balcony, the only place they were allowed to sit.

"I was so glad when we stopped wearing those itchy robes," said Roloc. "My male forebear was a stowaway on a vessel that made a trip to the Earth ruins, and he came back with an armload of real clothes. We took our pick, and he traded what was left for food."

Trieca gave him a look like he was stupid. "Come on. Let's go."

"But we just got here."

"I told you, we have things to do."

While the film was showing, they wandered into the hallway. Trieca picked a large stray rock off the floor and used it to pound one nail into the top of the image of the Rare Indigo and attach it to the wall. Next to it, she nailed the unfurled scroll.

LET ME INTRODUCE THE FAMOUS RARE ONE FROM THE COLORFUL LAND OF SWAZEMBI. THIS RAVISHING HUMAN IS THE FRIEND WHO AIDED ME IN MY QUEST FOR BETTER LIGHTING HERE ON KCLABEN. AS YOU REVEL IN THE DRIFTING PODS, REMEMBER I EARNED THEM BECAUSE I AM LOVED BY OTHERS IN THE GALAXY, DESPITE THE COALITION'S BAN. BUT THAT'S NOT ALL. I AM POURING MY SOUL INTO THE CREATION OF A MIRACULOUS HEALTH REMEDY THAT WILL BOOST OUR STATURE AND GAIN US ENTRY INTO OTHER WORLDS. SO, HOLD ON, DEAR ONES. KCLABEN IS ON THE RISE!
– Respectfully, T. Menton.

"But Trieca," Roloc said. "I thought it was your Toth contact? Didn't he secure the lights for you?"

"Yes, and so what?" Trieca huffed. "I told you before, the unders don't know that. They'll believe what I tell them."

"But will the chief believe it?" Roloc asked.

"He believes in me," Trieca said. "That's what counts."

She read over her scroll and gloated. "It's short, but I think it's pretty clever. When the moving slides end, the unders will read it and be impressed."

"I guess so," Roloc answered.

"I know so," said Trieca. "Come on. The film's almost over. Let's go."

Roloc felt like a band of rubber, but he didn't mind so much. Trieca had his hand in hers and he knew things couldn't get any better than that. When they entered security housing, she stopped in front of his door and placed a black rock in his hand.

"Black ore?" He stared at it in disbelief.

"It's yours, for keeping your mouth shut."

"I thought you didn't care who knew."

"Well, I'm a strategist. I needed your approval because you're going to take the fall."

Clear blood curled through the tips of Roloc's nostrils. He mashed his hands around the jagged edges of the ore and bit his lower lip. "Wh-What are you saying?"

"I'll say I have no idea what happened. Then I'll suggest that since you obviously have an amorous interest in me, you took it upon yourself to write a boastful scroll under the pretense of being me. Then, you clearly stole the rare one's image from the lab and hung them both without me knowing it."

"But –"

"But don't worry, I'll stand up for you. I have some clout. I can stop them from punishing you too severely."

Roloc found his voice. "Why are you doing this to me?"

"Think of it this way," she said. "*I* can't shoulder the blame. I'm needed because I've already done so much. I brought lighting to the unders. I discovered a product that will boost the standing of Kclaben. I write melodious ponderings that so many on Kclaben like to read. And you, what have you ever done?"

Silence.

"Exactly," said Trieca. She pointed to the ore crystal in his palm. "You use the black ore, and you fight. So, you must agree, I'm the more important one in this equation. They would never believe I did it anyway. After you say it was you who posted the image, the chief will be riled, but I won't let him lock you away with Bertram."

Placing her index finger on his temple, she guided it along his scalp and tickled him behind the neck. "There's plenty I can do for you, Roloc. Instead of jail, I'll suggest that you be sent away to handle the next phase of this mission."

"What mission? I don't know anything about a mission."

"Oh, but you will," Trieca said. "Now, go in your room and wait for my directions. You can soothe yourself with your crystal."

She walked away laughing, and Roloc felt his ribcage cleave to his chest. If he was still breathing, he couldn't tell. All he could feel was fear.

4

"Spills on garments turn into natural designs and flourishes. But the world doesn't see the loveliness. It sees a stain."
– From the journals of Ahonotay

The wall shuttle crept to a halt and Lileala walked through The Great Hall and down the limestone path to Mampong Ave. She'd had a restless night, fussing over skin eruptions, but by morning they had mostly vanished and all that was left were a couple of a tiny knots hidden under the hair shielding her ears. Relieved that her ordeal was over, she'd reported to her wave dance session and told no one about her calamity.

Now, she was glad to be hurrying back home to rest. But fewer pedestrians were around during evening hours and without the nods of strangers or the occasional friend waving as she passed, Lileala was beginning to feel pensive.

The marketplace haven owners had turned off their signs for the night, leaving the awnings as drab as ash. But every two minutes or so, a traveling light pod would float past, leaving behind a glowing trail.

She strolled beneath them, all the way to her compartment. Once inside, she stretched out on her bed without changing or prepping for sleep. A prickly tinge shot across her left cheek, but when she touched it, she felt nothing. She reached behind her neck and that pimple, or whatever it was, didn't seem

117

nearly as daunting. Too tired to check either of them in the mirror, she dozed off.

An hour passed, and she woke with her heart speeding. Something was stinging the lobes of both her ears. In the dark, she ran her fingers behind the rims. Lumps, two of them. She traced the crevices in the back of her neck and one more. She drew in her breath and suppressed a scream.

"Otto, Otto…" In desperation, she concentrated on her dial, then shook her wrist before she could disturb him. He was so busy outlining a Coalition project, they hadn't seen each other in days. And the last thing she wanted was for him to see her now, in such a compromised state.

Using her elbow, she tapped the pillar of her pod lamp stand while stumbling to her feet and rushing to her grooming suite. A poof of curls flopped over her forehead, hiding the tip of her eyebrows. Gripping a small mirror, she eased one finger under the curls and lifted.

"Whew! Not a scar," she said to her reflection. "What a relief." Convinced that the nightmare was all in her mind, Lileala did a brief wave dance before continuing her skin check. With a quick pirouette she used the mirror to get a wide view of the skin beneath the bounty of coils behind her neck.

What she saw triggered an unexpected cry. A lump of flesh hung like a tiny sack of fat and the sight of it made her hyperventilate. Lileala heaved and released another wail that vibrated across the room. Her knees unlocked and she dropped to the floor, letting the mirror tumble with her.

"What is going on?" she asked over and over. "What is going on?" Unable to stand or hold back tears, she lay in a crumpled mass before getting the courage to swipe her hands behind her ears again. They were hot. Just as she thought. Fever.

Lileala proceeded to the sink and leaned over it, trying to spit out her pain. With her hands clasped around her abdomen, she struggled towards the kitchen counter. In the corner was a large copper basin filled with Euc. She took in a whiff, a light, almost minty smell. The Euc was as fresh as clouds – it was part of a batch that had recently been shipped from Otuzuweland through Togu Ta City East. After filling the basin with the concoction and cool water, she immersed her entire face in the mixture. After thirty seconds, she looked up and moaned. Her Euc rinse had not helped.

Falling back onto her bed, Lileala summoned Otto, then shook her wrist, blocking him once again from her dial. She had to think. Who could she contact? Her elder Ma would get hysterical. Zizi? Wasn't she busy with her guard training? Her thoughts flipped to Cherry. The idea seized her, and she focused hard, hoping the clairvoyant would sense her distress.

Within minutes, Cherry's face bloomed on her wrist. "Ye, is this the Rare One?" she asked. "Cherry can feel hurting inside of you. But why does Cherry not see the smooth face as Cherry so remembers?"

"It's me." Lileala's voice quivered. "Me, Cherry. I'm afraid and I don't know what to do. Something horrid is attacking my skin. Cherry, I'm afraid."

"Clairvoyance is not needed to detect that, young one. Come to visit. Come soon. Speak with Cherry beside the fruit cart, no?"

Lileala sobbed. "But what about the Aspirants? Some of them gather in The Great Hall."

"And this troubles you? Young one, you have fear of your friends?"

"Not all of them *are* friends." Lileala sobbed louder. "And I can't bear the idea of any of them gloating. I'm the girl with the blackberry skin. No one can see me like this."

"Weep child." Cherry's voice softened. "Let the wounds find their escape. Cherry is in Boundary Circle. Cherry can come to you now."

Lileala nodded and hung up. Tears rained down her cheeks and she settled onto a swerving bundle of blankets and cushions.

* * *

By the time Cherry arrived she had sunk deeper into depression and her cheeks were a distorted mass of lumps.

"Oh no, no, no!" Cherry gasped. "How is it you came to this?"

The answer Lileala gave was incoherent. She let out a tumble of words before she finally came up with one that made sense. "Sleep," she whined. "Cherry, am I asleep?"

For a while, Cherry didn't react. Her eyes were sliding along Lileala's shoulders and arms. Finally, she spoke: "You are awake, but this malady is unknown to Cherry. Where is your elder Ma, Fanta?"

"On Toth with my Baba."

"Have you summoned her?"

"I wasn't sure I should but, yes. A few minutes ago. She's hurrying back home."

Cherry nestled between Lileala and the pillows, then threw both of her arms around Lileala's shoulders.

While Lileala wept, Cherry shut her eyes and spoke. "Cherry sees the odd ones fighting, so much fighting among these ones they call the Kclabs. And ye, for this reason they were cast out of Swazembi. Ah, but that was one hundred years in the past. They now try to change, ye."

Cherry wiped Lileala eyes then continued: "Many in Boundary Circle avoided these odd ones, for they came in anger then. Cherry does see them now and it is good that they struggle to be better. Before, ye, they were too mean and even Cherry was so afraid."

Tears flooded Cherry's cheeks, but Lileala was getting annoyed.

"Cherry, stop. Please stop." She tugged on her fingers and shoved her face into a pillow. "I asked you here because I need help. I'm sorry but I don't have time for stories."

When Lileala had quieted down, Cherry spoke again. "It is what came to Cherry, but Cherry does not always understand what Cherry sees and says."

A heavy yawn prevented Lileala from telling Cherry she didn't want to hear anymore that she had to say. She was cranky and regretted inviting her.

"I think I'll go to a medic and ask about oscillator treatments," Lileala said. "Maybe an electric infusion will help. That and an intoxicant. Maybe I'll drink some Mirth."

She looked at the door, hoping Cherry would leave.

"The ailment that troubles you is very old. Old as the Earth," Cherry suddenly announced, then quickly became silent again. Lileala could tell she was holding back.

"The Earth? My stars, Cherry, is this an Earth malady?"

The clairvoyant leered at her and grimaced. "Ah, so you have the ability! Cherry sees that now."

"No, I –" Lileala hesitated. "I don't even know what you mean. Ability? I have an ailment, Cherry. How do I get rid of it? Please. Why did you mention the Earth?"

"Young one, hush now." Cherry's eyes saddened and Lileala could see that they were damp. "This is too much talk."

"But I want to talk about whatever you know!" Lileala repositioned her body among the cushions and, while Cherry waited, touched the protrusions beneath her chin. Then a new blast of voices in her head startled her. She jumped but immediately blocked them out. "Cherry, I need to hear more."

"Cherry has told you, young one. The ailment upon you once existed on the Earth."

"I don't understand." Lileala coughed to mask the tremble in her voice. "Are you saying this disease is primitive?"

Cherry fidgeted and her speech came out muffled. "Don't ask. Cherry does not know much more. It is a hidden, ye," Cherry said. "This information, it is lost, ye. And in the Inekoteth trances, Cherry can barely see the home of the ancestors. Cherry must try very hard if Cherry is to dig it out." She sounded frightened and her words were moving so fast Lileala could barely keep up.

A whisper lodged itself in Lileala's right ear. She pressed the palm of her hand against it, hoping to ease the pain of the swellings and block out the sound at the same time.

"I don't understand," Lileala mumbled.

"The ancestors of Swazembi are of Earth," Cherry blurted. "And... and... They could talk to the stars."

"What?"

"Tnomo and his followers were the people of the Earth land, Africa. They were called the Dogon people, the great melanin bearers who made homes in the tall cliffs that did line the grassy soil of the Africa."

Lileala tensed and the hairs on her neck went ramrod straight. "Why have I never heard of these people?"

"Shh," Cherry whispered. "The Nobility does not believe in them. Never speak of them. That is why. Fodjour, dear, brave, Fodjour. When he and Cherry were first joined, he was permitted in a private chamber in The Grand Rising, but for a day to assist the Mhondora."

Cherry closed her eyes. "Ye, Cherry remembers how the Mhondora had praise of Fodjour then, because dear Fodjour is the scholar, ye, he did work so very hard. He stayed very long doing the research and he did fall asleep in the big chair. And in the night, there was the sound that woke Fodjour. Ye, Fodjour told Cherry it was a statue that had fallen from the shelf."

Cherry stopped and hugged herself as though the room was suddenly cold. She continued. "And when Fodjour went to pick it up, he saw behind the shelf a hole in the floor that was in motion and the round top covering this opening had been moved. How was Fodjour to know to stay away? He was curious, ye. Cherry's Fodjour, he stepped before it and was sucked inside. And oh did Fodjour wander among relics there that had a covering of much dust. And the masks and the tools stacked in heaps and made from the bodies of dead trees. And many sacks containing pendants and beads, ye, and papers too were there, locked together as one block and this block thing was called a book. It was the only relic like that Fodjour had ever seen."

Cherry and Lileala both sighed at the same time and Lileala pulled one of her blankets tighter around her arms and chest.

"When Fodjour told this to the Mhondora, he became enraged. The Nobility did not know about the relics and the Mhondora told Fodjour never to reveal them."

"Why?" Lileala asked. "That makes no sense."

"Because," Cherry lowered her head, "because they contained writings about the Dogon ancestors who traveled here from the Earth land. They claimed this world, named it Swazembi but they did not want to be known. They had a power, these ones, a juju that is a medicine and a protection. But the Mhondora keeps and hides it, he does, even from The Nobility, even from The Uluri."

The room filled with a dreadful tension. Cherry swallowed and went on: "But Fodjour did tell others of the writings, and this so angered the Mhondora he went to The Uluri. The Nobility accused Cherry's Fodjour of spreading falsehoods. Fodjour was ordered to leave Boundary Circle and never return."

Lileala shook all over. She didn't want to challenge Cherry, but she wasn't sure she believed her story. "Cherry are you sure you didn't pick this up in a trance, and maybe mix it up?" she asked.

"Rare One, this is Fodjour's story, not Cherry's. So how would it come to Cherry ever as Inekoteth?"

"But why is it such a secret, then?" Lileala said. "Why can't anyone talk about it?"

"The Nobility and The Uluri, how can they know what they do not know?"

"But Cherry –"

"Shhh… Cherry knows no more. Go visit Ahonotay. She will know. But do go soon, before she ceases to be."

"That's not going to happen. Ahonotay's only one hundred and one, right?"

"Ah, do not sass," Cherry ordered. "In the Inekoteth, Cherry surely has seen her. She walks the walk of the high seer, higher than the Mhondora. Ye, Cherry has seen her praying alone in the yonder regions of Mbaria. Something is pulling life from the cells of this Indigo and yet, still there is Shimmer. And it is greater than bushels of living light. Go be with her, young one. Ask her your concerns. See if she speaks."

"But you said my questions were foolish."

"For Ahonotay nothing is foolish. She knows more than Mhondora Chinbedza himself. So much more."

"How could that be?"

Cherry didn't answer. She reached into a large satchel and pulled out a bulky black robe with zippered pockets and an enormous hood. "When Cherry is busy planting, this is the main garment. Take it. Go to the oscillator medics and when you do, wear it. Wear and wait while Cherry does the Inekoteth. Can you promise Cherry that?"

"Yes," Lileala said, but as she spoke the lumps on her neck throbbed. She kneaded them lightly and groaned. But Cherry didn't look behind her. Without another word, she adjusted her headwrap and exited through the sliding wall.

Lileala couldn't look in the mirror. The last time she checked, her ridged cheeks reminded her of discolored melons, bumpy ones that had gone rotten. She refused to see them, but she still touched them. She was obsessed, pressing thin fingers into a patchwork of raised scars and over rough, uneven slopes.

She tried to stop but couldn't. It was her terrible new pastime. For a full day she tortured herself, rubbing, feeling, placing one hand onto a cheek then snatching it away as if she'd just stuck it into a blast of fire. Then she'd place it on her chin or forehead, and she would let out such a woeful groan. She sounded like one of the old horns bellowing through The Outer Ring.

When it became too much, she'd take a dip in the Euc again. But each time she finished her bath, her skin was unchanged. It wasn't working, but she was convinced it would. It *had* to work. That fact had been drilled into her as part of her Aspirant Training, and if Mama Xhosi found out about her ailment, she knew it would be the first thing she would suggest.

Without fail, the Indigo High Host appeared on Lileala's dial hourly, demanding to know why she hadn't shown for any wave dance or etiquette sessions. And before Lileala could block his image, Ataba Malik also appeared and shrieked: "Report for training now!"

Lileala hid within the robe, shielding her face. She didn't want either of them to know about her condition, even though she assumed Mama Xhosi would eventually figure out something was wrong.

"Release the heavy cloak," she demanded during her last call. In a state of panic, Lileala had shaken her wrist furiously and erased her, but she couldn't forget the High Host's commands. Like the voices, they burrowed in her ear, lingering until finally Lileala had no other choice. She blocked her from her dial.

Just as she prepared to try the Euc again, a slight buzz reverberated from her wall and her wrist glowed stronger than ever. Obviously, since Mama Xhosi couldn't break through Lileala's censor, she sent Yemisi, an Aspirant friend of Lileala's who hadn't been blocked. She fluttered above her dial in a cloud of intense vibrations.

"How did you sync with my wall and my dial at the same time?" Lileala demanded to know. "Did Mama Xhosi instruct the Pineal Crew to turn up your dial's power?"

Yemisi scowled. "I can't answer that," she said, not flinching.

"Waves, why can't I make everyone leave me alone?" Lileala said, wiggling both hands in hopes of making her vanish.

In a fit of tears, Lileala shook them harder, but the stubborn Aspirant remained.

"Can't get rid of you now, but once you disappear, I can block your return," Lileala cried. "You might as well go."

"Lileala, why aren't you trusting me?" Yemisi asked. "I'm your friend. That hasn't changed."

"I don't care. Don't you understand? Leave me be."

"No. I'm still at your door. I'm not leaving until you let me check on you."

"Who's with you?" Lileala asked.

"No one," Yemisi answered. "I have a gift from Mama Xhosi. It's a cannister of Euc."

"Oh no! Did Mama Xhosi find out I'm not well? Did she? Is she here with you? And Sonaguards, did you bring Sonaguards too?"

"I can't answer."

"Please go away. I don't want anyone to see me."

"I'm not leaving."

"I need quiet," Lileala snapped.

"What if I grabbed a dinner for you from the marketplace?" Yemisi asked. "What would you like?"

"I would like you to leave."

"No. Now, open your door!"

Pulling her hood tightly around her cheeks, Lileala gave her dial a hard slap and allowed the door wall to slide open a few inches. Through the crack, she saw Yemisi and a shiny Sonaguard uniform at a distance. She slammed the wall shut.

"You tricked me; you're not alone!" she yelled. "If you have a package, please leave it in front of the wall."

Minutes passed. Then an hour. The Aspirant still hovered.

More hours dripped along and yet there she was, haunting her like a bad dream. Lileala poured a small cup of Mirth and settled into her bed to sleep. When she awakened during the late hour, Yemisi was gone.

"Thank the Grace!" Lileala said aloud. "She finally gave up."

She checked the door and pulled in the package left by her visitor. The Euc would be her companion, her only solace. She couldn't afford to think about anything but that. And so, all night and well into her second day of isolation, she "Euced" herself, as Mama Xhosi would say. In order to escape the wrist tickles of other Aspirants trying to contact her via dial, she stuck it in her closet. She vacillated between sleeping and scooping Euc granules from the canister and immersing herself in its bubbles.

When Lileala prepared to do it for the third time that evening, she almost caught a glimpse of herself in the mirror. She turned her head just in time, snapping it around so fast the movement left her with a pinched muscle. Her nerves were frayed, so it didn't matter much. She reached again for the mixture and, discovering there was less than a fourth of a canister left, she tossed the container across her kitchen and slumped to the floor in a fit of tears.

Her elder Ma hadn't returned, and she was running out of the only thing that was supposed to help erase her pain. She needed to get to the market.

Housed in the bulky robe the clairvoyant had given her, she slipped out of her compartment and scurried through The Great Hall, her head bowed, eyes looking only at the floor. But her faceless presence, buried under an oversized hood, drew stares. Heads turned and whispers flew past. One was louder than the others, more of a shout. "Who's hiding under there?" an elder yelled and pointed. "Hey, who are you? Do you belong in Boundary Circle?"

Lileala pulled her hood tighter, ensuring there were no signs that she was the person beneath the dense fabric. But the elderly stranger kept shouting and threatened to call the Sonaguard if she didn't reveal her name.

He headed her way, but Lileala was swifter. The minute he glanced at his dial and turned to a passerby to point her out, she darted into a tapestry haven that was unattended and hid behind a barrel of rugs until he passed.

On trembling legs, she scrambled for the Grace Chapel, ran to the altar and landed on her knees, banging them against the limestone pew. She rubbed them and calmed herself by staring at a limestone statue, said to be a replica of Tnomo. The mounds on her skin stung, but the carving of the founder soothed them somehow. She admired the craftsmanship of the artist who created it but felt confused about Tnomo. *Was he a Mhondora?* She wondered.

Candles of varying sizes were lit, flickering in trays of sand that sat on either side of the statue at least three feet away. The candlelight shone from different angles, showcasing Tnomo's broad features.

He was a melanin bearer whose rounded lips and taut facial skin reminded Lileala of nearly every male Swazembian she knew. She studied him and struggled to believe he had lived during an age of antiquity and was part of a civilization that had settled on a cliff. Cherry's story was outrageous, and she was in too much pain to entertain it. She let it go, overcome by prickly sensations all over her skin.

Tremors coursed through her veins and fear consumed her thoughts, plunging her deeper into sorrow. She folded her shaking hands and prayed: "Grace of the ancestors, hear me please. Drown out the aches that nag me. Heal me and let me hear your truth."

Few are friends.

There was the voice again, bursting with a vengeance through her spirit.

"What?" she shouted. "You? You followed me here too? Why?"

All was quiet.

Lileala fell against the altar and wept.

5

Cherry's head never bowed, and she always took time to tell a story to any of the young ones she encountered sauntering through The Great Hall, but the meeting with the Rare Indigo had drained some of her strength.

Shaking her shoulders briskly, she tried and failed to stop fretting about Lileala. The only thing to do at this point was summon Mama Xhosi. But how she'd do that was another matter. She hadn't had much contact with the Indigo High Host, and without a bond of emotions she wouldn't be able to reach her on her dial.

Cherry found her stool beside her fruit, but instead of sitting on it, squatted next to it. On her haunches, she was more comfortable at times. It looked odd; she knew that. In Boundary Circle, respectable women were expected to rely on proper seating, not squat like a common villager. It was unbecoming. But Cherry was too upset to care.

When a trio of young women approached, she remained in her stooped position and handed each a free peach before bidding them to be on their way. They nodded in appreciation, all but one who stood before Cherry and surveyed the piece of fruit like it had to pass inspection. Cherry gave her a sideways glance and noticed a flicker of charcoal blue around her lips and cheeks. She was haughty, this girl, but she glittered like...

"Oh no! Oh no! You," Cherry said in a rush. "You are one of the Aspirant ladies, are you not? Tell Cherry, is this true?"

The woman brightened her glow then turned to leave.

"Young Aspirant," Cherry called out.

The woman hesitated as if deciding whether to listen. It was clear she didn't admire Cherry, not like her peers. Cherry had been told as much. She knew that some of the Aspirants felt it a bother to waste time hearing tales from a part-time farmer with a tiny headwrap and disturbed speech.

"Young Aspirant!" Cherry jumped to her feet. "Cherry does not know you, but Cherry recognizes the joy on your skin. It is Shimmer, is it not? You are Indigo Aspirant, ye? A friend of the Rare One, Lileala?"

The woman halted, but there was something unpleasant in her stare. Cherry didn't allow it to register. In her urgency, she shut out a warning that washed over her like a cold rain.

"Yes, yes, I know her," the woman said. She walked closer to Cherry and waited.

"Do find Mama Xhosi very soon," Cherry urged. "Do this, can you, please? Tell her the Rare Indigo badly needs her."

"What is it? What's so wrong?" the woman asked.

Cherry looked at her closely. There was a peculiar yearning in this woman, almost like lust, and she had just let loose a Shimmer that could wake the dead. It was so hauntingly beautiful Cherry wondered if it was against the Aspirant code.

Why does this woman permit such a loud glow at this hour? Cherry thought. *There is no performance, ye. She is not on the stage.*

"Tell me, please," the woman said. "I care about Lileala so. What is so wrong with the Rare Indigo and how can I be of help?"

Ignoring all the forewarnings, Cherry allowed her judgment

to lapse. She told the Aspirant of Lileala's condition and its possible link to the ancient Earth.

"Do take this message, please, to Mama Xhosi in a hurry, ye," she said. "The Rare One does not want Mama Xhosi to hear of such bad news as this, but Cherry does insist. You must seek Mama Xhosi and plead for the help. Right away now. Go, and when it is time, Cherry will let the Rare Indigo know who was asked to seek this aid. Please, young Aspirant, give Cherry your name."

"My name is Issa," the woman said, and Cherry felt a brittleness somewhere in her chest. The woman's eyes had opened a little wider and she hadn't bothered to hide the satisfaction behind her grim stare. At that moment, Cherry knew she had erred.

"This not a good woman," Cherry said to herself. "What a bad, wicked young Aspirant."

Cherry hugged herself and rocked back and forth in her seat. Had Cherry helped the Rare Indigo or caused her more pain? She went back to Otuzuweland that night and cooked a dinner of baby garnet yams and dandelion greens on a cast iron stove Fodjour had built by hand. While Fodjour ate, her eyes drifted to the window, and she watched faithfully while the sun set on their plots of mango and peach trees. After observing for a few more minutes, Fodjour recognized her sadness.

"My devoted," he said. "Why do you sit so quietly and without appetite? Is there some experience that has disturbed you?"

Cherry swallowed and wiped away a tear.

"It is sad that we have no authority," Cherry said. "You and Cherry. In Boundary Circle, there is no power for you and Cherry."

Fodjour took his devoted's hands. "Is that what you're fretting about? I gave up on that a long time ago and I thought you had too. You go to the Circle, I thought, as an outing, not to wield any real influence."

Cherry tore her eyes from the window and sighed.

"Devoted Fodjour, the Rare Indigo, she struggles with the unknown ailment, does she not, and Cherry has placed this news into the wrong hands. Cherry did not know what to do. Now, Cherry does fear the heart of this person. Cherry trusted her but now worries she will spread it as the gossip."

"The Rare Indigo has an ailment?" Fodjour asked. "Nonsense, nonsense."

"It is true, Fodjour," Cherry said. "Of the skin. An ailment has ruptured her flesh."

Fodjour lifted both hands over his eyes. "Is that possible?" he asked. "Who else in Swazembi knows?"

"At first only Cherry. And." Cherry paused. "But now Cherry is so afraid, ye, afraid that the one with the mean eyes has spread this very far. Cherry did feel this when Cherry was doing the speaking; but the feeling, it left, and Cherry paid no attention. Cherry is in sadness now, remembering the warning."

Cherry continued, "When Cherry can, Cherry will seek advice in the Inekoteth. That is the only authority Cherry has."

"No, we don't have authority," Fodjour said. "We never will." He patted his chest to control the jitters in his voice. "The Mhondora is afraid of us, you and me, so afraid of our truth. But you must never stop sharing, my Cherry. When you see trouble, you must speak."

"But the rare girl," Cherry said. "Cherry spoke and now will she hurt more?"

"You should always speak, Cherry, no matter what." Fodjour looked directly at his devoted. "Be of joy, Cherry. No one there in Boundary Circle truly believes us, but you had to speak out. You couldn't let the Rare Indigo suffer alone."

"No, Cherry could not do that," she said. "The pain, ye, did it not have to be told? It will end, this pain, but Cherry found the help the only way Cherry could."

Cherry returned to the window. Evening was descending like dreary dust over the Gwembian homesteads, but Cherry's eyesight was sharp, and she saw farther than most. She could squint and make out the tips of Mbaria's tallest huts and detect smoke curling from the communal cooking hovel in the center of the compound. She observed them closely, these symbols of simplicity. Afterall, it was such foolishness, this business of perfection, this belief that more beauty belonged to one than another. Cherry reminded herself that Lileala's woes were Capital City, High Indigo problems, so far removed from the peace of Gwembia and all of Otuzuweland. But she knew they were a core in the values of Boundary Circle and that a violation of those values meant deep agony for that young Rare Indigo. She sighed once more, then lifted her wrist and left an urgent message for her young friend.

"Cherry did fail," she confessed to Lileala on her dial. "Cherry could not think a soul in Boundary Circle could prick the reputation of the Rare Indigo. Now, Cherry cries because Cherry couldn't accept that there were bad ones about in the Circle. Please forgive Cherry, for Cherry only sees good."

6

*"Don't hold too tightly to any experience. Let go so that it might
become a note in life's eternal song."*
– From The Sacred Doctrines of The Uluri

Holographic images of Lileala clothed in a luxurious white
Aspirant gown coasted above the east end of The Great Hall.
They were accompanied by periodic updates about her condition
and an announcement that all tourists had been asked to leave
the Surface and The Outer Ring until further notice. Lileala
could barely watch or listen. All day, she'd seen the holograms
flowing across the viewerstream in her compartment, and the
constant reports were giving her a massive headache.

Ever since the word had spread about her ailment, she'd
been as sickened by that as she was by her ailment. Strangers
had loitered along Mampong Avenue, waiting for her to step
outside, and she'd exhausted her mental energy fighting
off callers who kept trying to penetrate her dial. It was all a
nuisance, and it made her feel even more trapped.

She knotted her fingers together and opened them again,
releasing the stress. Had she gone from beauty to oddity that fast?
The idea added to Lileala's misery. *Well,* she thought, *if they're
expecting me to make an appearance, I'll fix them. They're not getting a
single glimpse.* No one, not even Otto, would be allowed into her
private sphere, and she wasn't going to talk to Mama Xhosi either.

Lileala flipped off the viewerstream on the wall of her dining area before heading through a side exit that led directly into her forebears' space.

"Ma, are you there yet?"

She sank into a cushion in their foyer and cradled her head in her hands. Then she got up, and then sat back down again, choking for air.

"This can't be happening. It can't be."

With her stomach cramping, she stood and rushed back to her own quarters and into the kitchen. She cringed when she saw how unorganized it was. The area wasn't untidy, just too small for so many items to be left out in the open. Four new containers of Euc were piled on a slim cooking counter right next to an automatic fig grinder and a stack of self-heating bowls.

Her hands still shaking, she made a beverage of fig mixed with home-made juniper ale and cut through the foyer that separated the kitchen and living area. She drank the mixture in a few gulps, stepped down into a vestibule leading to a sunken bedroom, and slumped into her favorite chair. It made babbling sounds that mimicked the motion of a gentle river and carried her mind away, taking her somewhere that was free of worry. Her thoughts tumbled about and swam lazily through her agony. She thought she heard someone crying, but in her daze, the sound was garbled.

"Young one," her elder Ma's voice broke through her mental fog. "Can you hear me, Lileala? Please get up!"

"I can't." Lileala tried to lift her head. "Drank too much Mirth."

Fanta hovered and pulled on her arms. "Come on, I'll help you."

Trying to stand wasn't easy. Lileala steadied herself and hobbled to Fanta's side. At her instructions, she slipped on a metallic jumpsuit and the bulky robe Cherry had given her. She followed behind her elder Ma, one labored step at a time. The ale and the chemicals unleashed by the chair had made

her so dizzy that her mind felt disconnected from her body.
She had to force her fingers to move, and when she did, she
stared hard, thinking they belonged to someone else.

Then came her feet. Lileala pushed them and was surprised
by their willingness to lift. Slowly, she struggled out of her
compartment and along the figure-eight trail coursing through
The Great Hall and back to the Grace Chapel, grateful that it
was within walking distance.

The women entered and kneeled before an altar that had
one small candle surrounded by fresh Jacaranda petals and
several swatches of sage. Just as they began to pray, a low
voice rumbled behind them. Lileala was still as a brick, but
Fanta glanced behind her and into the face of the Mhondora.
He was walking toward them with an aggressive stride, his
posture defiant and eyes full of confidence.

"I was hoping to find the two of you here," he said. "Can I
kneel beside you and talk?"

Fanta said okay, but hesitated. "I'm afraid we're not in a
very good mood."

"I understand," he said. "You don't have to explain." He turned
his stare toward Lileala, but she refused to glance in his direction.

"Young one, please come closer."

Resentment simmered inside her. The fog had melted from
her eyes, but the Mhondora's coarse brown frock and round
face still looked fuzzy.

She glared at him, then whispered to Fanta. "I don't belong
here, Ma." There was a tug of war going on inside her and she
didn't want to be forced to talk about it. "Ma, you know this
isn't for me," she said, trying her best not to sound disagreeable.

When Fanta didn't answer, Lileala got up from the altar and
found a seat in a pew near the back of the chapel. She didn't
want to be around the Mhondora. Why should she trust him?

"We have never had disease on Swazembi. Never," he said.
"But this ailment will be conquered, ye, I know it will."

Fanta looked up at him and Lileala thought she noticed

uncertainty in her glance. "Mhondora, can I ask; why this is happening? Why have the ancestors given Lileala such a heavy burden?"

Mhondora Chinbedza slowed his speech. "My lady. Do not blame the Grace of the Ancestors. Bad energy doesn't flow from the Grace."

"From where, then? And why?"

"I'll need the Inekoteth to inform me of the cause of the ailment and explain the reason it has targeted the Rare Indigo. But I beg you again, do not attribute this to the Grace."

Rolling her eyes, Lileala turned away, but Fanta nodded. "I didn't mean to be disrespectful. I hold the Grace in high honor and while here in the chapel I'll honor the ye, so as not to offend the ancestors."

The Mhondora stroked Fanta's soft black hair, a mass of tight curls. She was two hundred and seventy-six years old, middle aged, comely. But she hadn't bothered to brush her hair or dab a touch of gloss on her lips. "Where did Lileala go?" He looked out into the pews. "Lileala, please. If only you would let me bless you."

Lileala kept her distance.

Leaning forward, Fanta tried to whisper, but Lileala could hear what she was saying. "She's slightly intoxicated, but she's coming out of it."

"Isn't that against the Aspirant Code?" he asked.

"It's not real Mirth, just a form of Juniper ale made from the fermented berries in her kitchen," Fanta said. "It's allowed before the Eclipse. It's mild and wears off quickly."

He didn't seem convinced. "I hear she's a fun seeker," he said, not hiding the criticism in his tone.

Fanta bristled. "No more than anyone else her age."

"But she's impulsive," he said.

"And yet she was given the moldavite key," Fanta answered. "Am I mistaken to believe that you were there when it happened?"

The Mhondora ignored the comment and directed his next remark to Lileala.

"Young one, please come to the altar."

"No, thank you," she whimpered. "I'm only here because of my elder Ma."

"My daughter," Fanta coaxed. "Won't you at least try?"

Without a sound, Lileala rounded her lips into a definite *no* and moved further to the rear of the chapel. Mhondora Chinbedza followed, but Fanta stopped him.

"Please." Her voice had taken on a higher pitch, and she began to weep. "Look, I'm sorry. Maybe we shouldn't have come here." At the sound of Fanta's sobbing, Lileala broke and hurried back to the altar to comfort her. The Mhondora stepped away to give them space, but Lileala thought he seemed nervous. He was pacing and fidgeting with the swirl of energy above his wrist.

"Let me help," he said to Lileala. "Allow me to go into the Inekoteth."

"Please don't," she said. She had sobered up now and regained her strength. "I'm not interested in a reading, and I wouldn't want to do it without my Baba anyway."

"I understand. Then maybe we can close our eyes before the altar and hope for an ancestral message?"

Worry lines creased Fanta's forehead. "Mhondora, I mean no disrespect, but please honor my daughter's wishes. My devoted is still on Toth planning the summit. I came back early, but he couldn't because of Swazembi's rank in the Coalition. He's not going to be able to leave for several days."

The Mhondora cleared his throat. "Why would you wait that long? This is not just a family concern. It's a Swazembi concern, a Boundary Circle concern."

She dried her eyes and pulled Lileala aside. "Listen to me. We're being so disrespectful. I think we should do as he says."

Lileala's hood and veil formed a canopy over her head as she stood beside Fanta and accepted the Mhondora's right hand. It was damp, and she was surprised by what she thought to be a slight tremor. Why, she wondered, do Inekoteth trances make one so intense?

"In the name of Tnomo," he mumbled. "For the sake of Lileala Walata Sundiata." He steadied himself and plunged into a state that Lileala found eerie. She'd listened to Cherry ramble now and then, but no one of an order as ascended as the Mhondora.

"Tnomo," he said. "Come forth, Tnomo, under the High Grace. Szewa. Szewa. Come forth in the Inekoteth tongue of the father." The Mhondora swayed and his chest rose and fell as if to the beat of a soundless drum. While his body twitched, his voice deepened. "Water will become stone and stream. Ye, in a void, an Indigo wears the veil and visions that burrow in crevices beneath her feet. Deceit will be unveiled, and she will ascend in the first of the high divination. A healer, ye, a healer. A clairvoyant. Rising in vision. Beyond the Pale Fox. Ye, an Aspirant hides. Ye, a High Indigo sees. This stone, like ice, grows colder. In the code of the Inekoteth, ye, will she climb."

He opened his eyes and Lileala saw a hot flush on his face. Sweat drenched his brow. The collar of his robe was wringing wet.

"Mhondora," Lileala said. "What were you saying?"

"I-I don't know. I seemed to lose most of my awareness this time. I don't know why."

"It was shocking," Fanta said. "I got the idea that someone here on Swazembi is up to something, and I got the distinct impression that I –"

He didn't let her finish. "I feel in my soul that Lileala is going to be alright. Someone from afar may have pulled this off, somehow, but they won't have the last word."

"From afar?" Fanta said. "You didn't say that in your trance."

"Didn't I? I only heard brief segments. I thought I'd heard… No, no, I didn't," he said. "But of course someone outside of Boundary Circle has to be responsible. No one in The Circle would be behind it."

Fanta observed the Mhondora closely.

"Just know that she is going to be all right," he said. "She will be restored. I do remember that much."

"But I won't be myself," Lileala mumbled.

"Not yourself? I don't usually ask this, but tell me, what exactly was revealed?"

"That I'm like you, a clairvoyant."

Mhondora Chinbedza stared at her as if she had erupted into flames. "Did I say that?"

Lileala shrugged. "I'm shocked, but then again I'm not sure I believe it anyway."

"Lileala, shush," Fanta said. She turned to the Mhondora. "Yes, I mean ye, you did." She prepared to leave then paused. "By the way, with all respect, I would like to apologize. We were both very rude."

"Can I do anything more?" he asked. "Would the two of you like to return tomorrow?"

"No, thank you." Lileala spoke up quickly. There was a passion in the Mhondora's voice that made her more relaxed, but she still didn't trust him, not after that conversation with Cherry. They walked out, and she whispered to her elder Ma, "You know I've never been fond of the prophecies, and I don't like him, not at all. But he's made some predictions I need to think about."

"Please do," Fanta said. "If you can't believe in the Sacred Inekoteth, what can you believe in?"

7

"Among the weeds of a selfish heart, the flower of wisdom suffocates."
 – Swazembi proverb

The wall made a clicking sound, a subtle tap followed by a gentle purr. It clicked again, louder, then gentler. Then stopped. More clicks. The wall vibrated. The clicks turned into heavy thuds. Lileala woke up, startled. She sat up in bed, grumpy. She looked at her dial and could see Otto standing outside of her compartment. "Otto, don't. Okay? Please don't do this," she yelled in the direction of the front wall exit. He had synced the guest alert button with Lileala's dial and turned a wall click into a rattling alarm.

The wall buzzed, shook and thundered again.

"Okay, Otto! Okay! Hold on and stop activating my wall." The vibrations shook her bed. "I'm coming, Otto! I'm coming."

She pulled herself to the edge of her bed and wondered if she should try and tidy up the room. Two empty jars of Euc sat on a crystal nightstand next to a large tin kettle. Her floor was smudged with sweat from her bare feet. Deciding to ignore the mess, Lileala slipped into her robe and veil.

The wall clicked once more.

"I told you, Otto! I'm coming. Hold on!"

The front wall slid open, and Otto rushed in. "Lileala! I've been so worried," he said, reaching for her arms. She tried to pull away, but he grabbed her close and held her firm.

"Oh no you don't," he said. "You can't get rid of me now."

After a few seconds, Lileala relaxed in his arms, head pressed against him forcefully. She cried. "I'm sorry, but I just couldn't see you. I didn't want to see anyone."

Otto touched Lileala's veil. "Why would you be embarrassed in front of me?"

She avoided his eyes and stared down at his sandals. He hugged her again and she kissed him once on his chin.

Otto stepped back. "Lileala, let me see what's happening to you. Please, for a moment, lift your veil?"

Her hands brushed the hem then froze. "I'm horrid."

"My devoted, don't ever say that! You'll always be beautiful." He stepped forward and hugged her tighter.

"No, I'm not myself anymore, that's what I'm trying to say," she gushed and smothered her face in his shoulder.

"Lileala, please. All I've been hearing is how bad you're feeling but no one can tell me what it is. Has anyone seen you besides your elder Ma?"

"Cherry. That's all."

"Ah, that might explain the way she's been acting. Like she's depressed or something. I heard that she let an Aspirant know about you and she's upset that the news was spread."

"That's my fault," Lileala shrugged, surprised by her own indifference. "I never asked Cherry to promise not to say anything and I know she's a talker. Who cares at this point, anyway? All I want is for people to either leave me alone or make this go away."

"Don't cry," said Otto. Her eyes had filled so much he could see tears through the veil. "Hon, it's okay. No matter what, I love you."

He held her close and Lileala wilted as she felt his heartbeat against hers.

"I want you to stop hiding and come with me to see a medic," he added. "How else are we going to figure out what this is?"

"I think it's primitive and so does Cherry." She cringed. "How can medics help with something they know nothing about?"

"I said we, meaning the Pineals. We're all going to help. We're the scientists. A few of us have been searching the knowledge stream for anything that fits the description your elder Ma gave us. There must be a cure, we've no doubt."

"What if the stream can't find it?" Lileala asked.

"Come on, be positive." Otto tried pulling down the hood on her robe, but she resisted.

"Positive? Why? I'm dealing with too much right now. My skin's diseased and I can't even ask questions about the source."

"Lileala?" Otto's mouth gapped and he stood in place. "My love, what are you talking about?"

"Something Cherry told me, but never mind, I can't share it. I'm just beginning to get frustrated. Maybe if The Nobility didn't have so much scorn for Earth's melanin bearers, maybe we'd know more about them, more about this ailment. Who knows what we could have learned from –" She looked at Otto's frown and stopped mid-sentence. "Sorry, didn't mean to rant."

"Not a problem. But seriously, beloved, do you really think you should be questioning The Nobility now? Especially since you're becoming part of it."

"Rare Indigos aren't Nobility. We don't even set policy."

"No, but you're symbolic," Otto countered. "And anyone who accompanies The Nobility or Uluri is seen as a leader."

"Right. Whether or not we actually do anything. Ahonotay didn't even speak for all anyone cared about her."

"Lileala, that's enough." Otto's jaws were clenched, but Lileala could tell he was trying not to overreact. He added, "You sound like an anarchist."

The statement shocked her, but she considered it. "Perhaps," she said, finally. Her voice was tinged with an unfamiliar bitterness that she didn't altogether welcome. She took a deep breath and switched tactics. "Come here, Otto," she said, leading him to a floor cushion. "I'm changing the subject, okay? Let's talk. I have missed you more than you know."

They sat on a plump gray cushion and Otto held the fabric of Lileala's over-sized robe. "This thing is awful," he said.

"I know, but I'm not removing it. The veil, either. But I would like to talk about the curse? I mean cure."

"Not funny, Lileala."

"Sorry. Go on."

"If the info I input in the stream is correct, then these growths aren't growths at all. They're scars called keloids," Otto said. "And, actually, you're right. They're an Earth malady – something that used to happen to those who bore melanin. And listen to this: apparently, some of the Earth melanin bearers were made to feel deeply ashamed."

"They were shamed because of these keloids?"

"That's only part of it," Otto said. "They were shamed simply because of their dark skin."

"What? Otto, are you making this up?" Lileala was in no mood for jokes.

"No, but that's not the point anyway. The fact is they could contract these keloids, some of them anyway, and having keloids added to their humiliation."

"What was the cure?" she asked.

"We don't know that yet. The first thing we need to do is get you to the oscillator to find out if we're on the right track." Otto hesitated. "And there might even be others."

"Other what?"

"Others who have keloids. I don't know yet, but the knowledge stream suggested that someone else reported similar swellings, someone on Toth. We'll just have to wait and see."

Lileala and Otto sat in silence. A few minutes passed before Otto spoke up again. "There's one more thing: the original melanin bearers would get an overgrowth of tissue, but it didn't do any real damage to them. Our atmosphere, however, is unusual. Whatever this is, it could have a far worse effect here on Swazembi."

Lileala sucked in a breath. "What are you saying Otto? That I could die?"

"No! No, I'm not saying that. We just have to accept that this ailment might be… harsh. We don't know yet. On Earth, nothing like this ever happened unless the skin was damaged in some way. If they experienced an injury, they didn't know how to use their pigment to heal it. So they'd let the wound mend itself slowly. That often took weeks, or months, depending on what it was. When it did finally heal, it sometimes left a puffy keloid in its place."

A lump swelled in her throat. She hadn't sustained any injuries; nothing had ever punctured her flesh. "Anything else?" she asked.

"Yes. The Coalition has been alerted that someone may have infiltrated our systems here and transmitted an unknown infection. Something that could possibly spread. They're prepared to declare an emergency and expand the summit, the one your Baba's been planning on Toth. Part of it is open to anyone who wants to attend."

"Waves!" She pouted. "My first time on Toth and I have to go looking like this?"

"No, Lileala. I'll be going. There are other plans for you."

The side wall clicked, and Fanta walked in, looking as if she hadn't slept in days. Her eyes were swollen and her purple and green headwrap hadn't been tied properly. Uncombed strands of hair peeked out from the top.

"Oh, I'm so glad you two are finally talking! Otto, how did you get her to let you in?"

Otto smiled. "I have my ways. And some good news."

"I'm not so sure it's good," Lileala said.

"But you didn't let me finish. While I was in the chamber researching, I discovered that spending a block of time on the Surface could be good for you. The drifts, combined with the pigment, might assist in your healing. And I'll go with you this time, not Zizi. I want to spend a few nights there with you before I leave."

Lileala was so astounded she could barely speak. Otto's announcement was a light in her cloud.

8

"All ceilings exist in the mind, not beneath the gabled roof. When the concubines understand this, they will rule."
– The Grand Prophecy of Una

Trieca was in the laboratory, hunched over a rusted microscope and sipping a cup of fresh water. "It's the best," she said to Mernestyle sitting next to her, trying not to gulp it down.

"Where did you get it?" asked Mernestyle, dripping micro drops of Mecca onto a petri dish.

"From the new rain barrel. Didn't I tell you? When our Toth contact picked up the serum, he brought us enough wood and metal to repair the barrels and to build one that's brand new."

"Are we allowed to accept gifts from Toth?"

"Why not? They're not the Swazembi. They're friends."

"I'm surprised at you, Trieca. We have one ally on Toth. One. That hardly qualifies them as friends."

Trieca laughed. "Taste this water. Go ahead. Then tell me it was a mistake."

Mernestyle was rigid, as always. She kept working and Trieca continued resisting the urge to guzzle what she had left in her cup. Clean, pure water was a luxury, and she wanted to cherish it. She took her time, let it roll around her tongue and, at last, ease along the creases of her throat.

She hadn't tasted water this pure since she was a younger, trailing her female forebear, Una, as they headed to a collection of rain barrels in the rear of the Sector Residence. Trieca and her forebears were part of a privileged clan that lived near the Sector quarters in a five-room wooden dormitory with a twenty-foot-high archway. The dormitories weren't fancy, but they were comfortable and nearly the size of the barns she had seen in old Earth films. Each family had sixteen-by-sixteen-meter quarters and access to a communal kitchen that was always stocked with beets, dried worms and the occasional turnip or carrot.

But it was never enough for Trieca. As a younger, she seethed at the sight of members of the Sector – overseers in starched white robes, and the chief with a bulbous pendant dangling from the thick chain he always wore around his neck. It was then that she wanted to be a man, wanted it more than anything. She yearned for it with such fervor, she was convinced thoughts could bleed.

When Una asked why, she complained that women were just concubines and didn't get to make any rules. But then Una shared something she never forgot: "Point your mind toward it, and one day you'll get your chance. My grand forebear told me that before she died. When she was being banished from Swazembi, she vowed that one of her female progenies would leave a mark upon the entire galaxy."

Trieca had stared at Una in disbelief. But Una kept talking on and on. "I don't know when that grand prophecy will happen, but for now, just know that you are better than the others. You will be prized by the Sector because of your facial markings. No one here has even a hint of color. *Everyone* will be drawn to you."

Trieca finished her water and let the words trip through her mind. She'd felt that way even before Una said it. She had always been beguiling. Why wouldn't everyone want to be in her space?

"Mernestyle," she said. "There is more to my plan that I haven't told you. And it's going to require a lot of Mecca."

"We can thaw the supply that's frozen?" Mernestyle said. "Or do you believe the Wilfins are coming back?"

"Who knows?" Trieca sniffed. "They've probably crashed somewhere by now. But we don't need them. Didn't you say the substance cells can self-renew?"

"I'm pretty sure they can," Mernestyle said. "But I'm still researching it."

"Maybe I'll make the imbecile help you," Trieca said. "That could be another part of his punishment."

"You mean Bertram?" Mernestyle looked up.

"Yep. The chief said he has to do some work on our Mecca project before he goes to jail."

"And what about that Roloc? Isn't he going too?"

Trieca picked up her cup then remembered it was empty. "No, not Roloc. I have another plan for him."

Mernestyle hesitated. "But he posted an image of that girl without checking with the chief first. Isn't that a jailable offense?"

"Never mind that," Trieca said. "He can be useful." Trieca stuck out her arm and showed off a wrist dial.

"Where did you get *that*?" Mernestyle gawked at what looked to her like a band of magical air. "I've heard about those, but I've never seen one." She inserted her finger in one of the spirals, but Trieca slapped it away.

"Don't do that, you might summon him."

"Summon who?"

"You know who. My Toth contact. He's getting pretty friendly with me."

"Wait just a minute, Trieca. Is this thing even allowed here? What did Chief Hardy say?"

"Mernestyle, stop fretting! No one ever said we couldn't accept personal gifts. And this man is valuable. We can't offend him by refusing. He's our spy."

"Our spy or your interest?"

Trieca shook her wrist and watched it light up. "Don't be ridiculous. You really think I could couple with someone from Toth?"

"No. We don't... appeal to them," Mernestyle mumbled, her voice trailing off.

"Maybe, *you* don't." Trieca looked indignant.

"Are you serious? None of us do. Not even you with your birth markings. Kclabs aren't that well-liked, not even on Toth, at least not since the Coalition banned us."

Trieca shook her head. "Damn, I miss those days. Before the ban, we were still in a stable orbit, remember?"

Mernestyle squinched. "Can't forget it."

"I was just a younger," Trieca went on. "But I still remember my family visiting the Black Mountain back then, except it was green and covered with dandelions. Una called them sun drops. She used to gather them for the dinner table."

"Yeah, we visited that mountain too," Mernestyle said.

"And the *sun*," said Trieca, dreamily. "We used to see it every day back then, instead of this now-and-then crap."

"Let's not talk about it," said Mernestyle. Her body had become tense. Clearly, it pained her to remember.

Her objections were wasted on Trieca though. "Did any of your grand-forebears visit Swazembi?" she asked.

"Don't know. If they did, they never discussed it."

"They didn't go then. If they had, they wouldn't have stopped talking about it. Una told me that after her grands went, they were never the same ever again."

Mernestyle closed her eyes and sighed. "Okay, yes. My great-grands went. But it was so sad. They were part of the group that was kicked out."

"Mine too," Trieca replied. "Una said my grand-forebears had a soap plant of their own, right behind their shack in the valley. Before Una left him, my male forebear worked there too. Used to pound salt and make it into detergent."

Something about the story relaxed Trieca and softened the edge in her voice. "After the plant started doing well, Una denounced the whole concubine arrangement and started working there too," she said. "That's why the plant flourished,

my two forebears and grand-forebears, all working and
sharing profits. Too bad it didn't last. The joy, I mean. Soon as
they earned enough salt, they moved to a better dwelling and
went to Swazembi on holiday. Never should have done that. It
broke their spirit, that trip. When they came back, they didn't
feel so good about themselves anymore. No matter what, they
knew they'd never have it as nice as Swazembi. My grand Una
resented them so much for it, she left them a nasty note."

"Please, Trieca, I don't want to discuss it."

"Doubt anyone ever saw the note, though. Probably didn't
matter anyway. They're happy, those Swazembians. Una's
grand-forebear said Swazembians were the happiest people
she'd ever seen."

"I asked you to stop," Mernestyle whined. "Are you even
listening?"

"They're only memories. Anyway, I just wanted to show
you my dial." Trieca dropped her wrist. "I won't be wearing it
again. I need to hide it."

"How are you going to do that?"

"I don't know, maybe Roloc. He'll do anything I ask. I might
stash it in his room after the other overseers finish grilling him
about the image," said Trieca.

"That was something, wasn't it," said Mernestyle. "I don't
understand Roloc's insubordination. What was he thinking?
And that stupid message…"

Trieca smirked. "Yeah, he's crazy, isn't he? Chief Hardy
thinks he did it to try to win favors from me. Get me to couple
with him. He might have even thought he'd get the unders
on our side. You know, convince them to love me and think I
have influence over Swazembi."

"Bad idea," Mernestyle said, shaking her head. "Now the
unders are asking questions about her."

"So what?"

"You know Chief Hardy; he doesn't want the unders to be
curious about other worlds. Thinks they'll rise up against the

Sector. He's so mad I don't think he'll ever let Roloc forget this."

"He'll get over it," Trieca said. "Give it time. Once he and the others finish grilling Roloc, they'll realize that he's more dependable than anyone else in Security. In fact, he's going to be the one to help me run our colony."

"Colony? You mean that site you've been telling me about? The one on the asteroid?"

"Can't say much more; you'll learn about it soon enough." Trieca wandered out of the lab and looked back. "Just wait."

On her way to Roloc's quarters, she continued brainstorming, but the conversation with Mernestyle nagged her. *Not appealing? How is that possible?* Trieca shook off the notion and congratulated herself on her upcoming plans.

By the time Roloc opened the door, her head was swarming with more ideas.

"My contact on Toth says this is a good time for us to make our move," she announced. "It's hard to believe, but he says the rare Swazembi girl might be infected with that rash that's going around and that she's going above ground to heal it. If you ask me, they're being arrogant. What makes them think those Surface colors can heal everything? I can't wait to show what we can do. We have to get a batch of Mecca ready. Now!"

Roloc was half asleep. He stood in the doorway in his gauze underwear, scratching his head and gazing at the strange circle of energy spinning above Trieca's wrist.

"I'm sorry," he said. "What is it I'm supposed to do?"

"Mix the Mecca sample so we can show it off. The Coalition needs to know that we have something more powerful than any substance they've ever been able to create."

"But it's late. Why now?"

"I just made a snap decision. A new Security addition, Dlareg, will be your partner. He's a mean one, but I'll supply him with crystals. He sleeps with his door ajar. Get over to his unit. B37. You can explain everything to him when you get there."

Roloc threw a crystal chip in his mouth and dressed quickly. His new partner's room was on the third floor of a wing that was two hundred paces away. When he arrived, he burst in without knocking.

"Wake up! We have work to do. We have a chance to cure the girl!" He reached down and shook Dlareg frantically, yelling as if talking to a disruptive child.

Dlareg groaned. "The girl? What girl?" He rolled over and lazily glanced at the time box on his dresser. It was Point Three of the late period. He frowned, blinked and inhaled. An aroma, sweet, mildly relaxing, had wafted through the night air and formed an invisible cloud over his bed. His eyes flipped open, and he saw Roloc standing there, smacking on a fragrant crystal, enjoying the sensation of being detached.

Dlareg jumped up in a frenzy. "I haven't taken an ore crystal, and here you stand, waking me during the late period."

Roloc took two awkward steps backwards. This wasn't going to be easy. "Calm down, will you? We have an assignment together."

Dlareg stumbled out of bed then felt his way through the darkness. "The light button," he said. "Help me find the frickin' light button."

Roloc waded along the edge of the wall, pressed a square on the side and stepped away. A choppy wave of light flickered on and off, lighting up the room just enough for Dlareg to see. He plopped onto the bed and cursed. But Roloc was safe, hiding behind the curtain surrounding the bathing area.

"Your anger surge will wear off soon," he yelled. "Let me know when it has. This is important."

Dlareg took a deeper breath, inhaling the sticky fume. "Who the hell are you?"

"Your new partner with news about the healing serum."

"You mean that Mecca stuff?" he asked. "Okay, shoot."

Roloc pushed the curtain to the side and approached him, holding up a five-inch bottle with a sealed spout.

"This is to hold the substance," he said. "Trieca wants us in the laboratory immediately. She wants us to make sure it's just the right strength. That rare Swazembian girl needs it."

"How do you know that?" Dlareg shot back.

"Trieca's source, someone on Toth," said Roloc. "He says the Coalition will meet on Toth in a couple of days, specifically to discuss her condition. I've never met him, but Trieca said he's sneaky and that he has the mind of a Kclab."

Dlareg stood up, tossing a robe over his puny arms and grabbing a coat made out of foamy cushion.

"Move a little faster," Roloc urged. "Please. By the time the Swazembian sun has come up and gone back down, the Toth contact needs to have more of the formula. He's going to come up with a sly way to use it on the girl. Then we'll announce we created it."

"What does that mean?" Dlareg asked. He trailed behind Roloc, scowling. "How can the Toth contact do that and not get accused of working with us?"

"How should I know?" Roloc replied. "But whatever this guy does, it works. Trieca really believes in him. She says he's been getting Mecca from her for a while and using it all kinds of ways."

The explanation seemed lost on Dlareg. He finished dressing and shrugged.

"You never said why we have to do this immediately," he said.

"I told you."

"Refresh my memory."

"The girl. Our contact has informed us she'll be on the Surface of the planet. If the rumors are true, she hopes to heal there."

"So?"

"So, this is our chance to demonstrate our prowess. Mecca can heal her skin condition."

"Someone's going to hand it over to her?"

"Nothing like that," Roloc explained. "Trieca's friend, or whoever he is, plans to hide this stuff somewhere close enough to affect her."

"Ah, I think I get it," Dlareg said. "We use it now. Then when we stop administering the Mecca, the problem will return. And when it does, the Coalition will run to us for the cure."

"Now, you're catching on."

They hastened outside, becoming silhouettes beneath the pod lights. The laboratory was approximately fifty meters ahead. "Damn, I hope we finish this in time," Roloc muttered. The pods of light floating above them seemed to be losing some of their strength, and Roloc had to squint to see. The lab building seemed so far away. "Damn," he repeated. "We're going to have to work feverishly, even if it takes the rest of the late period. It's critical that the solution be ready when Trieca's Toth friend arrives."

Dlareg's legs wobbled and he almost stumbled. His eyes were half closed, as if he were walking in his sleep.

"Tell me again," he said, his voice dragging. "Why are we in such a rush?"

Roloc's throat tightened. Bubbles of heat foamed in his cheeks. He glared at Dlareg and had to fight the urge to pounce on his new Security team partner. The crystal was wearing off.

9

"Are not colors and sound one and the same?"
– Scientific Pineal Crew Riddle

The whispers nagged her. She pressed her head into Otto's shoulder and tried to block them out, hoping he hadn't noticed. Lifting his hand to her face, she smoothed his fingers over her cheeks and chin. The keloids were shrinking in the morning heat of the Surface, melting among the painted mists. She slid closer to Otto and started to speak.

"Shhh," he whispered. "Wait. Just watch."

So, they waited, watching as the sun spilled over a deep green mountain top and curled into the purple and red drifts. Lileala and Otto moved on. This was their third day on the Surface and her keloids were nearly gone. Only a few scars remained, and they now resembled minor scratches. She could feel Otto's admiration, and she was determined, once again, to be the happy Lileala he knew – plucky, obstinate. She flexed her toes and dug them deeper into the sand.

"Remember this?" she asked, pressing her foot into the damp spot. "Remember back when we were chamber buddies, how we'd sneak up here after it rained and make footprints?"

On the clay bordering the shoreline, Otto kicked off his sandals and joined Lileala. He breathed in the warmth and stroked her hands. "Don't go in too far," he cautioned. The colors darting through the sea were playful, but the sea's electromagnetic tide was powerful enough to pull them under. She backed away with a sudden jerk, and he surprised her with a hug and kiss. She wiggled out of his grip. "We're still in the open, Otto," she said in a teasing voice.

Her words made him snicker. "There aren't many people up here; the ban on tourists is still in effect." He leaned in to kiss her again, but stopped. "Your Shimmer is more heightened than usual. Are you doing trinity breath right now?"

"Yes, and it's exciting. It's so easy now that I do it all the time, just like Mama Xhosi said it would be." She waved her hands over her head and brushed them through a flood of colors.

They continued walking. *The voices,* she wondered, *should I tell him?*

A male child scampered by and tumbled into a patch of red and blue sand. The sand exploded into a tantrum of powdered colors, dusting his satiny brown arms and legs. Otto and Lileala laughed.

They spotted a local female as she planted herself beneath a bouquet of green, yellow, and orange, letting them rinse her entire body. With both elbows above her head, the woman held her palms up and waited for the drifts to litter her face then cloak her arms and chest. She was a wizened elder, possibly close to four hundred sun years, radiant with knowing eyes. Her right leg was flexed, and a gash had sliced through her calf, revealing a wedge of bone. She was clearly about to engage in a common healing maneuver – allowing vapors to drip into the skin's natural melanin. She stood still for ten minutes performing the ritual. In gradual spurts, the gash on her leg began to close.

"And speaking of Mama Xhosi –" Otto pointed to another woman in a too-long garment, scooping a section of fabric into her arms as she trudged through the sand.

"Lileala! Let me see you," she called out. "Why did you hide from me? I needed to see you face to face." She didn't stop walking until she was so close Lileala could feel her breath on her nose. "You had no need to run from me," she said. "You're my favorite Indigo."

"I ran from everyone, not just you. I even ran from my devoted." She gestured toward Otto, but Mama Xhosi didn't glance in his direction.

"I was going to give you one more day to sulk," said Mama Xhosi. "After that, I would have ordered the guards to break in."

"Doesn't matter now, I'm okay."

"I can see that." Mama Xhosi scanned her forehead and cheeks. "You're not at all the way I heard you described. You controlled it with trinity breath, no?"

Lileala hesitated. "Not exactly. I mean, it didn't work, not at first. It works now, though; everything is working now."

A shadow of concern fell over Mama Xhosi, a pleasantness that reminded Lileala of the first time she told her she would be Rare Indigo. "Well, I want you to know your wardrobe is being designed. You'll have so many gowns – all of them breathtaking, absolutely breathtaking. So far, they're some of the best I've seen. As soon as you get back, summon me and we'll start the fittings."

"Thank you, Mama Xhosi." Lileala held onto Otto's arm. Lileala was hoping she would at least acknowledge him. But she didn't seem interested in anything but clothing styles.

"There's one that has so much gold in the material, it sizzles. Honestly, it shines so much you won't have to go into Shimmer. The dress will do it for you!" She let out a throaty laugh. Lileala suspected it was raspy because she wasn't used to laughing, or maybe it was the sound of her laughing and clearing her throat at the same time.

"I can't wait to see the wardrobe," Lileala said, trying to sound interested.

"Me too," Mama Xhosi said, as she shuffled off, still without a word to Otto. Lileala took offense.

"What are you thinking?" Otto asked. "You seem so serious all of a sudden."

"Nothing much. I'm just wondering – why wear pretty dresses, only to walk around here all the time, in Sangha province and no further."

They halted mid-conversation to watch another medicinal ritual. Climbing to the top of Blue Barrell, a muscular elder-child, twenty-ish, faced the east and absorbed sun rays into his pores as he anchored himself. The colors swarmed, basting the stubble on his chin and shaggy ropes of hair that bulged from his scalp and sloped down to his waist. With his eyes closed, he inhaled and kept four fingers outstretched, waiting while a stump on his hand sprouted into a bud then regenerated a new fifth finger.

"I guess I should consider my waves of luck," Lileala said. "How many people get to roam up here for a whole seven days? But…"

"But what? Love, what's wrong?" Otto slipped an arm around her.

"I don't know. It's like my reality was altered when I was afflicted, and all of a sudden, it's back again."

"Your point?"

"There's no point, really. Just a strange feeling," she said. "Anyway, I heard from one of the Aspirants that Issa is still complaining to Mama Xhosi about me. Can you believe that? She's still calling me the wrong choice. But you know what she said Mama Xhosi tells her every time? My Shimmer. No one can beat my Shimmer. That's it. And that's why… that's why… Otto, I'm sorry I hid from you, but that's why. Without Shimmer, I worry, who would I be?"

"You'll always be my Lileala, that's who," he said.

She clenched his waist and observed a hoop of color breezing past his nose. He swished his fingers through it and watched it gallop. "Did you know you're the only one who can make me forget about all the stress from my job?"

"What?" She giggled. "So tell me what I'm making you forget. The excavations, the experiments, the inventions?"

Otto fell silent, carefully observing Lileala's reaction to what he was about to say. "It's the strangest thing we've ever dealt with," he explained. "The Coalition and the Pineal Crew can't seem to get to the bottom of it. We believe there's a planet missing. Peculiar as it sounds, a planet in our Coalition is actually missing from orbit. Nowhere to be found."

"That's crazy!" Lileala said. "How is that even possible?"

"It's not. I don't understand it."

"So, besides the keloids, is that what you'll be talking about at the summit? Disappearing planets?"

"It's a big meeting," Otto said. "We'll discuss plenty."

His gaze bounced off Lileala and landed on a Surface vendor's crisscross of cornrowed hair. The vendor whistled as he passed, peddling mangos and pine nuts from a manual tray.

"Like the Earth's melanin bearers?" Lileala asked.

"No, what makes you ask that?" he replied.

"I'm just wondering. What were they like?"

"Like everyone else on Earth, I suppose. Too many weapons. Always fighting. Why?"

"Hmm, I guess I'm just questioning things. Ever since these keloids, I've wanted to know more about other worlds."

Otto stood directly in front of her, clutching both of her hands. "I'll be out there exploring them, and I'll share it with you. I can do enough world analysis for both of us."

Something about that comment sent Lileala into a soft pout, but she hid it skillfully. Rare Indigos, after all, weren't supposed to express strong political views with anyone and wouldn't be permitted to leave Swazembi.

Rotating his fingers in a slow, soft motion, Otto caressed her shoulders, and Lileala felt the admiration in his eyes. She twirled for him, showing off the flowing crepe crinkles of her dress and the strands of amber beads wrapped in layers around her hips.

"You're a special kind of elegance," he said. "Wait until visiting dignitaries meet you. You're going to wow them!"

The compliment flattered Lileala but also made her more cautious. She had to think carefully about how to respond. Otto wasn't ready to hear her burgeoning feelings and maybe she wasn't ready to share them. But when? Would she ever be able to tell him about the haunting messages?

"Otto, do you think you know me, I mean *really* know me?" she asked, just to test his reaction. "What if I had weird interests or secrets that I've never shared?"

"What kind of secrets? You don't hide anything..." Otto thought a moment. "I guess you did hide those keloids from me. Is that what you mean?"

"No, something else."

"Okay, tell me." Otto leaned forward and kissed her cheek.

"Well, I actually have developed an interest in the Inekoteth. I think about it sometimes and wonder what it is."

"The spirits of Tnomo and other ancestors, I guess. You're wondering about that?"

"I don't know. I might have to meet with the Mhondora again. If I do, I need to know how to behave. Should I act all stuffy? What if he tells me never to use S when I say yes? Should I mock him and yell 'ye, ye, ye'?" Lileala laughed so hard, she sounded like she was squealing.

Otto doubled over, laughing. "Come on, silly," he said when he caught his breath. "Let's get back to your dome." He dashed ahead of her, and she ran after, still giggling but still worrying if she should speak up. She, the future devoted one of a Scientific Pineal Crew officer, had been hearing strange messages. Shouldn't she say something?

She caught up with him, nuzzled against him and felt his strength. With their arms linked, they headed into the dome. Now was not the time.

10

"Never believe you are the superior culture. Brilliance is a cherry that grows in all worlds."
    – The Coalition Edict of Fair Negotiation

The conference area was not at all what Otto expected. He had attended many Coalition meetings in the past but never in such a cavernous hall. He was annoyed by the new setting. It made him feel as if he was visiting Toth for the first time.

"Why was the Aiden Center not used?" he asked a Sonaguard. "The summits have always been there ever since I joined the Pineal Crew."

His question caught the ear of Crew Colonel Rook Stevens, his former classmate on Toth. "And good day to you too, Officer Otto." The colonel smiled, despite his obvious displeasure with the remark.

"I'm sorry, Colonel Rook. Forgive my lack of manners," Otto said. "Waves of joy to you, as well. I don't know what came over me." Otto looked up again, distracted. The structure had an unusually high-ceiling and the width of a small space station. He thought it odd of the Toths to build something so ostentatious.

"I take it," Colonel Stevens said, "that you're not impressed with the Coalition's choice of venue."

"Venue, yes," Otto said. "Toth is the best choice. Always has been. But this particular room, this building – have I seen any of this before?"

"It was just built, designed by Ellis. You remember him, don't you? He attended school with us."

"Ah, yes. But I didn't know he studied architecture."

"He didn't. He's a geologist and some sort of expert on Earth structures."

"So he's an archaeologist?"

"No, just an explorer."

Unsure what that meant, Otto dismissed the colonel's explanation. He thought the building a tremendous waste of resources. Its panels seemed endless, stretching upwards almost half a kilometer, held in place by hundreds of glass beams and fluorescent planks. "Forgive me, but I always thought of Toths as conservationists. How is this sustainable?"

"It was an idea advanced by Ellis," Rook answered. "He can explain it better than me. Supposedly, he was able to create this with a minimal amount of lead glass and some sort of pearly mineral. I believe it's called gypsum. He claims to have some special method of stretching fibers. He says it uses less, not more."

"Excuse me for saying this but I always thought Toth's structures were designed for efficiency," Otto said. "This seems pretentious." His eyes skirted the periphery of the building again. On Swazembi, all structures were functional, even the rotating globes had practical upper rooms.

"Listen, let us show off a bit if we want. You have the pigment; we have the ingenious building capacity. Besides, Ellis is being generously rewarded for his contribution. He's next in line for the chief of building regulations seat."

"I see," said Otto. He thought Ellis was young for such a prime post. Otto mulled it over and decided he'd find him later and offer some form of congratulations. "Please excuse me," he said. "I haven't been in the best of spirits for the past few weeks. Of course, you know by now what happened to Lileala, my devoted."

"The Rare Indigo is your devoted? Well, well, good for you. I've heard that she's improving. Is that true?"

"Improving with the power of the galaxy," said Otto.

"And of course, the melanin," the colonel added.

"What do you mean?"

"I mean that Swazembi has more than its share of melanin. Isn't that why you're head of the Coalition?" There was a snide tone in his voice. Otto sensed it and became instantly irritated.

"You're so fond of saying that," he replied angrily. "Is this your way of suggesting we have an unfair advantage? Yes, the pigment can be a help. Like on Earth digs or anywhere there's excessive heat. But why bring it up? Be gracious. Isn't that somewhere in the Toth creed?"

For a moment, Rook seemed alarmed. Then he tapped his chin, a Toth custom meant to symbolize peace and walked off. Otto was left alone to deal with his private agitation and to think about the Swazembi-Toth pact: be curt during tense moments, say very little. Otto had violated it by raising his voice.

He felt momentarily ashamed. Toth was Swazembi's strongest ally, and he had demonstrated one of their worst taboos: poor self-control. Toths were disciplined and had a natural bluntness that matched their stern, controlled appearance. Lean with well-defined muscles and golden-white hair streaming down their backs, they had porcelain skin and a severe countenance. But that contradicted their trust and generosity. Unlike Swazembi, they allowed expatriates and had turned their world into an interplanetary mecca.

Two men then approached him, extended their greenish hands and said hello. Otto barely heard them. He recognized them as Jemtis, shook their hands and kept walking, his discomfort growing. It was a bit humid in the room and there was a sticky sweet smell that irked him.

"Otto, are you okay?" a voice called out. It was the Pineal Crew chief, Lileala's Baba, Kwesi. "Egads, man. You seem out of sorts. Is there more bad news?"

"No, not at all." He forced a smile. "She's fine. Believe me, she's fine. I know you haven't seen your daughter since all of this happened. But I've taken good care of her."

The room appeared to be getting warmer, and Otto wondered if the air was circulating properly. "Is it stuffy in here?" he asked. "Or am I the only one who finds this atmosphere troublesome."

"Troublesome? Why, no. But there is a strange odor." Kwesi's eyes shifted. "Strange hall."

"Indeed," Otto said. "Can I join you?"

The two men walked through a set of double doors and toward a long bench.

Dane Elliott, Coalition Chairman, and Coleman Spencer, Coalition Commander of Interplanetary Affairs, were calling the session to order. "We have a lot of work ahead of us," Dane announced, "and we need to move on it quickly. We have the matter of a planet – a Coalition member – that seems to have vanished. We also have an incurable infection happening within some of our other worlds."

Dane was a Toth native with bluish-green eyes and a complexion that was a blend of gold and beige. His voice boomed, projecting across the room without the aid of a volume enhancer. "Seated with me on the panel are representatives from the Coalition – from Neptune, Jemti, KaBa, Luton and Toth. And to my right, there's a disease specialist, Medic Sarami from Jemti. As far as we know, Jemti was one of the first planets affected."

Medic Sarami stood before he was asked. "We've never dealt with an ailment like this. It's something that our oscillators haven't been able to reverse," he said. "Now that it's hit Toth and Swazembi and still uncured, we're considering some archaic alternatives, maybe even biopsies."

"That's a last resort, I hope," said Dane. "But before you go on, I want to give the audience some background." His expression became grave, and he cleared his throat. "We don't know where this ailment came from or how it spreads. What we do know is that it causes peculiar scarring of the tissues. Several inhabitants of various Coalition worlds have been stricken with it. And it appears to attack those with melaninated skin, and by that, I mean natural melanin, not complexions like mine."

For the last two decades, Toths in power positions had learned a process called Mental Self Tan (M-S-T). Created and taught by Swazembian expatriates on Toth, M-S-T was a breathing technique based loosely on the Indigo Aspirant trinity breath practice. Those with strong lungs and disciplined minds could add bronze touches to their complexion simply through breath and willpower.

But it didn't induce the production of melanin. By adding that he could not be infected, Dane was making that point without making it. He waited until he had the audience's full attention before his next announcement.

"Please be advised," he said, "that we have another grave situation that's perplexing us as well. The planet, Golong, can no longer be detected by our telescopic radar. We're so bewildered we've even sent the Pineal Crew and a team of Sonaguards out to find answers. Three times they have failed to locate it."

The audience murmured and Dane paused. "I can't believe I'm saying this," he added, "but it's as if Golong never existed."

The noise in the auditorium thickened, and Dane raised his hand to request silence.

"That's not possible!" someone blurted.

"None of it seems possible," Dane said. "The disease or the…"

He stopped suddenly. Heads turned as two Sonaguards wrestled with a couple of intruders attempting to force their way through the doors. In silence, Otto observed with a nervous detachment, trying to ignore the anger fluttering in his belly. He recognized them as Kclabs. Though he'd never actually seen one in person, their appearance was unmistakable. Their skulls were out of proportion with their thin bodies and their skin didn't seem like skin at all. It was a sheer, hairless membrane.

Otto stood and raised one hand. Several others copied his gesture.

"Can we take this to mean that we are to allow these Kclabs to attend the meeting?" Dane asked, surveying the crowd. More hands went up, a unifying sign of agreement.

Dane signaled the guards. "Release them. I have no idea how they made it through our security barriers without the proper coding, but for the sake of peace, we'll allow them to attend."

Dlareg and Haliton brushed elbows, pushing their way to the front of the room, glancing behind them, in front of them and to either side. Dlareg's movements were wild and jerky, as if he was having a nervous fit.

"Your meeting is important to us," he said and bowed his head as if approaching a panel of dignitaries.

Haliton gawked at his partner and straightened his own shoulders, and, as if to distinguish himself, poked out his chest.

"Why are your eyes half closed?" he whispered under his breath to Dlareg.

"It's a habit," said Dlareg, but instead of looking at Haliton, he zeroed in on Dane. "We think we have an answer to your concerns."

Gently, Haliton tapped his security partner's wrist. "Not yet," he whispered. "We just arrived."

Dlareg spoke again. "Actually, I know we have the answer!"

Haliton took Dlareg's arm and whispered. "Let's wait. This is the first meeting we've attended, remember. We're here to give and get information."

With one surprisingly quick bound, Dlareg deliberately distanced himself from Haliton and shuffled closer to the podium. "My partner is shy, but I am not. I'm going to level with all of you. We, the Kclabs, the society you have rejected, have a wonder product that will cure this mysterious infection."

A rustle stirred through the room, making Dlareg drowsier. "We have a cuuuure," he said, stretching out the vowel. "I'm telling you, we can cuuure this."

"Hold on. Stop right there." Commissioner Dane stood and tapped his chin.

"What infection? Who told you about an infection?"

His speech was slurred, but Dlareg tried to squeak out an answer. Haliton blocked hm. Sweeping his hand in front of Dlareg's mouth, he spoke directly into his ear.

"Damnit, you took an ore crystal, didn't you?" he said. "You're dragging out your words and you're using poor judgement. We have to reveal a little at a time."

Dane's command drowned out both of them.

"I demand to know what you're talking about. Who leaked this information to you?"

Haliton stepped forward. "My partner isn't well. Excuse him. We're here to introduce ourselves and offer our services. But..." Haliton stalled. "We are privy to some information. We may not belong to your Coalition, but we have our ways of learning what we need to know, and right now, we happen to know about the illness and about a remedy."

While Haliton spoke, Dlareg staggered to the nearest bench and slumped over it, letting the sober Haliton take the lead. "You have no way to control this disease in your midst," Haliton went on. "We do, because... well, we dealt with it once before and we've studied it." The crowd buzzed, then quieted. Haliton continued, "Does that shock you? You with your moving rainbows. You actually need us, the species you banned."

Dane tapped his chin and interrupted. "You're trying our patience with your delusions. Just tell us your piece and explain how we can negotiate."

"That's easy," said Haliton. "Let us in. Invite Kclabs, like everyone else, into Toth and into Swazembi. Let us join the Coalition and we'll give you the cure."

Otto elbowed Kwesi. "I'd heard something about that planet disappearing but nothing about this foolishness. Since when do Kclabs have cures for ailments? I don't find it believable. What do you think?"

"It's buffoonery," Kwesi answered. "Pure Kclab buffoonery."
He massaged his temples and forced himself to pay attention.
He'd been on Toth for weeks and the Kclab antics were clearly
becoming too much to bear.

Dane remained still, saying nothing. He was detached while
the rest of the panel, seated in a row beside him, grumbled.

"We have absolutely no reason to believe any of this." He
looked toward the two Sonaguards standing on either side of
the door. "This is ridiculous. Remove them."

"Hold on!" Haliton shouted. "You want to help the Rare
Girl, right? You think it was you and your medics and your
electromagnetic colors that eased her symptoms? Not true. It
was us."

Silence shot through the room like lightning. Not a person
present spoke.

Haliton went on: "We were able to get ourselves admitted
into Swazembi and then sneak onto the Surface where the
Rare Girl slept. But don't worry. Our mission is one of peace.
We sprayed a serum called Mecca in the girl's quarters. And
that is why the keloids shrank."

"Shut up!" yelled Dane. "We've heard enough."

"But… don't you want to know more about Mecca?" Haliton
asked.

"I. Said. Enough," answered Dane. He turned the assembly
over to Commander Coleman Spencer. "My brothers and
sisters, please ignore the uncouth culture and try not to be
alarmed by their display," Coleman instructed. "Rest assured
the Coalition, with the help of our trusted medic, will resolve
this problem ourselves."

Coleman's message was accompanied by the rustle of
Dlareg's long, baggy tunic. He had awakened and begun
dragging himself to the front of the room.

"Resolved!" He chuckled. "You think the problem is
resolved? It won't be over until the affected ones come with
us. We have the only solution."

"It's true," Haliton added. "Mecca gets results. Without it, we're sorry to say, the keloids will return."

Other voices rose. There was an outburst of pleas and clashing shouts, everyone clamoring to be heard.

"Please, silence! Please!" said Dane. Anger flooded his voice, and he lost the mental control needed to maintain his tan. His skin faded to olive then turned a pinkish white. He and Commander Coleman faced the audience, their eyes riveted on Dlareg and Haliton.

"You want us to let her go with you?" Dane repeated.

"Yes, with us!" Haliton said. "There's an inhabitable asteroid not too far from Kclaben, so close, we've claimed it. We can't give you the Mecca because you might replicate it. Our proposal is that you let us treat the afflicted at a little dispensary we plan to set up on the asteroid. The only cost is our access to your worlds."

Dane could stand no more. "Jail them!" he shouted. "I'll have no more of this quackery. And I won't rest until I find out who's responsible for their presence!"

Four Sonaguards ran towards Dlareg and Haliton, and shook them to the ground. The Kclabs thrashed and kicked. They jumped to their feet just as the guards were inserting their hands into blue celluloid orbs.

Dlareg saw the weapons and shouted: "You can sedate us, but it won't do any good –"

Bolts of green and blue raced through the guards' fingers and zapped the Kclabs, bouncing from their shoulders to their ears and eyes. They blacked out, one behind the other, and their limp, unconscious forms were dragged out of the room.

Trieca fumed. Can't security do anything right?

She lifted her sleeve and checked her dial. Point Three in the afternoon and here she was, still in the Coalition meeting. She'd been there the entire time, enveloped in yards of smooth fabric the color of dandelions. She had wrapped it around her body and securely pinned the hooded veil to ensure her face was covered. With her eyes peeking through the garment's only opening, she had seated herself in the back of the room, on a bench that was occupied by several women, mostly observers like her.

Silently, she watched as the door slammed behind Dlareg and Haliton. She thought about how severely she would punish them. Now her Toth friend would have to waste time getting the two buffoons out of jail; she'd probably have to guide the ship back home without them. It would take time for the Coalition to realize they'd never get a cure if they kept anyone from Kclab imprisoned.

Just thinking about it was exhausting to Trieca. She thought about leaving them locked up and appointing a different team. Then she decided not to fuss over it, figured she'd leave the new team selection up to Chief Hardy.

She relaxed and smoothed her garment. It was yet another gift from her Toth friend and she adored it. She hadn't ever felt such exquisite fabric and didn't want to believe him when he told her it was made by worms. "The worm? The kind that is food?" she had asked, and she wondered why he'd made such an awful face. On Toth, they didn't eat of the worm?

She looked around, trying to see if he was nearby. Shouldn't he be at this meeting? Or was he avoiding it, fearing his presence would stir up suspicion?

But why would anyone suspect anything? She hadn't shared his identity with a single soul, not Chief Hardy, not even Mernestyle. When Haliton asked for the energy configuration that would allow them into Toth airspace, she had pressed the inverted pyramid on the ship's dashboard and secretly entered the code numbers RC1155. No one had seen a thing. So, where was he? Why was he making himself so unavailable?

"Simmer down, everyone," someone said. "Please simmer down." Then Commander Coleman stood and waited for the room to become silent. Trieca decided to stay and listen in on the rest of the meeting.

"We're ready now to open up the discussion," he said. "Quiet, please."

What an attractive man, Trieca thought – his hair tossed back, gold skin shining like a true Toth dignitary. He was high spirited and seemed to have the energy of all of the Kclaben Security Sector combined. But he was as restrained as he was handsome. To Trieca, he was a study in superb skill. Her spy friend had told her about the self-tanning technique called M-S-T, and explained to her that it was popular among the high-ranking natives of Toth. But not all of them had the mind mastery to sustain the hue as long as Coleman was sustaining it, and with such brilliance. The brightness and tenacity of his tan was a mark of superb mental prowess.

He stood beside Dane, unshaken by what he had just witnessed. "Now that the scene has ended, let's continue." The commander gestured to Dane to return to his seat on the panel.

Before Dane was seated, a hand in the crowd raised. Several others shot up like flags. "Go ahead," Dane said. "But one at a time."

A man in the first row waved both hands. He was part white, part iridescent gold. "I'm from Toth and I think we better do what they say. Just because they have an unseemly appearance doesn't mean they're not telling the truth."

Flashes of anger swept through Otto. "Do as they say?" he shouted, forgetting to wait his turn. "Lileala's not going anywhere! Besides, she's improving. Those damn keloids are almost gone."

"But you heard them," added the man with the golden sheen. "They're coming back."

"And you believe them? Just like that?"

Surprised by the resistance, Trieca pulled her body up to a standing position, careful not to release her veil. "Excuse me, since this is an open meeting, may I have a word, please?" She had one hand in the air, the other was gripping a flap of material that hid her nose and the white blotches on her left cheek. "I'm just a visitor, you see, but why not take them seriously? So, the girl is fine now. You don't know what tomorrow will bring. Maybe the skin contaminant will spread across Swazembi. Since you don't know what it is, I suggest you send her with the ones who claim they can cure it."

The crowd roared and Trieca continued. "You see, I happen to believe the Kclabs *do* have some knowledge of science. I don't think we should underestimate them."

"And who are you, again?" Dane asked. "Ma'am, what is your name and exactly where are you from?"

Trieca paused. "I am Tina, Tina from Jemti." She stopped without further explanation. She had enjoyed Jemti the time she visited. She had observed their shiny metal buildings closely and, if asked, could describe them in perfect detail.

From her side view, she saw her spy friend enter and head toward a row of benches on the left side of the hall. He was striking in a bold, commanding way, with a haunting, milky-white complexion and an ocean of salt-colored hair.

"I am tired, please excuse me."

She turned to leave, looking for a way over to him. She hadn't talked to him on this trip, and she wanted to see him now, in person, for longer than their usual rushed block of time. She wanted to ask him if he could arrange for her to stay a while longer on Toth so that she could enjoy fresh waves of sunlight and the two of them could spend some time together, perhaps even couple. It would be nice to cavort under the sun, she thought, and he would have an even better view of her ravishing birth marks.

Someone tall bumped into her and wanted to know how a woman of her low height could be from Jemti. She kept moving without a word. Where had he gone? Trieca made it to the far left of the room, near the rear, but her friend was nowhere.

She eased out of the back door, hoping to spot him in the hallway. It was humid and smelled of warm sugar. With the exception of several Sonaguards, it was empty.

"Excuse me," she said to one of the guards, a woman in the

requisite silver pants and shirt. "Did you see a human with pale hair leave the meeting? He left only moments ago."

The woman shot a glance at another female Sonaguard on the other side of the room. They both snickered.

"Um, excuse me?" Trieca said again. "I'm looking for a human who left the meeting early?"

The guard snubbed her again. Trieca sighed. "Okay, let me try once more," she said. "I'm looking for a man. He's white of skin with bright hair."

"Sounds like you're describing half of the men here." The guard laughed, and when she turned her back, Trieca reached out to grab her. She stopped herself quickly. Her friend had warned her that demanding and pushing were considered bad behavior on Toth. It was against something they deemed "rules of etiquette".

Trieca dropped her hands and frowned, irritated that the people of Toth weren't as gracious as she'd been led to believe. "Hypocrite," she mumbled.

The woman clenched her teeth in a pretend smile.

"Are you talking to me?"

"Yes, I am," Trieca answered, using a tone of authority. "I understand a social event is being held for those of us who are attending the meeting."

"Coalition members and the staff will gather later on the second level," the woman snapped. "But visitors aren't allowed. After the meeting, you're expected to leave."

"Oh, I figured as much," said Trieca. She stalled and tucked her tongue beneath the roof of her mouth to add more sizzle to her voice. "I completely understand, but I work with a new Coalition trainee. He told me that in the event of a gathering, I am to meet him there."

The female Sonaguard's jaws were tight and Trieca could tell that she was peeved. Pleased that her vocal power was having an effect, she smiled and waited for her to reply.

"Upstairs in the Amka Room. Go to the next platform and take the lift on the right to the fifth level."

Trieca said a quick thank you and headed toward the nearest set of stairs. At the top, there was a lift. Her heart pounded as she pushed button number five. He's there, she thought. I can feel that he's there. She walked down a wide corridor and, next to the third open door, spotted the word "Amka". As she approached, she could hear a familiar voice.

"I wonder if I should remain in here for a while or not. I'm not totally positive the person I'm avoiding was actually present."

It was him. Trieca's cheeks tingled. She couldn't wait for him to see her wearing the gown he'd given her. He would be so pleased, she thought. So impressed.

"You should leave now and come back later," someone answered. "We won't be setting up for another eighty minutes."

"Where else can I go? Not back in that meeting. Not now, anyway. You know how it is with the opposite sex and – trust me – they're the same no matter where they're from."

"Oh, so this is all about a woman! I didn't know you had a new woman in your life."

Moving closer, Trieca felt energized. *A new woman in his life. Me?*

"No, not like that. She's more of a business associate who's… not working out. Have you ever given gifts as a thank you to someone for a favor – maybe even as a bribe – and then realized they've taken it the wrong way?"

Trieca struggled to find her breath. Wrong way? But she was never wrong.

He continued, "She's an ugly one, too. I mean, whew!"

Trieca breathed in and then out through her nose. Suddenly, she could taste the salt from last night's dinner. A sour acid was rising up to her mouth. She covered it with both hands and pressed to stop herself from vomiting. Her eyes watered, and she threw her head back, letting the veil fall. Her breath was hot, stinging her lips and the sides of her contorted face. She gave in and let the anger surge through her body. Her legs crumbled beneath her, and she fell backwards, heaving as if the entire building had landed on her chest.

"Like I said, woman trouble." The other man was laughing and Trieca pictured her hands wiggling around his neck like snakes.

"No! I keep telling you. It's not that." Her friend laughed. "She's not even a woman, not a real one. I don't know what she is, but I have to figure out how to shake her off. Thankfully my business with her is almost done."

"Tell her then."

"You can't be serious."

"Either tell her or take her out on a proper outing. Come now, she can't be that bad."

With her hands smashed against the wall, Trieca managed to drag her body up from the floor and, one slow leg at a time, head in the direction of the lift.

"I told you, she's hideous."

She trembled and kept moving. The corridor was much longer than she remembered. And it had an echo now, a voice that reached deep inside of her and squeezed.

"That's the only word I could use to describe her. Do you hear me? Hideous."

11

*"I guess I needed so much more than their admiration could give me.
I couldn't tolerate the prison of their gaze. It made me feel like no
more than a spray of dust."*
– From the journals of Ahonotay

Lileala was in full Shimmer. Swaths of light swept around her
in vivid bursts, giving her flesh a glazed appearance. She was
incandescent and she knew it, took pride in it, swaying and
rocking her head from side to side. It was her first day home
since her Surface visit and she was calmer, still a tad confused,
but elated about the enormous improvement in her condition.
With the keloids gone, she could stroll through The Great Hall
again, face uncovered, bouncing to an old-time tune.

Otto had given her a new chip loaded with music he'd
collected during his last trip to Toth. Lileala listened to it and
grinned. The hymns were a rare find, discovered by Pineals
who had trampled through a pocket of Earth land that had
only recently been designated a safe zone, containing the least
amount of nuclear fallout waste. The Pineals roamed the sites
and transported remnants of appliances and cylinders of music
to Toth and Swazembi once every sun month. But this new beat
wasn't like the others. It was comical and deliberately playful.

*"We're gonna jump. We're gonna swagger on the dance floor. Yeah,
yeah, let's jump."*

She laughed out loud. A heavy laugh, the first good one

she'd had in weeks. Her fingers snapping, she munched on a molasses square and kept singing and walking.

Strangers turned as Lileala passed, acknowledging her radiance. She waved at some, but ignored the ones who were impolite enough to point and whisper. She was, for all practical purposes, healed, and she refused to be a curiosity, the Rare Indigo with a rash. That was behind her now and, thank the galaxy, she could move on. She could forget it, as Otto had said. Let the pain become a remote apparition of her past.

Lileala looked around for Cherry. She searched the spot where Cherry usually peddled her fruit but couldn't see her. If she had to wait too much longer, she would have to deal with people poking around and asking questions she wasn't ready to answer. She saw a former classmate, huddling with a gang of Centerfree rowdies. They were communicating in the boisterous tone used by minor-schoolboys and loafing around near Cherry's spot.

"I've been appointed leader of WITH, which stands for 'We Invite Travelers Here'," she overheard someone saying. "We don't have many members so far but we're already petitioning The Nobility for our rights to expand Boundary Circle. We want tourists to be able to visit below The Outer Ring. They should be able to join us down here in any way they see fit."

Lileala hurried past the crowd and pretended she couldn't hear the discussion. *Where was Cherry?* she wondered. Instead of interrupting her visit to the Surface, Cherry had left a surprising voice message on her dial:

"My dearest, dearest Indigo, there comes a time when one must do what challenges the heart. Cherry feels unwillingness in you, ye, to come out of the comfort. Break through it. Go see Ahonotay. Now. Contact Fodjour and he will assist."

The message left Lileala conflicted at first. If Ahonotay was mute, how would they communicate? And what if the former Rare Indigo was responsible for that awful note Lileala had discovered among the dried-up music chips? But Lileala trusted

Cherry's instincts even if she didn't always understand them and she wanted to talk to her before going, and find out what to say. Should she tell Ahonotay about the distant murmurings? Were the voices too muddled for anyone to figure out?

Lileala checked her dial, hoping she could summon Fodjour. If she was going to visit Ahonotay in Mbaria, she needed a ride across the lower pastures of Gwembia.

"Here I am," someone said.

Lileala looked down at her wrist with a start. Fodjour's face had flickered onto the dial. How could he feel her with such immediacy when they hadn't talked in years?

"Mr Crop, hello," she said.

"Why so surprised?" he asked. "Didn't you beckon?"

"I did, but sir, we haven't connected in so long, I rather doubted you would feel my impulses."

Fodjour faded in and out, a side effect of communication from a rural area. "I've been worried about you like a forebear brooding about his daughter," he said, once the connection resumed. "Cherry and I don't have offspring, you know. I suppose I adopted my students, even those from years ago."

"Waves of joy," Lileala said. "Thank you."

"It's true," said Fodjour. "Anyhow, I think I know what you want. You need to get to Mbaria."

"Cherry told you?" said Lileala, a little taken aback. "I would have hoped she would keep my private matters much closer to her bosom. That was just between me and her."

"My dear, Cherry and I are like trees intertwined in a forest. Our roots grew together long ago."

While Lileala considered his comment, she lifted her satchel off her shoulder and let it dangle from one hand. She used the other hand to play with an errant twist of hair.

"Now, I will take you to Mbaria," Fodjour continued. "Take a wall shuttle to the transit network. When you arrive at the Gwembia exit, board a lift down to the western Togu Ta region. I will be there with a land vehicle. I know you want to hold this as a precious secret but it's critical that I do this for you, and for Cherry. That's more important than a confidence. I'm just a man helping his devoted and his former student do what needs to be done."

The Otuzuweland province was a long drop below the northern border, at least a kilometer lower than Sangha's Surface and a half a kilometer lower than The Outer Rings above Boundary Circle. To get to there, Lileala had to ride a tram to Togu Ta City West.

There were very few travelers on the tram. Most were fruit sellers returning to their farms in Otuzuweland. Lileala caught one of the passengers eyeing her and she wondered if he was from Gwembia or Togu Ta. Residents of the port city used wrist dials and other gadgets, but in Gwembia, she'd been told that most lived simpler lives – in oval compounds and houses of old-fashioned brick. In the villages of Vandiagara and Mbaria, they preferred thatched-roof huts.

The young man staring at her was too modern to be from a village. He wore a crisp tunic over creased trousers, and from the question in his eyes, she figured he wanted to ask if she was the Rare Indigo. To avoid a conversation, she averted his gaze. She was so nervous; she couldn't stop tapping the rail beside her seat. What if Ahonotay wouldn't receive her? What if she refused to open her door or sent a message for her to leave?

Lileala wished she could sleep, but the tram's seats were made of a foamy, gelatinous substance – a new import from Toth – that molded itself around the contours of the body. It was intended to increase comfort and hold the passenger in place. Lileala thought it was a bad idea. It was clingy and hugged her bottom, an added nuisance on a ride that moved slower than she was accustomed.

An hour later, when she arrived in the Gwembia province, she was so anxious to get off the tram she almost tripped as she bolted out of her seat and rushed onto another lift and down a set of stairs in to... darkness?

Alone in the dark, she noticed a familiar sight – a cue of light pods drifting past the transit station and maneuvering through a plot of Cypress trees. Lileala relaxed. Pods were common in the Circle, but they were so different here, outdoors in such a black sky. They gave her the feeling of standing beneath a dozen moons. She inhaled. To her surprise, she liked the smell of grass and the minty fragrance of leaves. But where was her host?

"Lileala! Lileala!" Fodjour yelled. "Here I am!" Two hands waved beneath the brightness. She hurried to Fodjour and gave him a hug. "My, but you're beautiful," he said. "You were beautiful before, but –" he backed up and looked her over, "– but, yes, you're even more beautiful."

"Thank you!"

"And you're well?"

"Yes! I'm so glad to be well."

Fodjour led Lileala to his land vehicle. They seated themselves inside and quickly started their journey out of the Togu Ta city limits and along the labyrinth of its air base.

Otto had described it to her many times, but she hadn't imagined that it stretched for so many kilometers. Fodjour veered left, away from the port and toward a muddy terrain that lined the shores of the Bagoe River. The river was known for depths that no one had fathomed and a heavy undertow that, during a rainy season, would sometimes flood the coastal grasslands. It was tranquil now, tamed by the moist heat, but still Lileala was awed. She'd never seen flowing water that stayed the same color before, and she hadn't realized she would care about it.

Just as she was about to ask Fodjour the length of the river, she heard a bellowing, trailed by a low, somber whistle.

"What's that sound?" Lileala asked.

"You'll see soon enough," Fodjour said.

They rode another half of a kilometer and Lileala knew

without inquiring further that she had heard the ite irhe – the magical clams. She could see them not far from the riverbank, light wisps streaming from the mouths of their shells.

"How pretty!" she said. "I remember Cherry telling us about these beings."

"But you've never seen them because you've never visited us down here in the north," Fodjour said. "My dear, tell me something. What was the delay? I had hoped you would seek us long before now."

Lileala swallowed and fumbled through her mind for a good excuse, but there were none. "I don't know," she said. "I have my chamber studies and all the preparation for the ceremonies. And Mama Xhosi never suggested that I come here. Cherry never did either. Not until recently."

"That's just it. Why hadn't you taken it upon yourself?"

Selves, not self.

A voice flit through Lileala's ears and she couldn't tell where it came from. It didn't sound like Fodjour.

"Did you hear me? Why have you not taken it upon yourself?" Fodjour repeated.

You are many selves, many, many feet.

Lileala concentrated, but she couldn't tell who was talking or what was being said.

"What? Mr Crop, I mean Dr Fodjour, what did you say?"

He looked at her sadly. A spray of clam sparks sprinkled the glass windshield and he blinked. "I said you must learn to be an explorer, like the people here, the Otuzuwe. They're nomads who migrate from their villages in Mbaria and Vandiagara all the way here, and sometimes to the semirural settlements of Togu Ta City East. Then they go back to their villages, you see, with more information, more knowledge."

"I guess I didn't think there was much to see, just –"

"There's always much to see and so much to learn," Fodjour interrupted, "even in your own mind. Like Cherry. In one trance, she traveled to some high cliffs. She didn't know where she was, but she remembered melanin bearers being there and they were chanting and making objects rise from the ground. She was shaken and wouldn't say much more, but I believe it was the forbidden juju. That's not allowed here so you mustn't tell anyone, but Cherry and I tried it once. It helped us to create spontaneous seeds."

Seeds again? The ones Zizi talked about? Lileala said nothing. She glanced to her right and marveled at the ite irhe. There were more clams, dozens of white shells, the approximate width and height of a Surface dome, languishing on the sand. Undulating like gentle waves, the tender shells opened then closed, spurting a brook of whistling light that rose as high as thirty meters.

"When I was younger, I fought hard to prove the worth of these clams," Fodjour said. "They used to nest in the deepest part of the river, and they would awaken us with their awful hymns."

"You mean these are melodies?"

"Not quite, but they are part of a language. These clams are trying to tell us something. They're from Earth, you know."

Lileala's lips pursed as she tried to refrain from mocking Fodjour. He was foolish when he was a young teacher, and he was even more foolish now.

"I know what you're thinking," he went on. "I've been called a fool for my ideas. When I used to tell the folk here in Otuzuweland that the clams were our friends and that they'd be an asset to the community, they laughed and told me not to bother them with all my big city ideas. And now look, just look." Fodjour pulled the land vehicle over to the side of the road. "The ite irhe don't remain in their shells," he said. "They can leave them behind and go back into the river, and sometimes when they do that, they don't return. No one knows where they go, but the abandoned shells harden, and farmers use them as bartering posts and occasional overnight shelters."

Lileala's eyes nearly closed but she caught herself and forced them to stay open while she and Fodjour continued observing from the vehicle. One of the night vendors, a bushy-haired man in overalls, had just finished trading crops from inside of a vacant clam shell that was as large as one of The Outer Ring's outdoor pavilions. As he packed up to leave, the man tossed his leftover products into a long wagon.

With the foggy light surrounding his stooped form, the vendor approached one of the living ite irhe and thrust about four bundles of fruit into its wide-open shell. Then, still pulling the wagon stuffed with leafy greens and what looked like apples, he moved on to another.

Once they returned to the road, the distant music of the ite irhe began lulling Lileala to sleep, but Fodjour's brash lecture woke her.

"You must be assertive and take a stand in support of the old ways," he advised her. "As Rare Indigo, you can convince youth to remain in Swazembi. You can tell them more about the beauty of Otuzuweland and the ite irhe." He stared at Lileala's face and hands, now clear of any blemish. "It was the intruders," he said, "who visited such horrors upon you."

She yawned, hoping he didn't notice. She wished he would stop talking so she could nap. "Dr Fodjour," she said after a long pause. "I respect you so much but I'm not sure The Nobility would be pleased with a Rare Indigo who brazenly offered so many opinions."

"My young Indigo, you will be dining with guests from far away worlds, answering questions about what we stand for and explaining the mysteries of the pigment. You will be expected to be quick on your feet."

You have the feet of many.

"What do you mean, Dr Fodjour? How many feet could I possibly have?"

Fodjour scratched his chin. "Go to sleep, Lileala. You're obviously tired. I can drive while you rest."

And so Lileala slept as they rode across the pastures

and began a bumpy descent into the northern valleys of
Otuzuweland. For hours, they rumbled past corn fields and
potato patches, outstretched on wide open terrain. When the
farms were behind them, the road dipped over a narrow creek
and meandered through a forest of Cypress trees for nearly
one hundred and seventy kilometers. They arrived in Mbaria
just as the sun began peering over the escarpment.

"Wake up now. We're here."

Lileala squinted. "Where are we? All I see is dirt."

"They don't have twirling bars and wall shuttles here."
Fodjour smiled. "It's not going to remind you of anything
you've ever seen in Boundary Circle or The Outer Ring." The
vehicle rumbled onto another dirt road and whirred to a halt.
"Motorized wheels aren't allowed beyond this point. We have
to walk the rest of the way. Come, we're close."

The path ahead twisted, and Lileala trailed Fodjour along
it. They padded up a hill and onto another path paved with
amber pebbles. It swerved briefly then emptied into a village
that spread out into an orbit of painted stone huts. Some of the
huts were eighteen meters high. They reminded Lileala of her
octagon dome, but larger and without the metallic exterior.
Instead of gold or brass, each stone dwelling was brushed with
colorful dots, streaks and zigzag trimming. On one, there was a
silhouette of a couple laughing and dancing beneath a cluster
of Jacaranda trees.

"Amazing," Lileala said. "I didn't know they lived like this
here."

"Mbaria is simple, but it's a happy place," Fodjour said. "And
it's as close to the ancestors as you can get."

Lileala was so mesmerized she didn't know where to look
first. Men were pedaling by on shiny bicycles and barefoot
children were running in dizzying circles. Women, the color
of roasted coffee beans, wandered past, cloaked in material so
bright it appeared to be laced with pieces of the sun. Some
of them carried babies on their backs, swaddled in the sunny

fabric. A woman sat on the ground sorting spindly loops of straw and threading them into a mathematical maze of a basket. Beside her were two silver-haired women, elders who stood arm in arm. While Lileala passed, they began making noises that sounded like shrill hollers and howls.

"They're ululating," Fodjour whispered. "It's a celebration cry that's only done by women and children."

"But what are they celebrating?" Lileala asked.

Fodjour chuckled. "You, of course. They have seen me before, me and Cherry. But they can tell by your attire and by the way you're looking around that you're a first timer who only knows the Circle."

"That's... nice," Lileala said, not knowing how else to respond.

Another woman strut in their direction, seemingly oblivious to the massive bowl of oranges balanced atop her head. "Nam angaa def?" she said. "Xoibisimilaa neniha."

"She's asking how you're doing and welcoming you to Mbaria," Fodjour explained. "Most villagers speak an ancient dialect. I can understand some of it, but I'm not fluent."

Fodjour leaned toward the woman and took his time speaking, elongating his words. "Weee are look-ing for Ahonotay. Can you tell us where to find her?"

"Finder?" The woman looked puzzled.

Fodjour placed a hand on Lilieala's face. "Een dee go... Indigo," he said. He lifted the hand higher to indicate tall.

The woman's face lit up. She pointed to the far edge of the village and used her hands to indicate that they must go left and walk all the way to the end.

Lileala and Fodjour walked through the heat for close to twenty minutes. They stopped when they reached a white and gold dwelling that was wider than the others and higher than the Grace Chapel in the Circle. A bare-chested man stood out front with a sharpened pole in his strong grip and a white cloth tied around his waist and hips.

"Welcome," he said. "Go in. Go." Then he faced Fodjour. "You must remain here."

The interior of the hut shone with a harsh red light that bounced off its stone walls and ricocheted in all directions. Lileala walked through into a vacant, circular space. She waited.

"Hello?" she said, stepping under an archway drenched in pebbles and beads. It led to a pyramid where the red light penetrated every nook and cranny, flowing through like a bloody river. The area was empty except for beads made of amber. Clumped in a series of loops, the beads formed funnels, cone-shapes and concentric circles on the mud floor and the stone walls. Clusters of them were strung together on cords that hung from the ceiling like leaves.

"Hello?" she said again.

"Over here. Look. Look this way."

Lileala noticed someone then, but she had to focus. Through the red glare, she began to detect the subtle silhouette of a woman sitting in the center of the room, as if anticipating a gathering. There was a thin mist shielding the woman's eyes, and the red glow was coming from the pores of her skin. Lileala strained to see, but the light was too distracting. She squinted harder, trying to get a good look at the woman in the haze. This, she thought, is a former Rare Indigo? Ahonotay appeared to be much rounder than she had expected. It was hard to tell through the red fog, but her arms and bodice appeared pudgier than the holograms she had been shown.

"I can read your thoughts you know."

"What?" Lileala asked, panicked and guilty.

"You're thinking I'm fat and you're bothered by the lights. Come closer. I'm harmless."

She walked closer to the woman and spoke. "Are you Ahonotay?"

"Ahonotay Niani Gao. And you're Lileala Walata Sundiata."

"You know who I am?" Lileala asked. "How?"

"I saw you many years ago, you and a friend wandering the

Surface. I was innocent then too, like you, before the voices."

"You hear the voices too?"

"I do."

"But that doesn't explain how you know who I am."

"I know through your mind."

The shock of Ahonotay's statement left Lileala without a comeback.

"Don't be so surprised." Ahonotay flashed to her mind. *The ancestors often move through Rare Ones. They chose me, and they told me they would choose you. They may not do so again for another thousand suns, but for now, it is me and it is you.*

"Ahonotay, I don't know what's happening."

"Don't speak. Think hard. Think."

Lileala concentrated.

I don't like this, she thought. *Can you hear me?*

I can, came the reply.

I don't like these voices, Lileala thought. *Please tell me what this is? What happened to you. Is the same happening to me? Will I lose the ability to speak?*

You will not only speak, Ahonotay replied, *you will fly. Inside, you will fly like a winged creature. Did you see it yet?*

Lileala frowned. *Winged creature? Are you talking about the scuff, I mean twilight?*

Ancestral spirits take on wings when they want to warn us of something. Ahonotay paused. *Or tell us we're on the right path. On your journey, you're going to receive many warnings and signs. Let me show you something.*

The light from her pores dimmed, and without straining, Lileala could see Ahonotay seated upright in a chair woven from dried reeds and straw. Her generous curls were brushed out into a bush that sprouted upward and formed a halo of hair above her forehead and around her ears. She had a full face and her penetrating eyes, still veiled by mist, were like dark puddles. She was as striking as the image Lileala had found in her dome. She handed Lileala a tattered shard of bark paper from her right hand.

As soon as I felt you coming, I looked for this. In my mind you were clear, accompanied by the Cherry Willems' devoted one. Here, read it.

Lileala held it between her fingers. It was aged and crumpled, and the words so faded she could barely read them. The tip, on the upper left edge, was missing. When she noticed the torn corner, she felt a sudden prick. It reminded her of something. She couldn't remember what, only that it had bothered her terribly. She gritted her teeth and read.

Kclabs were visitors on your pompous Y. E. and now your kind dares force us out. I sting inside, and this burning, this boiling, this will come to you too.

Still trembling, Lileala nearly dropped the note, reminded suddenly of the rumpled message she'd found wrapped up in Ahonotay's crushed music chips. She only had an upper corner. Were these horrid words the part that had been ripped away? So Ahonotay *did* write this? Why?

No, Ahonotay answered sharply. *These are not my words. These are the words I found just as you did.*

Found? Lileala questioned.

Yes... Read more.

No, Lileala thought. Maybe this was a bad idea. Maybe she should go find Fodjour.

But Ahonotay's eyes wouldn't release her. *Read more.*

May it be merciless, raging like the wars that annihilated the Earth's inhabitants. Lileala looked up and stalled.

Ahonotay nodded. *Go on, please.*

The itch that crawls within me, it now crawls within you. This is my vow to the daughters of the future daughters I will forebear; for they are the ones who will rule the daughters of your daughters.

She stopped. *Why are you making me do this?*

I beg you, Ahonotay urged. *Please read.*

I can't. I just can't!

Ahonotay paused, eyes looking her up and down. *You are weak. Young Indigo, how long do you think you can remain this weak?*

Lileala gritted her teeth, hands trembling. *Okay, breathe,*

breathe, Lileala told herself. She dug her nails into the shard. She forced herself to read further out loud, her mind too preoccupied with her breath.

Who will rule the daughters of your daughters. Through them, I grow wings. Through them I will repay all of Swazembi for tormenting us. When I do, your access will be denied.

A tear inched down Lileala's cheek and Ahonotay joined her in her troubled breathing, pushing air in and out in the same rat-a-tat rhythm, as if borrowing some of Lileala's pain. There was quiet for a while. When Ahonotay turned her head toward her, Lileala thought she could see sadness behind the mist over her eyes. The red light around her had dissipated, revealing her fullness, the heavy thighs and round hips hidden beneath the folds and patterns of her garment. Lileala watched her take another full breath.

You're wondering about this light, Ahonotay said. *It comes from the eyes during the most prolonged state of the Inekoteth trance. I surround myself with amber to help me go deeper. I'm in perpetual dialogue with the ancestors.*

She readjusted her posture, making sure her spine was pressed against the back of her chair. *I maintain weight to keep me grounded in the body. Without it, sometimes I feel I'd simply fly away.* She laughed gently. *I wish I was like a winged being, like the twilights that sometimes visit me before they die.*

"But this? You didn't explain this." Lileala tried to give her back the paper note.

Ahonotay grimaced. *The author of that is from Kclaben. When they were banned from the Coalition, all they had left was that orphaned planet of theirs. Some claim it's a remnant of the dead Earth.*

"But that's where the Pineal Crew leads excavations."

No, no. Those excavations are on the charred Earth remains, the Americas mostly. The Kclabs are descendants of the ones who survived the planet's bloody terror. They live on a chunk of Earth that broke away, blasted off in the middle of the war, Ahonotay explained.

"So you actually met them, these Kclabs?"

Ahonotay pointed to the shard in Lileala's hand. *Only in*

the way that you are meeting them now, through this note. When I learned that I'd been named Rare Indigo, I fled to the Surface. While I was hiding, a voice entered my head and directed me to this scrap. That morbid message was on it. I stuck it in the vanity in my dome, but I accidentally ripped it. Ahonotay shuddered. *I'll never forget the first words I read: 'I loathe you.'*

Another wave of fear came over Lileala. She held in a gasp, concentrated on her breathing and continued listening.

After that, voices began haunting me. I stopped talking in hopes of hearing with more clarity. When I realized I was hearing ancestral spirits, they became more verbal each day. After a while, they were all I wanted. All my time was occupied with their directives. They need more of us on Swazembi to hear the tales of how they fled.

"Why did they leave and where did they flee? And how could they leave anyone behind?"

My, you have learned so little in that knowledge chamber. Our ancestors were among the many tribes to live there in the land of Africa. Some of them fled. Those who didn't flee were corralled onto vessels that sailed across great bodies of water.

Lileala felt a surge of confidence. "I think I know this. In the knowledge chamber, I learned about something called boats."

Ye, on sturdy boats. Big ones. Many of the ancestors were taken away on these. But in the cliffs of Mali, there was a group, the Dogon people, who had already been given a warning to leave. They learned this from visitors of a world near the Sirius star, known in their tongue as Po Tolo. Messengers from Po Tolo came to them. They were water beings that birthed light and nested in shells in the sea.

The clams that brightened the roads in Gwembia flitted through Lileala's mind and she was about to ask about them, but Ahonotay answered before she could begin.

Yes, the ite irhe descended from the Po Tolo messengers. They were guides who came to Earth to teach the Dogon tribe, who then passed the lessons onto other tribes. Even the nomadic ones.

Lileala could feel her pulse speed up. These were the people Cherry was afraid to talk about.

The illumination around Ahonotay faded. *Think, young Indigo. Think of when Fodjour tried to share.*

Embarrassed, Lileala recalled the day Fodjour was teaching and told the class he collected Earth fossils and planned to bring in an exhibit – a real animal tooth. A lot of her classmates were eager, simply because it was taboo. But Lileala and Zizi faked an illness, and the two sneaked out to buy music chips and flirt with tourist boys on The Outer Ring.

Ahonotay laughed until she shook. *You are a sneaky one, aren't you? Fodjour is learned and he has been sorting through discarded Earth lore longer than either of us has been alive. And yet, you hid from his teachings.* She tossed her head and continued laughing, making Lileala uneasy. She didn't like Ahonotay's laugh at all. It was too coarse, too accusatory.

No need for guilt, young one, leave it be. You must learn soon how to properly use the walk of the trinity breath.

"I know that, Ahonotay. I Shimmer all the time."

My Grace! Young one, do you really think that is the full reach of this power?

Lileala fidgeted. "I never looked at it that way."

Because you have used it foolishly. Vanity is not its true purpose.

Lileala wanted to ask what she meant, but Ahonotay had shut her eyes and begun another series of slow, choppy breaths.

Nine seconds later she opened them. *Here, I have taught others to rely on ancestral strength and use it wisely. I keep the entrance to my hut lit with the amber pearls to help me communicate in the Inekoteth.*

"Like the Mhondora?"

Ahonotay shook her head. *The Mhondora is weak.*

"But… he knows the Inekoteth."

True Inekoteth happens only when your inner travels fulfill the precepts that were lost. When the great ships came, some of the Po Tolo beings left their world and came back to Earth to try to save the villages. The ones who returned were lost, as were their precepts. But when you travel deep enough to meet the original melanin bearers you

*have found the first of six precepts: 'Give Balm to Burdened Spirits.
Comfort Their Minds and Souls.'*

A female elder-child walked in without introduction. Her
tightly braided hair was coiled into a half moon that was about
one-half inch in height. She carted a boiling pot of fig tea on
her head, and genuflected to pick up a cup, keeping the teapot
in place until she was ready to pour.

A long, still breath lodged in Lileala's throat. She was
stunned. When she saw Ahonotay observing her, she braced
herself for another round of subtle teasing. But she only smiled.

*She's in tune with the rhythms of life. That's a tradition here in
Mbari, but it's one that's been lost in the Sangha province.*

"They think of all Earth inhabitants as primitive." Lileala
edited her words carefully as she spoke. She was glad to
contribute something to the conversation but didn't want to
offend.

They have false pride, Ahonotay continued. *Since they don't
know the ways of the Dogon, they don't know their rhythms. The
second precept tells us: 'If we live and think in the spirit, we can control
any motion of the body.'*

Lileala tried handing her the note again. "You never told me
what this has to do with me?"

A stern look crossed Ahonotay's face.

"This cruel note, I don't want it." Lileala handed it over and
Ahonotay accepted without commenting. She turned to the
woman with the fig tea and the two shared a private mental
conversation. Then she looked at Lileala.

You will need to master all six of the lost precepts.

"But you've only told me two of them."

Later, young Indigo. They will come to you.

"When? I don't think I'm returning here."

*You'll learn. My personal hut is reserved for sacred communion.
This ancestral grace streams through you, and in scant moments,
through Fodjour Willems. But, his is sparse. He has tried, but he is not
a true seer. I'll have someone give him a nourishing meal of sorghum*

and millet before riding back with him to the province border to ensure his travels are safe. You will be with me for two days before returning to your studies.

A chill trickled down Lileala's spine and she fought the urge to disagree with her.

Ahonotay held up the note again and gave Lileala another stern glance. *The Kclabs have altered their demeanor and their conversations no longer reek of hatred. They have gone to the Coalition in a show of friendship.*

It's okay, young one, Ahonotay went on. *There is reason to believe the Kclaben beings are now benign. You haven't told me about your keloids –*

"Keloids?" Lileala asked.

Your scars. Yes, I know about them. I also know that you and other melanin bearers are affected and that these Kclabs will come to you with a cure. It is up to you to determine whether it is safe to go with them and whether their intentions are pure. Your skills will grow, young one, and in the forty-eight hours that you are with me, I will show you how to see with your spirit.

12

"Think of misery as a tube clogged with rubbish. Train your focus to cleanse the tube with happy thoughts that burst through it like the light of a laser."
— Indigo Aspirant Code Q, Provision Xiia

An abandoned church flashed in Lileala's mind. It was still intact, but its bricks were charred, giving it the appearance of a place that had been torched and yet had refused to break down. It was gravestone gray and moldy, and all around it flowed darkness and smoke and the eerie feeling that someone, or something, had just died.

Horrid in some ways, beautiful in others, the peculiar edifice stood alone atop a hill of blackened debris. Lileala had a clear view of the structure, though she didn't know from where it came or why.

Ever since her two days alone with Ahonotay, she now saw images. Vivid. Fresh. Startling.

The first happened on the tram ride back to Boundary Circle, but this, her third vision, seemed the most significant. She supposed that was why she couldn't quite shake it. It hadn't come with a message, and she hadn't been able to decipher its meaning. But she could tell it held some relevance and had once been a wondrous place of worship.

She had a strong inkling that people, on whatever world she was being shown, probably traveled from afar just to pray within the church's hallowed walls and beneath a steeple so tall and sharp it appeared to punch holes in the sky.

Just as Ahonotay had taught her, Lileala held the vision firmly in her mind, and observed it as if she were watching the viewerstream. It flickered for a few more seconds then fizzled, and she puttered around her compartment wondering what to do and who to tell. Not Cherry again. Not her elder Ma or Zizi or even Otto.

She mulled it over and figured she'd tell her Baba. Someone besides Ahonotay needed to know about her gift.

Otto surfaced on her wrist, and for a few seconds, she considered telling him.

"Lileala, are you there?" He vanished then reappeared.

"Yes, yes, Otto, I love you. Hello."

"Hello, my devoted," Otto said, sounding strained. "Lileala are you okay? I couldn't get in touch with you at all yesterday or the day before."

"Um, about that," she slowed her voice, searching for what to say next. "Well," she went on, "do you remember when we talked a couple of days ago and I said I was riding to Otuzuweland with Fodjour?"

"Oh! Yes, of course. I was shocked, but pleased. How was it? Did you stay longer than one night?"

She nodded. "Two nights. And… I learned some things, Otto. I found out what you and my Baba have been hiding from me. I have to say I'm not happy you didn't tell me the truth."

There was a conversation lull.

"Truth?" Otto finally answered. "What truth?" His voice faded again then came right back.

"Listen, Lileala we have to talk about that later," he said. "I'm being summoned back into another session in the knowledge chamber, the one at The Grand Rising. So be patient, okay? The Pineal Crew is designing an even better oscillator healing system. I know the keloids are gone, but we're working on it as an extra support."

"Otto, please stop," Lileala cried.

"Why? What's wrong?"

"You're hiding something."

"Lileala, what in the galaxy are you talking about?"

"Kclabs! When were you going to tell me?"

"Um," Otto's voice dropped an octave. "I thought I had..."

"Come on, Otto. Seriously?"

"It might be a hoax. That's what your Baba says."

"And what do you say?"

Otto hesitated. "I don't know."

"It's true, according to Ahonotay. I saw her and even spent time with her."

"Ahonotay? Isn't she in hiding?" asked Otto.

"Not quite, I mean yes and no, but I don't want to talk about her. I need to hear it from you. I want you to tell me what's going on."

On Otto's end there was silence, and Lileala thought she could feel the quickness of his breath. "Some Kclabs showed up at our summit meeting," he said, flinching. "Ghastly creatures. But... uh, your Baba and me, we decided not to tell you. We wanted to protect you until we could figure out exactly how much we could trust them."

"So, this is what you didn't want me to know? This is why you've been avoiding me?"

"I was trying not to scare you."

"I found out anyway," Lileala said. "Those beings want me to go away with them."

"Who told you that?"

"I told you. Ahonotay."

"Lileala, listen to me carefully. Ahonotay did not tell you this. She can't even talk." Otto was insistent.

Lileala grew quiet. Was now the time to tell him? How could she accuse him of secrets and not reveal her own? She braced herself.

"She talks when she wants to," she lied. The guilt stung

slightly, like a pinprick. She continued, "Those Kclabs want me to go with them somewhere."

"Don't believe that. They have no power to take you anywhere."

"But Ahonotay said..."

Otto resisted. "Forget about her. If she was so smart, why did she run away? She's a coward who's trying to cover up her own failure. She didn't even finish her reign. Has it ever occurred to you that maybe she's trying to ruin things for you?"

"Oh, but she wouldn't," Lileala said.

"But she would."

She thought about Ahonotay's wisdom and how much she'd just learned from her. It didn't seem possible that such a profound woman could be bitter. "Maybe, but I don't think so," she told Otto. "You're confusing me."

"Don't worry, I'm here to help. I love you and if I could, I'd take your place. We're still doing all we can." Otto gave Lileala a reassuring smile.

She did her best to return it. "At the Indigo rites tonight, I promise to give it my all. I'll be the best Rare Indigo they've ever seen."

"That's the spirit, my love. Of one accord, one beat, one protection." Otto blew her a kiss and faded out, leaving Lileala wondering why he was still in such a hurry. She'd wanted to mention the itch on her stomach, but it was just as well; she figured it was probably from one of those mosquitos in the village. She started to examine it, but the wall clicked aggressively and Kwesi's face appeared. He entered and pecked her on the cheek.

"You've come along so well," he said, smiling. "Look at you, splendid as ever."

"Hello, Baba," she said.

"'Hello, Baba'? That's all I get after weeks of being away?"

"Sorry. I'm confused, that's all." She leaned forward and hugged him.

"Sounds like things were pretty bad."

"Not really, Baba. The ancestors had it a lot worse."

Kwesi was silent a moment. "Waves of joy," he said. "But where did that come from? You don't even sound like yourself."

Lileala changed the subject. "I guess I'm feeling sort of patronized. Baba, why were you hiding things from me?"

"What? Who told you? Otto?"

"No, he didn't, but –"

"It's nonsense," Kwesi piped up. "I don't care who's saying it. Get that out of your head."

"But –"

"It's fine. Don't worry."

"That's not what I want to say. It's something else, something I haven't told anyone."

"I'm listening," Kwesi said.

"I can hear ancestral messages." Lileala tugged on a coil of hair and continued. "I know I should have told you sooner, but I couldn't believe it myself." She glanced at the floor and held on to the side of her seat cushion, clutching it as if it was about to blow away. "It only started recently, as a sort of... peculiar babbling. I told myself it must have been a music chip that someone discarded somewhere and that the sounds were filtering into my room."

Kwesi sat down on the cushion beside her, let his head drop. "Earth music?"

"That's what it sounded like at first. That's what I kept telling myself over and over until recently."

Kwesi stood up and paced. Lileala's eyes followed him.

"They started increasing only recently. I used to hear them now and then. Now it's daily. And they're coming with visions. Peculiar sights, strange words and, sometimes, a sound of yearning as if someone is in need."

Kwesi's eyes swept over his daughter. "In all the power of the galaxy. Lileala. You," he said. He stroked his chin and sighed. "But if this is the will of the ancestors, then so be it.

hardened into protective shells, then slowly unfolded, and an Indigo twirled out on her disc. Lileala was last.

"And now, our Rare Indigo," Mama Xhosi called out. "The ultimate example of the trinity breath in its full, divine Shimmer. Lileala Walata Sundiata, please emerge."

The cocoon containing Lileala parted slower than the others, one sectioned layer at a time. As she entered full Shimmer, a light pod descended and enveloped her. She spun out in a glistening prism of colors, greeted by a burst of applause.

Cherry had a seat close to the stage, but she stood up and planted her feet in a space that provided a full view of Lileala's open cocoon. The ceremony ended with a blast of colors that scattered everywhere, and it made Lileala smile to see the soft sticky powders landing on Cherry. Her eyelashes turned pink and her lips various shades of green. Lileala waved at her. She hadn't seen Cherry since returning from Mbaria, but she could detect an unusual yearning in her spirit. There was an intensity, as if the clairvoyant was preoccupied with some ancient tale and had a desperate desire to share it. Now. At a time when Lileala needed to greet people and thank them for their support.

Lileala wondered what was provoking Cherry's sudden clamor for attention, so she headed down the stairs. Cherry weaved her way to the end of the stage and Lileala was overcome by the terror she saw crouching in her eyes. "My, Grace!" Lileala exclaimed. "What is it?"

A plea gushed from her mouth. "Cherry must speak with you alone, my dear one. Allow Cherry to speak."

But Zizi pushed her way through and butt into the conversation. "I'm so proud of you Lileala," she said. "Apologies you haven't heard from me, but that was because of my Sonaguard preliminaries, not you."

"You had preliminaries?" Lileala stood beside the stage, and a crowd swarmed around her. She had to sort through a flurry of congratulations, just to hear her friend.

"Yes, I'm doing them already, right here in the Circle," Zizi said. "It happened all of a sudden, my approval I mean. Before I leave for Toth, I want you to know that you're still my friend. And I'm so proud."

Cherry tried to speak even louder and force her words in between Zizi's, but the commotion all around them was overwhelming, even for a gusty voice like Cherry's. Vendors were touting the fig tea that twirled atop their automated push carts and a couple of small boys were tussling and arm wrestling in their seats. A trio of farm women in patterned cloth dresses stood on the sidelines ululating and singing Otuzuwe folk anthems.

"Cherry must share the warning!" Cherry's voice boomed. "You must take heed of now, before your Eclipse." There was a cold silence in the surrounding crowd. Zizi seemed startled and the men and women mingling with the Aspirants paused mid conversation, their ears perked to listen, no one finishing what they were saying or doing. Lileala swallowed, but couldn't hide her embarrassment. This kind of an intrusion was so unlike Cherry. Lileala couldn't fathom why she would blurt out such a loud and stark demand.

She rushed toward her, assuming she'd figure out a way to follow Cherry to a more convenient spot. But Zizi spoke up again before she made it to Cherry's side. "Can you meet me in the chamber tomorrow morning?" she asked. Lileala agreed. They talked for fifteen minutes, and Cherry became distracted by a presence no one else could hear or see. Her mouth was sluggish and her eyes distant and the conversation she was having seemed directed at the invisible. The trance took her in deeper and she spoke out loud as she shuddered and sauntered along the figure eight of markets.

By the time Lileala went to search for her, Cherry wasn't easy to find. Lileala checked with a tea vendor and peeked twice into the corner where she peddled fruit. Her cart was in place and held one bag of purple grapes, but no signs of Cherry. Assuming she had left, Lileala went home.

Unbeknownst to her, the clairvoyant had strayed to an empty booth and sat behind a counter stacked with bundles of fabric, not sleeping and not awake. If Lileala had known that she was still there in the darkness, she would have seen the tears that Cherry had fought so hard to control. She would have seen her lips moving like ripples of water, up again, then down. Hopeful, quivering, praying lips. She would have seen Cherry weaken, nearly limping as she struggled to get back to her fruit stand. She would have known that Cherry, still in a daze, kneeled there in that empty corner, lips still throbbing, speaking in anxious repetition.

"For Lileala Walata Sundiata," she prayed. "Spare her, spare her, spare her, Cherry begs of you. Cherry comes to you with desperate heart, pleading in the Inekoteth tongue of the father. Cherry bleeds within for this one. She is the only one, ye, the only Swazembian to drink of such a cup. Let her stay in bliss, here, ye. Of one beat, one accord, one devotion. Spare her. Spare her. Oh, Grace, please spare her. She has no idea, you see. No idea of what is to be."

13

"Judge not another's vice for you may fall into an equal trap and when that happens who will you tell? The disgrace is..."
– Trieca's unfinished scroll message from Toth

The room seemed to be spinning. Fast. So fast Trieca couldn't remember where she was. It was the first time she'd ever consumed a wedge of black ore and she had no idea it would be so potent. It overpowered her. Far more than she expected.

Again, she looked around the room. Where was she and how did she get here? She rubbed her eyes and looked at her yellow robe. It was soggy in spots, from sweat, she supposed. And it was torn around the collar right behind her neck. She didn't care.

If only the room would stop spinning, if only she knew how she ended up there. She tried struggling to her feet and keeled over, hands outstretched in front of her in a failed attempt to break the fall. She whimpered and felt around the floor with her palms. It was cool, hard, but comfortable. Some sort of smooth surface, so different from the concrete she walked on in her room on Kclaben.

It was too much to absorb at one time. Trieca gasped and pulled herself back up onto a plush armchair. It was all coming back to her. This place, this room. She had passed out in the hall, that long hall above the assembly area on Toth. She remembered being trapped in an air that was boiling, an air without oxygen. She remembered being hot, struggling to control the blood poisons that were stampeding her heart. But it was no use. The anger surge had overtaken her, and the more she tried to hold it back, the weaker she had become.

Somehow, with her hands unsteady, she'd managed to drag the black ore out of her pockets, fat chunks that she had with her to give to Dlareg and Haliton. In her desperation, she'd taken one herself. She wasn't too sure what happened after that. Vaguely, she remembered someone carrying her, someone making awful comments about her face. But she'd blacked out and hadn't heard much else.

The room she was in contained an ample-sized bed, but she was not lying on it. She was propped in a sturdy chair that tilted backwards and her body was facing up toward the ceiling that, for some reason, had a brass object stuck in the center. She stared at it, curious about the glass pendants and baubles that streamed from its nucleus, projecting a dim light. Her spy friend used to try to describe Toth to her, and she wondered if this was what he had called a chandelier. He designed chandeliers, that lousy oaf. The pretend friend. The bastard. The dirty, lowdown bastard.

She rubbed her eyes again and continued looking around. The dizziness was subsiding some, and she could see that the walls were the color of a pale apple, and the room was filled with such opulent furnishings it could have been the home of one of those kings that had ruled ancient empires of the Earth. But he was no king, that rat who betrayed her. Was this his shelter? Was he the one whose arms she felt scooping her up as she surrendered to blackness? She stroked the cushions beneath her body and tried again to stand.

Steady. Steady. Slowly, she moved one leg off the chair and onto the floor. Another leg followed, and she stood. But she was still woozy. She took her time and edged toward the brown wooden surface ahead of her. The door. If only she could make it to the door. Trieca straightened up and tried to walk without wobbling. She was overseer of Security, she told herself, the first woman ever allowed into the Sector. She was better, had always been better than others. She reached for the shiny brass ball on the side of the door and turned it.

Yes, that's it, she said to herself. She was better, better, better. But the word didn't feel so good anymore. It had a bitter tinge and it taunted her so much that she stopped saying it, stopped thinking it. She wasn't better, she was...

Her body quivered, and she tried hard not to remember. But the blow of her spy friend's words had created a vacant space deep within the cavity of her body. And the words just sat there, stuck, so shocking they just wouldn't go away.

The ore crystal was wearing off, and her memory was returning. It was a miserable memory and she thought, for a strange second, that she needed another piece of ore to deal with the shame.

Trieca pushed herself through the desire and kept walking. Another hall, another row of doors, another lift. She pushed a button and got on. This was a curved platform that spiraled through a sea of lights as it dropped to the bottom floor. For a moment, Trieca was terror stricken. But as soon as she reached the first level, she forgot about the confusion, stepped off the platform and out into a wide lobby. The next door she approached was programmed to open without assistance. A robot that she didn't need to push.

She stumbled through it and sunshine enveloped her, stinging as it warmed the thin membrane covering her bones.

"Ah," she breathed in, and a second later said, "ouch!" She wondered if her skin had become too fragile to handle the sun. But it refreshed her for now, helped stabilize her body so that she could walk with a steady gait.

Now, the space rocket. Where was it? Time to return home. Alone.

"I don't know. All she does is stare," Mernestyle complained to Chief Hardy. "Ever since she returned, she's been in her room just sitting there. I think she went to the lab once, real late at night, but I don't know what she was doing. I can't explain it. She just... stares."

Hardy held up a petri dish and tried to force himself to listen. He no longer cared about Trieca. She was a screw-up now, just like Dlareg, just like Bertram and the others. She'd gone to Toth, and she had failed. "I'm going to have to trust you with this mission," he said to Mernestyle. "You know the chemical makeup of Mecca and you have the plans."

Mernestyle cleared her throat. "I don't know. You really think I should? I don't want to leave her out."

"She's leaving herself out," Hardy snapped. "Look around. Do you see her? Where is she?"

"I don't know, sir."

"She's where you said she was, in her damn room, sulking. And from what I understand, she's been taking black ore. Trieca, of all people. Whoever thought she would become an addict?"

"Sir, I don't think she's –"

"I'm sure she is," the chief snapped. "One of the Sector youngers told me he saw her in the hallway yesterday. Said she could barely walk."

"She'll be better, sir," Mernestyle dropped her head. "Give her time."

"She's taking too long," the chief sneered. "I don't know what happened to her on Toth and, between you and me, I don't care. I don't. I just know that someone has to make sure this new batch of Mecca gets to Swazembi by tonight."

"It's already there, sir. We left it. I mean, Haliton and Dlareg did when they were there. They increased its potency then took it with them to the meeting," Mernestyle said.

The chief kept studying the petri dish. "It looks dry to me. Are you sure there's enough?"

"Enough what, sir?"

"Damn it, Mernestyle. The Wilfin serum. Is there enough?"

"Trieca always said there was plenty," Mernestyle answered. Chief Hardy slammed the dish onto the lab table and turned to face her. "I don't give a damn what she said. She's incompetent."

"She knows what she's talking about."

He looked down at the cracked dish. "Go and get her. Get her and bring her in here now!"

Mernestyle headed toward the door then stopped suddenly. "I guess I should tell you something."

"Oh, really?" the chief said.

She stood still, waiting.

"Go on," he said.

But Mernestyle remained quiet, unsure if she should proceed. "Um, well, I said she was in her room because... she, well, that's where she's been for the last few days, ever since she returned from Toth and..."

"And?"

"And now she's not there. I saw her last night, but when I checked this afternoon, she was gone."

"Has she given you any direction?" the chief asked.

"Yesterday. She confirmed that the Toth man, that spy, already has the new batch and is awaiting further instructions."

Chief Hardy smiled. "That's good then. At least one thing went as planned."

"But..." continued Mernestyle.

"But what?"

"Trieca. She's missing."

The chief raised an eyebrow and gave Mernestyle a polite nod. "I must say, you're dedicated. Wouldn't you be honored to take over the whole mission?"

"She's my friend, sir."

He laughed. "I know, and like I say, I admire your dedication. But I need to remind you this project was never my idea. Trieca wanted it. You wanted it. Before I get stuck with it, I'll cancel it. We can always come up with another plan to get into the Coalition." The chief hesitated. "Once more, are you willing to take charge?"

Mernestyle was quiet a while, carefully mulling over her

response. She had worked hard and had been the one to dissect the Wilfin gland herself and discover this new way to use its secretion.

"Speak up," the chief said. "I'm waiting."

She stood very still. "Yes. I mean, no," she stammered.

He narrowed his eyes and gave her a nasty look. "I need an answer."

She sighed. "I, I... I'll tell you later. Right now, I'm just concerned about Trieca, wondering where she is."

"I can't say I'm surprised that she's missing. With those other buffoons locked up on Toth, I was short of security officers and had to let Bertram out of jail this morning. It was the fair thing to do anyway, especially since his partner, Haliton, was part of that damn failed trip to the Coalition meeting. They must have been quite the spectacle, why else would the Coalition guards jail them?"

"I wish Trieca would tell us what happened," Mernestyle said. "But she won't talk about that or what's troubling her."

"Maybe she's upset that I let Bertram out," the chief said. "She hated him, you know." He deliberately slowed his voice. "Or maybe, just maybe, Bertram found her and told her she'd been demoted and that he's the new overseer."

"What?" Mernestyle couldn't keep the shock from her voice.

"You heard me."

"But... you just asked me to take over the mission. You didn't tell me that you'd already stripped her rank. It's only been four days, sir. Can't you give her more time?"

Chief Hardy didn't hesitate. "Both you and Bertram will be in charge, and the answer is no, I couldn't give her time."

"How can you expect her to deal with losing her post, just like that! She was already depressed enough."

"That's not my concern."

"Chief, can you imagine how that made her feel?"

"I said it's not my concern. And it all depends on Bertram, on whatever he said. If he told her that she'd be reporting

directly to him, I guess maybe that might be cause for upset."

Mernestyle was quiet a moment. "What do you mean directly to him?"

"What does it sound like I mean? Besides..." He paused and chuckled. "It's better than forcing her to be his concubine. Don't you think? We discussed that too you know."

Mernestyle was too sad to answer right away.

"It's your serum anyway," the chief went on. "You discovered it and Trieca took over and began carrying it out with a vengeance."

"That doesn't excuse what we're doing." She stared at the chief. "What about her other project, not the colony, that thing she's doing with the unders? Who's going to run that?"

"You. And maybe Bertram."

"But... I don't know a damn thing about it. I need Trieca."

He stared back. "I don't know what it is either and I don't care. Whatever she was up to, I just let her get on with it. I figure she'd get it done."

After another long pause, Mernestyle bit her lip. "I understand but it's hard not to worry."

"Force yourself," he said. "She'll be alright, that one."

It took a full minute for Mernestyle to respond. She rubbed her forehead and did what she felt she had to do. She agreed with the chief. "Yeah, she's a real fireball, isn't she?" She glanced at the petri dish on the lab table and thought about how she'd repair it. "Wonder what they did to her? Maybe that Rare Indigo taunted her."

"Ridiculous," the chief said, then he paused and seemed to rethink his statement. "But something drove her to the ore crystals. Never thought I'd live to see that."

"Me neither. Chief, I'll take on the mission for a while, just until she gets better."

Chief Hardy laughed again. A long, irritating laugh.

"If you don't mind," Mernestyle said, "I'm going to find her and ask about that colony and, um, that program she had going with the unders. And I'm going to need Trieca to tell me the best method for handling Bertram."

The chief continued laughing. "Well, well," he said, "You do have a fire in your belly. And now that I'm thinking of it, did you see that one out behind the Mealing Center? There was smoke, lots of it. I thought we'd run out of charcoal and of wood."

Mernestyle remembered the wood Trieca's contact had given her. She snatched a lantern off the shelf for extra lighting and took a step toward the door. "Excuse me, chief, I need to leave."

"Don't forget to talk to her about Bertram," he called after her. "She's going to hate that, I tell you. The two of them working together and with Bertram as her superior and then you in charge. That's going to be something."

His laughter continued. Mernestyle walked on, ignoring it. She'd never liked the chief and had only tolerated him because she had to, and because Trieca did such a good job of keeping him in check. "Methodic Molding" is the term she'd used, and she'd done it so well. She stood up to the chief, told him what to do, controlled him, all while getting him to think it was his idea. But without her, the man was like a silly, fussy younger.

Mernestyle spent the rest of the evening hunting for Trieca. She went back to her empty room again and sorted through a scattered pile of black ore pieces and old bark paper curled up on a table next to the unmade bed. The room smelled of a floral perfume her Toth friend had given her, and the crushed ore crystals added an acrid odor. Mernestyle found the perfume bottle, tilted on its side, still open, the liquid dripping onto the floor. She stood it upright and picked up Trieca's perfume-stained scroll. She read a portion:

"One day soon, Kclabs will be able to stand before the waterless oceans on Swazembi's Surface and watch colors colliding in the sky..."

Finding no clues in Trieca's bedroom, Mernestyle went to the Mealing Center. There were only two people inside, an overseer and his concubine, feeding from a plate of slivered potato peels. Walking out of the center, she found the smoky

remains of a fire smoldering in the back. Clearly, someone had
been burning something, but she couldn't fathom why.

Mernestyle decided then to retrace her friend's usual habits.
There was the Old-World Earth Corner. It had an information
and reading area that Trieca liked to visit. She sometimes
lingered around that place for hours in the evenings. While
everyone else was preparing for bed, she'd sort through the
ragged halves of books or listen to audio ribbons that had
been salvaged from rummage piles on Earth. One night, she'd
pounded on Mernestyle's door, clutching a chunk of bound,
crumpled pages that were just clear enough to read.

"I just found this, a whole book, in one piece!" she'd
proclaimed. "It's some type of scout survival guide on how to
adapt to life in the outdoors, I think. It's going to come in good
use for that colony I'm creating."

It was a fond memory that made Mernestyle smile. She
figured Trieca had to be curled up somewhere in the Old-
World Corner researching her next move. But when she poked
her head through the door of the reading area, all she saw was
a spider crawling over a stack of dusty papers.

Next, she tried the Viewer Room, but the screen was blank,
and a couple of youngers were hiding behind a back row of
seats, coupling. From there, she tried the old barn, the former
shelter where Trieca was raised. She peeked inside but it was
empty space, then gazed up at the backdrop of Black Mountain
and shivered. What if Trieca, in her despondent state, had
ventured somewhere along the mountain?

Mernestyle recalled the smoke and tried not to worry. But it
haunted her. Trieca knew how to make charcoal out of synthetic
materials and had once built a fire so that she could scorch a
robe to stop the hem from fraying. She had used a piece of it
later to make a rope belt. Mernestyle held her breath a moment.
She was wearing an ankle-length cotton garment; surely it
would tear during such a journey? She proceeded anyway and
held the lantern in front of her as she struggled up the muddy

mountain. The ice was gone; that made it safer, but there wasn't much grass to walk on and not a single tree to grab for balance.

For more than forty minutes, Mernestyle moved along the mountain's periphery, looking for signs. At Point Five exactly, she saw a pair of Trieca's rubber boots trashed in a mound of dirt beneath a shelf of rock jutting from the side of the mountain. A rope made from charred nylon and swatches of burlap swung in the darkness, a noose at the end.

The beam of light from Mernestyle's lantern flickered past it and on to a set of evenly spaced eyes. Trieca's eyes. They stared helplessly as she lay on her back, her limp body slumped over a long, jagged ledge.

Mernestyle dropped the lantern and stumbled toward her, bawling.

"Trieca!" Mernestyle wailed. "Trieca, how could you do this?" Mernestyle moved her numb fingers with precision, slipping them beneath Trieca's shoulders as she carefully pulled her off the rock and hauled her body up toward her chest. Surprised by her own strength, Mernestyle kept lifting until Trieca was in a jackknife position, half of her in front of Mernestyle and half folded over her back.

Dirt-streaked tears lined both of their faces and Mernestyle's loud sobs floated around the gritty foothills below. She could feel the soft pound of Trieca's heart against her. She wasn't talking, but she was conscious and forcing out shallow breaths.

"Trieca! You're still alive," Mernestyle tried to shout. But her own breathing suffered under the heavy weight. Carefully balancing Trieca, she eased down the steep incline, slowly, one side step at a time. It took nearly forty minutes, and by the time she reached the bottom, Trieca was softly moaning.

"Come on now, keep fighting," she rasped. "You slid out of the noose because you're meant to be here. You're a survivor. And whoever pushed you to this state is going to pay. I promise. They're going to pay dearly."

14

*"Problems are wobbly miscreations generated by fear. You can solve
them by decluttering your mind."*
– From the Sacred Doctrines of The Uluri

*Lileala could hear the sound of her own footsteps, loud, quick, and filled
with a terror unlike any she'd ever known. She moved faster, hurrying
down a twisting road. The soil was cracked, the land treeless. Lileala
kept walking, heard her feet pounding, watched her lone shadow.
She saw a brown tuft of something grassy, a blade battling for life.
Lileala bounded past. The dirt road curved and she paused. Ahead, on
a skinny, bending pole hung a sign: NO KELOIDS ALLOWED. She
broke into a run and breathed in the dust. She felt her skin tingling
and she moved faster. Faster. Faster. Faster.*

Lileala awoke, shocked. She closed her eyes again and tried to
calm down. She stirred and felt a prickling, then an outbreak of
itching. Sweeping one hand across her neck, she encountered
something rubbery. The shock made her clamp her teeth down
a bit too hard, just missing her tongue. She dragged herself
out of bed, sobbing and aching. The discomfort quelled some,
only to then start tickling. The sensation eased down her lower
body and spread around her back and knees.

She opened her mouth to scream but found she couldn't.
Her mind became a blur, words fusing together, thoughts
muddled. She looked in the mirror and shrieked. The fibrous

scars were back and even puffier and larger than they had been a week ago.

Lileala slipped on her hooded robe and hurried out of her compartment. It was Point Five of the early hours as she made her way over to the knowledge chamber, quietly sobbing. When she arrived, it was deserted as expected. Lileala touched the wall to summon a pod light, then settled into her assigned seat and allowed a bubble to envelop her station. A static band of energy swerved in front of her, awaiting the first question.

"This is Lileala Walata Sundiata" she announced. "The hour is Point Five, but I have only one term left of courses and want to complete them soon."

Dots darted across the stream, and it teetered and beamed two words: *Welcome Lileala.*

"I spent days on the Surface," Lileala said in a rush. "I nourished my body and spirit. I gave the kelolds extended time to wither under the drifts, which they did. Now they are back. Please, tell me why? Why are they larger and more painful?"

She waited.

Nothing.

"Please send me an image, some words. I know this isn't part of my lesson plan, but it's something I desperately need to know."

Still nothing.

Lileala winced. It was so late at night and there were so many vacant seats, why would the knowledge stream be so sluggish? Tomorrow, she'd issue a complaint to the educational faction of the Scientific Pineal Crew, and while she was at it, she'd ask them to update and expand her lesson plan.

"A message, please?" she went on, almost shouting. She caught herself and lowered her voice so as not to alert any Sonaguard who happened to be in the vicinity. "Please," she repeated. "This is urgent."

An old image flaunted itself: That Rare Indigo with the wheel around her neck, wearing the same haughty expression.

For a moment, she disgusted Lileala, and instead of reading the words that unfurled beneath her, she reached out and tried to slap them away.

What's happening to me?

She massaged her arms with a fury. She needed a friend, someone besides Otto. She didn't want him to see her right now... and she wasn't sure she wanted to see him either. He idolized her too much. The idea of him reaching toward her now, beholding her, a scarred icon, would only make her feel worse. She thought about summoning her elder Ma, poor Fanta. She'd been so frazzled by the ordeal, so worried. Lileala glanced at her wrist and concentrated on Zizi, summoning her out of her sleep. They had planned to meet at Point Eight. Maybe she'd come early.

"Lileala?" Zizi's dazed face fluttered above her wrist. "What's wrong? Are you okay?"

"No, no I'm not." Lileala's voice shook, and she sobbed openly. "I..."

"Where are you?"

"The chamber."

"At this hour? Never mind, just stay there. I'm on my way." Zizi disappeared and Lileala slumped in her seat. Her face hurt; her skin burned. Why did she bother Zizi? What could she do? Would she even be that supportive?

Lileala stood, but found her legs too heavy, and she sat back in her bubble. She could trust Zizi. Whatever disagreements they'd had, she was her best friend.

Lileala was half asleep by the time Zizi rushed in, calling for her. Zizi's voice broke into a dream she was having about the charred church from her vision, except this time the church had a dingy annex, a smaller, even gloomier building.

"What is it?" Zizi shouted in her ear.

Lileala's eyes shot open.

"Lileala?" Zizi bent down and hugged her. "Why are you here? Let's call Cherry or the Mhondora. Why aren't you with the Mhondora?"

"No, no Inekoteth, not now. I have to get answers, plain answers," Lileala said.

"Answers from where, though? I have no answers." Zizi stopped and thought awhile. "Wait a minute! You have the moldavite key, right? Doesn't that give you access to The Grand Rising's headquarters?"

Lileala's eyes fogged. "I haven't been able to think. I'm confused, but y-yes. I could enter. But I don't know which Sweep route to take."

"I know the way," Zizi said.

"You? But how?"

"Don't sound so surprised. I'm training to be a Sonaguard, remember? We guard everything."

"Right, I just didn't know..." She stopped talking, afraid she'd say the wrong thing.

Zizi grabbed her hand. "Hurry, we have to get there before anyone else arrives." When they reached an upper platform, they took a Sweep above The Outer Ring for ten minutes. Moving her shoulders, Zizi guided the energy stream to release them near a lift to Ring One.

"What are you doing?" Lileala asked, confused as to why they were exiting The Sweep so soon. "Are we there?"

"No. Follow me," Zizi said. The two women walked down a platform ramp and to a concourse around Ring One. "You can't enter The Grand Rising from a concourse."

They took a lift to another Sweep Station that Lileala had never seen before. It was much smaller than the others and perpendicular to The Grand Rising headquarters. After marching up a gleaming silver ramp, they were gently absorbed by a quiet, subdued cloud that whirled along a path at a pace that seemed slower than most Sweeps. It dropped lower and lower until they were traveling in a lane on an obscure side of the Circle, through a hidden route.

They swooped between stone pillars that were chipped around the edges and alongside archaic structures smeared with odd drawings. Zizi explained that they were moving through an anthropological Coalition Museum and that the etchings were called graffiti and the stone pillars and buildings were artifacts lifted from the ruins of the Earth. As they drifted lower, Lileala got a closer peek at a peculiar, dilapidated wall. It was made from crude cement and the scrawled letters formed unfamiliar words. She blinked, trying to decipher them.

Zizi flung her hands in front of Lileala's eyes. "Don't read those," she teased. "They're the dirty vocabulary they used during the olden days."

The currents were spooling past a third-floor balcony of the sacred headquarters of The Nobility. The shock of seeing the place up close was more than enough for her to process. She beheld The Grand Rising Dome to her left and found it to be as glaring as sun rays. Beaming strands of color were fused into a blinding nest of jewels and light. The S hovering above it hung in place as if by magic, suspended without any visible support.

Out of respect, she said nothing. The Sweep charged forward for a half a kilometer and deposited them in front of an illuminated pyramid with no doors.

"Where are we?" Lileala whispered. "I've never seen anything like this."

"The Grand Rising knowledge archives. I've only been inside once, but I've seen its exterior several times while on practice patrol. You're going to be spending a lot of time here after your reign begins. For now, we have to hurry."

"There's no rush," Lileala protested. "The Uluri invited me."

"I don't care what they did or said. If they see you here now at this early hour without consulting them first, they won't like it. Where's your key?"

Lileala reached beneath the collar of her blouse and lifted the key and chain from around her neck. A light sizzled from it and pierced one side of the pyramid, creating a narrow portal and syncing the key to her dial. The portal expanded and the two women wandered through a hallway of glass, a brief foyer, another corridor, then a sprawling room of drifting globes. The globes were about the size of human hands, and each bore tiny labels bearing titles of their worlds. Forgetting about the keloids, she let her hood drop and clapped her hands.

"I'm overwhelmed," she said.

Zizi grinned. "I know. I was too the first time I saw it."

Lileala and Zizi strolled past Toth, Jemti, Luton and nineteen other Coalition planets and into a space of nothing but spiraling, bubble chairs and floating words.

"Waves of joy," Lileala exclaimed. She looked up towards a wall of Screeners: A herd of huge, furry animals rumbled across grassy terrain. Strange amphibious creatures swam through vast stretches of water. Shiny vehicles motored up and down cobbled brick roads and feathered beings flapped tremendous wings as they streaked across blue skies.

"I've never seen beings like these before," said Lileala. "These creatures are from all over the galaxy, aren't they?"

"Every world, every possibility, every experience is right here," Zizi answered. "But come on. We don't have time to waste." Zizi led her to a smaller space that contained nothing except numbers that dissolved and reappeared at random. "So much for the tour," Zizi said. "Let's see what we can find out." Zizi sat down in the nothing, and currents of an invisible chair formed itself around her. Reluctantly, Lileala did the same.

"You're the one with the key," Zizi said. "Speak up and let the energy circuits know why you're here."

A flood of tremors made Lileala hesitate. She didn't know what she was about to learn, but she feared it wasn't good.

"Lileala Walata Sundiata here," she said, trying not to sound afraid.

"Go on," Zizi coaxed. "And talk louder."

"What is happening with the keloid cure?" Lileala asked. "Why do I still have them?"

Instantly, three bulbous heads appeared in front of her. Waxy with sagging skin, the Kclabs were seated at a long table in a room that looked like one of the convention center offices on Swazembi's Outer Ring.

Lileala gasped. Otto was seated at the end of table along with her Baba, Chief Kwesi and several uniformed men she didn't know.

"Zizi. What is this? And what's Otto doing there?"

"It's a re-creation, I think," Zizi said. "Grand Rising archives take you into the actual experience."

"Gentlemen. Let's get started," one of the Kclabs said. He wasn't as frail and didn't look quite as frantic as the others, but his face was just as translucent. "I'm Chief Hardy and to my right are Haliton and Bertram. Thank you for releasing our men from your prison, especially Haliton. We needed him at this meeting."

Aghast, Lileala wiggled her toes and gave her left thigh a hard pinch. But when she shut her eyes and opened them again, the setting was still the same. This was not a dream.

Otto? Her Baba? How could this be real?

"So where's this Mecca you've been talking about?" Kwesi asked, apparently not interested in small talk. "I don't need any formalities. Just give it to us so we can be on our way."

"Patience," said the chief. He turned toward the door. "Mernestyle, please come join us."

The Kclab named Mernestyle was portly, and Lileala noticed a veiled indifference shining through her unevenly placed eyes as she walked in. She placed a half-filled vial of syrupy liquid on the table along with two glass saucers. She placed these beneath a device that hung from the ceiling and shone light onto them, which projected their images onto the front wall. Lileala inhaled slowly. On one saucer was a swatch that looked like lumpy, pale-violet flesh. On the other was a brush no longer than her thumb.

Mernestyle picked up the brush and dropped some of the liquid from the vial onto the empty dish, then swept it over the swatch.

"This sample is only one-and-a-half inch in diameter," she explained. "But it's enough to make our point. It is the skin of someone with the keloid ailment. Now, pay close attention."

Barely five minutes passed before the keloid lumps on the skin started receding. In another ten minutes, every keloid had withered.

Otto shot up, waving his hands in disbelief, but Kwesi reached for his arm and pulled him back into his seat. They both gawked at Mernestyle like they'd just seen an apparition.

"Fifteen minutes flat," she announced. "That's all it takes."

Haliton congratulated her then looked around the room and boasted.

"We're not bad after all, are we gentleman? And to think you threw us in jail when this is all we were trying to tell you. It's a cure and we're kind enough to share it with you. After all, why should Swazembi be the only one bearing gifts?"

Both the chief and Bertram chuckled, but Mernestyle maintained her glum façade. No one else in the room broke a smile.

"So," said Kwesi, "I believe you and, yes, a thank you is in order. My apologies for the skepticism. But, of course, we had planned to test it ourselves before handing it over to our Rare Indigo."

Bertram laughed through clenched teeth. "I don't think you understand. It's not being handed over at all. We will dispense the treatment."

"You're right. We don't understand," said Otto. "Why can't you just give us some samples of your Mecca or, better yet, let us pay for it and take it back to our planets so we can use it as needed? Why are you holding on to it?"

"Because it's ours," said Bertram. "And because we don't want it reproduced."

"And that's what we have a problem with," Otto added. "It's supposed to be a cure. You don't have to give us a major portion of it. Let us have a small amount, a few drops. We don't care. Just let us take it with us."

One of the uniformed men Lileala didn't recognize tapped his chin, a gesture that was foreign to Lileala. Otto reacted by pounding his knuckles on the table.

"Officer Otto," the man said. "I've given you the Toth peace signal and still you refuse to be silent. There are other Coalition worlds represented here and we'd like to speak. This thing is interplanetary; someone on Toth has it and some other planets have reported similar issues."

The man looked toward Haliton.

"Let's consider the big picture. This thing might spread. A few drops of this product aren't nearly enough."

Bertram stood and walked to the front of the table.

"I want all of you to understand that we are not turning over vials of Mecca. So far, we are the ones who have been preventing this outbreak from getting worse. We have proven that. Now it's your turn to do your part. We want the ban against Kclaben lifted. If we hand this over to you, how are we to know that you won't back out of your promise? We want to have a signed pact that Mecca will give us access to your Coalition worlds, all twenty-two of them."

He picked up the vial. "This is our ticket. In return, we have set up a special Mecca dispensary on a cozy little asteroid near Kclaben."

"When can we go to this 'little dispensary'?" asked Kwesi.

"No one will be allowed there but the patients. We want to ensure that the cure isn't leaked, at least not before our entry into the Coalition."

Kwesi was incensed. "We need to see this place in advance, and verify it for ourselves, before we even think about sending our Rare Indigo there."

"There's no time for all that, not if you want a cure quickly," said Bertram. "The time you spend traveling back and forth is time wasted. The disease is progressing and could infect others in your world. Every day and every minute should be invested in the cure, not frivolous trips."

Bertram walked up to the two uniformed men who had been silent for the entire meeting.

"Tell them," he said, casting a hard stare at both of them.

"Some of your people are on the asteroid already. Tell them what it's like."

One of the men stood.

"Apologies. We did not wait for Coalition approval." He held his head high, a gesture that usually meant solidarity. "We always stand with the Coalition, but this time we had to move on our own. At least four of our residents are afflicted and they're desperate. So, we let them go, sir. That's why we're here now, to let you know the place is safe. We've heard from our people many times."

Otto raised his hand in protest but seemed to think a minute and go silent.

"I kind of thought you'd see it our way," Haliton added. "Listen, if you believe in what we're doing, then tell the afflicted about our free dispensary. We'll house them and heal them at no cost while we negotiate the new pact that allows us into your worlds. Given our past interactions with your kind, you must understand our reluctance to hand over something so potent. After we prove the viability of our solution and everything is going as planned, then we turn over the formula. Everybody's happy, see?"

The screen disintegrated and Lileala and Zizi sat in the empty space, dumbfounded.

"Treatment on an asteroid?" Lileala murmured. "And my Otto and my Baba? They didn't tell me a thing."

"Maybe they haven't agreed to it," Zizi said. "It's too ludicrous."

"Sounds like I'm the one who has to agree to it," Lileala mumbled.

She crossed her legs, then uncrossed them. "Otto's been rushing off to a lot of mysterious meetings," she went on. "And last night after the rites ceremony, he disappeared. He didn't even take me to The Outer Ring to celebrate. Maybe he was here trying to come up with a different solution?"

"There are laboratories in the back," Zizi said after a while.

"If Otto was in here last night, he was probably back there trying to reconfigure programs for the healing oscillators. Maybe to replicate that liquid?"

Lileala crossed her legs again and dabbed the tears burning the corners of her eyes. "Those beings aren't allowed on Swazembi. How could they have been treating these keloids without even coming near me?"

"No one seems to know," Zizi answered. Her voice was so soft it made Lileala bristle. Zizi had a strong voice. It didn't normally sound anything like pity.

"You've never seen them, have you?" Lileala asked.

"Seen what?"

Lileala removed her veil and let her robe drop around her shoulders. "You saw them covered. Now look at them in the open. Look at them. I know they're unsightly, but I don't need your pity."

Zizi lowered her gaze and struggled to come up with a response.

"Don't look away," said Lileala. "Don't you dare look away."

Zizi frowned. "Why are you... why are you showing me?"

"Because, I want to, that's why. And I'm changing, just like you. Didn't you tell me you were learning and growing? Well, me too, I guess."

The tears gushed and Lileala pulled her knees to her chest, hugging them.

"I wish I knew what you were talking about," Zizi countered.

Lileala said nothing, thought nothing. She rocked silently and let her mind dance in its own pain.

"Come on, let's go before the Pineals show up," Zizi said.

Something curdled inside of Lileala. She was irritated by the sound of Zizi's voice. It was whiny and so unlike Zizi, so unbecoming. She swayed dizzily and closed her eyes. Would she go to that keloid colony? Would she?

"What would you do?" she asked Zizi. "If you were me, what would you do?"

"I'm... I'm not sure. I don't know."

"I'm devastated, Zizi." Lileala's lips quivered. She lifted her robe back over her shoulders and hid her face in the hood.

Zizi hugged her, and she hugged back, slightly.

"I think I saw it," Lileala said. "In a dream, I believe I saw that asteroid. There is no grass there and there are no colors singing their own praises in the sky. But... I'm going to go. I've decided. I need to be rid of these scars."

"Think about it some more," Zizi whispered.

Lileala pointed to her chest. "I feel this heavy throb inside, like I'm being pounded and hammered. I feel like the rains are coming down hard and they have no colors, like they're pouring through me, and I can't make them stop."

Zizi started to speak then stopped. Lileala could tell that she was also in pain. She observed her friend closely, admired her silky, brown skin.

"I ache in a way that no one ever aches here on Swazembi," she said. She lifted fingers to her face, let the tips slide over the keloids. "I hardly know myself anymore." She paused a moment. "I might as well tell you – I'm just now discovering that I'm a clairvoyant."

Zizi's mouth fell open. "What? Does Otto know?"

"No, he doesn't." Lileala searched her face. "Are you shocked?"

"About what? The clairvoyance or Otto not knowing?"

"Both."

"I don't think you should hide it from him."

"I'm uncomfortable telling him."

"Is that good, do you think? Shouldn't you be able to share everything with your devoted?" asked Zizi.

"I suppose."

"Come on. We have to leave." Zizi was talking in that whining voice again.

"No, wait," Lileala said. "If this stream can show me anything I ask, then I have one more request."

Lileala turned to the space and confronted it: "This is Lileala Walata Sundiata again. I've been asking about the past, about Earth for a while. And now... now I'm dealing with this Earth ailment. Can you help me understand why it's happening? Why me?"

The stream blurred and then a name appeared: Gwendolyn Bennett, twentieth century Earth Poet. Below it, was a poem:

"*Something of old forgotten queens*
Lurks in the lithe abandon of your walk
And something of the shackled slave
Sobs in the rhythm of your talk."

Lileala read without comment, then rose and made sure her hood was in place.

"What does that mean?" asked Zizi, still staring at the cryptic passage. "What's a shackled slave?"

"I have no idea," Lileala answered. "But I get the feeling I'm going to find out."

PART III
The Six Precepts

1

*"Every dilemma is a messenger summoned by you. Every pain
is an envoy."*

– Swazembian Proverb

The vessel came to a halt midair and performed a sluggish
rotation as it lowered onto the flatlands of Togu Ta City Port.
The path was clear and spread wide to the north and to the
south – a much larger landing strip than Lileala had anticipated.
She'd never visited the port, and it hadn't occurred to her that
it would take up so much space or that it was on the border of
such a bustling town.

She'd been hustled through the town under cover, wearing
her robe, veil and dark glasses to avoid being recognized. It
had only been three days since she made her decision and the
Sonaguard had not succeeded in hiding it. Although the Kclab
meeting with Swazembi was supposed to be kept under wraps,
someone from inside leaked it to the public and everyone
seemed to know Lileala was leaving. Since all else had failed,
the Pineal Crew issued an emergency mandate – absolutely
no unauthorized person was allowed anywhere near the strip.

While waiting, milling around a team of Toth and Jemti
officials she'd never met, Lileala didn't care who saw her. Not
anymore. She had listened all morning to a soothing melody
and the lyrics to *Keep Your Head to the Sky* were still running
through her mind. The sentiment calmed her anxiety as she

prepared for departure. Her elder Ma stood on one side and Otto on the other. She wrapped both hands around his right arm and watched the vessel containing the Kclabs.

When it landed, her hands shook so Otto squeezed them so close to his, his perspiration felt like her own. Neither said a word. She wanted to ask how it was that such awkward beings could manufacture a vessel, but then she heard her Baba whisper, "That's a Toth ship, I believe." He was standing on the other side of Otto and next to two golden men who had flown in from Toth, Chairman Dane Elliott and Commander Coleman Spencer. "Am I right?" he asked them. "Doesn't that thing belong to your crew?"

"It looks like one of ours," Coleman said after some hesitation. "I don't understand what this means any more than I understand the ailment. But... give us time. I promise you. We're going to find out."

The door of the vessel opened and Lileala felt certain her mind had curled up inside of itself. She didn't budge right away and neither did Otto. Their joined hands were numb, like ice that had been clumped together in a frozen box for years. Ten members of the Pineal Crew stood behind them, along with nearly thirty Sonaguard, all of them with their fingers jutting from their orbs, poised to fire just in case.

A being stepped down from the vessel and headed in their direction. The closer it came, the more unpleasant it looked. When it was in front of them, Lileala thought she would faint. A gross membrane coated its nose and cheeks. Was that skin? Then it spoke, and she knew that it wasn't the face that disturbed her; it was something else. Something was hidden within the being, something Lileala couldn't pinpoint.

"Hello. Call me Bertram. My partners will introduce themselves shortly." It turned and gently raised its voice: "Hurry. I don't want to keep our patient waiting."

Lileala's heart raced. Seeing Kclabs in person was so much worse than watching them in the knowledge stream. Two more stepped out, one with a smaller head and a thinner body, and one who was rotund and dressed in a long gauze gown. Lileala recognized her immediately – the female Kclab she'd seen in The Grand Rising Archives. She walked up to the crowd and shouted, "I am Mernestyle. It's nice to see so many of you here today sending off the Rare Indigo but I... we... don't have time for extended greetings. Where is she?"

Otto tried to leap forward and swing at the beings, but Kwesi grabbed his right hand and pulled him back. "What are you doing?" he hissed. "Lileala agreed to this. And no matter what you think of them, they have proven themselves."

The pain in Lileala's eyes seemed to trigger Otto more, but she calmed him with a single pat on his wrist.

"It's okay, my Baba's right," she said. "Promise me, Otto, you won't follow and won't try to visit. That's not part of the plan." She shot a stern glance at Kwesi. "You too, Baba. The agreement, strange as it is, states that I spend some weeks with the Kclabs, at least three or more. And while I'm doing that, they don't want visits to break my focus and make me homesick."

"They're not worried about homesickness," Otto said. "They're scared visitors might get their hands on that cure."

"They don't trust us, and we have to take responsibility for that," Kwesi muttered under his breath. "We rejected them."

"Right," said Lileala. "I just want to get this over with so, let's just follow the rules."

"You've never been anywhere that far, never..." Otto hyperventilated.

"Otto, please. If something goes wrong, you'll hear from me. They guaranteed a cure and vowed to let me stay in touch. And I will, okay? So, don't interfere and don't try to send rations because if you do, I might be tempted to leave, or they might get frustrated and postpone treatment. Just wait to hear from me and get their reports. Okay? Either we trust this process, or we don't."

"I don't know where you're getting this bravery from,"

Kwesi said. He gave Lileala a side hug and she tried to pretend she didn't feel tension building in her shoulders and neck.

A third Kclab began to speak, but Lileala kept her eyes on Kwesi. He was holding his breath and deliberately standing close to Otto, blocking his movement.

"Just so you know, I'm Roloc," the Kclab said. "Rare Indigo, come forward, please."

No one moved and Lileala felt Otto tighten his grip on her hands.

"I don't know about this," Fanta said. Her eyes darted between Roloc and Otto. "I didn't know they were this frightening."

"They're not," Kwesi said gently. "Calm down. They're just different."

Fanta reached out for Lileala and when Lileala turned to hug her elder Ma, she saw a familiar round face. Ahonotay. She was draped in tightly woven brown sack cloth and standing in formation with the Sonaguards, just a couple meters away. She edged closer to Lileala and parted her lips.

"Bring her forward," Mernestyle announced. "We'd like to make it to the asteroid while the sun still sends it rays."

"That's her," Lileala whispered to Otto. "That's Ahonotay." They both stared and Ahonotay, her lips still parted, seemed to be using all of her breath to create a sound.

"Sz-ze-w-w-w-a," she breathed out loud, struggling to force air through the letters. "Sz-z-szewa, sze-wa. R-Rem-member Szewa."

The Kclabs listened and waited. "We can leave in our space rocket and come back another day," Mernestyle yelled out. "But we prefer not to. The longer the Rare Indigo delays the longer her treatment will be delayed."

In her state of anxiousness, Lileala yanked herself away from Otto and hurried toward the ship without allowing herself to look back at him or her parents or Ahonotay. She heard her Baba shout a loud goodbye and amid the frenzy she could tell that someone, maybe it was her elder Ma, was fainting. The Sonaguard were trying to control Otto. Lileala could hear his wails.

The noises were hazy, as if memories from a distant past, as she made her way inside the ship. She settled in a seat and refused to allow herself so much as a glance out of the window. She knew the mayhem, if she saw it, would change her mind. If she was to heal, she knew she had to focus her energy. She had to nurture it, toughen it.

She pushed herself to peek at the Kclabs around her – their opaque layers of flesh, glassy faces and hardened, rock-like eyes. A wave of guilt hit her. What right did she have to condemn their appearance?

As the ship lifted off the ground, Mernestyle glanced at her and scowled. "What did you do to her? What?"

A lump swelled in Lileala's throat. "What did I do to who?"

"She was one of us. She was wearing all yellow. Does that bring back memories?"

"I'm sorry, I-I don't know what you're talking about."

"Speak up, please," Mernestyle snapped. "And stop lying."

Lileala trembled and Roloc rushed to her seat, sandwiching himself between her and Mernestyle.

"What happened to all those manners we've been rehearsing?" he asked. "For days, we've been practicing 'yes, it's nice to meet you fine people' and 'have a good day, gentlemen'. How can you forget so soon?"

"You're right." Mernestyle backed away from Lileala and spoke to her in a tone that was almost tender. "You are our guest and our patient," she said. "I lost my head for a second because my friend, you see, she's dealing with grave injuries."

"It's okay," Lileala offered. But she spoke with her neck stiff, and shoulders hunched, too tense to move her head.

"Don't be alarmed by this," Roloc told her as he pointed to the membrane surrounding his cheeks. "This is our skin, but other than that, we're just like you. You're here to get well and we promise to do our best."

"Leave her be and let her rest," Mernestyle said. Then she looked down at the whirl of vibrations curling above Lileala's wrist. "Devices don't work on the asteroid," she said. "You might as well give that to me."

Without looking up, Lileala took off her dial and handed it to her. "It won't work for you anywhere," Lileala said. "It's tuned in to my emotions and the emotions of the people I contact."

The band of energy rotated and died just as Mernestyle was sticking her finger through it.

"Let me see that," said Roloc. "I remember Trieca having one of those things. Where is she, anyway? I haven't seen her in over five days."

She pointed at Lileala. "Ask her."

"She's the patient. She doesn't know," Roloc rumbled. "Tell me where Trieca is?"

"She's not here and I can't talk about it." Mernestyle rotated her wrist, trying to force the dial to operate.

"Where is she?" Roloc repeated. "She kept me out of prison, just like she promised, just to send me on this mission, but I haven't seen her, and when I ask about her no one answers."

Mernestyle studied Roloc for a moment before responding. "She hurt herself, but she's healing up fine, regaining her strength."

Roloc rubbed his knee and closed his eyes. When he opened them, Lileala saw that he had one hand over his mouth and another on his stomach. "When did this happen?"

"In the late hour. You were asleep."

"But why didn't anyone tell me?"

"The chief didn't want it spread. He didn't want anyone saying that he'd been too harsh."

"Oh, I don't think he's that bad," Roloc said. "Especially with Trieca's. He's an old softie around her."

"Well, he turned harsh, and that's all I'm going to say about it."

"Maybe he found out about that wrist thing. I don't think

Trieca was supposed to have it. She was going to give it to me."
He reached for the dial in Mernestyle's hand.

"No, no," Mernestyle sneered. "This belongs to the patient."

Patient? The word made Lileala queasy. "I told you," she
said timidly. "It's not going to work for anyone but me."

"Well, we don't need it anyway. We have something better."
Mernestyle held up a couple of pieces of black ore and grinned
at Roloc. "I'm in charge for a while and it's going to be up to
me who receives this."

Roloc fell silent.

"Just as I thought," Mernestyle said. "You're not going to do
anything to jeopardize your ore, are you?"

She waggled it above Bertram too, but he didn't seem to
care. He slid into the space beside Lileala, eyes racing up and
down her heavy robe. "Can you lift the hood?" he said, finally.
"I've never seen a keloid."

Mernestyle placed a finger in front of her lips. "Bertram,
shhhh! Now everyone, listen. We all agreed to keep our
attitudes in check and handle this mission with dignity. So,
please, stop questioning the patient."

Bertram shrugged and changed the subject. "I'd like to
thank you for those pod lights. I was mad at first but now that
we're sort of on even ground, Kclaben and Swazembi, I'm not
bothered. Besides, the unders needed it."

Lileala took the deepest sigh she could. Nothing made sense
to her. The strange accusations, the constant descriptions of
her as "the patient". She crossed her arms and hugged herself.

Comfort. No comfort.

Is that you? She asked of the voice in her head. *You're
back.* She felt her body gradually relax. The messages were a
welcome break from the Kclabs.

*Stacked tightly, we are. As stalks of corn at the marketplace. Bound,
we are. Suffocating in our own urine.*

Lileala smiled. *My stars, I can understand more. How is it that
you speak to me so plainly?*

Understanding will grow, so far away from the confines of Boundary Circle, you will hear.

"Hear? What will I hear?" Lileala said out loud.

Bertram jumped out of his seat. "She's crazy," he said. "No one told me Swazembians were crazy."

Mernestyle and Roloc backed up with him, making sure they kept their distance. "She's delirious, maybe," Mernestyle said. "Should we give her an ore crystal?"

Bertram stomped his foot. "Those are for us!"

"We will see." She patted her right pocket and moved toward the front of the ship.

"We have about three more hours before we get to the dispensary." She glared at Lileala. "Your treatment will begin upon arrival. For now, you might as well sleep."

But in her state of terror, Lileala couldn't even close her eyes. She had gone into shock.

2

"If the road you trod leads to a valley, learn to fly."
– Mantra of The Nobility

They landed on an open plain that was less than a hundred meters wide – too small and poorly lit to comfortably accommodate a spacecraft. Tiny glass reflectors were positioned haphazardly around the site, but there were no circular markings to indicate landing perimeters. The descent was so jarring it roused Lileala from her daze.

She looked around and, for a minute, forgot who she was with and why. Bertram was still slouched in his seat, snoring. But Mernestyle stood at the helm and Roloc was taking his time rousing himself from his spot on the floor. Lileala clutched her stomach and worried that she felt queasy.

"Is this it?" she asked, glancing out of the window. "How is it that life can be sustained here?"

No one answered and she caressed her forehead, trying to sooth a headache along with the stomachache that wouldn't ease.

The ship settled down and Mernestyle turned her attention to her passenger. "Try to move quickly," she said. "We want to get home."

"But where is this? Who's to be here with me?"

Roloc struggled to his feet. "I'll take her outside and introduce her to the others."

She trailed him and tried to contain her shock. She hadn't

expected a great deal of foliage, but she had assumed she'd see a bush here or there. There wasn't a plant in sight. The cracked ground was dry and barren. Dust was swept up by the wind and tossed over boulders and scattered rocks.

"Where do I check in?" Lileala asked Roloc.

He scratched his head and shot her a blank stare.

"What do you mean by 'check in'?"

"At the facility? The facility for treatment."

"Oh," Roloc said. "Um, I don't know about a facility." He called out to Mernestyle. "Hey Mern, did Trieca mention anything to you about facilities and check-ins of some sort?"

Sudden peals of laughter tore through the spacecraft window, causing Lileala to jump and strike her foot on a nearby boulder. Were they making jokes? It was too dark to see what she was doing, or know where she was going. Did they expect her to deal with jokes too? She wondered if the Coalition-Kclab pact could be rescinded.

Mernestyle stuck her head out of the door and shouted an answer to Roloc. "That Trieca, you know how secretive she was about all this. I didn't hear about a treatment center, just the serum."

She covered her mouth and Lileala could tell she was stifling another laugh.

"Okay, well, will you show me where my room is?" Lileala said. "All I want to do is eat some dinner and go to sleep."

"About that," said Mernestyle as she walked part way down the stairs of the vessel. "Rare lady, you know this is a very new project and that my friend, Trieca, was the one who came up with it. She's real secretive, and told us little about this asteroid. So, I don't know about rooms and fancy dinners. This is no hotel. But we'll all have better answers, you know. After she recovers."

Lileala's jaw dropped. "There's no hotel? I've never seen a more depressing environment!" she moaned.

Her hope lifted as soon as she saw silhouettes behind a cloud of dust that had been stirred up by the ship's landing. There were more than a dozen people, waiting, eyes cast down as if afraid of what they might see. She walked toward them. Roloc followed one awkward step at a time.

"The long ride aggravated an old knee injury," he said, and she wondered if he actually expected a shred of sympathy. She looked at him with disgust and continued toward the sad cluster of people. Not a single head raised and, though their mouths appeared to be moving, no one spoke.

"What's going on?" she asked Roloc. "What are they doing?"

He grimaced. "I think they call it praying. That's what they do right before the late hour, hold hands and mutter something over and over."

Lileala watched quietly, wondering if it would be improper to interrupt.

"Go ahead and join them, but take these with you," Roloc dug into his pocket and scooped out two narrow capsules, four inches long and made of a thin metal. "One is your breakfast, and the other is lunch or dinner, whichever you choose," he said.

She took one in each hand and scoffed. "Are you serious?"

"They're powdered meals," he continued before she could ask another question. "Just pour on your tongue and that's it. You're nourished."

She rolled the metal around in her hands and made a sour face.

"It's safe," Roloc said. "You're our patient. We're not going to feed you anything harmful."

Lileala scowled at the puny Kclab in front of her and considered shoving him as a form of protest. How could this undeveloped little asteroid and these little capsules heal anyone?

"Do *you* eat this?" she asked.

"What are you trying to say, that I'm an under?" Roloc bit down hard on his bottom lip. "I had a lot of that back then, a lot of that powder and the skrull. But it was the skrull mainly, gritty lumps of smashed grains that I couldn't stand."

A cool breeze blew dust in his face, and he flashed a smile that Lileala knew was fake.

"You'll eat the skrull too, one day a week," he said in a tone that was suddenly more formal. "If it was good enough for me, it's good enough for you." He bit down hard on his lower lip. "Is that okay, Miss Rare Indigo?"

Lileala thought it was best not to answer.

"We have chemists on Kclaben, damn good ones," he said sharply. "They know physiology, that's for sure. Each capsule has all the minerals you need, dug out of rock and mixed with dried roots."

Roloc gathered part of his robe into his right hand and lifted up one side so he could rub his swollen knee. Lileala grimaced. His knee was like a mass of hardened bubbles. "We'll be back tomorrow. Anything else you need, ask those people mumbling over there." He limped toward the ship, and she resisted the urge to follow and bombard him with more questions. Ore crystals, unders, skrull, powdered food... She had so much to learn.

You are here in body so that your spirit may thrive.

Her pulse slowed a bit. The voices were beginning to feel like friends.

You will see, you will see... They faded out.

As the vessel lifted off the ground, Lileala shuddered slightly. Should she do this? Should she stay or send word to her Baba that she'd changed her mind? She turned around, checking to see if the line of people still awaited. The soft twilight made them seem like mere shadows, but she could see one pair of eyes shining and lots of hands waving in the dust.

"Hello?" she called out. "Hello?"

"Come closer," someone said. "Come."

Lileala moved closer, clutching her hood and slanting her head to hide her scars. A round-faced youngster approached.

He had pudgy cheeks and large, kind eyes. Keloids were concentrated on the periphery of his brown face.

"I am Garrette," he said, smiling. "How do you do... Lileala, is it?"

Lileala smiled back at the child. "Yes, but how do you know my name?"

A woman walked up beside him but didn't speak.

"We all know you. We arrived last week, and we were told you'd be here soon," Garrette said.

"But aren't you kind of young to be here, so far from home?" Lileala asked.

Garrette laughed. "Yes and no. I have been alive thirty-four years, but my maturation process is locked in at fourteen and my physical aging stopped at twelve. That's typical among those who bear the heavy pigment on my planet, Xale."

"Xale, yes," Lileala said. "I've heard of it."

"Then you know about us," the boy continued. "There are a large number of us there, like me. And this is how we have been for a millennia. We remain this way until we pass on."

Lileala tried not to appear startled. "On my planet, you would be a mere babe."

Garrette laughed again. "I assure you, I'm not a baby. We Xalians are quite responsible, except we do avoid Coalition meetings. We tried one once. It was no fun."

"I've never been to a meeting, but you're probably right," said the woman standing next to him. She nodded at Lileala and smiled lazily. Her eyes had a mysterious probing quality, and her skin was a hazy gold.

Garrette glanced at her and then back at Lileala. "I have been here six days and I can tell you it's sad. You will find that out, Miss Lileala. The Kclabs are okay, but this place, it's very sad."

Several more men and women in long cotton frocks joined Garrette while the golden woman extended her hand to Lileala. "Your scars are worse than any we've seen," she said.

She lifted her right hand to her forehead and onto one of the two blemishes on her temples. "Mine are starting to heal, but they're still there, just not as large as yours." She lifted her head so Lileala could get a closer look. A series of golden keloids clustered beneath her chin.

"Are you from Toth?" Lileala asked. She'd met Toth tourists whose skin flickered back and forth between white and gold. But this woman was different. She had the brightness of an early moon and it remained intact.

"Yes and no," the woman said. "You must forgive my bluntness. That's the Toth side of me. I'm Swazembian also, on my elder Ma's side. And she always taught me to be more tactful. So, if you don't mind, I'll start over. My name is Martore and, I'm a native of Toth."

As she spoke, the woman's hair tumbled about her shoulders, swaying without the aid of the wind. Long and delicate, it was a dusty beige and arranged in an array of braids. Lileala found it distracting.

"Your braids," she asked. "Why are they moving?"

"The gravity is thinner here," Martore explained. "My coils fight the gravitational pull, I guess." She glanced at her own feet. The tips of her toes brushed the dirt, and her heels hovered half an inch above the ground. She laughed. "My hair coils are tugged hither and there, and my feet never quite touch the dirt. Not completely. I don't know, maybe the pigment in my skin reacts one way, and my Toth DNA pulls me the other way."

"I've never known someone to have the DNA of two races before," Lileala said.

"Of course not," said Martore. "You were groomed to be an Indigo Aspirant. You've never left your homeworld."

"How did you know that?"

"Miss Rare One, I am the one who became infected right before you. On Toth, we were made aware of you and your affliction. I thought you were told about mine?"

After a moment of silence, Lileala answered. "Yes, I guess I did hear of you." She spoke quickly, trying to hide her shame. Until now, she hadn't inquired about the Toth woman with the ailment. She hadn't even wondered.

If Martore hadn't been watching, she would have pulled her hood closer to her cheeks to mask her embarrassment, but it was too late. Martore was searching her face. Lileala noticed that her eyes were glowing.

"You never gave me a single thought, did you?" Martore asked.

"I, I..." Lileala stammered.

"Too bad you don't know about me," Martore went on. "Because I know so much about you Indigos. Have you figured out how to use the trinity flame breath properly? Or do you still think it's just a cosmetic thing, just to make yourself all shiny and pretty?"

"What are you implying?" Lileala asked, abruptly irritated. It was enough that she'd come to a strange place, that she was ailing. Now she had to deal with criticism, too.

"Didn't mean to insult you," said Martore. "And I'm not knocking trinity breath. My elder Pa does the M-S-T and says there's a connection between the self-tanning practice and trinity breath. He's always wishing trinity breath was more widespread. My elder Ma tells me that it's only on Swazembi and only taught to Aspirants."

Lileala found her voice. "Yes, well, come visit when you get out of here. Why don't you come as my guest?"

Martore laughed. "Miss Indigo, you don't get it, do you? After my forebears were joined, my elder Ma never visited again. She resents the fact that my elder Baba's not allowed in Boundary Circle."

One of the men beside Martore placed a hand on her shoulder. "Ladies, it's starting to get dark. Let's head to our sleep stations."

But Lileala was still agitated. "But we are tolerant," she said to Martore. "We allow everyone onto the Surface and in The

Outer Rings. We entertain tourists from all over. I even like the Earth hymns."

"Do you?" Martore sounded defensive now. She looked again at her own feet, trying to press them closer to the soil. "My elder Ma tells me you only listen to music internally on chips, and that there is very little external music in that circle of yours. She thinks your ears have been dulled."

"They hear just fine, and they enjoy lots of sound. Lots of it," a man standing near Martore blurted out. Extending his right hand, he greeted Lileala with a firm grip. "I'm Brian. We're not going to be around each other forever, but while we are I think we should try to respect all our different cultures." He gave Martore a firm look. Then he raised his index finger toward a stack of boulders. They balanced atop one another precariously, as if they were tipping over but were held in place by invisible hands.

"Look to those beauties," he said. "They lift our moods somehow and they help us find our way. After sundown, it tends to get pretty dark here, but the rocks sort of glisten, and that helps some."

Martore's pupils narrowed. "The only good thing is that, once you adjust to the darkness, your eyes will be more activated here," she said.

"My eyes too?"

"Especially yours, since you're the Rare Indigo," said Martore.

Lileala tried to ask another question, but Martore chattered on. "I need to show you something," she said. She rolled down the sleeves of her robe, held up a golden arm. It was covered with keloids from wrist to elbow. "My face was spared somewhat, I suppose because I don't have as much melanin as some people here," she said. "But I have enough for whatever they did to take effect."

"You're still lucky," Lileala said. "They're on my arms, legs and face."

Martore rubbed her arms and sighed. "I was sort of special

too, I mean, before this. On Toth, they look up to us hybrids because of our eyes. They depend on us to decipher hidden mental patterns among allies and adversaries and among planet inhabitants. We use our eyes to reveal truth. I was one of the better ones." The heat of Martore's eyes warmed Lileala's face. "Let me know if there's any way I can help."

A man's voice resounded behind her in a loud, slow shout. "What do you mean any way you can help? Tell her the list of dos and don'ts."

The crowd spurned him. The man was almond brown and not much larger than a twelve-year-old child, and everyone hurried out of his way. He took notice and sneered. "Is anyone going to orientate the newcomer, or should I?" He chuckled and faced Lileala.

"Number one, take your serum. They call it Mecca and they give it to us daily. This isn't a real colony, but we think of it that way, since we're stuck here a while. That treatment's not going to happen overnight. Now, for don'ts: you should know that the Kclabs have a little metal 'no keloid' shed here on the asteroid. It's their private office. Don't go near it, and don't ask too many questions about it.

"I'm LaJuped," he said finally. "The others don't like me 'cause I don't have as many keloids as they do. So, they think I'm a spy, but I'm a patient here like everyone else. My skin had more of them when I came, but they're clearing faster than everyone else's."

He turned and made an ugly face at the crowd. They were waving at Lileala and slowly walking away. "Some people here, like that Martore, think their culture and their ways are the best," he said. "Don't let them get you down, and if they do, go to that rock tower and get some sun rays. Earlier today, a corner of sun appeared briefly over the horizon, and it made those rocks over there light up like a star."

"Where?" Lileala asked. She raised her eyes and squinted.

"No," he said. "Not the sky. Look ahead. Straight ahead."

About forty meters away loomed another cluster of boulders, nearly twenty of them stacked on top of the other in one shining heap.

Lileala stared for a full minute. "That's beautiful, even more beautiful than the first one."

She turned to thank LaJuped, but he was gone. She stood alone and watched the others, wandering past various rock piles and headed toward a narrow trail. She followed them down the trail and passed a few miniature flying beings that looked eerily like the mosquitos she had seen in Mbaria. One of them landed on her shoulder and made her squeal.

"It's only an insect," a passing woman said. She was an elder, with a cheek mole the size of a pebble and faint creases around her eyes. She wore a cotton bonnet and a gray wool blanket of a dress that sagged around her hips and stopped just above her ankles. "The tiny dirt insect is the only lifeform natural to this environment," she said. "It burrows in holes in the ground."

Lileala regarded it cautiously. It was nearly three times the size of the mosquitos in the Otuzuweland. The woman continued. "They're harmless. The Kclabs are too. They're gone now, but they'll be back tomorrow, hopefully with enough Mecca to go around."

Lileala opened her mouth to speak, but the woman shushed her.

"Come on," she said hurriedly. "Don't tarry, not here. I'm Hattie, by the way."

Without looking back, their steps quickened. She and Lileala hurried along together past a curving trail of rocks. Lileala paused momentarily to loosen the collar of her hood and let the air soothe the keloids on her cheek. As soon as she lifted her hood, the vision of the old cathedral burst into her mind. Clear as crystal, there it was again, a smoke-drenched church that had survived despite an obvious fire. While the others hurried on, Lileala surveyed it and searched for new details, anything to give her a clue of what it meant. Her mind fell upon the church's marquee message behind a sheet of busted, singed glass. She concentrated, carefully tracing each letter with her inner eyes.

Hattie stopped and yelled, "Come on, Lileala, we need to get to our sleep stations." Just as she turned to follow, the marquee flashed, and she could see its announcement bright and clear.

NO KELOIDS ALLOWED

The following morning, Lileala awakened in a cave to loud chatter as the colony's inhabitants crawled out of their resting places. Most had slept with their bodies pressed against the rough, stone wall and curled beneath wool blankets the Kclabs stored in piles on the ground. At the first glint of sunshine, they began moving about and trying to find enough space to stand upright. The front area of the cave was barely five meters high and only the shortest among them could walk through the space without bending forward.

Lileala lay still and watched as a couple of long-legged women hunched over their belongings, debating about something called a letter. She wasn't sure what a letter was or why they seemed so excited.

"Today is the day. I'm sure of it," one said. She was young, fifty-something, too tall to stand comfortably in the cramped space as she flipped through her knapsack. Lileala noticed that the two women speaking were identical, with the same coffee bean complexion and broad, rounded noses.

As Lileala pulled herself slowly to her feet, she heard a heavy voice coming from the rear of the cave. It sounded like Brian. "Hey Wasswa sisters, tone it down. All that noise is disturbing the peace. You think I can't hear you just cause I'm in the back?"

"Watch your words, you," one of them teased. "We know you're not sleeping. You're writing, aren't you? In the darkness with that little flashing light of yours."

Brian laughed along with the twin sisters. "Can't use my

portable light any longer. The current died and there's no way to charge it here. Besides, I finished writing yesterday," he said. "You better have yours ready too."

The women shook the grit from their blankets and made eye contact with Lileala. "Excuse us," one of them said. "We were in such a hurry we forgot to welcome you last night. I'm Virtue." She smiled slightly and glanced at the woman beside her. "And this is my twin sister, Honor. I can see you're nervous, but you don't have to be that way around us. In our world, Aarasalon, everyone is expected to live up to the name they were given. And we –"

Honor piped up. "We do our absolute best. So, get that worry off your face and come on and out of this cave. It's daytime." In unison, the twins began fluffing their braids and stepping across the stone floor. The sisters giggled again and Lileala watched them sweep their long braids to the side and awkwardly ease through the cave's opening that Lileala thought was too narrow. The night before, Brian had remained with her awhile, gently coaxing her to go inside.

She was shocked when she realized the interior had plenty of space. A floor of grainy calcium deposits stretched for nearly ten yards and the uneven bottomland near the rear slanted and dipped to form a bed of rock-hard soil. Brian liked it back there because the ceiling was so much higher – at least seven meters. But Lileala had opted to create a palette in the front near Hattie. The two had spread thick blankets over a stretch of limestone and Lileala had whined for nearly an hour about the discomfort. Hattie didn't seem the least bit interested in her complaints, and when Lileala tired of yearning for a bed, they both gazed out at the falling stars until finally falling asleep.

But where was Hattie now? Lileala looked around, puzzled. It was very early. Did Hattie leave while it was totally dark? She peeked out. It was dewy outside, and the distant sun was casting jigsaw patterns of light across the grounds. She folded her blankets and tucked them under her arm.

"Excuse me," she said to one of the sisters. "But why are we sleeping in a cave? I asked about it last night, but no one seemed to be in the mood to explain."

The woman's smile froze in place, and she gave Lileala a quick pat on the head.

"A little naïve, aren't you?" she said, not unkindly. "You'll learn, my child. The Kclabs, yes, they are nice to us, and when we return home our condition we will be healed. But we are patients, not friends. Think of this as a business. They'll do all they can but with as few resources as possible."

"But a bed?" Lileala countered. "Why would a bed be too much for us to ask for? Could it be that you're the naïve one?"

Brian bent over so he could interrupt them without bumping his head. "You'll adjust," he said to Lileala. Then he looked at the sisters. "Leave this discussion to me."

"Come," he said. "Leave your blankets in the pile in the corner and let's talk."

Lileala obliged and stepped with Brian out of the cave. "Boy, you're all so energized and jovial. What happened? Last night, everyone seemed so cold and distant."

"We're less inhibited in the morning," Brian said. "The Kclabs aren't around, and we get a dull spot of sun. It's just a wee bit, but this is when it's best here. The morning might not seem like much to you now, but after a few more dark evenings you'll start looking forward to it, just like we do. But listen, that's not what I want to talk about." He paused and went on. "We haven't been here long, only a week before you, but we already understand how this game works. We have something the Kclabs want. They have something we want. So don't worry your pretty little head bothering them about beds and what was that other thing you asked for? Oh yeah, a treatment facility. When I heard you say that last night, it took all my willpower not to laugh out loud."

"But that's a reasonable expectation," Lileala protested. "Don't you think?"

"Let it go," he went on. "They're simple, those Kclabs. From what I know about them, there's not much technology on their world. Only the stars know how they got that rocket ship. But all we want to do is get through this experience and get home."

Lileala was quiet for a minute, weighing Brian's words before she spoke.

"But they're breaking their promise. They're not sticking to the pact."

"The pact said cure, not a cozy resort." Brian observed Lileala's pout and kept talking. "You're pampered, I get that, but don't mess it up for the rest of us. If you make too many waves it will delay the whole process. We want to get out of here fast as we can." He looked at her again. "Besides, the cave's not bad, and those blankets, whooh-boy are they plush. Kclabs' must have had them made just for us."

Lileala choked back her next question and ignored the knot swelling in her throat. This was nothing like what she had in mind, but it would have to do. Brian studied her shrinking smile and softened the tone in his voice. "Look around you, Rare One. This is all there is to this place; it's an asteroid. There's not much that can be done with it."

"But there's space over there." Lileala looked beyond a tower of rocks and toward a hill. "What's over there?"

"I don't know, I think it would take years to develop the landscape," Brian said. "Come on now, if they could do all that, wouldn't they want to be here instead of that dump they live on? Last I heard their population was thirteen thousand. If they could make this work for them, they would."

"Well." Lileala shrugged. "Guess we're stuck with it for now. Lucky us."

She looked up at Brian, doing her best not to stare at the keloids crowding his neck and chin. She zeroed in on the depth of his dark eyes, the bell-shape of his nose and his black, velvet skin. Handsome, she thought. "Thanks. Obviously, you're coping a lot better than I am right now."

"No worries," he said. "I was one of the first to come to this galaxy-forsaken spot. I spent one day and night here all alone. I was the one to find the cave. Come on, let me show you the pond."

They walked a few meters to the left of the cave and toward a natural basin filled with cool, stagnant water. A bundle of torn towels and a stack of clay bowls and cups were piled around the basin on a ledge made of loose rocks.

"This water was once like stone," Brian said. "That's how cold it was here before. Now this asteroid gets some sun at times and the stone – they call it ice – has melted." He reached for a cup, lowered it into the pond and drank. "This melted ice is very good, even the Kclabs like it," he said. "Sometimes they come here just to fetch water."

Several inhabitants joined them, filling up canteens, then scooping water into the clay bowls and gingerly dabbing their keloids with wet sponges. The Wasswa sisters stood about two yards away. They were taking turns holding up a large towel while the other hid behind it, dousing her naked body with several bowls of soapy water. Lileala walked over, pulled a bar of soap from her knapsack and asked if they would shield her as well.

When she finished bathing, she found Brian and Martore sitting on adjoining boulders, drinking powder from their capsules.

"Wait till you taste the other stuff they give us, the skrull," Brian said. He made a face. "It's some kind of mushy grain mixed with milk they squeeze from potato peelings."

Martore stuck out her tongue and groaned. "It's bad. It's so bad."

"Who feels like eating anyway?" Brian said. "I'm too disgusted."

A pair of eyes alighted on Lileala, and she could feel Martore watching, probably thinking she would drink the powder and gag. Lileala gulped it down without reaction. It wasn't that unpleasant, and it got rid of her troubling hunger pains. She was considering drinking her lunch capsule ahead of schedule when she noticed Hattie at a distance, talking to LaJuped.

"Hattie!" she called out. "Hattie!" Hattie didn't glance in her direction. She kept her head straight ahead and hurried off with LaJuped.

"What are you doing?" Brian asked.

"That lady, Hattie, befriended me last night but then, I don't know, it was so weird, this morning, she was gone."

"Let her go. LaJuped's going to hang around her until he gets what he wants. Then he'll probably hurt her. Whatever you do, try to avoid that jerk. He's a spy." He turned to walk away, then stopped. "By the way, this is letter day. When the Kclabs get here, they'll collect them and take them to Toth. Our loved ones pick up the mail from there."

"Brian, excuse me, but what is mail?"

Brian studied Lileala like a pilot going over the vital control panels of his ship. "In your world, do you ever use your hands for anything? Are you really that spoiled?"

Lileala didn't know what to say.

"Never mind," he went on. "Mail happens when you pick up a tiny utensil that makes markings, like your name for instance. You write out the words that are forming in your mind. We call that a letter and when we send one to another, it is labeled mail."

"Oh, instead of using a dial?" She thought about the crude message Ahonotay had insisted she read.

Brian contorted his face, and Lileala could tell he was trying not to make fun of her. "Yes, instead of a dial. And, read no more into this than was intended. This letter, if you choose to write it, won't be that hard. Just picture each individual letter in your mind and figure out how to recreate them with your hand."

The idea was more than Lileala could fathom. She had never picked up a device and drawn shapes to communicate. She thought about the words that streamed in the knowledge chamber and tried to understand why they couldn't stream from her writing utensil in the same way. How would she express her deepest thoughts just by moving her fingers and wrists?

Eager, she rushed back to the melted ice pond and grabbed a wide, but flimsy, swatch of paper and writing utensil from the plate of tools – spoons, brushes, hard blocks of soap – at the end of the ledge. Lileala thanked Brian again for his guidance then wandered off and found a sunny patch of ground.

The sun had risen, and the flying speckles were back. As she prepared to write, the creatures pestered her, and a long fluid shadow slipped into her view. She blinked, assuming it was the silhouette of a passing colonist. The shadow swelled and she blinked again. A speckle flew past, and she waved her hands in front of her, hoping to knock it out of her way. But it hovered.

"Go away, away," Lileala whispered. Two more came and she spoke louder. "Shadows, insects. What next?"

An impassioned voice answered, startling her. *There are certain things you're not going to change. Why not tuck them gently under your arm and ask them, 'What meaning do you bring?'*

Lileala waited and listened.

What meaning rests inside of your experience? Ask yourself that. When in pain, seek.

Lileala put down the writing utensil. "Why do you now come as a shadow? And why don't you ever reveal who you are?"

Nothing.

"Please give me clear direction," Lileala said. "Please tell me what your intentions are for me."

Look at the meaning.

The message was clearer than it had ever been. Lileala listened closely.

We are many, we ancestors, growing now in living images, experiences, snatches of what you have labeled as history.

She held her breath and a woman appeared, dressed in rags.

There were traces of blood on her wrists and ankles and her bare shoulders were a blistering mess of scratches. The woman screamed and vanished. Lileala shut her eyes tight and placed her hands over her face.

Precept three, the voice whispered. *The third precept urges you to 'Dig deep inside misery and pull out a secret gem'.*

"Thank you," Lileala whispered back. "I'll try."

She prayed a while then opened her eyes. The letter to Otto lay in the dirt and she was pressing against it, soiling it with her clammy palms. She was shaking, sweating. But she felt no fear. On this world of deprivation, she'd have ancient guides. Nervously, she pulled a sponge out of her satchel and cleaned her hands. Then she picked up the blank letter. It would take a while to learn how to do words manually, but she had to figure it out and get a message to Otto. It was time he knew the truth.

3

*"Physical comeliness is a self-aggrandizing bias pushed by worlds
with power and privilege."*
– Trieca Menton's scroll from her sickbed

An hour passed and Lileala had written a series of uneven
letters that formed a single jagged line. She read the line over
and over, then decided it wasn't good enough and dragged her
pencil through it. Yet something within her spirit fought back.
She steadied her hand and tried again. After just a few strokes,
she had etched out three cryptic words: *A Protective Talisman.*

Lileala studied the phrase, thinking of it as yet another
nonsensical message, except this one had come from her own
fingers. How could that be? She kept going and scrawled out
eight more words: *Juju, Drumming, Dancing. They kept us from harm.*

Frustrated with her lack of progress, Lileala crumpled the
letter into a tight ball and tossed it in the dust. She stretched
out her arms and legs, figuring she'd try again tomorrow.

Then the thrumming started. A boisterous, festive thrumming.
A confusion of musical moans and raw drumbeats that thumped
through her mind. Lileala slapped her ear. She hadn't had a
music chip since leaving Swazembi and had been told that, just
like dials, they wouldn't work on the asteroid even if she'd tried
to sneak one in her satchel. There would be very little to comfort
her here. Just messages. Visions. And now, music?

The music frightened her, and when she tried to relax it seemed to get louder. Lileala was torn. Part of her wanted to welcome this banging in her head. Another part of her saw it as yet another mental intrusion that she'd have to struggle to understand. But some of the drumbeats seemed to hold her under a spell and she felt an invincible power resting within each note. And with each boisterous pound, came a surge of strength.

So she embraced it.

She closed her eyes and saw and heard drummers; the rhythms resounding through her mind were more electric than any she'd ever experienced in Boundary Circle. Men wore wooden masks, kicked their legs high, undulated their torsos, leapt five meters into the air. Stilt walkers rattled beads draped around crinkly grass skirts. A cascade of female dancers slinked about in a wild palette of yellows, reds and greens. The drumbeats intensified and the colors quivered.

Lileala bobbed her head, fully immersed, until an intruder broke into her happy place. Little Garrette stood before her, a wilted look in his wide eyes.

"Miss Lileala, Miss Lileala," he said. "I've been trying to get through to you for a long time. Couldn't you hear me? The Kclabs are here and –"

Lileala didn't wait for him to finish. She shook her body vigorously to clear her head and scrambled to her feet just in time to see the Kclab spacecraft ahead, its entrance closing.

"They're not staying today," Garrette said. "I came to tell you that there would be no serum. The Kclabs said they're in a hurry and aren't dispensing it until tomorrow. But here's your food capsules."

The tin bottles clinked as Garrette dropped them in Lileala's hand and she plopped back down in the dust. Another day of no healing. Another day she had to stay in this dusty wasteland.

Near the end of her third day on the asteroid, Lileala finished her letter to Otto. Just as she was signing her name, a loud ruckus jarred her and, thinking it was yet another message, she listened intently. When it came again, louder, she pocketed the letter and rushed over to a huddle of colonists who had gathered around the landing strip.

The Kclab ship had landed, and Bertram and Haliton were unloading a lumpy bundle of rolled up mats with great difficulty. Their groans could be heard for miles. Finally, they handed their load over to Brian.

Lileala rustled in her pocket for her letter. She was so proud of it and couldn't wait to give it to the Kclabs. Bertram pointed at her, and she held it up above her head to make sure it couldn't be missed.

"I hope you're happy," he said, ignoring the letter. His eyes were sunken and Lileala could tell he was flustered. "These bundles are because of you," he went on.

A nervous wave flit through Lileala's stomach. Everyone's head turned in her direction, then flipped back to Bertram, looking at him with accusing eyes.

"What did Lileala do wrong?" Brian asked. He had hefted the entire load onto his broad shoulders but appeared unaffected, not nearly as overwhelmed by it as Haliton. "She just arrived," he continued. "How could she have upset you so soon?"

In an instant, Haliton's attitude changed. "Never mind, we're joking," he said. "What I'm trying to say is that all of you should thank the Rare Indigo for this present. We went all the way to an Earth auction yesterday and didn't return until morning. That's why we're late. The pickings were slim, but we were able to find these beds. And it's all because of her demand."

Several colonists cheered, but Lileala didn't join in. She hadn't asked anyone about beds... except for Hattie and the Wasswa twins. How could the Kclabs have known?

"We got them for all the patients," Bertram went on. "They're called sleeping bags."

A few more cheers went up and most of the colonists followed Brian as he carted the bundle to the cave. Lileala decided to stay behind, more anxious for her first dose of Mecca.

A slight clamor sounded from the spacecraft and Roloc and Mernestyle teetered out, clumsily dragging a burlap sack filled with potatoes.

"Everyone needs to go to the pond," Bertram said, glancing at the crowd. A few of the colonists were still with Brian but a couple of the women were relaxing on the ground near the rock towers, drinking their powders and soaking in the final flashes of sunshine. Some were still writing letters, and little Garrette was kneeling in the dust, playing a game with a stack of stones.

"It's Point Fifteen, and the sun's going to be gone within an hour," Roloc announced. "Let's hurry up. Everyone, get to the pond."

Dropping the potato sack, he headed back to the ship and returned with a spouted tin cannister under his arm. When everyone had assembled, he ambled over a path of rocks and toward the nearest colonist. Mernestyle stopped him.

"Wait just a minute," she said, then shouted into the crowd. "Will the newest inhabitant come forward please? We want you to be the first today."

Lileala hesitated. She was desperate to be cured, but something about this ritual seemed demeaning, and pride swallowing wasn't a habit she'd ever formed. Pushing her reluctant feet toward Roloc, she realized more than ever what it meant to humble oneself.

He lifted the cannister and allowed one drip to fall on the tip of her nose.

"Rub it in," he ordered.

Dutifully, she rubbed it in and stole a quick glance at her hands. "Is that all?"

"Scoop water from the pond now and drink it to help your skin absorb the serum. You'll see your first improvement in less than an hour."

One after the other, each colonist accepted a drip and moved on. All except an elder man with a walking stick. "We should get two doses to make up for yesterday," he complained. "Why is it always so sparse and why is the cure taking so long? I want to talk to whoever is really in charge, cause if I don't get results soon, I'm going home."

Mernestyle squinted, apparently watching someone from the corner of her eyes. "Osiris, the one you want to talk to is tired," she told him, "but Trieca's coming now. She said she needed to take her time." Still squinting, Mernestyle pointed at a hazy, slow figure moving as if each step was a calculated decision, a goal that had to be weighed.

When she came into full view, Lileala's heart rattled. This Trieca, whoever she was, had a stern presence and such unusual white smears on her face.

"Why did you leave the ship, Trieca?" Roloc called out. "Your throat's damaged and I don't think it's wise for you to be breathing in the dust."

An unspoken command shot from Trieca's eyes and Roloc shut up and kicked at the nearest rock. Trieca looked through him and stationed herself beside Mernestyle. "I'm well," she boomed. "Let it be known that I'm as well as anyone. I'm ready..." She concentrated on Bertram. "Ready to resume my original command."

Bertram wore the deflated expression of someone who had been excluded from a celebration. Trieca watched him, and when his jaws sagged, she laughed. "Show me what I came to see," she demanded. "Bring the Rare Indigo."

"Me? Why me?" Lileala asked, tightening her hands around the hood of her robe.

"Why not you?" Trieca asked, her voice dropping an octave. She stepped up to Lileala and glued her gaze on her.

"Ah, is this what all the to-do is about?" Trieca barked. "You're not so much, not now anyway. Probably never were. I should end your malady and dismiss you." Trieca swallowed and readjusted a loose sash that was draped around her neck and chest. "But we have unfinished business."

The word "dismiss" bolted through Lileala's mind and her voice cracked. "Ma'am, did you say I should leave? Before I've finished my Mecca treatment?"

"Of course, you'll finish it. I said that in jest." There was a sudden dullness in Trieca's tone. As she spoke, she placed one hand on her throat. "I meant we have a matter to attend to. Tell me, what gives Swazembians the right to sway the Coalition with their narrow standards? Melanin is the only measure for glamour and Swazembians are to blame for it. You have turned the entire galaxy against Kclabs."

"I don't know what you're talking about." Lileala looked at Roloc, hoping he could explain. Trieca stared at her coldly and inserted one finger beneath her cumbersome sash. The fabric fell to the ground, and she held up her head. Her neck membrane was shallow and translucent and part of the flesh had caved into a clear gelatinous ring. It encircled her neck like an indentation in an aged tree stump.

"This is from the rope," she declared. "It's a souvenir of an anguish I never should have felt." She motioned toward Lileala. "This was caused by someone like you."

Enraged, Roloc butt in. "What a sight you are!" he said. "Just look at the fear on our patients' faces. Just look at the scare you have induced!"

"Such big words for such a low-ranking Sector member," Trieca mused. "Where are you getting the courage to speak to me like that?"

"Demote me. Lock me up," said Roloc." I don't care. I want to stick to the pact. You're always blaming someone else," he said. "You blamed me, got me in trouble. Now you're blaming everything on this Rare Woman."

She shot him a curious glance. "It's not just this Indigo, it's all Swazembians."

"You're blaming all of us here?" Brian shouted. "You're punishing anyone with a trace of pigment!"

Indignant, Trieca stalked off without another word. Roloc

stepped beside Lileala and spoke into her ear. "I apologize for all of this. She likely needs some black ore."

The comment made Lileala uneasy. Why did he tell her that? She had no idea what Kclabs did with black ore. Did they eat it? Was it similar to the skrull?

"Us Kclabs can turn a little jittery and mad. When we do, we have a hard time controlling it," Roloc continued. "The ore crystal calms our anger surges. We get a little woozy, but not out of control." He stopped talking and gestured over his shoulder.

"You see that bag over there, the one I was lugging? Boiling potatoes. I talked the others into letting me bring them. They're small and have a lot of bruises, but they're edible and this is probably the only time you'll ever have anything like it. And here's a couple of matches in case you need them."

He stuffed the matches into Lileala's left palm and she closed her hand around them in a tight fist. She wished she knew what they were and what he was talking about.

While she eyed Roloc suspiciously, Trieça returned with a startlingly different presence. The white blotches on her cheeks had a smoother chalkiness and the dent around her neck had taken on a watery shine.

"I just needed to refresh," she announced. "The sun here is so bright it reminds me of my days beneath the black mountain. I have calmed and now, I understand what my subordinate was trying to say." She nodded her approval at Roloc. "So, before I go, let me be the first to accept a letter from the Rare One. Lileala, is it? Lileala, do you have a letter ready?"

Lileala adjusted her hood and reached in her satchel for the words she had learned to etch onto paper a few days earlier. Her hands shaking, she handed the letter to Trieca.

"Thank you," Trieca said. "Forget about that earlier outburst. I want you to know that I'll always respect the pact." She observed the folded paper and let it rest a minute in both hands. She played with it and seemed to delight in the rustling whistle of paper. Then she let it slip and swiftly caught it, appearing to accidentally tear one side then the other until she had torn the letter in half.

"Oh, I'm sorry. I'm so sorry," she said. "I don't know how that happened but, oh well, it's no good now, might as well get rid of it." Trieca ripped the letter into various pieces and walked away smiling as bits of paper floated to the ground.

Lileala wailed and Osiris raised his cane and aimed it at Trieca. Brian grabbed him and Trieca spun around with one hand over her heart. "My dear Indigo. You will forgive me, won't you?"

Roloc dropped his head and continued gathering the mail. "Sorry," he muttered as he passed Lileala. But she could barely hear him through her sobs.

Brian wrapped his arms around her and Garrette walked up and patted her on the back. "Don't worry about it, Miss Lileala. Maybe she's doing this because you're new. Anyway, we'll be out of here soon."

"They can only go so far," Osiris said. "They have to answer to the Coalition, and if they don't honor that damn agreement, believe me, all over the galaxy the Kclabs' name will be mud." Osiris groaned as he walked away shaking his head.

Lileala wiped her eyes and watched as Roloc dumped a pile of letters collected from the other colonists into a burlap bag.

"Whatever you do, please don't tell anyone about this," Roloc begged her. "Give us another chance. Stay with us. And in your next letter, don't tell anyone what happened, I promise it won't happen again."

"We won't," Brian said. He faced Lileala. "Roloc's right, you know. One of them messed up, but don't judge all of them for that. If you tell anyone in your homeworld, they'll rush out here, and where does that leave us? The Kclabs already made it clear that one violation like that and the pact's off. Don't let one run-in blow it for all of us."

"But what if Coalition officials show up on their own?" Lileala said. "This place is a mess. What if they see how we're living?"

"How?" Brian asked. "They don't know and we're not telling them. Why would we do that? They'd come get us and we'd go home to suffer without a cure."

Lileala thought for a second, trying to shake herself out of a daze. "Seems they could cure us in a few days."

"Not all sixteen of us," said Brian. "They need time to mix up batches of Mecca, negotiate with the Coalition and all that."

Martore walked up and stood between Lileala and Brian. "Just checking to see if you're okay," she said. "That's the rudest thing I've seen since I've been here. Normally, they're pretty decent."

When Lileala didn't react, Martore turned to Brian. "Let me talk to her. We can go for a walk, and I'll help her sort things out."

"Fine," Brian said and moved on.

"I don't understand them," Lileala said, stealing glances at Martore's wandering hair.

"Most people don't understand any culture but their own," Martore explained. "Maybe that's why the ancestors brought us all here. To learn tolerance. Oh, and to get that cure. You can do it."

"I'm trying but, I guess, I don't know. I just think it would be easier if we could get in touch with home more. It seems kind of unfair." Lileala's eyes watered. She wiped them with the back of her sleeve.

"The mail situation's not the Kclabs' fault," said Martore. "Don't take it personally. Until they're officially in the Coalition, all they can do is drop our letters at the Toth air base and leave."

"I get it, I think," Lileala said, but she was looking through and over Martore's braids and only half listening.

Martore continued talking, not noticing that Lileala's mind wasn't with her. She had entered a daze and drifted into a void of gray skies and a field of white, plump flowers. Lileala got lost there in the stillness, and for what seemed to her like hours, she was absorbed in a living dream. A dream

of troubled eyes. Lileala looked through them, and she felt
herself run.

*Running. She was running through the field of flowers, but they
weren't flowers. They were little cushions, globs of condensed clouds
with hard, prickly bottoms. Dark fingers were pulling on them,
bleeding. Lileala felt a jolt.*

*One of the women stopped yanking on the white puffs and started
screaming. Lileala groaned. She felt herself inside of this woman,
breathing her breath. She heard herself shriek. She recognized her
– she was the woman who had appeared earlier, the woman of the
shadows with blood on her wrists.*

Someone cried out and Lileala shrieked again.

*And she raced through the field, still screaming, scraping her elbows
on the white clouds on top of tall, jagged stalks. A man on a four-
legged creature called out a name. Della. Lileala kept running. Was
she Della? The man on the animal came after her. She pelted toward
a barn, toward a tree.*

*"John!" she screamed. A young man, of no more than fifteen sun
years, was tied to the tree there. Another man, older, his face the color of
the strange, flowerless field of clouds, was swinging a long, serpentine
belt. A lash?*

*"Quiet, Della!" he snapped, looking at Lileala. Her stomach caved
in. The man swung again. Lileala felt Della wail.*

*The man jumped off the animal's back and ordered her to "get back
in the field." She pushed and kicked.*

"That's my son! That's my son!"

*Lileala heard the lash cut through John's flesh and she screamed
with Della. Della's howls became hers and Lileala's heart almost
forgot to beat. The boy screamed louder, and she doubled over, anguish
pouring from every cell.*

When Martore looked over at Lileala she was on the ground,
sobbing.

4

"Yesterday never left. Tomorrow's already here. They both live and breathe in our collective soul."
– From the journals of Ahonotay

Martore waited, watching her with kind but frightened eyes.

An hour passed. And another. Martore remained. She was still there when Lileala's head began to rise. Lileala regained her senses, blinked and looked around. "Where am I?" Everything was so dusty, so blank. She blinked again and remembered the colony. But that woman named Della and her son, John? Were they going to be okay?

"You were in some kind of a trance," Martore said. "What happened?"

"I-I don't know what happened. I'm confused."

After Martore helped her to her feet, the two walked toward a block of three boulders that were tilted on their sides, leaning against one another. They sat on the ground in front of them, saying nothing for a while. Finally, Martore spoke. "You're seeing things. Is that something you normally do?"

An overpowering grief came over Lileala and she began to tremble and cry. "Yes, but never like this, never this bad."

"Do you think it's because you're afraid here? Maybe you're hallucinating because you're so far from home."

"I wish I was home. There are no horrors like this there. It was terrible, Martore. I saw someone being hit with a long cord."

"When you're overwhelmed, it's normal to behave strangely, to see things, maybe. Stay close to me and Brian. We can help you make this adjustment."

"I don't know. I think this is more than an adjustment."

Martore wrapped one arm around her shoulders. "It's getting late. Time to sleep."

Lileala resisted. "I'm okay. I just need to be alone," she said and gazed at the sky. "You go ahead."

"Sure, take your time."

When she left, Lileala felt grateful that she had not pleaded with her to go along, that she had gone off to be with the other colonists. She could see them crawling through the dark and narrow opening of their sleeping quarters, the bowels of the cave.

For reasons she couldn't explain, she was feeling more confident, brave even, brazen enough to stick her hands beneath her veil and touch her cheeks. She felt the lumps. They were smaller, and they didn't sting nearly as much.

You're here because of them. They led you to where you need to be.

There was a difference in the voice, a more nasal pitch.

"Ahonotay?"

Yes, it is, young Indigo. Szewa.

"But… but are you here in the colony?"

Why do you refuse to speak with me properly? Please speak with your mind.

How is it you can reach me all the way here? Lileala responded.

She heard Ahonotay's shrill laughter then, soft and brief. *You are silly, indeed. What does distance matter to mind and spirit?*

It's dreadful here, so dreadful. I'm glad to hear someone I know, thought Lileala.

You will know others as well. And in that knowledge, you will become one. On the great ships, your groans will be their groans, melded with living cargo, chained in corners that are as dark as the night is long.

Do you know who I just saw? In my daze, whose soul overtook me? Lileala asked.

The past ones. Your presence eases their suffering, Ahonotay answered.

I'm scared of returning to them. I fear their pain, but I'm also worried about them.

Still your thoughts and wait. I have been in communication with the water beings of Po Tolo. They said you are now ready to link with them fully.

"Yes," Lileala said, and she folded her legs. As she watched the last drop of sunlight spill behind a small mountain, she wondered what existed on the other side.

There's a trail there. Get up and follow it.

She did as Ahonotay instructed. She watched a dim spark in the sky, a star she hadn't noticed before. She stared at it and wondered from where it had come. Po Tolo, she wondered. Is this Po Tolo?

Walking with a sense of aimlessness, she made it around hundred meters past the cave where the others slept and headed toward a narrow path that snaked toward a hill. She trod carefully over a bed of sediment and climbed up an incline toward a clearing. It was dark, yet she could easily find her way along the path.

"Po Tolo?" she asked.

Without waiting for an answer, she proceeded. When she reached the clearing, she headed to the top of a hill and from there spotted a massive, copper cave that was supported on each side by steep, rugged mountains. The passageway into the cave's interior was the width of a spacecraft and its ceiling was like a honeycomb of pure gold. But it dead ended and twisted, leading to a brief tunnel with porous walls and a ground splattered with sharp rocks. It was less than five meters, but Lileala had to tiptoe carefully to avoid gashes in the soles of her sandals. At the end of it, she exited onto an enormous ledge.

"Ahhh," she whispered. "Breathtaking!" The land was a dry floor of packed red soil facing a copper and diamond wall. It was so beautiful. There were no trees or blades of grass, but the air was fresh, cleaner, free of dust, and the wall had a blinding sheen. Lileala walked closer to the edge and looked down into a deep gorge that appeared to have no bottom. She was stunned by the vast indentation and realized from her chamber studies that it was a crater. "Beautiful," she said. "As beautiful as the Surface."

Here, you will help them, a voice interjected. *Those who did not flee, need you. The Dogon live in many lands, many countries and some, who lived near the Akan, The Ashanti and the Bano tribes of Ghana.*

Lileala's heart palpitated.

"Po Tolo?"

We are the water beings of Po Tolo who counseled your ancestors and sent rays of light from our star. When it reached its highest peak, hundreds of Dogon, carrying favorite treasures and tools, joined the light force and rode the beams that cast them into a new world.

"Traveling by beams?" Lileala asked. "But how long did that take?"

A moment of transfer. Is that not how light travels through space and time?

"Yes," Lileala answered. "I understand."

But some became captives. You must help them carry on.

"How could I possibly help? Their struggle is in the past."

As the beings answered, Lileala felt a calmness surround her. *There is no past,* they said. *That is precept four. Your forebears are still with you. You can think what they think, feel what they feel.*

"I feel pity for that young man and his elder Ma."

Send them strength, not sorrow, the Po Tolo's beings instructed.

"I will. I will."

We leave, they said with voices like a whistle. *Wait for the Dogon.*

Perched on the perimeter of the high cliff, Lileala couldn't stop gazing into the crusts of gold and platinum that lined the gorge below her. More than once, she had to remind herself that this was no ordinary crater. When she got the chance, she'd ask the Dogon if the metals surrounding her were fine tuning her capacity to hear within.

Yes.

The answer came. It was chilling. A chorus had fused itself into Lileala's thoughts and begun to echo around the rim of the crater.

We are the Dogon, speaking as a collective, the chorus said. It was so loud and had so many voices that Lileala thought her ears would burst.

Yes, the metals and compounds of this environment help you calibrate and help you hear us. You'll cope better once your body's electrical impulses adjust.

"I'm still struggling with the fact that you're real, and that you're part of me, part of Swazembi."

Ah, but we have been waiting for you. Your blackened skin, the open quality of your mind, your curiosity, we can use it, you see for we have centuries of stories to tell and the anguish of it is still with us. There is no death, but in the land regarded as the past, we suffer, we yearn, we cry. We, the Dogon who strayed to the Gambia and the coast of Ghana, speak to you from dungeons.

A sharp ache twinged Lileala's spirit, and she saw a dank, dark dungeon.

No, she resisted. *I don't want to go.*

The Dogon chorus plunged her into it anyway and she felt herself falling into a deep sea of moans. Around her, bodies writhed. Convulsing. Crying. Bathed in their own sweat. A vulgar stench was trapped in the walls, and the smell of it, the smell of the bodies sickened Lileala. She tried to wiggle but there was no space to turn, to breathe. A scream encircled her, and it took a minute for her to realize it had come from her.

She yanked her arm from beneath a dead body pressed upon her shoulder. A spit of mildew dripped from the ceiling. The whole room radiated death and she stopped trying to see. She was blind now, or was the space sealed from any light?

Lileala opened her eyes and cried.

"Why did you do that to me?" she asked the Dogon chorus. "I felt like I was suffocating! I wanted to die!"

And so do we, they answered. *We cope by coming to the future ones, begging you to hear. So do all of our ancestors, the Dogon of Mali, the Ashanti people of Ghana, the Wolof of Senegal, the Igbo, the Yoruba of Nigeria. We are many, in agony. Propelling our spirits beyond is the only way out. There is a belief that we permitted ourselves to be enslaved. But we lay in damp dungeons for months, lying in our own excrement, awaiting long ships. Our spirits are being destroyed even before we reach the new world.*

Lileala let the thoughts sink in, praying and pleading that she would never have to experience another vision like that. In the midst of her prayer, she leaned over a silver slate of bedrock and vomited.

The Dogon chorus spoke up immediately and with urgency.

Our anguish is an enormous cargo, but it is vital, for it is only the sensitive who can feel and carry the message.

"So I can feel it. So there's no distinction between my place in time and yours. So what? What can I do with it?" Lileala asked.

Young one, you are a portal. Let us tell our story through you.

The water beings still speak with us, they continued. *Here in these dungeons, we can hear them.*

A shock shot through Lileala, and she sat up upright.

Oh, the water beings, they have shown us your Sweep. That is the residual energy from those who traveled among the stars. Those who left this land were told to take the bones of the lion and the antelope, the predator and the prey. When those bones were charged with Po Tolo's beams of light, many Dogon villagers vanished into them. They returned to the solid physical state of their bodies once they arrived in their new world.

"Did they leave without the water beings?" Lileala asked. "What became of them?"

Some beings of Po Tolo went with them to Swazembi where they have mutated. Some left their shell and let the river's currents take them back home.

After an hour of discussion, Lileala still had questions. "But how long will I see the horrors of those left behind?"

We don't have the answer.

"I still don't know if I can do it."

Remember the fourth precept, said the chorus. *We are the past, the present, the future. Use our chant, Szewa.*

A weariness seeped into Lileala's joints that ached from sitting up all night. And yet, her mind was exhilarated. She returned to the colony energized as if she'd had a good night's sleep.

Brian spotted her in front of the rock tower and ran toward her. "Thank the galaxy! Do you know how distraught we've been? No one knew where you were! We thought something had happened."

A smile dominated her face. "Hello, Brian."

"You're glowing," he said. "Lileala, what's going on?"

"Must I share? Isn't anything private here?"

"We share everything here."

"Then Martore already told you of my trance?" she asked.

"She was concerned."

"Don't be. I've found a place, that's all. A secret place, it's almost magical. When I was there, I could hear the spirits with more clarity. They are ancestors from beyond Swazembi."

Brian gave her a pitying look. "You're not coping. Martore told me you're not."

"I'm coping well," she argued. "A new energy has flooded my spirit and I have entered the bodies of the early melanin bearers."

"And you think this is normal?" Brian asked.

"You're worried," Lileala said. "Don't be, please. I'm fine."

Brian shot her another sympathetic glance and grabbed her hand. "Come on, let's go have our powdered breakfast and chat. The Kclabs will be here soon."

When they arrived near the melted ice, the colonists who had gathered there rushed to Lileala and began pelting her with questions. She didn't answer most of them and tried her best to sit with them and make bland small talk. After a half hour or so, she could feel the Dogon beckoning. She promised that she would return to the spot again that evening. And she did as she promised and stayed with the presence all night long and well into next day.

5

"One who wrestles with fate is like a twig trying to evade the ebb and flow of the mighty river."
– Swazembian proverb

A circular object floated through The Great Hall, just a few inches in front of Otto. He sauntered along behind it, allowing it to move freely. The gadget paused, made a buzzing noise and just barely avoided crashing into a marketplace booth.

He ignored the mishap and paid no attention when someone he didn't know stopped and gawked. He liked the Wmet communication device and planned to use it no matter what anyone said. Considering no one had relied on a Wmet in nearly four hundred years, it was a marvel. It just needed a little tuning.

He kept going. The Wmet spun in front of him in a jagged semi-twirl, and heads turned to watch it. Sonaguards snickered. Otto was oblivious. The Wmet, twirling at a slow pace, about two meters above the ground, suddenly sped up and nearly sideswiped a young woman walking past. Otto grabbed it just in time.

"Sorry," he said. "That was close."

The woman stared at him, then stared even longer at the spinning object.

"It's a Wmet," Otto said, unabashed. "It used to belong to my great grand-forebear."

The woman was silent. Her eyes skipped back and forth between the Pineal Crew officer and the crude device.

"You don't know what this is, do you?" Otto asked. "From what my Baba tells me, it was created at least one thousand eight hundred years ago. I found it in an old storage vault."

Otto released it and moved on. Ever since Lileala left for the asteroid, it frustrated him to use his dial. They had always chatted on it, and he'd grown accustomed to the constant stimulus on his pulse. Wearing a dial reminded him too much of her absence. He kept expecting to see her image fluttering above his wrist.

The Wmet began ringing and halted in place. He bent over, opened a flap, picked up a long handle and spoke. "Otto Keilta Gonga, Pineal Crew officer, here."

"Hello...? Hello?"

A puzzled voice traveled through the receiver handle.

"Are you there, Officer Otto? Are you there?"

"Yes, I'm here."

"This is Javien. I'm at the Sonaguard headquarters. I'm using an enhanced, high-frequency dial to reach you, but you're breaking up. Your device isn't adequate enough for full reception."

"It's adequate," said Otto. "Trust me. I'm afraid that it is me who's not at my best."

"Very well. I'm calling to tell you that two of our task force members stationed on the Toth air base have a piece of mail for you. It was left there by the Kclabs and believed to be from the Rare Indigo."

Otto almost tripped over the Wmet. "Waves of joy," he said. "I can check out a vessel and be there within a few hours."

"Slow down, Officer Otto. It's on its way. Our Sonaguard team is treating this as an emergency. They dispatched someone this morning. He should be there shortly."

"You've known this since this morning and you're just now telling me?" Otto demanded.

"Officer, if we'd told you sooner, you would have rushed to Toth needlessly. Be patient. We'll deliver it. You're in The Great Hall, aren't you?"

"Yes, I am," he answered.

"Then stay there. The Sonaguard will meet you near the marketplace."

"Yes," Otto sighed.

"And, officer, one more thing."

"Yes?"

"Please get rid of that piece of junk."

"It's not junk," Otto said. "It works just fine."

Otto heard a click and placed the handle back inside a flap atop the Wmet and pressed a button to deactivate. Carrying it under his right arm, he found the nearest bench and sat there, in front of a busy clothes haven. An hour later, a Sonaguard appeared, thrust a brown paper envelope in his hand and left.

"Thank you. Waves of joy!" Otto called out. With his heart racing, he opened the envelope and began to read.

My Dearest Otto

Please bear with me as I struggle to make words on paper. I think of you and I long to talk to you but this is the only way. My heart is bursting and I'm feeling pain I've never known before and I don't know what to do with. It saddens me to burden you with this. I know you're hurting too. And we can't even help each other, comfort each other.

You were so sad that day I left and that is troubling me too. I see your face and feel your sorrow. I hear my elder Ma's screams and I keep thinking about my Baba being so strong and wanting to hold me back.

But, strangely, it's not all bad here. It's not happiness, but I'm getting help and that's what matters. The Kclabs are not cruel and I am fond of one of them. A couple of them can be grumpy but I always think that is probably because no one wants to be here, not even them. That means a lot though, the fact that they came here just to cure us. So I guess that sort of gives them the right to be in a bad mood now and then.

Otto, I have to tell you something now and I want you to try not to be mad. Before I left home, I was holding in a secret. I hear voices. There, I said it. Voices were in my head and they are here now, still in my mind. They started before I left but I just didn't know how to tell you. The Mhondora implied it was the Inekoteth, but he didn't know for sure. I'm sure now Otto. I am speaking with the ancestors. Their ancient tongue flows through me in streams of words and visions. I hear their aches and their moans. I'm sorry I never told you. I couldn't because I didn't understand them myself. Now, in this desolate bed of dust, I am certain. But please don't worry. And please do not travel here and do not let my Baba come. Visits would be a distraction and would only slow progress. I want to get well. I want to come home.

I must go now. The Mecca is being dispensed. I love you.
Your Lileala

6

ANTIPATHY
We will clothe our cocky stare neatly of mercy
And they will not reap
Scars and pains, upon them like their rains
Let them not weep
– Poem by Trieca Menton

Roloc limped down the stairs of the spacecraft, dragging his bad leg, and yelling out for Lileala.

"Come over here!" he shouted, beckoning her toward the ship. "I have another surprise."

Lileala turned to scoff at him. "More surprises? Roloc, you don't have to bring something every time you visit. The only thing I want is a faster remedy. That's all any of us want."

He hung his head and she quieted. There was a sting of rejection in his eyes and the glint of it was more than she could take.

"Okay, Roloc." She rushed over and outstretched her arms. "Toss it. I'll put it in an open space by the pond."

The thing Roloc threw to her was a crumpled, unrecognizable mass of plastic. When Lileala carted it to the pond and unraveled it, she waited for him to explain.

"It's a table cover," he said. "I know there are no tables here but maybe we can get one later. For now, you can place it on the ground, make yourselves more comfortable."

"Great idea, Roloc," Lileala said then signaled for a few other colonists to take a look.

Brian and Martore had been having a conversation in front of the cave. They ended it and joined Lileala.

"Very nice," Brian said. Martore regarded it in silence.

"I knew you'd like it!" Roloc clapped his hands and jumped up and down on one leg, stopping abruptly to pat his knee. It had become arthritic, though Lileala and the others couldn't tell he was suffering. On the rare occasions when he did frown, Lileala wasn't sure if he was upset or simply reacting to the pains.

"What is this anyway?" asked Martore.

"A tablecloth," said Garrette.

Virtue objected. "Well, I don't know about all of you, but I plan to use it as a shield for our hygiene rituals." She nodded at her sister. "We'll hold that up instead of a towel."

"Never mind that for now!" Haliton called out. Carrying the cannister of Mecca, he slow stepped out of the spacecraft with Mernestyle and Bertram behind him, each toting buckets containing tins of powder and several servings of skrull. Lileala joined an assembly of colonists but glanced over their heads, anxious to get her treatment so she could wander the hills and canyons.

The queue was moving slower than usual. Bertram seemed agitated and not in the least interested in his job of doling out the daily Mecca. Put off by the long wait, Lileala wrestled with a string of sketchy visions, coming and going erratically in her mind. The scene fluctuated between a Dogon chief in a tall, checkered mask that resembled a ladder and a busy throng of drumming dancers, more joyous than ever, shimmying in a circle and waving rustic metal pendants and wooden figurines. She observed a few minutes before concentrating hard to clear her head. But the serum? What was taking Bertram so long to pour a few drips of serum?

As soon as she focused and regained her own equilibrium, Lileala noticed the distraction. Trieca, hands on her hips, had planted herself in the doorway of the spacecraft and begun frantically waving her arms. After setting a large clay bowl of skrull on the edge of the pond, Mernestyle left in a hurry.

Lileala, who would have been next to receive her treatment, stepped out of line and joined the procession of colonists and Kclab crew members marching to the spacecraft.

"I have an important matter to share," Trieca said after they all made it to the vessel. "Through our spacecraft's communication device we sometimes get scant messages from Toth and – everyone listen to this – the Coalition is pleased with what they're hearing from all of you, and they are ready to start planning our entry into Swazembi. Our Chief Hardy has been invited to Toth to negotiate with the Coalition. He plans to meet with them in a week."

Applause erupted. Trieca shook her shoulders with delight and continued: "The Coalition has learned, as I predicted, that your condition is improving here. Congratulations, patients. Good job!" She paused. "Questions? Anyone have questions?"

"I do. I want to know how soon we can leave?" It was Osiris. He shot a threatening glance at Trieca, and though she frowned, Lileala felt a glee in Trieca's spirit and began to tap into a string of haphazard thoughts. She picked up that Trieca felt emboldened now, comfortable in her reclaimed strength. She had begun putting extra corn starch in her cotton gowns and stopped covering her neck with fabric. The scarf was a needless accessory that made her feel less defiant. Her days of sorrow were over. In her mind, she was still an enchantress – had always been one. She had even come to appreciate the uniqueness of the hollow circle around her neck. Lileala flinched and shook Trieca's ramblings out of her mind. She eased to the back of the crowd, hoping she could sneak away. Osiris was still awaiting an answer to his question and Lileala was aware that Trieca was dodging it in a sly, edgy manner, not paying attention to much else.

"I want to know when we can leave," Osiris demanded again. "How often do I have to ask you this?"

"You already know the procedure," Trieca hissed. "If you go home as you are now, the problem escalates. Your Coalition knows that and, like I just said, they know we are doing all we can to ensure you are healed."

"But it's still taking too long!" Osiris shouted. "I want you to speed up our cure." The other colonists murmured, but no one else spoke up directly.

"Listen, we have another surprise for all of you today," Trieca went on, ignoring Osiris. She gestured toward Haliton. "You can come forward now."

Haliton walked up with a burlap mail bag which he quickly turned upside down, spilling an array of shirts, jackets, coats and dresses all over the ground.

"Kclaben once had a relationship with a person of high influence from Toth," Trieca said. "We don't deal with him anymore, the traitor. But at one time, he worked closely with us. He goes to more Earth auctions than we do and gave us this clothing."

There was silence.

"Why so quiet?" she asked. "Shouldn't you be happy? On this one day, shouldn't we get a bit of gratitude."

"Thank you," Garrette mumbled. He sauntered over to the pile and began sorting through a bundle of coats.

"Anyone else?" Trieca asked. "How about the privileged Rare Girl? Doesn't she want anything? Where is she? Why isn't she here with everyone else?"

"She's coming," Roloc lied. He squinted and peered through particles of dust.

Lileala had left, assuming Roloc would cover for her. There was more dust in the air than usual, and she knew the Kclabs would have to squint to detect her cloaked form heading in another direction. But she thought she heard Roloc shouting for some reason. Was he warning her that Trieca was watching?

She turned and saw him jumping up and down on his bad knee, waving for her to come back. Leave me be, Lileala thought and kept going. The next sound she heard was a yell for help. Someone on the asteroid was in need and the person's pain swelled up in Lileala's heart. She moved farther along a dirt path, headed to the top of a hill, and tightened her hood around her face to block out the dust. Here, she was far enough away not to be seen, but close enough to feel what was happening in the colony. She heard a loud screech as she tuned in.

In her mind, she could see that Roloc had fallen and that the colonists had dropped everything and run to his side.

"Ahhhhh," Roloc howled, writhing and holding on to his knee.

"What's wrong with Lileala?" Brian was asking. "She's wandering off before she receives her treatment."

"She's fine. Let's help Roloc," Martore told him. "I can't stand watching him suffer." Martore picked a soft robe from the bundle of clothing, folded it, and propped it beneath Roloc's head.

The Wasswa twins were fetching water from the pond and then ripping up a flannel shirt to use as a compress. "We'll wrap it as soon as the swelling goes down," Virtue said.

Roloc was watching her and trying to smile. "You have my gratitude," he said in between groans.

"Tell me," asked Martore. "Why are you so different from the others? They act nice, but you really *are* nice."

His eyes misted. "I don't know. I was like them, well, not quite as irritable, but close. I used to take black ore crystals to calm myself down. Maybe that had a permanent effect, who knows? Maybe that and my knee pain. It hurts so bad I can't even think some days. I think the pain masks my rage."

Brian kneeled down beside him. "Shouldn't you get someone to look at that? A medic, maybe?"

Roloc thought for a moment. "We have chemists, those with skills like Mernestyle and Trieca. That Trieca, she's a genius."

LaJuped approached with Hattie alongside him. "What are you people doing?" he asked. "You better go find Lileala. I heard all that talk about the negotiations being finalized. Now's not the time to get Trieca annoyed."

"She's in a great mood today," Martore said.

"That can change at any time. Believe me, I know."

"And just how do you know so much?" asked Martore.

"Don't worry about that, just find your friend and let her know what's going on. Hattie and I will stay here with Roloc," he said.

Brian, Osiris, Garrette and Martore went to look for Lileala while LaJuped, Hattie and the remaining colonists gathered around Roloc. Lileala watched him look up at them, though he was clearly too dizzy to focus. She felt his ache easing and, as it lifted, he was being overtaken by an odd mix of sensations. From somewhere deep within him, orneriness was creeping along but foaming into a nagging desire for peace. He wrestled a while with the conflicting emotions and then felt a set of hands – or was it four hands? – squeezing drops of milky fluid from a bowl of leftover skrull onto his knee. His anger was fighting to come to the surface, but an eerie calmness was fighting back.

He fell asleep.

The colonists didn't know where Lileala had gone. Nor were they aware that she could still see and hear them. She continued her high watch, remotely viewing their actions and wishing she could stop them from what they did next.

They walked more than twenty minutes along the flat, barren plain, with Osiris leaning against his cane and Martore's feet barely touching the ground, her hair like fragile leaves dancing in the wind. Garrette took one of Martore's hands and she thanked him for the support. But for half a kilometer, there was nothing on their path, and no visible hiding place. To Lileala's relief, this was the sign they probably needed to force them to give up. She knew that most of them thought their quest a waste of time, and she was pleased when she heard them begging Brian to stop. Just before they turned back, Garrette spotted a hill.

"You don't think she went over that, do you?"

"I'm afraid she must have," Brian said.

"But what if she didn't?" asked Martore. "I'm not going any farther."

"Well, I'm going to check." Garrette started up the hill and stopped in his tracks. Everyone could hear the sound of falling pebbles and the crunching of sandals on gravel. They waited. Lileala came over the hilltop and toward the group. Then she froze. Before beginning her descent, a soft warmth surged through her body, and she was met with a recurring sight – the vision of the same burned cathedral she'd seen days ago. Except now it was shrouded in dense smoke. She paused and stared.

"What is it? What's she looking at?" Martore shouted up at Garrette.

"I don't know," Garrette answered. "It's like she's stuck in some sort of nightmare."

Lileala closed her eyes. *What is this?* Lileala asked in her mind. *Why am I constantly being shown this church if no one is going to tell me what it is?* Her body quivering, she fell to her knees and prayed.

"Of one grace, one accord, one protection. To the Grace of the Ancestors, please, what is going on?"

Standing up, the grassless hill beneath her was slick. In her dazed state, she kept going, hoping to escape that drab, singed church. The vision hovered, and after a few more minutes, Lileala stopped again and sat.

"What are you doing?" Brian yelled, loud enough for Lileala to hear. "Are you okay?"

He nudged Martore. "I'm going to get her."

"Leave her. We have time," Martore shouted. Lileala picked up every word.

The distant sun had begun its slow descent into a bleak evening sky. Still, the group waited while Lileala's vision turned into a trance.

Bubbles of intermittent blue light wafted from a window that was no larger than a dinner platter but provided an easy view of the goings and comings inside the old church. Concrete walls were coated in black ash and floors were a worn red cobblestone covered here and there with a smattering of silt-drenched rugs. The room was a meeting place containing a log table and sturdy chairs.

Four men, their bodies cloaked in blue robes sat at the table and one struggled to speak.

"Is this all that is left? A church? Is this all that is to be ours?"

Another man, no, a woman, wearing a sturdy white gown, stood before them holding up a vial of liquid. "No, the church is ours too. You have this," she said, handing him the vial. "This is all we promised you."

Lileala placed both hands on her heart, hoping that would help her understand what she was seeing. The woman's face had a strange opaque quality, and her cheeks and forehead were a patchwork of white smudges.

"Trieca?" A sudden anxiety came over Lileala and she lost the vision.

"What is it?" she demanded. "I need to know! Po Tolo!" she begged. "Tell me, is this you that I'm hearing from? Are these images from your water beings?

Yes, we are here.

Lileala was relieved and elated.

Then came another reply: *No. That image has nothing to do with Po Tolo.*

"What's going on then? Why is this happening?"

You are using your powers in many ways. Your heightened senses probe beyond the ancestors and into spaces we have not penetrated. When we explore it, all we hear is the muffled scorn from your captors, the Kclabs.

"But how can the Kclabs be captors?" Lileala asked. "They have the medicine."

They are your captors, said the Po Tolo beings. *Their rants speak of other captives, and of the remains of a world they destroyed.*

"No, no, you have them wrong! Kclabs don't destroy. They may not always be the easiest people to deal with, but they have good intentions. They're healing us."

Lileala nearly tumbled, ambushed on both sides by Brian and Garrette. Brian caught her and held her close to his chest. "I don't know what's going on with you, but this is scaring us," he said. "You're not well. Come on, so we can get you to safety."

"What are you doing here?" Lileala huffed. "I told you I don't want you spying on me."

"Hush," Brian said. "The Kclabs are closer to securing an entry onto Swazembi. That means they're finishing the cure and we'll soon be out of here. Let's get you back to our little community before they think you're up to something. We can't afford for anything to go wrong."

By the time Lileala and the other colonists had walked the remaining distance back to the settlement, it was late evening and the vague imprint of the sun had already vanished. They were surprised to find the Kclabs still waiting, white silhouettes in the dusk. Roloc was propped against a boulder at least ten meters from the rest of the crew.

Unafraid, Lileala walked out in the open and stood in between Brian and Martore. Mernestyle gasped.

"Have you been hiding from us?" Mernestyle asked. "Why? Haven't we been more than fair?"

Lileala looked at her but didn't see her. She was looking through her to a different time and place.

Again, she saw John. Her body ached. She was John, lying on a pallet of rags, tossing and bleeding in a shack with a mud floor. The wood of the shack had cracks that were splitting into larger cracks that were spreading into gaping holes. The ceiling sagged and there was no door. With Della away in the fields, all John could do was lie there, on the verge of death.

His agony consumed Lileala, slicing through her mind, her legs, her arms. She fought to sit up and went into convulsions. John's pain was like nothing she'd ever felt.

Again, she collapsed.

* * *

Two purple eyes beamed down at Lileala.

"What are you doing?" she asked. Her head felt like a boulder, and she was having trouble lifting it.

"Don't you worry. Just rest." Lileala recognized LaJuped's voice. Her head rested on his lap, and he sat on the ground, watching her come in and out of a dizzying stupor. She tried to lift her head again. "Not now," LaJuped said sharply. He was wiping her forehead with a damp cloth.

Lileala felt the ground spin and grind to a halt. She noticed Martore and Hattie standing beside LaJuped, but they spoke in a tone that was too soft for her to hear.

"Don't worry about me," Lileala said, struggling to pull up to a sitting position. "Take care of the boy. Please, he needs help."

"Stay down," LaJuped ordered. "Right now, you're the one who needs help."

"But the boy, John. What about the boy? Where is he?" she asked, voice desperate.

"Who, Lileala? Where is who?"

"The young man. Della's son. I told you, he needs help." Lileala was shaking.

"You're seeing things, losing strength. You slept out here all night. The Kclabs were so worried they stayed over last night in their shed. That's the first time they've ever done that."

She quieted down. She was in a scattered state and could just barely see LaJuped above her, a hazy, bent figure, giving her orders. He was abrupt and distant.

But where's the boy? she thought. If only she could get him to care for that young man. "John," she said out loud. "Please help John."

LaJuped shot her a mean look. "You're still half dazed," he said, making no effort to feign patience.

Lileala caught a strong whiff of wind and tried again to pull herself up, using slow, strained movements. The vision was gone, and her mind was silent. She sat erect and watched the steady march of Martore's braids.

"You're coming out of it. That's good," Martore said and smiled. "This is the second time I've seen you like this. You're not well."

"It's probably just an adjustment phase," LaJuped said. He dropped the cloth into a bucket of water, wrung it out and placed it on her forehead. The cold water trickled down her eyes and nose.

"I thought that at first, but not now," Martore argued. "I didn't go through this and neither did you. She says things I don't understand. She's seeing things, having hallucinations of some sort."

"I'm okay now," Lileala said. "I'm alert. I can see both of you and I can hear you." She stroked her neck and head. The ache had turned into a dull throb. "You can leave me now. Seriously, I appreciate all you've done for me, but I'm fine now."

"I'm staying," said LaJuped. "I've been instructed not to leave your side." He continued bathing Lileala's forehead.

"Instructed?" Martore was indignant. "Who gave you such instructions?"

"Mernestyle and Trieca told me to watch her. None of the Kclabs left. They're still here."

"They really are investing in us," Martore said. "When this is over, I think the Coalition should give them a special reward."

LaJuped didn't answer, but Lileala noticed that his eyes had changed from purple to red. From what Brian had told her about LaJuped's people, she realized his eye color was changing every few pulse beats, indicating a severe mood swing. She suspected he was on edge. His face twitched and he talked faster than normal. He paced about in a circle, sat down again, then reached in his robe pocket for a thin folded strip. It looked like writing paper, rolled up into a tight wad. LaJuped squeezed the center and a teeny flame appeared on the paper's tip. He puffed on the thing, breathing in and out as if he needed it to survive.

"I guess you've never seen a cigarette," he said to Lileala

and Martore. "On Dolu, my people inhale these." He blew out a noxious stream of smoke. "It's a habit, you know, helps us to relax."

Curious about LaJuped's peculiar habit, Lileala sat up to watch. With each puff, his pupils switched back and forth from red to a brilliant green. Lileala wasn't bothered but she sensed that Martore was repulsed. "Your pupils are changing colors," Martore said. "What is going on?"

"Your hair is wiggling," he answered. "What's going on with you?"

Martore laughed and patted him on the shoulder.

"Now that's a surprise," she scoffed. "I never thought of you as clever enough to say anything funny."

A look of scorn crossed LaJuped's face. "I'll stay with this Rare Girl if you don't mind," he said. His eyes had turned brown, and his demeanor had an authoritative quality. Martore gave up and walked away. LaJuped looked up at the sky and Lileala knew he was wishing for a glimpse at the sun. It had come and gone that day in just one hour. "Hey girlie," he said to her. "Tell LaJuped what is going on. Why are you hallucinating?"

"I'm doing better," Lileala said. She gawked at him, unsure what to think. One minute he was callous and the next he seemed like a friend.

"You had a terrific spill out there, falling and talking out of your head. Tell me, who you were talking to? What did you see?"

"Nothing. I'm just adjusting. You said so yourself."

"No. You're doing more than adjusting. You have some secret. All of the colony can see that. You're changing here. And you've discovered a place to hide."

Lileala raised herself off the ground and found a seat on a nearby boulder. "And how do you know that I hide?"

"I know it. Everyone knows it."

"I hide so that I can go deeper within, so I can learn."

LaJuped squatted in a patch of pebbles. "Learn what? From whom?"

"From the voices. Just like Martore said, I hear them all the time and see visions. I feel them as if I'm living in the madness of a dream."

"Tell me," LaJuped pressed further. "Is this normal where you come from? Does everyone experience this?"

"There are just a few of us, I'm told."

His eyes danced. They were purple again and so intense Lileala wondered if he could see right through her skin. "What do you see?"

"You wouldn't understand."

"Maybe I would. Maybe if we go for a walk, you can explain it."

"Maybe," Lileala said, but she felt an eerie sensation as she and LaJuped walked toward the pond. She saw Brian standing beside a tower of boulders nearly forty meters away; she sensed he wanted to tell her something. LaJuped inhaled smoke through the skinny white paper, then noticed Brian and waved.

"Where does your mind travel and what does it see?"

"I have a clairvoyance, but it's all new to me and I'm still being surprised all the time. It's overwhelming, the way it just comes on me suddenly. I see so much pain. I feel it through the melanin bearers who lived on the Earth. But today I..."

"Yes, go on." LaJuped's eyes turned orange.

"Don't tell the Kclabs, but today, I think I saw Trieca," Lileala said. "It was bewildering. She was standing with some strange men in a building that had been torched."

Lileala and LaJuped moved closer to the rock tower.

"Are you sure it was Trieca?"

"Yes, I'm fairly certain. And it didn't feel right. The situation she was in seemed sinister. I don't know what it means yet, but I'm going to warn the others, let them know there's more going on than we think."

"Remarkable," said LaJuped.

She continued: "But I've only seen Trieca that one time. Mostly it's the original melanin bearers from Earth. I'm gaining strength from them and they're gaining it from me. That's why I go to the cliff."

"The cliff?"

"It's a crater, really. I found it accidentally one evening when I went too far south where the path of rock comes to a dead end. I climbed a hill and found a passageway that cut straight through a cave."

Lileala arrived at the boulder tower and stood before Brian. "Would you like to join us?" she asked him.

"Who is 'us'?" Brian posed the question like an angry statement. "Who would you like me to join?"

"Us, LaJuped and me." She whirled around, searching. She looked at Brian, startled.

"He was just here. Brian, you saw him. He was just…"

Brian nudged Lileala and pointed toward a pebbled trail. LaJuped was running as if under siege. "He ran off a few minutes ago."

"But why? Why would he do that?"

"He left you because he got what he wants. Several meters before you reached me, he disappeared. I knew he would and that's why I watched you. He was excited about something, something you were naïve enough to tell him, no doubt. I could tell by the expression on his face."

"Oh no. Oh no!"

"Don't worry. Let's see where he's going." Brian and Lileala scrambled down the path, but LaJuped had an ample lead, and they had a hard time keeping up. He turned down another trail and almost slipped out of sight.

"There he is!" Lileala said. "I think I see the back of his head near that boulder on the right."

They followed. He slowed his pace and meandered for a couple of yards. On one side, the path split into two. Lileala held her breath. Ahead, on a skinny, bending pole hung a large sign: NO KELOIDS ALLOWED.

"We should hide," she said.

"He won't notice us," Brian whispered. "We're too far behind him and he hasn't looked back once."

LaJuped trotted to the end of the trail and stood before a long, rectangular shelter made up of shabby, wooden planks and a corrugated metal roof. Peering from behind a boulder, Brian and Lileala watched LaJuped pull on a metal lever and waited while a wide, blue tube snaked its way through a hole in the front door. He lifted it to his mouth to it and shouted, "Trieca! Mernestyle! The girl has linked you to a building that had been annihilated. I don't know what it means but it's in her mind and she thinks it's real. Come out and I'll tell you more. Trieca? Anybody? Are you there?"

Brian grabbed Lileala's hand, tugged it. "Let's go," he said. "Now!" Brian sprinted ahead and Lileala ran behind him. She remembered her dream and ran faster. Her lungs filled with air, and she gulped. Brian stopped, waited for her and together they picked up speed.

From afar, they could hear LaJuped screaming: "Finish my cure now, and I'll tell you exactly where she hides!"

Inside the shed, one of the Kclabs chortled and several others argued about whether or not to let LaJuped inside.

"Go and open the door," Mernestyle said. "I want to hear what he knows."

"Not now, I get the feeling someone's watching," Trieca said. "Let him yell. I want to make sure he's alone. And besides, I have another plan to discuss, and I don't want him around."

"Yes," Bertram said. "We're waiting."

Trieca pulled an optic of Lileala from the pocket on the front of her gown. She lifted the flimsy disc up as high as her arms would allow and made it a point to turn and face Bertram.

"If you ever doubted me, and I know you have," she said directly to Bertram, "here's evidence of why you should hold your tongue. I got this from the lab that day I demonstrated the potency of Mecca. I hung it, but the chief had it taken down. So, I kept it."

Bertram was more nervous than impressed. "We're nearing a truce. Why would you need an image of their Rare Indigo?"

The glance Trieca gave him was rather hostile.

"She's the one who's most important to them, isn't she? Why would I bother getting an image of someone else?"

"Okay. But what for?"

"Don't be coy," Mernestyle broke in. "This woman is their coveted prize. She's leverage."

"We don't want leverage!" Bertram shouted loud enough to drown out LaJuped's raucous screeching. "We want fairness! We want to be admitted into their lands and the only way to do it is with the cure – not, not some foolish blackmail scheme."

"Who said anything about blackmail?" Trieca retorted. An amused smile formed on her lips. "This is the proof we'll use, don't you understand? We'll send this to let them know she's fine. I want them to know that just because we're close to an agreement, there's still no need to visit."

"*Are* they coming to visit?" Haliton asked. "This is the first I've heard about it."

"No, they're not. But at one point, about a week and a half ago I think, I did hear from the spy that they were planning to," said Mernestyle. "He's the one who talked them out of it."

The mention of the spy made Trieca flinch. Since her setback, she had refused to talk to him and only knew what was going on when Mernestyle brought it to her attention.

"Glad he's still of some help," she said bitterly. "But we don't know how long he can hold them back. Until we can wrap things up, we need to take extra precautions, do something that says, 'the colonists are okay, don't fret'."

"I don't know." Bertram still seemed hesitant. "How did you get the Rare Indigo's optic in the first place?"

"Never mind that," Trieca answered. "If you don't know, they won't either. They'll have to assume we created it. Get it?

A brand-new image of her, healing and resting in our colony."

"The whole idea scares me," Haliton said. "What if the Coalition finds out you had the optic all along? They might stop trusting us and think we're plotting something and not trying to cure her at all. Or any others for that matter."

"We aren't just trying, we're succeeding. That's what we want to show them," Trieca said. "They have no way of knowing this is an old image. How would they?"

"They won't," added Mernestyle. "I mean, the girl is healing, so why shouldn't we send this to the Coalition as proof?"

"But if the girl *is* getting better, why use an old image?" Haliton asked.

"'Cause optic flashes don't work here," Mernestyle reminded him.

"Save your breath." Trieca laughed and glanced at Mernestyle. "Stop explaining and show them, please."

Mernestyle held up a thin mirror that contained a permanent reflection of the laboratory on Kclaben.

"You see this?" she asked. "Well, of course I can superimpose the Rare Indigo into this setting. After I fuse them, we'll have a convincing new optic that shows her getting well in a nice laboratory, so professional it's even equipped with optic capabilities. No one has to know what it's actually like here."

"I still don't get it," Bertram said. "They know they're not allowed on the asteroid. That's part of the pact."

"You don't understand humans very well, do you?" said Trieca. "They say one thing and then they walk it back. We don't want that. We want them to keep trusting and continue waiting. We can't have anyone suddenly showing up, poking around and getting hold of our Mecca. Get it?"

"Got it!" chimed in Mernestyle and Haliton.

Bertram still wasn't so sure. "So… this is just a precaution?"

"Correct," Trieca answered.

"So…" he went on, "who's going to get this optic to Toth?"

"I think I'll send you and Mernestyle. Just do it quickly.

We'll return to Kclaben tomorrow morning and doctor up the optic. Then all you have to do is fly to Toth, make the delivery and come right back."

"Good plan, Trieca," Haliton said. "I think this can work."

Trieca didn't reply.

LaJuped's voice outside was getting more strained and she didn't know how much longer he could hold out. She glanced at the door and waved at Mernestyle.

"He's waited long enough. Let him in."

7

"Warriors of the spirit are not worriers in the spirit."
        – Swazembian Proverb

There was an unusual amount of activity in the Interplanetary Center for Analytics on Toth and the normally placid facility was packed with researchers, astronomers, astral physicists, biomedical experts. All manner of authorities representing planets from across the galaxy had flown in for a weekend conference intended to address the Coalition's greatest dilemmas – the troublesome keloids and the grave mystery surrounding the missing planet.

Otto found the whole thing sickening. It was the second day and all that had resulted so far was a bunch of theories and streams of confusing data flowing through stuffy knowledge chambers. By midafternoon, Otto was ready to give up. If the best star gazers and chemists in the Coalition had failed, then there wasn't much the Scientific Pineal Crew could do.

He'd always trusted his peers. Though some of the engineers and excavators were based on Toth and the rest stationed on Swazembi, they were a team – a damn good one, he thought. But they had reconfigured the programs in the healing oscillators on Swazembi a dozen times. And still, they'd ended up with nothing but hand wringing. Their morale had declined as a result. Patience was short and tempers were high. And this conference of errors wasn't helping.

Most of the afternoon, Otto had dawdled in the foyer, doing a bit of nonchalant people-watching. Peers passed and he'd greet them half-heartedly, but mostly just keep his head down, making it clear he was in an antisocial mood.

The foyer doubled as an assembly area that drew some individuals he wanted to avoid. He sat on a long bench in an empty corner and stretched out his legs. The site was becoming crowded, and the blare of loud and constant chatter was an assault to his ears. Still, it was much roomier than the knowledge chambers and it provided an escape from meaningless panel discussions. At least here he didn't have to listen.

He massaged his eyes and forehead, trying to remember what life was like before Lileala's crisis. It would be nice to recall it, to feel it. But he couldn't do that either. Nothing about this conference was conducive to reflection. How could it be with so much irritating, non-stop commotion?

Otto left his seat and wandered over to a far wall to clear his mind and survey the screens of various planet landscapes. From one side of the wall to the other, magnified views of rivers, mountain ranges and valleys were spread, superimposed with the circumference depth and the longitude and latitude of all twenty-two Coalition planets. All except one. The absent Golong planet. The planet's title was emblazoned above the screen, but beneath it was dead space – an empty black void dotted with stars.

Otto cracked his knuckles and tilted his head sideways, gently stretching out the tension in his neck. He reluctantly returned to his bench seat in time to hear a familiar voice that made him feel slightly encouraged. Ellis Bourka, Toth's new Chief of Building Regulations, was preparing to address the gathering.

"I've been told to ask everyone to take a seat and to compose their questions as quickly as possible," he was saying. "The more organized we are, the quicker we can finish."

Finally, Otto thought. He plopped down on the bench and sat at attention, hopeful but curious as to why Ellis was the speaker. He hadn't found him that impressive back when the two were both enrolled in a mind-science course on Toth. Otto had mastered the class along with his Pineal Crew engineering requirements, but Ellis had not. He'd always wondered how Ellis had made it so far career wise, as he wasn't close to being the most insightful student.

Otto decided he was going to give Ellis the benefit of the doubt, but as he listened to him field questions, all he felt was aggravation. Why wasn't anything working? After the oscillator had failed to revert keloid tissue back to its natural state, the Scientific Pineal Crew made unsuccessful attempts to alter a culture of keloid cells using an archaic cryotherapy technique. No one, even with all the specialists in the room, seemed to have an adequate alternative to offer.

Otto's breathing escalated, and he began fidgeting. He wanted everyone to shut up already, particularly Ellis. His talk sounded more like rhetoric than anything else. Instead of solutions, he was explaining how a substance he'd discovered could bend building materials and make them more pliable.

"But can this substance help us cure keloids?" someone asked.

When Ellis said no, Otto got up to leave but was stopped by Kwesi. "Sit down, officer, and wait. It's a dud of a meeting so far. This young man, Ellis, I don't know what he's talking about, but let's hear him out anyway."

After Ellis finished, he headed toward Otto. "Waves of joy, officer! Didn't we attend school together?" He gave him a firm handshake.

"Yes." Otto shrugged. "I was surprised that you switched to architecture. How did that happen?"

"Long story, and I'm not going to bore you with it," Ellis went on. "But listen, I thought I saw you at the last meeting, the one on Toth, but I couldn't get your attention."

"Sorry. I was too tired and distracted. I guess you know that it's my Lileala in that damn colony. Eighteen days now and we still haven't come up with a damn thing."

Ellis cleared his throat. "I didn't realize. I mean I knew about the girl, the Rare Indigo, I just didn't realize the two of you were –"

"To be joined, yes."

"Joined? Well, well, you will be one lucky man!"

"Will be?" Otto was miffed.

"I mean, when she's cured, of course. She won't be stuck there forever. Anyway, the Kclabs will be part of the Coalition soon, so what will it matter?"

The comment ripped through Otto, but he kept talking. "If the Coalition doesn't finish those negotiations soon, I'm going to go to that place and retrieve her myself."

"You'll do nothing of the sort!" Kwesi ordered. "That would only make things worse!"

Otto glared at Kwesi. "I think we're being too complacent, that's all."

"Dammit, Otto. We have to finish our talks with the Kclabs, make sure we're all on the right track. And we have given them time. They're the only ones who can heal this malady."

"Yes, but what if they don't? Then what?"

"Then," said Kwesi, "Lileala and all of the other colonists will return home and be stuck with a condition that could cause them a lifetime of pain and embarrassment."

"Excuse me for butting in," Ellis said, dismissing Otto's discomfort, "but I have something you need to see."

Ellis walked back to the podium and returned with a palm-sized metal case. He pressed it gently and an optic popped up on the front.

Otto's face lit up. "Lileala? That's Lileala! Where did you get that? Where was it taken?"

"Looks like a laboratory in the background. It's a bit crude, the facility, but not bad. I was told that the Kclab who delivered it said it was taken at the treatment center."

"On the asteroid?" asked Otto, reaching for the optic. "I thought devices didn't work there."

"Apparently this one did," he said. "Pretty nice, huh? It arrived on Toth yesterday, and when a Sonaguard brought it to the Coalition office, I was the only one there. No one else has seen it yet."

Kwesi grabbed it from Otto and inspected it from all angles. "Just look at her! Happy and not a scar in sight!"

"I'm stunned," said Otto. "When were you going to let us know?"

"I told you, it only just arrived." Ellis sounded flustered. "I was going to pass it to the Coalition now."

"Never mind, just give it to me," said Otto. He kept staring at it. "Seems like she's okay... But damnit, when will she be home?"

"I thought I'd heard that people on the asteroid have been writing their homeworlds and saying they're doing just fine? And, in fact, getting better by the day," said Ellis. "They can't seem to say enough good things about the Kclabs."

"We know that!" Otto snapped. "It's just not moving fast enough."

"Be calm. Please," Kwesi snapped. "We're all anxious, Otto. How do you think I feel? I've watched my daughter go to some remote galaxy-forsaken place. Her elder Ma's so ill she barely leaves home. Did you know that? Have you ever thought about what this has done to Fanta and me?"

Otto didn't answer. He felt ashamed, but it faded seconds later, replaced by more frustration and self-pity. "I'm sorry, but I'm coping as best I can."

"It does seem futile, though," added Ellis. "It's odd that the Coalition can't control something that's being so easily cured by a group of primitives."

Anger flared in Otto's eyes. Something about that remark, the casual tone: *cured by a group of primitives*?

"What makes you so sure we won't come up with something equally effective?" Otto snapped. He was trying his best not to challenge Ellis to a verbal confrontation – in violation of the Swazembi-Toth pact.

Sensing tension, Ellis tapped his chin and shrugged his shoulders before stepping out of their way. Kwesi turned to Otto.

"I know you're not sleeping. Fanta and I aren't sleeping either. But remember, Lileala is supposed to be a seer. She is going to be okay."

"I'm trying to believe that," Otto said. "I was going to leave but I think I'll stay and wait for more answers." He plopped down in a vacant chair and examined Lileala's optic. It was really her, that much he was sure, dressed in a heavy black robe, sitting in a treatment center run by a species with sparse technology. And smiling. Was she really that content? He flipped the metal image on its back and tried instead to see her in his memory, in his arms in full blown Shimmer, but he couldn't.

He jumped to his feet as a Sonaguard burst into the room, shouting. He ran toward Otto.

"This is for you," he said, breathless. "I believe it's a letter from Lileala."

Dear Otto:

My love, I can only send you mild waves of joy but I want you to know I am better than before. So if you're worrying, please know that the keloids are shrinking, and I don't agonize over them any longer. I'm getting strong, Otto. I've practiced time and again the art of stilling my mind. It's a practice Ahonotay taught me. During our visit, she showed me how to hold the image of golden red beaches, the greens and the blues wafting across the Surface. It's comforting, but sometimes it makes me ache because I so miss being home.

My emotions bleed, Otto, and my body and soul now know what it's like to endure pain. Real pain, Otto. You know that sting you felt after you cut your hand? Remember? You had fallen against one of your Baba's old-time woodcrafting tools and had to be rushed to the top of Blue Barrell and lift your hand up to be healed in the vapors?

If you remember that pain, Otto, then try to prolong that memory. Now, prolong it further. That sensation would be barely a prick to the ancestors who endured so much more. What I'm trying to Say is that I have walked roads you have never known and when I return you will not know me. I am so different you won't understand me and we would be such a bad match. I have opinions, so many of them and I don't feel at all suited to flaunt myself at parties, to behave as if beauty is some type of medal My love. this concerns me greatly. What I'm saying is that I can no longer fit in your world.

Otto, I am no longer the Lileala you knew and the things I once called problems, how I would laugh at them now. I will return to Swazembi soon and when I do I will be a stealthier being with a spirit that has deepened and a desire to impart my new wisdom.

For that reason, I can no longer be your devoted one Otto. I'm so sorry, but I love you enough to let you go. I love you too much to hold you captive, to force you into the shadows of what I hope to achieve. I want you to find someone who can stand tall before the cascading colors and not question why she must remain on Swazembi. Find someone, Otto, whose spirit is as untouched as mine once felt. Do not write me, and do not trouble the Toths for mail, for I will not etch another letter.

This is goodbye.

Lileala.

8

"Adversity is a muse wearing a clever disguise."
– From the journals of Ahonotay

A small fire was crackling, sending ribbons of smoke into the dark, chilled air. Several colonists sat around it, enjoying the bursts of warmth. This was the first fire they had created, and they had done it as a team, collecting wooden writing utensils that had broken, discarded letters and torn garments found in the pile of Earth clothes. One piece was a tattered coat, made from a rough, scratchy fabric. In its deepest pocket, Brian had discovered a handful of hardwood cubes, perfect for kindling a fire, and Lileala had rummaged through her satchel and pulled out one of the matches Roloc had given her.

By striking it against a flint of iron rock, they generated a flame that made them cheer. It felt magical to them. Their first accomplishment as a unified colony. Their first collective project. They hugged one another and smiled, despite their inner turmoil. It had been thirty-five days for some of them, twenty-eight for Lileala. With the exception of LaJuped, Hattie and a few malcontents, they were like family now. They leaned on one another as they huddled around their fire, wondering out loud why the asteroid had developed such a cold front.

"I guess it's what they call the frost season," said elder Osiris. "We don't get this where I come from. It's warm all the time. Don't believe we've ever known cold on KaBa."

"Well, luckily, it's only this way at night," said Lileala. She scooted closer to Brian, hoping the body heat would add a little more warmth.

"At least the cold brought us together," said Martore. "And now that we have a bit of light, we don't have to go to bed so early. I was tired of saying prayers and then, as soon as the sun dips, rushing off to that cramped cave."

"I wish I had my dial," said Lileala. "That would have kept me occupied and I could have stayed in touch with my parents and friends. I think I'd share more than I talk about in my letters, you know, about my visions."

"Oh, good," said Martore, a mix of bitterness and sarcasm in her voice. "We get to hear about more visions."

Brian shot her a sharp glance. "Martore, please," he said, then turned his attention to Lileala. "We want to hear more about them, I mean if you can handle it without it being too emotional."

Lileala laced her fingers and spoke slowly. Martore's comment had made her uneasy.

"I'm not going to bother you with most of it," she said. "They're my ancestors, mostly, but there's something that's really troubling me about the Kclabs."

"Kclabs?" Martore said. "I thought we were talking about visions."

"We are. I saw Trieca in one of them and I'm telling you it was worrisome. She was in an old burned up house and she seemed to be out of control."

Elder Osiris laughed. "That woman's always out of control. That's her personality."

"Seriously?" Brian added. "That's your big vision? Trieca and her antics?"

"Brian, everyone, listen. These weren't just antics and temper tantrums," Lileala said. "There's something going on. I just don't know what it is. I don't know if we should continue trusting them."

"Lileala," Brian went on. "You know how much I respect you, but if I can be honest, those hallucinations worry me. You're jumping from one to another. And now, the Kclabs are involved too? Come on, Lileala. They've been nice to us. Look at us; we're practically keloid free!"

"*That's* what we should be toasting!" Honor pitched in. "I'm not worried about the Kclabs. They're the ones who saved us. And how long do we have here, anyway, maybe another week?"

Feeling defeated, Lileala changed the subject. "You're right," she said. "We are healing and it's because of them. Maybe I read that vision all wrong. Guess I shouldn't have brought it up."

"I want to hear more about Swazembi, not Kclaben," Garrette piped up. "Can we get back to those dial things? How do they work?"

"They light up," Martore explained. "We use them on Toth. If you think of someone strongly, you summon them, they feel you contacting them, and their image appears on your wrist."

"Now, that's a much better topic," Brian added, winking at Lileala. "Are they dependable?"

"Yes, unless the person you're trying to reach is busy." Lileala shrugged. She was thinking of Otto juggling meetings and wondering if he had received her last letter. Just the thought of him reading it made her solemn.

"I'm also told that in your home world you have rainbow waterfalls, kind of like the rains of my world but with color," Brian went on. "Is that true?"

"Sometimes," Lileala mused. She looked up at the black sky, remembering. "When the rains come, they're all sorts of pretty colors, but they turn into vapors and most never hit the ground." She spoke quickly before anyone could ask a question. "The colors last all the time, all year round, but they're even more intense during the rainy seasons. But it's only that way on the Surface. In the rural areas, rain is just rain."

"I wish we could get some of that 'just rain' here," Martore mumbled. She was massaging her cold fingers and fussing over the dry cracks that were spreading across the palms of her hands. "And I wish I had cream for my hands and feet," she complained. Then she noticed Lileala observing her.

"My, we're vain, aren't we?" There was a mocking sarcasm in Lileala's tone. It gave her satisfaction to see Martore fretting over her appearance. She looked at her and smiled.

"Okay, forget the cream," Martore said. She peered into the fire and shook a cold breeze away from her shoulders. "But a little rain would be nice." She looked around. "It probably would turn to ice here, but that would be okay too. I don't know if anyone has noticed but the pond is starting to shrink."

"Yes. It's starting to get gooky," Garrette said.

"What?" Lileala laughed. "What's 'gooky'?"

"There's a corner that's starting to look like gook," he said, annoyed by the teasing. "Haven't you seen it?"

Brian shook his head to suppress a laugh. "We'll try not to drink from that section, young one."

"I'm serious," Garrette protested. "Most of it is frozen and the rest is gunk."

"Shhh," Lileala said. "I have something to show everyone. When you see this, you'll stop worrying about that pond and that other stuff – what was it? You know that weird chalky stuff we had to eat a few nights ago?"

"Skrull," the twins said in unison.

"Well, watch this," Lileala said. She reached into her pocket and pulled out something that was around the length and diameter of a baby tooth.

"It's a seed," she added. "A friend on Swazembi gave me this robe and her devoted must have placed these seeds in the pockets. I had no idea that I even had them until one day when I was standing by the cliff, and I happened to push my hands deeper into the pockets. I kept hearing about them before, that they were special. Out of curiosity, I thought I'd plant one to see what happened."

"And, what happened?" Osiris leaned forward.

"It produced right away. I was trying to plant it, but as soon as it hit the soil, it just... sprouted!"

The colonists scoffed at Lileala's comments and called her ridiculous. Osiris slapped his knee and laughed out loud. "Was this another one of your visions?"

But Lileala didn't say another word about the seed. She simply tossed it and waited as it landed a foot from the fire and began creating a rumble, stirring the soil. The group fell silent. The rumble continued, and the soil rose in spurts, moving like some small creature pushing from beneath the ground. Then it quieted, and the sharp stem of a vegetable plant knifed its way through the dirt.

Honor was the first one to react. While everyone else sat and stared, she stood up. "This is a little frightening. Between this and the talk about visions, I think I'd better leave." She asked her sister if she was ready to go to the cave, but Virtue ignored her and remained seated, mesmerized by the strange eruption.

Lileala walked towards where the seed landed and tugged, pulling up an oblong yellow squash. The colonists shrieked. They all started talking at one time.

"I'm bewildered!" Brian said. "But thank you, Lileala. You never cease to amaze me."

For the first time since they met, Osiris looked at her with admiration. "And here I thought you were crazy. But this – this, is something." He stretched his long fingers over the squash and stroked it to make sure it was real.

"I don't know what this means," Lileala said. "I've never seen this happen before. But you have to admit," she held up the squash, "this is going to taste a lot better than those nutrient powders."

Everyone laughed, including Honor, and the colonists continued to chat and share stories about their home worlds.

"I guess this is an ongoing night of mystery," Martore volunteered. There was a self-satisfaction in her statement that made Lileala tense. "This fire and Lileala's seeds aren't the only creation here that was brought on by the cool weather." She glanced at Virtue and seemed to gloat. "The Wasswa sisters have created sweaters; did you know that? Sweaters from their own hair!"

Virtue, who was sitting sideways on her knees, began rocking, something Lileala noticed that she always did when she was embarrassed or trying to appear humble. She was shy and didn't like showing off. Lileala nudged Honor because she knew she didn't mind.

"We're wearing them," Honor said, stroking the curly fibers of her sweater. Then she pulled off her headwrap and touched the tight coils of hair. Her long braids were now a short curly mass, much closer to her scalp than when she first arrived.

"Wooly hair is perfect for knitting," she said. "She tugged on one sleeve and held it up to her cheeks.

"Can I touch it. Please can I touch it?" Garrette squealed. Everyone gawked, but his hand shot up first and he was leaning across Osiris, reaching.

"Sure, I'm quite proud of it," she said. "You can make one yourself too, from your own hair. I'll show you how. Maybe later though, not right away."

Martore avoided the sweater and instead peered at Honor as if expecting more information. "Why do you lie?" Martore asked. Her eyes were intense, but her voice was gentle.

Honor said nothing. All the joy had drained from her face, and she wore a look of sheer terror. "My name is Honor," she said, and her eyes welled with tears. "I do not lie."

"Then forgive me for pointing one out," Martore said. "Just as you struggle to speak lies, my eyes struggle to avoid them."

Tears dampened Honor's cheeks, and for the second time that night, she prepared to leave.

"Please, don't go! Please stay." Lileala jumped up to defend her. "Martore what have you done?"

"We had help, okay!" Honor cried. "I-I am guilty of a small lie, a very small lie of omission."

She tried walking away and Lileala blocked her path. "Stop crying. Please. What's wrong?"

Honor wiped her eyes and Virtue looked at the ground. "I'm ashamed," Honor said. "We took credit for something we don't even understand. We don't know the source of this ability. Our elder Ma taught us how to see flame when we prayed. She said she learned it from a woman she had befriended during a trip to Swazembi. The woman had the darkest of skin, like a High Indigo, like the Rare Ones."

She stopped and pointed to Lileala. "Like you. And when she visited my elder Ma in her dome, she didn't speak. She used her hands to demonstrate and point, then she handed us bark paper that contained instructions that my elder Ma was never to share her secret with anyone. The mute Indigo came to her every night for four nights, helping my elder Ma practice. When she returned home, she practiced for weeks before she taught it to us. Nothing happened at first, but Virtue and I kept trying. After a while, we could conjure up a tiny flame behind our eyes. This is the way Virtue and I made these sweaters, one night while everyone else was asleep. We can't teach this because we don't understand it ourselves and we were told never to talk about it by my elder."

"That's okay," Lileala said. "I'm sorry too. In my home world we call this the flame breath or the trinity breath and, you're right, we are pretty closed about it. We don't share it a lot and we only use it for… I'm ashamed to say it, but we use it for cosmetic purposes."

She glanced at Martore. "You tried to tell me this, didn't you? When I arrived, you implied that we abused this power."

"I didn't mean harm," Martore said. "I just wanted it known that trinity breath isn't just for Shimmer. Honestly, I didn't mean to wound the sisters."

Lileala and Virtue stood and hugged Honor. Martore, who had quickly run to her side, hugged her too.

"Can I suggest something?" Brian asked, carefully observing

the twins. "If you don't mind, I'd like to suggest that we share all of our talents and figure out a way to benefit from them, just like we did this fire."

"But how?" Lileala asked. "I've only used it to produce Shimmer."

"Lileala, you can teach us what you know, and we'll practice," said Martore.

Honor and Virtue settled back down, and the colonists examined their sweaters, studying the mastery of the sisters' technique and the bulky texture of the fibers.

Brian moved next to Honor and placed his hand on her shoulder.

"I'll learn too," he said. "I have a small nail-cutting device that I can sharpen. If we all give ourselves haircuts then before this cold season ends we'll all have new sweaters, not just junk from that Earth rag pile. Even you, Martore. You think you can part with your fluttering braids?" Martore agreed and Brian continued. "Let's sleep. We've got a big day coming up."

"What?" asked Garrette. "Is it letter writing time?"

"No, no, something better." Brian had a sly grin on his face. "It's the skrull. My fellow colonists, the next time we get another bowl of the skrull, we won't have to eat it." He glanced at Lileala. "We can have squash."

9

"This tribe defies all understanding. They live on a cliff in mud dwellings that lack basic, modern comforts and yet their knowledge of the cosmos is far greater than the volumes of data collected by our most powerful telescope and most advanced satellite in space."
– A scientific notation found on a road near a Dogon Village, Author Unknown

The fear on her face had frozen into a mouth that could not smile, and eyes that would not blink. In stark silence, the barefoot child scampered across warm, parched land. The house she'd left behind, a three-room square of bricks beneath a low cement roof, had erupted in flames and she had fled without a whimper, escaping through a side door hatch and running all alone through streets tinted with smoke.

The sight of her running, the lack of emotion in her listless stare, made Lileala clench her teeth. A siren was sounding, and with it, an announcement:

"Evacuate now. Leave your homes and report to shelters. Stay clear of anything that reads 'no keloids allowed'. That is the forbidden zone."

The little girl ran amid the clamor, and though Lileala didn't feel the jolt this time, she became the child, went inside her, absorbed her utter terror.

With numbed awareness, she darted past a charred church that was coated with ashes and soot. Particles of the soot, like flakes of black snow, landed on her lashes. Lileala stopped to blot them and kept going. *Several yards ahead of her, a hefty chunk of cement lay on top of a bed of dirt. A dozen or so children sat in front of it, on singed blocks of cinder and oil cans that were dented on the sides.*

Lileala, moving in the child's pained spirit, made a breathless dash toward an empty crate and sat, tugging on the burned, splintering wood. She waited in stoic silence until beings with transparent faces waded through the soot that dusted the air and took their places on the cement.

"For weeks we have trained you for this moment," said one of them, the woman with splotches on clear cheeks. "You have learned well. Except..." She paused and her face seemed to tilt toward Lileala for what seemed like a very long ten seconds. Lileala's spirit squirmed about in the child's body. She knew that stare, those markings.

"Now is the time we have prepared you for," Trieca said. "We have led you through many, but those were drills. This is not a drill."

"I hate you," a small boy wheezed, breathing in particles of ash. "I want my elder Ma. Where is my ma?" His pleas coursed through the wind and died.

"We trained you for this," Trieca said. "And we told you this day would come. If you wanted to be with your elder Ma, you should have been around when we led the adults into the shelters. How am I to find her now?"

More whimpers flooded the hot air, followed by fits of sneezing. And a loud, piercing cry.

"Everything you know as planet Golong has been eradicated," Trieca went on. "Your forebears have reported to shelters, and from this day on, you will remain here. There will be no more drills. You are now part of The Children's Day School of the Horizon of the Second Kclaben Society. You will be groomed to serve us, adopt our customs and assimilate our culture. We are your new rulers."

Lileala jerked her spirit out of the scene and began coughing deliriously to clear her itching throat.

"What kind of school is this! Outdoors in the dirt?" she asked aloud, staring at the piles of rocks surrounding her. Then she realized that she was leaning against boulders, not old crates.

She pulled back and ran her hand over one of the slick rocks, looking for signs of soot.

"Why were the children outside?" she repeated. "Why is their city buried in ash?" She rubbed her eyes, smearing them with the dirt on her palms. Someone tapped her shoulder and she jumped.

"Hold on. Hold on, girlie. It's only me, LaJuped."

Her stomach churned. She didn't want to look at him. Not today.

"Hey now, girlie, I said it's only me."

Contempt cast itself over her eyes, her cheeks, dragging her mouth into a frown. "Go away!" she shouted.

LaJuped frowned. "Okay," he said. "But you're going to wish I was here when the Kclabs come back. You're going to want my protection then."

"Why? What did you tell them?"

"Just about your visions. And that other little thing about Trieca."

"I don't have anything to say to you."

"Well, just thought I'd warn you that no one's going to believe you anyway. So, if I were you, I'd keep it to myself." LaJuped smirked. He had one eye closed and one eye open. "You know what? You're pretty. I can see that now that the keloids aren't so bad. You're the best of the bunch where you come from, aren't you?" He reached in his satchel, pulled out a small plastic jug and drank from it so fast the water splashed over his lips and spilled onto his chin. "Aaah," he said, wiping his back hand across his mouth. "I'm leaving soon, you know. I'm the only one here whose skin has completely healed."

Needles shot from Lileala's eyes, and she looked at him, perhaps for the first time. A small, crooked form, his face entirely smooth, not a single keloid in sight.

He wandered away. Lileala watched and said nothing. She wished she had listened to Brian and not trusted him so much. As he roamed the trails leading past the rock towers, colonists hurried out of his way. But when he saw Hattie, she stopped and the two entered a lengthy discussion. Lileala watched with interest, and suddenly had an insight: it was Hattie, she thought. She must be the one who told the Kclabs that Lileala had complained all night and requested beds. Since Lileala's first night in the colony, Hattie had never returned to the cave. In exchange for secrets about the colonists, were Hattie and LaJuped getting special favors, promises, extra doses of Mecca?

Tired of trying to figure them out, Lileala scrambled to her feet, then walked over to a small group standing around the pond. "Where's Roloc and the rest?" she asked. "It's past the noon hour."

"Oh, they'll be here," Brian answered.

"They might be on Golong," Lileala said, a tinge of bitterness in her tone.

"On where?" Brian gave her a suspicious glance.

"Some planet called Golong," she said. "I just had a vision about it and the Kclabs. It was deadly, and they –"

"Lileala, please," Brian said. "Not that Kclab conspiracy again. I don't know what Golong is, and I don't want to know. The Kclabs have been nice to us, and this is how you repay them?"

Lileala walked away, biting her lip. Then she saw Osiris and quickened her pace. "Elder Osiris!" she called out. "The Kclabs! They're doing something to planets! I saw them. I saw the vial of serum. I saw burned buildings. I saw them destroying everything."

Osiris leaned against his cane and pointed a shaking finger at Lileala's forehead. "Young one," he said. "Brian is more tolerant than anyone here, and even he's getting tired of your nonsense. I don't appreciate it. No one does. Why do this now when it's almost time to leave?"

"But elder, I think it's a trap. They're using this cure as a ploy! On this other world, I even saw them with the vial of –"

"How do you know what was in that vial?" he snapped. "And how do you even know where you were? I can't say I believe any of it." He switched his cane from his right hand to the left and gave Lileala a hard and fast once over. "You might be pretty, but you're not too bright. Myself, I think you're crazy. When you get back to Swazembi, young one, get help."

The elder hobbled away and Lileala rushed to a group of passing colonists she barely knew. "The others aren't listening, but someone has to," she pleaded. "We have to get word back to our worlds. We have to stop the Kclabs."

"Leave us alone!" shouted a young woman, light green with a bush of green hair. She walked off, linking arms with two men on either side of her.

Frustrated, Lileala turned toward the cliffs and broke into a trot.

Brian hurried onto her path and stopped her. "Listen," he said, standing in her way. "I'm sorry. I didn't mean to be so rude, but Lileala you're babbling and saying things that make no sense."

Not answering, Lileala tried to go around him. He stepped to the side and blocked her attempts to pass. "I'm sorry about this, but I'm not letting you go to that cliff or whatever it is today," he said. "It's making you act too strange."

Lileala tried again to dodge around him, but he held her still. "Come on, now. It's for your own good."

"Brian, you don't understand. I know what I'm talking about. I thought you were one of the few people here who actually believed in me, but clearly you don't."

"Apparently, LaJuped believes you," Brian said. "Supposedly, he dug up enough information on you to upset the Kclabs. It's the strangest thing, though. Why would they take his gossip so seriously? When something's not true, why not just ignore it? It's absurd."

"I resent that, Brian. Did you come here just to insult me?"

"No, to help you!" Brian grabbed her wrist and leveled with her. "Lileala, I've thought it over and… I'm starting to believe you, okay, at least partially. I'm sort of confused that this cure is taking so long, and I think it's odd that they'd get so upset about accusations you can't even prove."

Lileala stopped resisting, grateful that he was loosening his grip. "You believe me?"

"I'm, I'm torn, Lileala. Like I said, I'm confused, and I'm worried about you. But whatever is going on, you have to stop talking so much. Where I'm from, we believe that you should never let your right hand know what the left is doing."

Lileala studied Brian's demeanor. "So... you don't think I'm crazy?"

He smiled. "Never have. There are two sides to everything. I just don't want you to –"

"Block our progress?" Lileala asked. "Is that what you were going to say? Don't do anything that might keep us here longer?"

Brian didn't answer. The Kclab vessel was landing, clanging as it touched down on the tight and misshapen landing strip. He tried to take Lileala's hand and coax her toward the landing site, but she backed away and lingered near the pond. After LaJuped's revelation, she figured the Kclabs planned to embarrass her, maybe try and taunt her with everything LaJuped had shared.

Her mind went into a fog. Brian looked behind him and waved for her to come stand beside him. She was beginning to be able to hear private thoughts now. In Brian's, she could hear that his desire to protect her was causing him to ache. Internally, he was saying that he and Martore would stay by her side. But the fog in her brain triggered a heaviness she couldn't escape. Instead, she plunged back into the reverie of the Dogon Dancers and bounded through their village with them.

Lileala stretched a tall and gangly body toward the sun, letting sweat trickle down an unkempt beard. Infused within the form of a middle-aged male drummer, she pounded and stomped. There was a fury in each pound, a joyous ferocity in each wave of her arm. Tribal dancers bounced around her in circles, their chants making her giddy. An imposing drummer swayed his hips and pivoted toward her and shouted: "Hogan, she is here! She is here!"

A crowd of women squealed and ululated. Children romped by and shrieked: "Hogan, Hogan!" until he appeared – an elder with skin as taut as leather and glints of soft light framing his countenance. He walked up to Lileala and bowed.

"You have come," he said, skipping introductions. "Thank the ancestors, for you have come."

"You know me?" Lileala asked. She kept her jaw clenched and flexed her calf muscles as she tried to get comfortable in the body of a man.

The Hogan gently took her hand. "You stand before me as a warrior drummer, but you are our daughter of tomorrow who sends us strength from beyond the thousands of years ahead," he said. "Now you have come, our daughter, as proof of the world that awaits. As proof that the ancestors never fail, and that the juju will always work."

Though he spoke in an ancient tongue of the Dogon, Lileala heard it as English and instinctively knew what it meant. In his hand were misshapen seeds, much like the ones enchanted by Fodjour, but brighter and more robust. He scattered the seeds on the ground in front of Lileala, but instead of vegetation, an image appeared of a planet in skies bathed in striking colors.

"This world will be our own," the Hogan shouted to the crowd. "And we will take with us the teachings of Po Tolo."

While the crowd cheered, the Hogan opened his other hand and revealed two tarnished bronze pendants, one bearing the image of a striped eel and the other covered with intertwined leaves.

"Rare One," the Hogan said. "This is our juju medicine. Have you seen these anywhere in your world?"

When Lileala said no, the Hogan loosened his grip on the pendants. "They are a hidden magic, and it is good that they are not used in your great city." He observed her closely. There was a ghost-like outline of the real Lileala flowing from the crown of the drummer's head.

"Your presence is strong," the Hogan said. "But the warrior whose body you have assumed does sleep in his spirit now and has no awareness of your mark within him. When he awakens, he will know you as a dream and will have the benefits and knowledge that your energy has left behind. You have given us hope by coming here from the many-colored soil. You are our truth."

"What truth? Who are you?" Lileala asked. "And how do you know me?"

"I know you because of the glow that never leaves you and the haze of a seer's spirit in your eyes," he answered. "I am the Hogan, the one who recognizes all spirits and advises healers of the village. And I am the chief of this village. My name is Tnomo and I will be the founder of Swazembi."

Lileala gasped and the man's body she inhabited nearly fainted.

"This bronze stone bearing the creature gives me powers," said Hogan Tnomo. "And this, the coiled pendant, is medicine for protection. I used them both in my rituals to call out to Po Tolo. I asked that one be sent to us from the farthest shores of the sky to show us the glory that is to be."

He held the tools higher. "I used these with the powerful herbs, rooibois and bocho. I threw the cowrie shells in a circle while I entered Inekoteth trances, and I ate the blessed seeds to see the future of our tribe. Some call this the Juju, but it is the sacred medicine we use to prepare us for our journey."

The Hogan nodded and pointed to a white light spiraling around two animal ribcages that lay on the ground at a distance of no more than seven or eight meters.

Lileala's face twitched, and he gently touched her chin. "It frightens you now, this energy that pierces through bones, but Po Tolo has shown me that this light will become wind and this wind will sail through your city and allow you to fly like birds in the sky," he said. "For the Dogon who choose to leave this land, that wind tunnel is like the sea that bears the great ships. It will take us to our new home."

Hogan Tnomo kneeled in the sand and with one finger drew the figure of a being shaped like the ite irhe clams of Gwembia. "We asked Po Tolo for a sign, and we have received it," he said. Pressing the medicine pendants against his heart, he stood and beheld a scattering of villagers who waved at him from hovels carved into the high cliffs.

"The Rare One has beckoned!" he announced. "It is time."

Lileala eased toward the burning light and her spirit was immediately catapulted back onto the grounds where she still stood next to Brian. But her senses had traversed many realities, and because of it, her mind had wearied and her surroundings – the pond, the boulders, the Kclab ship – seemed to flash in and out of her awareness.

Ahead, she thought she could see Mernestyle and hear her announcing that it was time for the daily Mecca to be dispensed. But her scratchy voice was vague, drowned out by a clash of competing commands that were making Lileala light-headed. She had to pick one and tune in.

Run! Run, Lileala! Run now! Run!

Ahonotay?

On swift feet, she did as she was told, running and listening as Ahonotay's guidance squeezed itself between the spaces of her own private thoughts.

If only you knew how often your image comes to me in my altered states, Ahonotay intoned. *In my meditations deep within my hut in Mbaria, I saw you many times. And I see you now hurrying toward the orange and copper walls of the crater. I can almost touch you. Young Indigo, it is you who will be the link, not me. Po Tolo's beings needed me to prepare you. I was never the link. It is you the children call out to. It is you the ancient Dogon raise their voices to. You are the link to our homeland's scattered forebears. You are their source of comfort.*

Lileala choked out a reply, "Please, I don't want to do this anymore. Make it stop, please… Make –" Midsentence, she caught herself and remembered to speak through her mind.

Make it go away. Please, Ahonotay, please help me. I don't know what to do. I'm having so many visions I can't take it. I'm scared.

Breathe, Lileala, Ahonotay soothed. *Take deeper breaths.*

No, Ahonotay. You don't understand. It's non-stop and I'm tired.

But she refused to yield. *Lileala Walata Sundiata, you will not give up. Remember what I taught you. Find your center.*

Still running, Lileala blasted *No, no, no!* through her mind. *I'm dealing with multiple shocks. You said it would be up to me to determine if the Kclabs are genuine. They are not. They have entered my visions in a horrible way. And people in the colony won't believe me.*

You don't need their belief. You need solace, young one. You need inner fortitude.

But Ahonotay, these visions are too many. They haunt me so. I can't handle this jumping from one life to another. I'm with Dogon ancestors one minute and the next I'm in this strange church watching the Kclabs do things I can't comprehend. I feel like I'm losing my mind.

Ahonotay's communication drifted into a slower cadence. Lileala stopped to catch her breath and absorb one last directive:

You will survive this mingling of worlds because you are using your third eye. It is an invisible eye that sees from within. The pain of unveiling your third eye is unbearable. I understand. But it is wide open now, young one, and you must use it to find answers. Rely on it to excavate the gems of peace and creativity buried within your very being. In doing so, you will finally discover the true purpose of the trinity breath.

Lileala sat beneath the midday sun, her hood around her shoulders and, for the first time in weeks, her face fully exposed. She hadn't made it to the cliff. Ahonotay's revelation was making her rethink the trip. As a seer, she could get cues from anywhere, near or outside the crater. And now that LaJuped had revealed her private spot, she felt she needed a better place to hide.

Lileala tried to piece it all together. The Dogon, the Kclabs, the sad children. All discordant scenes and all of them cramming themselves into her brain. Could her third eye help her make sense of that?

Tugging on the collar of her hood, she shielded her neck from the cool air and reflected on Hogan Tnomo's comment. *"I asked that one be sent to us from the farthest shores of the sky to show us the glory that is to be."*

A chill rushed through her. That's it. If these intrusions were the will of the ancestors, then she needed to be a healer and a muse. In the Inekoteth state, she'd ask even more questions and search for methods to quell the anxiety of every forebear she met. Maybe it was possible to breathe in their pain and blow it out through her nostrils, psychically medicating them and soothing their physical trauma.

"That is five, the healing precept," the Dogon chorus interjected, speaking clear as a bell in Lileala's thoughts. *"'Heal with mind and breath.' Tap into the flame that burns inside you. Use it for a greater good."*

With her eyes closed, Lileala went into trinity breath.

Breath One: Imagine a new flame.

Breath Two: Walk upon hotter embers.

Breath three: Be the fire for change.

In a few minutes, her mind was aquiver, and a new clash of images seized her.

A young man flees. Arms in the air, he dashes across a yard with thunder in his heart. Men pursue him on foot and his fear of them drives his legs. Lileala feels the burn within him, and a clammy fever clutches her body. The men behind her are clothed in deep dark blue, but they are not in Shimmer. They are angry, in a hurry to harm.

They hold up a device. Lileala has seen one before on the viewerstream and her mind associates it with danger. A shattering boom sounds and she is hit with a hail of hot metals. Lileala's knees buckle. There's an explosion inside the young man's back, inside Lileala. Crumpled on the ground, she breathes hope into his spirit and a balm of comfort into his pain. His abdomen contracts and Lileala's entire soul contracts with it. His weakness is now her weakness – his agony, hers. She fights through and allows her energy to pour like medicine into his wound. It silences the fierce rippling in his spine, letting him rest as he dies. She pulls out of his body and watches his life force depart.

Lileala opened her eyes and prepared to head toward the hill, but she was stopped by a voice, loud and real.

"Hey, Miss Lileala!" Garrette yelled. He was running, flagging her with his hands.

She shivered. "Garrette, what are you doing here? Did you follow me?"

He tried but couldn't mask his guilt. "I had to. I had to know what you are."

"What I am? What does that mean?"

"You're not a normal woman, Lileala. What are you?"

Still unsure how to answer, she locked both hands and took a long look at Garrette, noting the changes. Life in the colony was making him appear older. His large eyes had a withered appearance. Lileala could see the tension hardening into his face.

"*I* don't care so much what you are," he went on, "but the others want to know – the Wasswa sisters and Hattie. Especially Hattie. She's been coming around us more, but all she does is talk badly about you and she's making me sad."

Seeing the concern on his face, Lileala patted the ground next to her. "Look at you, getting all grown up," she said after he sat. She leaned over and gave him a hug. "It took a strong person to say what you just said. A big person, someone with courage."

"No, not at all. I think it just took someone who likes you so much, like me and Brian and Martore. We all like you. And the Wasswa sisters. They like you too. But they act nervous sometimes, like they're scared of you or something."

"But why? Is it because I'm no longer there at night?" Lileala asked.

"It's because of Hattie and LaJuped, I think. They keep saying things, and the others are starting to believe it. Last night, after our prayers, I heard one of them calling you something I've never heard of before. Something called a witch?" He stopped talking a minute, then continued. "Miss Lileala, what's a witch?"

For a while, Lileala couldn't think of an answer. She looked up at the sky, worried that it would soon be dark. "I don't know," she said finally. "I heard about them once in an old Earth tale, but I can't say exactly what they are or why I'd be called one."

Garrette pulled himself up. "You better come with me now. The Kclabs will be looking for you."

"No, you go on. I have a lot to attend to," Lileala said. "I haven't even made it to my destination yet."

"So, are you going to tell me what you are?" he asked. "If you tell me something, I can get the others to shut up."

She smiled, perhaps the biggest smile she'd ever allowed herself in the colony. "I'm happy you're thinking about me. But don't worry, okay? I'm just a clairvoyant that's all. I don't think that's nearly as special as Martore with her dancing hair and eyes that look through you to see if you're telling a lie."

"They're going to find you," Garrette said. "The Kclabs, I mean, not the others."

"Goodbye, Garrette," she whispered. "Go on back. I'm going to walk a little farther and think."

"Don't you always," he said and skipped away.

A half hour later, when Lileala had made it to the trail leading to the cliff, she felt the urge to slip back into trinity breath but with increased intensity. So, instead of one heavy inhalation and two exhalations, she went for three heavy breaths, two releases and then a long hold.

Next, she stood before the mouth of the jeweled cave she discovered before and retraced the procedure, breathing like someone who was being apprehended. Content, Lileala inhaled and broke one of the key Aspirant provisions – she tweaked the trinity coding:

Breath One: Diffuse the smoke. Let not the veil fall only on one.

Breath Two: Scatter the embers. Let not the spray benefit me alone.

Breath Three: Spread the fire!

The flame climbed through her spirit and shot like lightning into her heart. Eyes open, she trekked through the golden cave before her, but when she reached the tunnel there were no spiked rocks or jagged pebbles marring the floor.

Lileala walked across it with ease and exited on the other side onto grounds that were covered in damp green moss and several husky plants that resembled the Baobob trees of Africa. A leafy array of branches spread out from bushes that were as thick as drums. Crescent-shaped clay formations she had never seen before loomed above the cave, flanked by several scarlet red peaks. Lileala's heart galloped, and she heard the Po Tolo's beings: *You did this. You. Your mind.*

She breathed quicker. *But how?*

Lost Precept Six. 'Use your innate power to Create'.

She looked down. Beneath her feet, the ground was still a cushion of clay, only firmer, clear of dust and the color of a rich fig wine. She yanked off her sandals, walked across the cold ground in her bare feet, tipping as close as she could to the narrow rim of the cliff. She peered over it then stood still and tapped deep into another version of the trinity.

Breath One: Bathe in the smoke that saturates a wide valley.

Breath Two: Wade in the embers sprinkled over a plateau.

Breath Three: Swell the fire.

The flame in her spirit created a wreath of mist around her physical body and sent vibrations through her throat and heart. She spoke aloud in the Inekoteth.

"To the old ones who live in desolation, to the young ones who know torment, see the majesty that always is. Move from sorrow to joy and let it sizzle in the gladness with the forking tendrils. The one who is being chased is now the victor, madly charging in the opposite direction. Szewa, Szewa. Know Joy. Your souls are not tarnished. Go to joy. Lift."

But on the crater, there was no reaction.

She tried again, and on the second try she sat cross-legged and absorbed the sultry heat of the inner flame. Her mind went into the quiet. She waited. Her thoughts began to waddle through the ashes of past lessons, and she heard another command from Ahonotay:

Take all lessons back to the colony and pour healing forces into their hearts.

Lileala thought how depressed they'd been of late and filled with such longing. The pond was drying, and illness was coming upon a different one each day. Lileala breathed deeper and whispered to the Hogan Tnomo that now it was his turn to send her a sign. Had her Earth visits had an impact? Had her mergence with the languid souls helped? She waited. Still nothing.

"Szewa," she pleaded. "Szewa." She said it over and over until her voice began to sound like a whistle. There came a mild popping in her left ear followed by a murmur from the beings of Po Tolo:

Use your power for change. Their words faded and a light floated above the crater, whistling, sharp and soothing, like the giant clams of Gwembia.

With whistles reverberating through the mouth of the crater, a stream of dark faces appeared punctuated by a vague mumbling, *Inventor. Fighter for freedom, Leader of millions. Maker of laws. Teacher. Maker of music, Athlete, Author of great tomes.* The faces streaked in and out, on and on.

A man surfaced, speaking words that sailed in a rocket of emotions and burst like a thunderstorm over a mesmerized crowd. Lileala listened to him plead for justice. Then the lines of courage around his jaw, the determination in his countenance fizzled, and the tired image of a woman hovered in its place. She trod through woods unafraid, carving out her own road amid the thorny burrs that had fallen from the trees. More women and men appeared, but they were on paved city streets, marching, chanting. Many were young, wearing the denim Earth wear; some were melanin bearers, and some had skin as white as Toths. They marched together, droves of them, shouting, and waving posters with the words: *Black Lives Matter.*

Lileala didn't know what the signs meant, but they were followed by more. She tried to read all of them:

I Can't Breathe
Reform The Police
It's History; Not CRT.
We Are Not Target Practice
Ban Assault Weapons
Save Our Books.

Lileala's mind spun. Books? Wasn't that what was taken from Fodjour? History? Ah, that's what had been denied to Swazembians for too long? The posters blurred in her mind, and when she opened her eyes, she heard the word, *Miracle*. "We can be their miracle," she thought. "With our rituals we can touch our own ancestors. We can reach back and help them rise." She let her eyes sweep across the wide expanse of cliffs. "The past is still now," she said and lifted her hands. "Melanin bearers of the Earth, Szewa. You are more than the pain of your oppression. Chase away your fears, brave ones, for you are triumphant." She stood still. The images were no more and the chant of *Szewa* was carving itself into the air and echoing against the copper and gold canyon walls.

Szewa. Szewa. Szewa.

"I understand the meaning of Szewa more than I ever have. It's 'everything is now'." With her palms upraised, she repeated it out loud. "And so it is done. Szewa."

She turned to leave, unafraid of whatever awaited her at the colony. But as she backed away from the cliff, she felt a sudden nervous lunge inside her spirit. Something caustic was nearby, getting closer. She waited. Hearing nothing, she took a few more steps. Before she reached the cave, it came again – a voice so irate she felt like she was being hunted. She listened.

"Hurry. There she is. There! There she is! Ow! Dammit, that hurt."

Bertram exited the tunnel leading to the cave, groaning as he stumbled off the prickly floor. Without Lileala's breath there to change it, the ground had resumed its natural gritty state.

"Grab her!" Haliton yelled. He leapt out of the tunnel but took his time catching up to Bertram on feet that were obviously sore. Lileala cooperated while the two apprehended her, tying her wrists in a burlap rope so thick and tight that it scraped her skin.

"How did you know about Golong?" Haliton asked. "How could you possibly know something that even our own chief doesn't know?"

"And why are you telling others?" Bertram grunted. "That's the real problem. Stop it! When we're back at the colony we're going to take some of those fibers from around your wrists and loop them around your mouth."

Clamping his hands down on her wrist, Bertram forced her to walk in front of him.

"We're not being gentle anymore," he said. "You ruined it. The plan, that nice act, we're done with it."

10

"Can the wind not push objects, make them toss about? Does not the soul do the same to the body? Like the wind, the soul will scuttle forms for only a short distance. Then it blows on."
– From The Sacred Doctrines of The Uluri

Mhondora Chinbedza bounded across the Surface and sneaked around the outer perimeter of Lileala's private dome. He approached the door, stood on his toes and reached upward. Losing his balance, his thumb scraped against the door handle, and he heard a faint clatter then a ringing.

Naja. Naja. Naja. Jrr. Jrr. Jrrrrr. Rrrrrr.

He kept going, ignoring the noises.

Naja, Naja. Jrrr. Jrrrrrrrrrrrrr.

Chinbedza grasped at a triangular ornament that jutted from the top of the door, just below the roof of the dome. Distracted by the clatter, he leaned too far to one side, almost slipping in the sand. His arms flew forward, his back arched. A fierce buzzing surrounded him, turning into a deafening ringing in his ears.

Naja Naja Naja Naja Naja Naja Naja Nja Jrrrrrrrrrrrrrrrr.

The frequency was so painful he had to suppress a scream then open his hands, place one on each ear and push.

Naja Naja Naja.

His whole body shook. The sound persisted and he steadied himself, took a quick step and leaped. He fell backwards onto a bed of pink sand and cursed under his breath.

Naja! Naja! Naja!

The high pitch accelerated and reached another octave. It sent him into convulsions. He rolled over on his belly, careful to hold his head high to avoid swallowing whirling vapors of color. He lifted himself, moved back to the door of the dome and eyed the ornament. The triangle was a burnt copper, about six inches tall and served as a keystone to support the initial L for Lileala. It was sturdy but detachable. All he needed was one good yank to remove it from its base and retrieve the chip inside.

Chinbedza stood still and rested. This struggle was so much more than he'd anticipated. He wiped his brow just as a torrent of vibrations began swerving above his wrist.

Ellis Bourka of Toth appeared on his dial. "Mhondora, where are you? Are you finished?"

"Not now," Chinbedza whispered. "I'll contact you when I'm done."

"But I need to know how it's going," Ellis said. "Did you get the chip?"

"I'll get it."

"What's the hold up? I expected you to contact me an hour ago."

"Will you leave me alone? I'll summon you."

"Chinbedza, I'm going to be on Swazembi tomorrow and you better have that chip. I managed to get a special day pass for The Outer Ring, but with the current restrictions, I doubt that I'll be able to get another one."

"I'm trying. Now please, go away."

Ellis' image wavered then brightened. "You're acting strange," he said. "You know how important this is."

Chinbedza became annoyed. The noise was getting louder, and he had no idea of the source.

Naja. Naja. Naja. Naja. Rrrrrrrrrrrrrrrrrrrrrrrrrrrrr!

"What's that?" Ellis asked, startled. "What in the galaxy is going on there?"

"I-I don't know." Chinbedza's arms were extended over his head, high enough to grab the keystone. But his balance failed him. He slipped and missed again. The fall was harder this time, and the noise was deafening. It entered his ear and stayed there, nagging. Chinbedza felt as if his insides were being mashed and stirred.

Jrrrrrrtrtrrr. Jrrrrrr.

"What is going on?" Ellis demanded. "I need to know what that noise is."

"I told you, I don't know," Chinbedza snapped. "It starts up every time I reach for the keystone. It must be coming from that chip. Did you program it to do this?"

"Program it? What kind of a question is that? What would I want to program... Wait a minute." Ellis said nothing for a beat, then shouted. "Dammit! I hope this isn't some sort of backlash from Trieca."

"I don't know who, in the galaxy, Trieca is, but I do know we're in trouble. This chip must have been engineered to react to any removal attempts. The noise has a painful effect. It's almost paralyzing."

"I suggest you figure out something," said Ellis. "We can't turn to the Kclabs. We can't let them know we're trying to remove the thing."

"Looks like we're going to have to." The Mhondora was watching the keystone. "I'm beginning to see the outline of the tiny chip inside. It's shining and emitting rays of color."

"What are you talking about now?" Ellis asked.

"I'm talking about the chip! It's glowing somehow."

"Great. First it was making noise. Now it's glowing. Grab it, Chinbedza. Can't you just reach out and grab it?"

Chinbedza took a step forward, reached up again. The ringing reverberated in his ear.

Naja. Naja. Naja. Naha. Najajnajanajanaja. Jrrrrrrrrrrrrrrrr!

"For the galaxy's sake, man! What have the Kclabs concocted?" Ellis asked.

"I wish I knew," Chinbedza said. "I didn't have any problem removing the last one. I replaced it with no problem. Did you do something different this time?"

"Nothing. I added the serum, that's all," Ellis said.

"You or someone else must have tampered with this one."

"I told you Chinbedza. I didn't do anything," Ellis snapped.

"But look at me," Chinbedza said. His clothes were torn and rumpled. Sweat poured down his face. "I can't believe you let things get so out of control."

"I had no way of knowing they'd try to take it further," Ellis answered. "I promised them two people of color, one from Toth and one from Swazembi. That was it. That was the agreement."

"Agreement," scoffed Chinbedza. "What were you thinking? What was *I* thinking? It's clear they have no respect for the term."

"Well, you went along with it," said Ellis.

"I didn't know they would take it this far!"

"Far? Mhondora Chinbedza, you cast a spell that helped them cloak an entire planet and make it invisible to the Coalition. *You* did that. And now you're saying something was too far?"

"My role was minimal at best," said Chinbedza. "I showed up on Golong and performed juju rituals. That was it. They're the ones who burned all the buildings to the ground."

"I thought you said that was the only way to create the screen of invisibility?" Ellis said. "Didn't you tell me everything on the planet had to be blackened?"

"Ellis, listen. The Kclabs said that, not me. Are you even hearing me? My role was juju. I didn't know they'd torch the place."

"Stop worrying," Ellis said. "There has to be a way around this."

"That's what I told myself," said Chinbedza. "I saw this coming. I foresaw some trickery, I really did, but I told myself they were just Kclabs, that they weren't advanced enough for that. I figured we'd find a way around any deception on their part. Now, look at us."

"Calm down," ordered Ellis. "We'll think of something."

The Mhondora sighed. "It seemed so simple. If they acted up, all we had to do was throw away the damn chips." He gazed at the keystone. "What pain these things have caused!"

"I'm worried about how long this is taking," Ellis said. "Does anyone know you're on the Surface?"

"No. After the tourist ban, Sonaguards stopped patrolling this late on weeknights."

"Good. Then stay where you are. We can figure out something. Damn that Trieca. I'm not going to be outsmarted by a useless Kclab."

"Well, it looks like you were," Chinbedza said.

"If I have to, I'll spend the night working on this," Ellis countered. "I'll go to one of my labs and determine the chemical composition of the substance in those chips."

"Ellis, don't you think you should have done that a long time ago? I thought you knew what this stuff was."

"The only thing I know is that it emits sound waves that I can use to distort matter."

"And?" asked Chinbedza.

"And make it easier to mold. That Mecca makes it pliant."

"That's not helping. Don't you know anything else?"

"What else is there to know? It's inside the chips."

"Even the ones with music?" Chinbedza asked.

"Chinbedza, we've been over this before. The skin altering chips are totally separate and different. I've handled them, even poured serum, so I know they didn't go inside of the music chips," explained Ellis.

"Then what's going on with this one? Something is causing that sound?"

"I said calm down about it," Ellis snapped. "If it contains the chemical, then there's no music. Do you understand?"

Lurching forward, Chinbedza leaped again and grasped the keystone, holding on until the sound made his knees buckle. He landed in the sand, moaning.

RJJJJJJJJ! Rajarajaraj rrrrrrrrrrrrrrrr!

"Did you get it?" Ellis yelled.

"Ouch! Does it sound like I have it?" Chinbedza growled.

Ellis thought a minute. "Trieca made another batch of Mecca after she returned from that Coalition summit. I wonder if she did something different."

"Clearly, she did," Chinbedza said. He held on to the side of the dome and pulled himself off the ground.

"Either that," said Ellis, "or someone else here on Toth tampered with it."

"For what reason?" Chinbedza asked.

"No reason. I'm beginning to wish I'd handled the last pick up," Ellis said, after a long pause. "I sent my assistant, Trevon. He's pretty young, only twenty-one years. I hope... No, never mind, he's responsible. I'm sure he didn't let anyone touch it."

Ellis was quiet again. "Damn, I hope Trevon kept an eye on that Mecca... I'm going to get a handle on this even if it means putting a temporary ban on Earth music."

"I hate to state the obvious, but what good is that?" Chinbedza's tone was hostile. "A ban can't help us now."

"I'm trying to make sure no stray chips got infected. I'm the chief of Building and Regulations and Excavated Materials. I can insist on a ban."

"Not on Swazembi, you can't."

"Why are you suddenly so pessimistic?"

"Because we're no longer in control! And to add insult to injury, the girl turned out to be clairvoyant. I should have known then that –"

"Goodbye Chinbedza," said Ellis. "Just get the damn chip and I'll meet you as planned. Tomorrow, the Hotep Office Center in The Outer Ring. We'll continue our discussion then."

"If I'm there," Chinbedza mumbled.

"What's that?"

"Never mind." Chinbedza's voice trailed off and his mind became a blur of jumbled thoughts. He breathed in the freshness of the drifts and looked out at the sea of vapors. His eyes leaped from hill to hill, and he reveled in the misty environment, wondering why he'd been willing to risk it all and how the plans had turned so deadly.

For Ellis, it was simple. He used the Kclab's peculiar serum for his constructions on Toth. But Chinbedza's goal, a singular ambition to rule the Golong world invaded by Kclabs, had turned into one of the worst disasters in Coalition history.

Chinbedza sat in the soft colored powders and tried to soothe his mind. Puffs of windblown reds and yellows were falling and rising, creating a frenzied vortex. He soaked in the beauty. It was majestic, this planet.

He shuddered and let his eyes take in the grandeur of Blue Barrell mountain while he thought again about his stupid scheme. He'd tapped into forbidden juju and activated spells that had been dormant for several millennia – all for some damn Kclab takeover!

What a petty goal I had, he said to himself. *What a damn, stupid, petty goal! My galaxy, ancestors, what must you think of me?*

When he was an elder-child and his Inekoteth trances were just beginning to take root, the great ancestor Tnomo had once visited Chinbedza in a dream and given him his blessings. As he savored the memory, Chinbedza pictured Tnomo, the face with a smile that seemed powered by sunbeams, a deep set of creases and a wisdom that he wore like a crown. Composure and kindness were Tnomo's cornerstones, and if Chinbedza had let it be known, he could have been the galaxy's greatest icon – Swazembi's original clairvoyant, a Dogon Hogan from Earth who left tons of treasures behind.

Did you abuse our sacred medicines? Tnomo seemed to ask in Chinbedza's mind. *As gatekeeper were you not to shield these secrets? How can you call yourself a son of the Dogon?*

The Mhondora pressed his back against the dome and put his face in his hands, cringing at the sand on his fingertips stinging the corners of his eyes. He knew Tnomo's visit was a figment of his imagination; no ancestor would honor him with a vision now, and it was his guilt that haunted him, filling him with angst.

Chinbedza wrung his hands, trying to suppress his shame. But it overtook him. *That was it, wasn't it?* He asked himself. Shame. Wasn't that the emotion that made Swazembi's founders enforce restrictions? Weren't they ashamed, after all, of their choice to abandon their village? Isn't that why they cut off their legacy to the African land? Out of embarrassment, weren't they trying to forget and deny the world they'd left behind?

At Hogan Tnomo's bequest, every Mhondora for generation after generation was to be keeper of a history they never could share. Like all Mhondoras before him, Chinbedza had not leaked a word about the Dogon Earth tribe, the huts on mountain cliffs and grasslands that were home to four-legged beasts. And like the others, he was expected to fiercely protect the forces of juju medicine that had been accumulating for thousands of years.

Chinbedza rested a trembling hand on his chin. He had failed, and if nothing else, he would make it right. Tonight, he would remove that Kclab apparatus from Lileala's dome. He would not go home until he did.

Stepping backwards about ten paces, Chinbedza ran, leaped toward the dome's roof and threw himself at the hidden chip. The noise jarred his mind and pain rippled down his spine. He grabbed the keystone and held on despite the sudden and haphazard stinging as the ringing intensified. He felt as if his brain had burst.

Najnajanajanajanajanajanajnajanajanajanajana janajanajanajananajjrrrrrrrrrrrrjananana. NaajaJaNajajrrrrr. JRRRRRRRRRR! RRRRRRRRRRRRRR!

Chinbedza's body was racked with spasms. He held on, pulling and tugging at the keystone. Pain gripped his shoulders. He trembled and kept going.

Najanajanaa. Naja. Naja. NAJANAJANA. RRRRRRRRR!

He felt another jolt. It shook him violently. He spit up blood, sputtered, begged within for the ancestors to help. And still he held on.

Naja. NAAJA. NAJ. RRRRR!

He shriveled inside, but continued to clutch and tug on the keystone. With a final yank, it loosened.

He collapsed, holding the triangle securely in his right palm. It shone brighter and a path of colors appeared above it. The Mhondora lay on the ground, motionless, his mouth foaming with blood. He heaved suddenly, and then he lay still.

The ringing softened, and another color patch spurt from the keystone. A burst of quiet vibrations turned into a wave of color in motion. It circled his form, brushing against the blood trickling down his chin.

He took one last breath.

A funeral procession wound around the jagged grasslands of Gwembia's northern pastures. The sojourn was being made by foot, just as tradition called for. But tradition meant so little now. Tradition had crackled under the steamy glare of a society stunned by an ache it had never known: the shock of early death.

The Mhondora was only four hundred and twenty six. No one had succumbed so young. None on Swazembi had joined the ancestors before their five hundred and fiftieth sun year and no one understood the trauma of an unfinished life. That the Mhondora could leave more than a century too soon was an unutterable travesty. Who could advise mourners, when no one had ever walked this path? The Uluri? The Nobility? No one, even those with a legacy of centuries had the tale of an early death to tell.

So mourners, thousands of them, waded alone in their confused anguish, uncoached, dragging emotions that wore odd faces and a wound so tender they could not even force a smile. The entourage had taken rail trams to the transit station then marched for two days in the green pastures of the valley where the Mhondora's body was wrapped in a handwoven curtain of Jacaranda petals, dosed with fragrant anise seeds, and then torched.

On the third day, the procession started up again in Boundary Circle and ended on the Surface, near Lileala's golden dome.

"Is this the spot?" Chief Kwesi asked. He was leading the ceremony that would bring the three-day ritual to a close. "You are sure this is it?" Kwesi asked a second time. "We must be definite."

A Sonaguard member beside him pointed and nodded. "Yes, stop here," he said, squinting. The evening sun was dripping behind the blue hills, and he strained to see the imprint the body had formed during the hours it lay in the sand. "This is definitely the place," he repeated, voice shaking. He was on duty that morning and had stumbled upon the limp body curled up by the dome. "This is where we found him and where we confiscated the strange instrument that was in his hand," he said.

"You mean the chip?" Kwesi asked.

"Yes, but, actually, it was a keystone. An imitation keystone from the dome. The strange chip was inside."

"Very well," said Kwesi. He turned and motioned for the procession to halt. "The Pineal Crew is examining the chip. We'll discuss all that later. For now, I just needed verification of the exact location."

A nervous young woman found a spot beside Kwesi. "I'm Adilah," she announced. "I'm an Indigo Aspirant and the Mhondora's eldest granddaughter." Adilah was a haunting presence with a pinch of blue in her blacker-than-berries complexion. She raised her left arm and spoke louder.

"May his soul unite with the spirit of oneness," she said, addressing the crowd. "May he watch over us. May he become part of our continuing being."

She wiped both eyes. Two Pineal Crew officers handed her a chrome box containing the Mhondora's ashes and a small gold pouch packed with toxic yohimbe leaves. She pried open the box and sprinkled the ashes with a handful of Ka, a potent spice grown only in the Xandiagara village. She poured the ashes into the pouch and tossed it, trembling as it exploded into flames that shot skyward and faded into the vapors.

"The herb is meant to purify the air, to create a safe passageway for the Mhondora's journey," she said. "May any furor be still, and any crimes exonerated. May patience and love reign supreme." She raised both arms and wept. The other mourners did the same. Kwesi, still standing near Adilah, was lifting his arms when he noticed Otto.

"Otto," he called out. He removed himself from the ceremony and walked in his direction. "I haven't seen you in days. If you're becoming a hermit, I think you're overdoing it."

Otto hunched his shoulders. "You obviously have more hope than me," he said. "I don't have any left. I prefer to remain alone these days, after Lileala's last letter."

"Last letter. I didn't know you had heard from her again."

"I did."

"And?" Kwesi asked.

"Haven't wanted to talk about it. That's why I stayed away. From everyone."

"Otto, your sense of endurance is not what it once was."

"I don't mean to be disrespectful, Chief, but what is that supposed to mean?"

"I mean you were once a champion of higher mindscapes. It was you, in fact, who encouraged my daughter to praise The Grace. Always it was 'of one beat, one accord, one protection'."

Otto caught his breath and the two walked a while in silence.

"I'm ashamed," he said finally. "I'll admit it, I'm ashamed.

But what can I do? I was positive. With me, it was waves of joy. Constantly, waves of joy."

"And what has changed?"

"Circumstances. Challenges. Real challenges. Maybe I'm not as strong as I thought, as everyone thought," said Otto.

"But maybe you are," said Kwesi.

"Aren't you contradicting yourself? A minute ago, you were pointing out my faults."

"No, I was pointing out your unwillingness to rise up, to show your true spirit. It's as if you're defying all of your Pineal Crew training. Otto, has it ever occurred to you that it's easy to spread joy when all is well? But when the flame is too hot –"

"That is the true test," Otto said. "Yes, I understand."

"I'm hurting too, son. Really hurting."

"Lileala refuses to be joined." Otto blurted out the words without thinking.

Kwesi stopped walking.

"I'm not ignoring your pain, Kwesi," Otto said. "Believe me, I respect your strength and wonder how you can carry on but–"

"What did you say?" Kwesi's voice was quick and sharp.

"That I wonder how you carry on."

"No, before that."

"That Lileala refuses to be my devoted. She's cancelling our joining."

"I thought I didn't hear that right," Kwesi said.

"You did," said Otto. "I don't believe it either. She's changing so much. She talks about things I don't understand. I don't accept most of it. Did you know that she considers herself a seer now?"

Kwesi looked directly at Otto. "Listen to me," he said. "Listen closely. She *is* of the High Order, an empath and clairvoyant. Before the two of you went to the Surface, Lileala and her elder Ma visited the Mhondora."

Otto had to steady himself. "I knew she went to see him, but she never told me what he shared. If the Mhondora told her way back then, why did she keep me in the dark for so long?"

"How was she to tell you when she hadn't yet accepted it herself?"

"I don't know what to think." He searched Kwesi's face. "And you say the Mhondora actually confirmed this? Then what was he doing lurking around her dome? And why was there a music chip in a keystone, for galaxy's sake? What was his role in all of this, anyway?"

"That's a good question," Kwesi said. "That's a very good question."

The day after the final ritual, Sonaguards from Swazembi and Toth combined forces and marched single file down the middle of a congested boulevard in Toth's largest municipality, a festive community known as Sirap. Mini transporters jettisoned along the edge of the boulevard and crystalline balls, carting two or three passengers, twirled overhead. Somehow, a gangly boy riding an air bike had sneaked into the area unsupervised. He hovered over the guards, pelting them with sticky wads.

"Ouch!" Zizi said. A wad the size of a fingertip had landed on her uniform. She looked at it with suspicion then touched it. It was like water, but it wasn't wet. It clung, searing through the metallic fabric and rapidly changing from a gelatinous wad to a sheer, molten liquid.

"What is this?" she said, rubbing the smear.

"Ha, got you!" The boy waved his right arm and sneered. "Got you!"

Zizi jumped out of line and ran down the boulevard. The melting wad was still leaking through the cloth and now stinging her skin. She needed to let it cool. Gingerly, she touched it again, disgusted as it rippled along the tiny creases of her silver sleeves. Her fingers turned red, irritated by what appeared to be a current. A warm, mysterious current. Grabbing the corner of her sleeve, she shook it, hoping to air it out and minimize the damage.

She headed back to the boulevard and tried to catch up with

the other Sonaguards. But the crowd was too thick. She couldn't see them. The minor-child, still watching her from his bike, pointed and laughed. Zizi overlooked him and kept walking. She didn't have time to argue; she had to get to a meeting – the Sonaguard, the Pineal Crew, Toth and Swazembi Leadership and representatives from five Coalition planets were gathering to discuss findings surrounding the Mhondora's death.

Zizi dashed down the busy boulevard and forced her way through a throng of slow-moving pedestrians. An acrobatic dancer passed, and the crowd lingered, marveling as he did somersaults and remained upside down, suspended in midair.

Zizi kept squeezing her way in and out of the throng. Earth-style music blared, and a three-member band skated past her on wheels so fast they were almost invisible.

"Toth is always having an extravaganza of some sort," a stranger blurted. He was a rotund man with a double chin and bulky cheeks. He nudged her with his elbow. "I'm here from West Neptune, vacationing. Care to join me? I came here to meet people like you." He winked one fat eye.

"No, thank you," she said, and hurried off, pushing through the crowd. Up ahead, about four and a half yards, she could see an octagon building surrounded by swinging balconies. Whew! She dashed to the entrance and fell in place with the rest of the patrol team. They had arrived several minutes earlier and were marching to the rear of the room. Zizi fit right in and darted into a seat just as Coalition Chairman, Dane Elliott, was signaling Commander Coleman Spencer and asking him to begin the session.

"I'll give it to you bluntly," said Coleman, skipping the formalities. "The Mhondora was killed by a stress reaction and physiological trauma caused by some sort of ear chip that did not contain music. Apparently, this chip emitted a sound that Swazembians can't hear under normal circumstances. From what we can tell, those sound waves can have some kind of effect on cell development and the central nervous system. The chip has been deactivated at this point. When the Mhondora tampered with it, it must have gone beyond its highest octave and hit a pitch that ruptured his ear drum. The intensity is what we believe killed him."

He continued, "We don't understand the chemical composition of this chip. I must stress that the makeup is very different from the typical music chips we see here on Toth. We're alarmed because we haven't verified the source of this instrument and we don't know how many of them exist. We do know that this very strange chip was tucked inside an imitation keystone perched on the personal dome of Lileala Sundiata."

The room was a flurry of chatter and Coleman had to raise his voice to be heard.

"My friends, it is possible that the Mhondora Chinbedza knew more than he let on about the keloid disease. The Rare Indigo, Lileala, is the only one on Swazembi to develop a mutation of her skin cells. As far as we know, her dome is the only one with a chip in the keystone. If you can stretch your minds the way we have been forced to stretch ours, then you might question, as we have, whether or not the honorable Mhondora was somehow involved."

A young man from Swazembi jumped from his seat, yelling, "This is disrespectful! We're still grappling with our shock."

Coleman regarded him with a detached interest. "We asked that you remain silent until the report is –"

"Silent? How can we be silent? A man of only four hundred and twenty-six sun years has left us! I can't be silent, and I can't stand here and let you tarnish his reputation like this!"

With his arms crossed, Coleman remained quiet for half a minute. Mentally, he was signaling M-S-T techniques, turning his skin a light bronze. "We must investigate, and we cannot do so without your cooperation," he said, keeping his voice firm. "For that reason, we'd like those of you who have had contact with the Mhondora during the last ninety days to come forward and provide us with any information you might have about him, his activity, his behavior. Also, we have conferred with Ellis, Chief of Building Regulations. Where's Ellis? Can you stand, please?"

Ellis stood, wearing the frightened gaze of a fugitive.

"Ellis has suggested that we consider a temporary ban on music chips, for safety."

The audience began to grumble, then suddenly gasped. There was an outburst of screams and dull banging noises, the sound of chairs being knocked over.

"Relax! Please, relax!" Coleman shouted.

But everyone was frantic. A woman and a man from Jemti began trembling and embracing. Several Swazembians shielded their eyes with dark glasses. A couple of women from Toth ran out of the room.

"What's going on?" Coleman shouted over the noise. At that moment, he became aware of a scraping sound, then a loud thump. He heard the scrape again, and another thump. Coleman turned his head toward the open door behind him. An awkward, elongated being was bumbling through it, wriggling along the floor and toward the podium. It was sloppy with glazed eyes that bulged from the sockets. Two slits formed air vents around its tiny mouth.

For a fleeting minute, Coleman considered screaming and running. But he regained his composure as the thing stopped moving. A slit beneath the being's eyes opened. Finally, it spoke, "Hello. I am Egna 7, a Wilfin from Kclaben. Our torment at the hands of the Kclabs has reached such unbearable proportions that only eight members of my species remain in existence. We would like to request asylum on Toth."

Coleman's mouth gaped open; he couldn't stop staring at what was in front of him. A Wilfin? What in the galaxy was a Wilfin? Coleman couldn't bring himself to speak.

He chastised himself for standing there, dumbfounded, unable to respond to a creature just because... because...

"Because," he blurted out, "because of what? You're saying we should grant you asylum because of Kclab abuse? We have no proof of that."

Coleman's heart pumped with the ferocity of a warrior in the midst of battle. Was this Wilfin really that revolting? If not, why did everyone look so terrified?

"Excuse me, commander," Dane said, stepping back up to the podium. "Perhaps, we should hear the Wilfin's story. Let it talk." Dane had to force himself to look straight at the beast.

"Thank you very much," the Wilfin said, and it clucked in a pitch that sounded a lot like a scream. "I am pleased that you are willing to oblige me."

"We haven't said we're willing to oblige you, just to hear your story," Dane said. "Why are you here?"

"I am here because this is the planet we have chosen as our future home," the Wilfin said. "I am not alone. I have come here with my friends, the whole ragged eight of us. We have been traveling quite a long time, you know... since... since. I will have to check with Egna 8, but I believe we have been trying to get here for nearly two moon semesters. We lost our way several times and the rusted ship was sluggish. I, we, did not think we would ever get here. We started out on a fluke, you know."

"Go on," Dane said. "What kind of fluke?"

"The Kclabs were fighting about the skin contaminant they created, and we escaped in one of their vessels."

"Wait. Back up. Back up!" Dane shouted. "Created? Did you say *created*?"

The room roared in disgust.

"Quiet, please!" Dane shouted. "How do you know this?" he asked the Wilfin.

The creature craned its neck, twisted it like rubber and focused its bubbled eyes on all the Coalition officials in front of the room. The officials sat at attention; eyes downcast to avoid staring. "My, but you have a large gathering," it said. "And so calm. On Kclaben, this would never do. At an assembly this size, they would be bouncing about punching one another. Did I tell you that was how we escaped?"

"Yes, you did," Dane said. "Now quit stalling. We want to hear whatever it is you know."

"You must give me my answer first. Will we be granted our wish?"

"You're making me angry," said Dane. "We need answers, not games."

"We need answers too, and we want desperately for you to honor our wish."

Dane seethed. "That's blackmail."

"No, it is mercy. We are seeking your mercy. That is something we never received on Kclaben."

"Look, just give us an idea of what it is you know." Dane lowered his voice.

"Very well. But first let me consult the others."

The Wilfin craned its neck again and clucked seven times. On command, they oozed into the room. Each one introduced itself as Egna, along with its specific numerical designation.

"We all needed to be present," Egna 7 said. "Now that we are, I can give you the whole story, all the sordid details. I can tell you that we, the Wilfins, have an unusual chemical in our adrenal glands. It is quite pungent, something we secrete when we have been alarmed."

"What does this have to do with skin contamination?" Coleman broke in.

"Oh plenty, plenty," said Egna 6. "You see, the Kclabs frightened us continuously. They flogged us. In the process, they discovered that the fright aroma Egna 7 just told you about can become so potent that it transforms into sound waves. It was a gurgling sound that affects their skin at certain octaves and—"

"No, no, no, no," said Egna 2. "That is not the way it happened."

"It is not?" The Egna 6's voice creaked. It sounded hurt and confused.

"No, you are forgetting an important detail," added Egna 1.

"And what was that?" Egna 3 said.

"Stop it. Stop it, right now!" Coleman shouted. "Either one of you speaks or no one speaks. Please appoint a spokesperson. Let Egu 7, is it? Let that one tell the story."

Egna 7 slid closer.

"I would be delighted," it said, neck twisting to get another look at the room. "We all should avoid talking at once."

The Wilfins clucked and Egna 7 continued: "The Kclabs began extracting the substance from our glands. They liked the aroma and wanted to use it as some type of perfume. But the minute the stuff hit their skin, it burned. It lost its smell, too. The fluid would evaporate and, instead of a fragrance, it became a dull, noise. Then, one of them – I believe it was a lady Kclab – decided she rather liked the noise. She said it reminded her of the Earth music. So…"

Egna 7 stopped talking. Dane and Coleman nodded for it to continue, but its eyes were closing, and it was falling asleep.

"Wake up, please!" said Coleman. "Somebody, one of you Eggas, please wake it up."

Egna 6 clucked and Egna 7's eyes shot open. It said: "Please forgive me. That is one of our worst habits, sleeping during all the inappropriate times. But we are tired. Did I tell you we have been traveling for nearly two moon semesters?"

"Yes, you did," Coleman answered quickly, losing patience. "Continue."

"As I said, the lady Kclab liked the sound. And that is when it all began."

"What began?"

"The experiments. They began experimenting with the secretions, trying to come up with various usages. It was one of the most exciting new substances they had ever discovered. They were ecstatic. They got so worked up they started cutting us open and actually removing our adrenal glands."

Egna 7 stopped again. A gooey tear dripped from one eye.

"We cannot live without that gland. That is why there are so few of us left. We started huddling together, sharing one name and remembering one another as numbers. We count one another every day."

"And the substance," said Coleman. "What about the substance?"

"They became obsessed," said Egna 7. "They opened a night laboratory and the lady and... and another one – Tric, Trecca, I believe that was her name. The two of them would work on it during the early and late hours. Then one day, they said someone from Toth had figured out how to insert this stuff into something called music chips. The fluid had such an odd effect on the skin, they wondered about the impact the sound would have."

Egna 7 paused and breathed air in through its slit. "Funny," it said, shaking slightly. "But this room, it has a sweet sort of smell like, if you do not mind me saying, like our gland."

"Get on with your story please," said Dane.

"Oh, yes. The skin," said Egna 7. "The skin was their next step. They began solidifying the fluid into a gummy wad. I know because that Trecca talked about it in front of me. She said the substance in our gland was going to help her to achieve power over individuals with a certain hue."

"But they had no one in their world with dark skin to pass it on to?" said Coleman.

"Oh, but they did. The person from Toth agreed to help them. They had some sort of pact with him, and they often gave him our gland secretions," Egna 7 continued. "I know this because I heard the lady Kclabs praise this man from Toth. They called him a genius. I wish I could remember his name."

"Please try," urged Dane.

"I am... It just doesn't seem to be there. I suppose all the floggings have affected some part of my functioning."

"Were all of you flogged so they could induce this fear byproduct?"

"Yes, you see, it was far better for them that way. But at times, they chose to remove it. Did I tell you that because of the gland removals there are only eight of us left?"

"Yes, you did," Coleman and Dane both said in unison.

"All I remember is that one named Trecca really liked this man. She said she couldn't believe he was a Toth; that he actually should have been a Kclab. After the Toth man had figured out how to insert the secretions in small chips, she said the two of them were going to do more research and then report their findings back to all the Kclabs."

"And what were the findings?"

"That, for some reason, humans of high color content, could not hear the high frequencies our secretions could produce. They couldn't hear it unless it was turned down to its lowest peak. At its highest, they didn't perceive the sound waves at all. They only experienced the awful side effects. The Kclabs called them keloids. They said they were some kind of scar tissue."

The room was so quiet, Egna 7 took a break. The Wilfin seemed tired of hearing itself talk and startled by the sudden quiet and petrified stares. "Does this mean that you are going to grant us asylum? Is this going to be our future home?"

Dane made eye contact with Coleman. The officials on the platform were tapping their writing utensils and mumbling. Hands in the audience were upraised. "The answer is a collective yes," said Dane. "We don't even have to vote on it. You may not realize it, but you could be the answer to our prayers."

"Prayers? What are prayers?"

"We can talk about that another time. What we need now is the name of that Toth. Have you remembered the name yet?"

"No, I am sorry. My memory suffers because of –"

"I know, the floggings," Dane sighed.

"Thank you for understanding," Egna 7 said. "We will go now. We have an old Kclab ship. It had been discarded. But for us it is like home. If you do not mind, we would like to go back there now and try to get more sleep." Each Wilfin lifted its scaly foot and prepared to thump-slide toward the door. They all clucked. Egna 7 paused and said: "We have fantasized about this place. We have heard the Kclabs say that you opened your doors to anyone but them. Too bad they actually found someone here to cooperate. And hard to believe, too. Imagine, he was willing to harm others so he could synthesize new building fibers. The Kclabs said the human from Toth wanted to revolutionize the landscape."

The room erupted.

"Ellis!" someone shouted. "Ellis!"

Ellis was in the rear of the room, sneaking out of the back door. The Sonaguards grabbed him, and everyone stood.

"Ellis?" said Coleman, his voice trembling.

Ellis dropped to his knees. "It wasn't my idea!" he screamed. "It was Chinbedza! Blame him! It wasn't me, I tell you. It wasn't just me!"

11

"Life happens in your mind, for that is the only place you truly reside."
– From the journals of Ahonotay

Lileala hopped along a path leading to the caves, stopping now and then to catch her breath. "Keep moving. I'll catch up," she called out to Brian.

He waited anyway. "I'm not going to leave you, Lileala. Not as long as you are tied."

"Stop making a fuss. I'm not helpless."

"You're not helpless, but you do need help," he said and began walking toward her.

She wagged her head. "No, I'm fine. I have it all under control." She bent over and tried to loosen one of the ropes Bertram had wrapped around her ankles.

"I wish I could help you with that," Brian said.

"Don't bother," she said. "LaJuped might be watching. You and Garrette take the gag out of my mouth every day. That's enough."

"I don't understand why you won't let us get you out of that thing too."

"They'll only make another one," Lileala said, tugging at the rope, leaving bruises where she once had keloids. But each day, the friction became more bearable, and she had learned, with some effort, how to maneuver her way around the colony.

"Here I come. I managed to twirl the rope a bit and give myself a little more room to move."

"You're amazing," Brian said, shaking his head. "No one but you would persevere so."

"That means I can be an example."

He laughed. "Sure, Lileala, sure you can."

"Don't be so cynical. At least I've accomplished one thing."

"And what is that?"

"I made you laugh. That's something you never did before." She smiled at him.

"I take offense to that. I laugh all the time."

"Maybe in your world, but not here. How much do you really laugh here, on this place?"

"I suppose not much, and now that you mentioned it, I'll stop completely. I have no intention of laughing again, not until I get home. I'm tired of this place."

"That's just it." Lileala kept hopping. "You're making yourself miserable. By refusing to laugh, you, me, all of us, we're choosing misery."

His voice dropped. "Not now, Lileala. I'm not in the mood for this today."

"You have no choice. I'm going to talk about it anyway, and as soon as we arrive at the cave, I'm going to tell them the same thing."

"I don't know how much of a reception you're going to get," Brian cautioned. "People think you're a troublemaker."

"Why? Just because the Kclabs aren't accepting any more letters?"

"Not just that, Lileala, it's the rumors you're spreading. They're tired of all your negative talk about the Kclabs."

"But it's true," Lileala said. "I know what I saw."

She and Brian stopped in front of the cave and peered inside. The Wasswa sisters were tucked in their usual space, and Garrette and Martore were about a half of a yard behind them. Lileala could see clumps of lumpy blankets and sleeping bags somewhere near the rear.

"Don't wake them," Brian whispered.

"I'm not, but why are they still asleep? You're up already."

"I told you, I can't sleep."

"And I told you I have the remedy. Joy."

"That's enough," Brian said. Thin lines were spreading across his forehead. "Let's keep walking. I don't think it's such a good idea to hover."

They moved further along a twisting trail that led to a garden Lileala had created in the dirt several meters from the cave. When Lileala stopped hopping and caught her breath, Brian sat on the nearest boulder and began studying the newly sprouted crops. "Carrots and grains," Lileala said. "And over there are some nettles. This is what I can't wait to show the other colonists, the ones who weren't with us by the fire."

An insect, smaller than most, flew toward Brian and landed in the middle of his chest. Brian swatted, then frowned when he noticed that it had managed to entwine itself in the dense hairs of his sweater. "I'd hold off, if I were you," he said to Lileala. "They might think it's unnatural. I'm worried that they're going to get even more suspicious of you."

"Go on then, leave me here by myself," she said. "I don't like listening to you when you're this negative."

Brian got up, but didn't leave. He waited, watching Lileala struggle again with the rope around her ankles. She turned her back, burying her thoughts in the cool, dry ground. She knew how much he hated the cold, the nothingness, and that not a single night passed without him tossing feverishly, longing for a lush setting of grass and trees.

"Some evenings, just believe," she said. "For a second, believe that you actually see bushes growing miraculously in the compound. See it and pretend it's not a mirage."

He glared at her, and she fought off a creeping resentment

that had lodged in his spirit. Was there any way to get him to find some joy in these conditions?

"Yes, I know it's like a cold desert here," she said. "But at least the insects are starting to vanish and at least I found a spot where the air doesn't have so much dust."

A frown crossed Brian's face. "Yes, I see," he said. "I know you're clairvoyant, but don't use it on me. Particularly when I'm in a bad mood."

Lileala continued as if she hadn't heard him. "My skin doesn't sting anymore and neither does yours, Brian. Not like it did when we were covered with keloids. Isn't that something to feel happy about?"

Brian sucked in the air and feigned indifference. "How can anyone suffer like you and yet appear so noble?"

"Is that your problem?" she asked. "You don't believe I could be content while enduring so much pain?"

"If you're going to read my thoughts, then you have to answer them." He paused. "Will you do that?"

"Perhaps." Lileala squirmed.

"I do believe in you. I respect your abilities," said Brian. "I'm just wondering what good they are. How are they helping us in this galaxy-forsaken place? The Kclabs aren't letting us write and no one at home knows what's going on. Where are your ancestors now? Why haven't they done something?"

"You're difficult, Brian."

"This is a difficult place," he countered.

"But it doesn't have to be."

"Lileala, stop it already. We're rotting here. It's no longer a dispensary. It's more like a prison and our home worlds don't even know it."

Leaning all of her weight on one leg, Lileala put pressure on the right and strongest side of her body and hopped in Brian's direction. "Let's go," she said. "The sun's about to rise, the others will be getting up soon."

He reached to help her, but she moved with a quickness that surprised him.

"No, it's okay," she said. "Let's get back."

The sky was turning a blurry yellow and a wand of light was forming on their footpath, making it easier for them to see. They lumbered along the path, Lileala hopping, aware that Brian was toying with the idea of making up. She read his mind and answered before he could switch to another thought.

"It's okay, you're forgiven," she told him. "I'm not mad at you. I just don't want you and the others to become embittered."

"It's a little late for that." Brian raised his voice. "Everyone's already bitter. But they're blaming *you*, not the Kclabs. They feel the Kclabs have abandoned us because *you* keep getting them all worked up. Look at yourself; they've got you tied up in ropes."

"I can handle the ropes. But what do you mean they're blaming me?"

"They feel the Kclabs have become crueler, that they're meaner to all of us in an effort to get back at you."

"I'm the one in ropes, not them." She looked away.

"But the conditions are tougher now," Brian said. "The pond's dirty and there's so little water left. What happens if it dries up completely? I doubt there are any more ice pockets on this asteroid."

Lileala reached for a calabash, the big jug strapped to her back. "This is a present from Garrette," she said, oblivious to Brian's remarks. "He crafted it himself out of the dried remains of that squash that grew the night we all sat around the fire. After it hardened, he fused both halves together by wrapping them in burlap strands. I've filled it with beverage."

"A beverage of what? That water stinks."

"It's melon. I never know what's coming. Melon sprouted yesterday. Just one, but I got it to yield extra nectar just by dicing the rind and the peelings. I'm taking it to those who

haven't felt well lately." They continued down the path and
Lileala sank deeper into Brian's mind. Something pricked her,
and she nearly jumped.

"What?"

"Nothing." She shook off the painful thought he was having
– a memory of his dead elder Ma – and moved into something
easier: his yearnings. She was careful not to storm into his
mind like she'd done earlier, keeping Brian oblivious to her
intrusion. She tiptoed and sorted through his fantasies with
a feather-like touch. She felt him imagining the two of them
walking down a road flanked with leafy trees.

"I believe that if you trust in something enough, it will hold
true," Lileala said as they reached the caves.

The colonists had risen, and many were rolling up their
sleeping bags and heading out with their towels. "We won't
have clean water much longer," a young man griped. He had
an ash-brown complexion that was a lighter shade than the
two men who stood near him. "The supply is so low," one of
them added, then scowled at Lileala. "And it's not getting any
better."

"Oh, it will." Lileala said, slowly easing into the cave. She
stooped over an ailing woman who was curled up in a blanket
on the ground. "Don't let them worry you about that pond,"
she said, patting the woman's hand.

She looked up at the men and sighed. "The Kclabs don't have
the power to fill it," she said. "They're probably as frantic as we
are. Has it occurred to any of you that, before we arrived, there
had never been a single occupant on this asteroid? Without
inhabitants, how were they to know how much water was
needed? It's up to us to figure out what to do. If we make a
fire, can't we clean the water by boiling it?"

Turning her back to the skeptics, Lileala kneeled beside the
woman, wishing someone would come help. Without a word,
Garrette walked from the rear of the cave and stopped to hand
Lileala his bowl. He poured the juice mixture from Lileala's

jug into the bowl and watched as she held it up to the ailing woman, letting it soothe the corners of her mouth. Her skin was dry and cracked, though Lileala supposed she was only in her fifties.

"Here," she said. "You're sick, but it's not your body that has burdened you. Your state of mind is what's taking your strength."

The woman grabbed Lileala's hand. "Everyone thinks you're a nuisance." Her voice was hoarse, and her eyes were a flaming red.

"You're in need," Lileala said. "I'm here with you, sending you good thoughts. That's the way I help." The woman took a sip of the sweet juice while Lileala supported her head with her arms. "You're losing too much strength," she said again. She handed the bowl to Garrette while she pulled a rolled cloth out of her satchel. She unwrapped it and offered the woman several large, freshly plucked leaves.

"No," the woman protested. "It will make me sick."

"You're already sick," Lileala said. "Here, eat. They're beet greens. I'll place pieces in your mouth that are small enough to chew raw."

The woman ate it dutifully, then sat up and leaned closer to Lileala's breast. Lileala felt a sweet satisfaction in her stomach, a feeling that the vegetable was nourishing the woman's body. With each chew, Lileala could taste the chlorophyll in the leaf and the revitalizing minerals in the stems. She thought of how strong this woman had been when she first arrived in the colony. She remembered how swiftly she walked and how much determination she had rattling around in her spirit. "It's still there," Lileala cooed, and she sent the woman an image of her former self, fearsome and vibrant.

"My child," she said to Lileala. "Whoever sent you, thank them." She looked up at Garrette. "Thank you, little one, and thank the Grace of the ancestors."

"Get away from us! We don't want to be around you!" It

was a bystander, a woman Lileala knew only vaguely. "If it wasn't for you, we'd probably be back home. You and your lies have slowed down everything!"

"They're not lies," Lileala countered. "The Kclabs aren't what you think. They're using us as part of some elaborate plot."

"You don't know what you're talking about!" the woman yelled. "Once we're cured and back home, some of them will move to our home worlds, and that's that. If you know something more, you should explain it to us, not just ask us to trust you. What do they plan to do?"

Lileala paused. "Um, I can't tell you, exactly. All I know is that on the planet I saw, buildings were burning and Trieca was herding scared children into an outdoor school of some sort."

"What planet? What damned building? If that's all you can tell us then you don't know anything," the woman scoffed before backing away. The others followed, keeping their eyes fixed on Lileala as they moved out of the cave.

Lileala and Garrette sat with the sick woman a while longer then made their way to the pond. The odor was so foul she could smell it before it came into view. Almost all of it had turned into clumps of sludge, and she noticed a young Jemti man crouching near the pond's ledge, holding on with both hands, licking his lips as if he was taking a drink. She leaned over and stroked his dull green hair. "Here, drink," she said.

He lifted his limp head and drank. "I have been here so long on this place that I can't blame you. Even if you are crazy, I can't blame you."

"I'm not crazy," said Lileala. "I'm different, but far from crazy."

The man wheezed then rubbed his throat. "Some people here like you, mainly your friends. The rest say you're a lunatic. They say you have strange visions and that you do things just to provoke those Kclabs."

"I don't provoke them," Lileala said patiently. She drew in

the strength he'd lost and imagined it flowing back to him. "Not deliberately."

The man kept rubbing his throat. She could feel his will fading. She breathed in and exhaled life back into his thoughts. She reminded him that he was defiant, that his soul was filled with humor. "You're going to need that humor now."

"Some say that you like causing trouble," he said and coughed. "They think you make the Kclabs angry on purpose so you can show off your powers. LaJuped said the Kclabs told him this. He said you want us to rise against them; you want us to fight so you can use your powers to kill the Kclabs."

Lileala processed the accusations and disregarded them. But her images to the young man continued, a mental compost of his past self, the vigor he had when he first arrived in the colony. "I don't believe fighting would get us anywhere," she said to him. "That's just what LaJuped wants you to believe." She could feel him getting stronger. "I have no reason to pretend. I wonder why the people on this place have so much trouble believing me."

The man paused. "I trust you. I'm not afraid."

"You *are* afraid," said Lileala. "That's why you're in this condition. If I can get you and the others to release your fears, you wouldn't know so much pain."

The man wheezed and Lileala cradled his head in her arms, feeding him pieces of beet leaf.

"You leave him alone!" There came a sudden shout. Lileala turned to see a woman approaching. She was younger than the others. Her arms were thin, and her dark face was gaunt. "Leave him alone," she shouted again. "Leave us all alone. We don't want you around."

Several colonists chimed in. "Go away. Leave this area and don't bother us."

Lileala backed away, staring into the eyes of her tormenters. She noticed Martore among them. Her braids had been cropped, swaying only slightly and her eyes were cast downward.

"What are you so afraid of?" Lileala asked. "My courage? Are you afraid because I am not afraid? So, I stand up to the Kclabs. Is that so terrible? You've never stood up to them and where has it gotten you? You're still on this asteroid. And many of you are wasting away. You're sick. Do you know why that is? Because of your own fears, your own refusal to reach out and help one another. There are weak people in this colony and most of you haven't offered them anything, not even your leftover skrull. Why aren't you sharing with the sick ones? Is it me you're afraid of? Or are you afraid of yourselves?"

"We're just trying to survive," the woman said, but Lileala thought she now looked ashamed. "We don't know what to make of you. You talk to yourself, you wander away to strange places, and you have upset the Kclabs."

"The Kclabs," said Lileala. "The Kclabs will be upset no matter what we do. Why do you think we're here?" Lileala backed further away, hopping at a slow, deliberate pace. "LaJuped is right about one thing," she said angrily. "No one can talk to you. You're so content to wallow. You won't do anything to help yourselves. When I tried, that traitor, LaJuped, used it against me. He turned the Kclabs on me, so I couldn't reach out to you, and now he's turned you against me too. All so he can win their favor. And it's working. You're walking right into his trap."

Lileala adjusted the jug on her back, picked up her satchel and prepared to leave. Her eyes wandered to the young man on the ground, and she noted that he was lifting his head on his own. He was sitting with his legs outstretched in front of him, but he wasn't strong enough to stand just yet. Lileala nodded to him before walking toward the rock tower.

"Wait!" Martore was standing near her, shortened locks completely still.

"Did you say LaJuped deliberately turned the Kclabs against you?" she asked. "Are you saying the Kclabs and LaJuped are making you part of a scheme?"

"What do you think?" Lileala said. "From the beginning you and Brian told me that he couldn't be trusted."

Martore directed her gaze on Lileala and used her rotating pupils to detect signs of a lie. "I see you're telling the truth," she said. "I don't know why I didn't do a probe sooner. Perhaps I wanted to believe the little runt. I can't believe I was really that –"

"Jealous?" Lileala's tone was confrontational.

Martore looked away. "Yes, that was it, I suppose. I'm sorry. I'm truly ashamed."

Lileala sighed. "It's okay." She gave her a warm nod before turning toward the crowd, "I mean that for all of you. Whatever you have thought of me is okay. I realize you're confused. I'm confused too. But I'm not what the Kclabs have told you. I'm not what LaJuped has claimed. And I'm not crazy."

The crowd was silent.

"But you *are* bringing us pain," the woman who had accosted her said. "And our water supply is drying up."

"I don't bring pain, and – and I have my seeds. You've seen them, even in a world like this, they can create food."

"Witch!" someone yelled, and the crowd began muttering again.

"Listen to me!" Lileala shouted. "If nothing else, please listen. If the Kclabs were as honorable as you think they are, do you believe they would be treating us this way? Lately they only visit the asteroid every other day, and when they do, they don't always have the Mecca or nutrient powders with them. What kind of healers abandon you in a time of need? You can believe me or not, but either way, just ask yourself what reason they have to deny letters and stop doling out our treatment. If they really wanted us to heal, would they keep it from us? So, yes, my visions about them were sketchy. But look around, please. Look at how we're living. Doesn't this environment tell you that something is very wrong."

The crowd looked on. Brian and Martore were standing

beside Lileala, and from the corner of her left eye she noticed that Martore was silently beckoning the Wasswa sisters and the elder Osiris to join them. She was moving her lips, asking them to come forward, but the sisters stayed where they were in the back of the crowd.

The woman spoke again, "We're just trying to survive. But... well, perhaps, I don't know, maybe our fear made us selfish." She raised an arm to help Lileala walk. "I can't say I believe everything you said but some of it made sense and you're making me ask a lot of questions."

"That's all I wanted."

The morning air had a sharp bite, the aftermath of a strong overnight wind that had blown across the asteroid, scattering sediment and broken chips of rock. Despite the chill, Lileala was determined to lead any colonist who was willing on a sojourn along the trails leading to the mystical crater. After enduring their verbal attacks the day before, she had won their trust and didn't want to take a chance on losing it.

As soon as they awakened and clambered out into the open, she told them her plans and was surprised that all of them, even the sick ones, wanted to make the trip.

"It's not that far, really," she assured the group. "I've done it in forty minutes flat. But we can't do it without a good breakfast and –" Lileala paused and peered into their eyes, looking for signs of doubt or suspicion. "I'm going to do something now that some of you have seen but most of you haven't. Please, do not be alarmed."

She instructed them to sit in a half circle around an expanse of dirt about five meters long, maybe four meters wide. While they observed in silence, Lileala swept a towel across the dirt, clearing it of pebbles and assorted debris. Martore stood to help, but Lileala was too carried away to notice. Wiping her hands on the towel, she leaned over her makeshift plot, plonked down three large seeds and whispered: "Now watch this."

Barely seconds had passed before the ground began spitting up dirt and churning like a dull theater of the soil. A vine of yellow zucchinis slowly bored through its surface. Onions popped up. Next came fennel, peas, massive cucumbers. In a matter of minutes, there was an explosion of cabbage, corn and sundry root vegetables. Instead of fleeing as Lileala had worried, the colonists clapped and cheered.

"We'd already heard about this," said the elder woman, Hattie. "But it's something else to actually see it happen and know it's real. I guess LaJuped would have –" She caught herself and stopped talking for a few seconds. "Sorry," she said. "I didn't mean to bring him up. I promise you, that traitor and I are no longer friends."

"Who cares? Who's thinking about him right now? I mean, look," said Brian, motioning toward the garden.

Without Lileala asking, Brian rose and busied himself making a small fire and used his sharpened nail file to slice potatoes and carrots. The Wasswa twins simmered the cucumbers in a long, iron saucepan Roloc had given them, stirring until they had generated enough water for cooking. Martore added a blend of root vegetables and boiled them for twelve minutes, stirring in sweet peas and crumbled fennel leaves.

After they had eaten, Lileala cast her final seed. It sprouted into a wild blueberry bush that bore a tart fruit to stash in their satchels and save for the trek back from the cliff.

"Okay, let's go," Lileala said. "It's getting late, and I want us there before dark. But – and I mean this – take all the time you need. If you have to rest, please say so and we'll wait."

Lining up behind Lileala, they began their journey up the inclining road and over the hill to her hideaway. Along the way, the strongest assisted weaker ones. The woman who had been cared for by Garrette had regained much of her stamina, but her movements weren't steady and Martore had to take her arm to help her over the hill's peak. Still bothered by the asteroid's low gravity, Martore's heels barely touched the ground, but she pressed harder. When Lileala suggested she rest she waved her away.

"We're almost there," Lileala announced once they'd made it to the other side of the hill. "We'll enter a cave I found soon, and it will twist toward a tunnel with a floor of spiked rocks. But I'll smooth them, you'll see. Come on."

They gathered around her, so eager Lileala could feel it. The young Jemti man she had comforted the day before began running and she had to plead with him to slow down.

"Okay, I will," he said. He broke into a trot then a quick stroll, before grudgingly accepting her suggestion to allow the twins to walk with him, each on opposite sides in case he lost his balance. But the diamond-flecked copper roof of the cave up ahead sent him into sprint.

"Look at that!" he shouted, racing ahead of the others. He gushed even more when he entered the cave and discovered that the porous ceiling dripped with gold.

When the cave reached what appeared to be a dead end, Lileala came to a standstill and closed her eyes.

"Follow me," she said after a five-minute lapse. "This area has rugged spikes along the bottom, but now it should be smooth."

The colonists ducked into a squat tunnel with a paved quartz crystal floor. Once on the other side of the passageway, they shrieked in delight.

"It's beautiful," said Martore. "Now that I see it, I get why you come here all the time."

"I see more than this though, Martore," Lileala said. "That's why I brought you all here, to show you. I see the original melanin bearers of Earth. I see their despair, but I also see their triumph."

"But," said Martore, "didn't you see them back at the colony?"

"Yes, but I couldn't heal them," Lileala said. "I had to come here to tap into curative powers and renew my strength. And all of you can do the same. Many of your ancestors were probably melanin bearers like mine who found a way to escape the persecution on Earth. My people are the Dogon from Mali, but so many of our other ancestors came from all over the Africa land. And in those areas your ancestors are waiting for you to mine the strength that flows within your own spirits and flow it back to them and help them heal."

The colonists sat in a circle, spellbound by Lileala's message. "You must be like the mythical fox being tracked across the plateaus around the Dogon villages," she said. "This pale fox turns from the pursuit and chases the pursuer."

Lileala suddenly stopped and told them to clasp hands and chant. "Rise up, rise up, rise up." Then she requested their silence as she moved closer to the precipice of the cliff and, despite the cool air, began to sweat.

With closed eyes and hands upraised, she sank into an Inekoteth trance so deep that for a moment, she seemed lost to her companions.

Ten minutes later, she opened her eyes and spoke: "A week ago, a few of us made a commitment to learn trinity breath, but all we did was use it to make a few sweaters." She laughed. "Martore, Virtue and Honor, don't you believe we can do better than that?"

The chuckles that came from the group sounded nervous. Martore spoke up. "You think everyone can do this?" she asked. "Even the uninitiated?"

Lileala smirked. "Martore, take a good long look at this beautiful escarpment. It's a natural enclave of gems. And there's power here, given to us from the stars of Sirius, Po Tolo, and my ancestors. With energy that pure, everyone up here will be electric."

She rose and suggested that all hands be placed above abdomens to allow breath to be harnessed from deep within the diaphragm.

"Do it three times and exhale," she said. "Now twice. Now once. Now, everyone, we're going to do this again, but each time, picture a flame and repeat after me:

"Breath One: Imagine the flame.

"Breath Two: Walk upon the embers

"Breath three: Be the fire."

At the end of their trinity exercise, Lileala encouraged them to relax and trust. "During the two hours we have spent here, you have communed with a Higher Power and allowed this power into your spirit," she said. "I'll show you how to use it when we return. Right now, let's get out of here. I know the Kclabs have been inconsistent lately, but we better get back just in case they choose today to visit."

"Smart thinking," Brian said. "We need to hurry, so let's undo those ankle ropes."

Lileala nodde, allowing him to cut the ties.

Brian walked beside Lileala and squeezed her hand. "You really empowered those people. I'm amazed. The sick ones seem to be nearly twice as strong as they were before your ritual."

A sense of gratitude filled Lileala. Instead of pulling away, she tickled his palm. "Thank you for appreciating me," she said. "And thanks for removing my ropes."

"That was easy," he said. "I just don't get why you didn't let me do it before today."

"Come on Brian, the Kclabs know we're friends and that you're likely to be the one to assist me. They're bound to show up again and when they do, now they're going to turn their rage on you too."

Brian said. "I don't care."

"You're not afraid?" Lileala asked.

"Should I be?"

"Probably."

Lileala paused. "I have another surprise."

When the group made it down the hill and reached the rock tower, Lileala addressed them. "For days, Brian has yearned for a rainforest like the ones on his home world. In his mind, he sees a canopy of trees with water dripping from their branches. In his mind, heavy rains fall, dripping into thickets and bushes with leaves larger than our hands. It has been a mirage only because he's left it there.

"There was a time when I didn't believe in illusion," she said. "Now I do, and I want to show you how to live inside of your own minds. Close your eyes," she ordered. "Now that all of you have learned trinity breath, we're going to put it to good use."

"But what about the crater, the magic of the cliff?" someone asked. "How can we do trinity breath without that?"

"You learned a lot at that crater, but I'll add Inekoteth too," Lileala said.

"What's Inekoteth?" asked Garrette.

"That's when my ancestors talk to me or through me," Lileala said. "I'll tap into it to strengthen our vision. But this time, when you see the flame, add the images of your choice as well. When you become the fire, feel the blistering heat and add your own words.

"Okay, go!" she shouted. "First, do your breath work."

Murmurs followed and Lileala could feel everyone around her absorbing the flame. "Now, close your eyes and feel a light spray of water. See it falling. Feel its touch. Go inside and see the branches of hundreds of trees swinging in the wind. Let them brush against you." She paused and, after a moment, began to pray.

The colonists joined her, repeating the incantation Lileala had recited on the cliff, acknowledging the power of Po Tolo. "Rise in the energy of the fox, one who chases away fear. Rise, rise, it is fine. Szewa." They spoke with a fervor that shocked Lileala. Eyes shut tight and lips aquiver, they prayed with her. She opened her eyes and felt her pulse accelerate.

"Look around you! Please, everyone!" She laughed as she shouted.

The colonists shrieked. They were flanked by tall grasses and green, low hanging vines. A creek cut through the center of the dust trail. Bushes surrounded it. Palm trees encroached on a narrow waterfall that meandered over a hill and splashed into a cool, clear brook.

Virtue was the first to speak. "It's a rainforest! Is this really here?" Her face was full of awe.

"Yes, it is here for all who are willing to see it and for you, it is very, very real," Lileala said, smiling as the water drizzled onto her cheeks. "But for the Kclabs, this will not exist."

Lileala heard water sloshing and saw Martore and Garrette trampling though a bed of soggy weeds. Osiris followed behind them, then stopped and pointed up at a cypress tree atop a nearby mountain.

"That can't be," he said. "That looks like a tree from my homeland. Is it here?"

"The forest and all the trees are our collective reality," Lileala said. "*We* created it." Osiris let out a loud sound and joined Garrette among the wet leaves. Brian stood alone, and Lileala was so entrenched in the mindscape that she couldn't pick up his thoughts. Could he see it? Had he really been able to manifest the woods, the creek?

Lileala watched him sadly, wondering if the pain gnawing inside him was so great that it simply couldn't be penetrated.

"I can't stop you from driving away your own feelings of joy," she cried out.

"Don't bother," he yelled back, a tear trailing down his cheek. He turned in a circle, allowing himself to be drenched. "Don't bother with me," he said. "Help someone else, someone who might not believe."

A sudden grin dimpled his cheeks, and he broke a promise he'd made to Lileala only days earlier. He stood in the center of the Keloid Colony and laughed.

12

"To the cells of our bodies, we are deities to be worshipped and served. Healing begins when we listen to their cries."
      – Scientific Pineal Crew by-law

Egna 7 slinked around the Toth science laboratory, a mere box of a room, compact and tidy with sharp corners and sterile white walls. The Wilfin seemed uncomfortable in the sanitized surroundings. It rolled onto its back and squirmed as if it was beginning to itch. "I find things disconcerting here," it complained. "Why are there so many vacancies?"

Egna 7's neck wobbled. It twisted around to the front and to the left, disturbed by the silver and chrome sink, the scrubbed canisters, the long, glass countertops and the empty spaces. "Wilfins aren't used to empty spaces," it said, alarmed. "Why are there vacancies?"

Kwesi peered through an elongated instrument and knocked his knuckles against the lab table, ignoring Egna 7 and its incessant whining.

"You mean you can't tell me anything?" he asked, handing the instrument back to a technician. "And you of all people, Rhonda. You're the best biochemist we have on Toth."

"We're getting close," Rhonda answered. Grimacing, she placed the instrument Kwesi handed her on the table and pushed a pair of rimless magnifiers above the tip of her nose. The microscope lenses floated in place about two inches from

367

her forehead, enhancing her view of Wilfin cell mitochondria.

"We haven't figured out the respiration process of the cells in the Mecca sample provided by Ellis," she said. "But Tres and I have a theory about their frenetic movements."

Tres, Rhonda's lab partner, strode from the other side of the room.

"These cells don't behave like anything we've ever experienced," he said. "But we think we can manipulate them. To do that, we need more input from Ellis."

"Sonaguards are in the next room, interrogating him now but –" Kwesi gave the table a hard whack. "I walked out. I couldn't stand being around him. I'll hear him out now, though," Kwesi said and rushed out of the room.

Egna 7 wobbled behind him, speaking though its nose. It contracted in quick, short spurts. "Wait. I would like to go," Egna 7 squealed. "Please, sir. I want to get out of this room."

The door slid shut and Kwesi vanished. The Wilfin began wrapping its body into a lumpy ball.

"What's wrong?" Tres asked, keeping one eye on his instrument. "You've been acting bizarre. Do you really want to leave that badly?"

"Yes, please," it said. "I do so want to leave. I want to join the other Egnas. And…" It looked at the room as if it was on fire. "I want out of this awful place. There are too many vacancies."

Tres scanned the room and chuckled. "What vacancies?" he asked, grinning. "I'm not sure what you mean."

"The vacancies. The many empty spaces. It is so open here. Every spot is not crowded in the way I am accustomed to. The edges are so severe, so perpendicular. I feel as if I am twirling. We Wilfins prefer dark areas and many, many objects. We like being around many objects that have aged."

"You like clutter?" Tres said and he laughed at the Wilfin. "I'll let you go, then," he said. "We don't need you now. We have the serum. All we need to do is study it."

"I am most grateful," said Egna 7, looking into Tres's eyes.

He shuddered. He couldn't stand it when the creature peered right at him. He didn't like watching it purse its tiny pinhole nose as if it were a pair of lips.

He prepared to press the wall exit button, but it opened suddenly and Kwesi walked in with Ellis.

"Where are you going?" Kwesi said to the Wilfin. "Sit."

"He wanted to go, sir," Tres said.

"He'll do nothing of the sort." Kwesi's eyes were riveted on the Wilfin. "Egna, I want you to listen to this. If he says anything that you recognize as false, then tell me right away."

"Right," said the Wilfin. It sidled up to Ellis and let its eyes droop.

"You can let it go now," Ellis said, settling into a lab chair. "You won't need his service. I have another sample chip with me, and I'm prepared to share it, to tell you everything. It was a bad idea and I'm remorseful."

"Shut up!" said Kwesi. "My daughter is in that damn colony you helped concoct. I don't need your remorse. Right now, I just want the facts."

"The chip Chinbedza had in his hand was filled with Mecca," Ellis explained. "Every time the Kclabs increased or diluted it, I'd go there to pick up a portion and infuse it in another chip. Then I'd take the new chip to the Mhondora to place in the keystone. It penetrated the walls of her dome and continued to affect her, no matter where she was. The Wilfins have an intense connection to one another. They feel one another's moods and emotions, even from a distance of millions of kilometers. The serum in the chips functioned on the same principle. Lileala was exposed to the chip during her nights on the Surface. Granted, those nights were rare, but it was enough for her cells to absorb the frequency."

"But she was directed to spend *more* time on the Surface," Kwesi said. "And when she did, her symptoms faded."

"Like I said, they diluted the formula and passed it on to me. They knew she was trying to heal. Chinbedza told me and I told them. At the Coalition meeting they told you they made it past your Sonaguards and sprayed Lileala's dome. That's a lie. I gave the new diluted Mecca chip to Chinbedza, and he went to the Surface in the late hour and switched the chips."

"But Otto was with her. Why wasn't he affected?"

"He was with her when the Mecca was weak, meaning it was healing, not producing new keloids. That's what helped them convince you that they had the cure without revealing more."

"More what?" Kwesi's voice was tight. "You're talking in circles."

"More about their role in this," Ellis said. "Sir, it was the Kclab's fault. They used the Mecca chips to cause the disease in the first place."

The rage Kwesi felt at that moment numbed his senses. While the lab techs scoffed at Ellis's story, his mind swung back and forth between shock and rumbling thoughts of vengeance. He coped by pretending he was extinguishing tiny little explosions in his chest.

"I'm having a hard time managing my temper," he said, trying not to lunge at Ellis.

Ellis grimaced. "Sir, I'm sorry."

"Damn your fake sorrow!" Kwesi snapped.

"By opening up, I'm hoping that now I can help. Truly, I am sorry."

"Just tell me what I need to do to get my daughter back."

"Well, the vibrations are strange because, as your science staff will tell you, the chemical make-up of the cells in a Wilfin's gland is irregular. I was able to use the serum to impact construction materials. I'd place it in a chip just to contain it. By exposing any material to the chip, I could change its molecular structure, stretch it or bend it. It actually makes matter more pliable, then sturdy."

Kwesi glanced at the Wilfin for verification. Its head was twisted toward the back wall, and it was sound asleep. "Dammit," Kwesi said. "Wake up that thing."

Tres shook it and laughed at the way it jerked.

"Sorry, sir!" it yelled.

"Proceed," Kwesi said to Ellis.

Otto walked in the room at that moment but was not acknowledged by Kwesi. His behavior had become troublesome and Kwesi wasn't relaxed enough to deal with it.

Otto grabbed a chair and tried to make eye contact, but the Pineal Crew Chief kept his gaze on Ellis. Kwesi knew without turning that Otto was disheveled, that his uniform was probably soiled, and that his hair was unkempt. He was growing a heavy beard these days and Kwesi didn't approve.

After a few moments, Kwesi allowed himself to observe him, and wished immediately that he hadn't. The damn fool! He was out of uniform and his hair was a matted, uncombed mess.

"Proceed," Kwesi said again. He was trying hard not to give Otto a second glance.

"As I was saying, I was able to alter building materials simply by exposing them to the vibration of the chip. Well, just think what that would do to skin, even skin that's not directly exposed?"

"And what about you? You were..."

"It didn't affect me because I knew which frequencies to use and which to avoid. And I wore protective clothing, stuffed with lead."

"But you're saying that just temporary exposure was enough to affect my daughter?"

"Yes."

"Absurd."

"Absurd, yes, but true."

Kwesi checked the Wilfin. Its head was bobbing up and down in agreement.

"Keep in mind that the vibrations are noises," said Ellis. "And that's how..." Ellis quieted.

"Yes? Continue."

"That's how Chinbedza died, sir, trying to remove the chip from the dome. He and I both wanted it removed. We honestly didn't know the Kclabs would go as far as they did."

"What do you mean?"

For a full thirty seconds, Kwesi could see Ellis's lips moving but he heard nothing.

"Speak, Ellis, speak!" Kwesi commanded. "What is wrong with you?"

"It's h-hard s-sir, that's all," he stammered. "I'm having a hard time saying t-that, well, the Mhondora went deeper, much deeper than me. For years, I mean centuries, he… he was hoarding some ancient type of medicine. At least that's what he called it. He said Swazembians originated from a mystical tribe and that when he was named Mhondora, he and he alone became privy to their wisdom. All of the wizened Mhondoras learned of these secrets and all of them, including Chinbedza hid Swazembi's legacy from Earth."

Kwesi sucked in his breath. "Earth? Did I hear that right? I'll be damned! So that really is our heritage, our past. And he knew it! Why, in the galaxy, would he hide something like that?"

"According to the Mhondora, your founders wanted it that way. But as the sole gatekeeper, Chinbedza had access to their potent medicine, something called juju. The Mhondora told me that, as far as he knew, it was pure. Its incantations hadn't been uttered more than once or twice for thousands of millennia."

"Meaning?"

"Meaning he wanted to grow it to almost unimaginable proportions," Ellis went on. "He was driven, that man. He wanted to use it to take over and rule his own world."

"That doesn't make sense. What possible world would the Mhondora —" Kwesi halted midsentence and clenched both fists. "Oh, no! Golong! Are you talking about that missing planet, Golong?"

Nodding his head, Ellis continued. "But the Kclabs reneged on their part of the deal. After the Mhondora cloaked Golong and hid it from the Coalition's view, they cut off contact with him." Ellis hid the upper half of his face in his elbow and discretely wiped away a tear with his sleeve.

"Wow," said Tres, his mouth gaped. He poked Rhonda and she spoke into her dial.

"Janelle, you've got to come hear this. Hurry."

Three women and two men wearing white vests identifying them as medics and biologists entered while Ellis stumbled through the rest of his story.

"With the Mhondora's abilities, if he had wanted to, he could have cast a spell to maim or even destroy the Kclabs, every last one of them. But his guilt got the best of him, and he no longer wanted any part of the Kclabs or their plan. All he wanted was to get that chip out of the Rare Indigo's dome. But he couldn't. The Kclabs must have added a chemical that locked it in place and made it ultra-sensitive to any disturbance. When the Mhondora yanked it, well, I was in communication with him at the time. That's when I heard the sound."

Ellis stopped and cleared his throat. "Sir, do you know how many decibels that was?"

"The crew that examined his body believes it was something like three hundred," Kwesi said. "A deadly intensity."

"If only the Mhondora had known they'd do something like that," Ellis added. "I bet there was some spell he could have used to get that chip, but by the time he realized it had been sabotaged, it was too late. He was already on the Surface, grasping that thing, manually pulling it out of the keystone."

"It bombarded him and left a ring of color in its place," Otto suddenly interjected.

Kwesi reprimanded him. "What do you know? You've been missing meetings. You weren't even on Toth when the Wilfins arrived!"

"But I do know what I learned from the knowledge stream," Otto said. "And I know what Lileala wrote me in her two letters. She said Swazembians were too focused on aesthetics and that our ability to hear had suffered."

Kwesi leered at Otto. "I don't even know why you're here."

"I'm here because I want the truth! Ever wonder why

massive streaks of colors straddled Chinbedza's body? Go ahead, explain it to me if you can."

Kwesi didn't answer.

"That was the sound we can't hear," Otto said. "What we don't hear can enter our realm in a different form." His eyes began to water. "Just like my Lileala. She's entering another realm in another form I don't understand. She's like the sounds I can't absorb. Vanished."

"Escort him out of here," Kwesi said to Tres, though his voice was softer now.

Tres led Otto out of the room and Kwesi glared at Ellis. "You're despicable. Do you see what you've done? Can you feel it? And for what? You've committed unspeakable acts for nothing!"

"Sir?" Ellis dropped his head.

"Shut up. Dammit. Shut up!" Kwesi balled one fist and rammed it into his left hand. "Dammit," he said again. "Think. I have to think."

"You didn't hear our theory," Rhonda volunteered. "If you don't mind, I'd like to share it?"

Kwesi waited.

"The Wilfin substance seems every bit as powerful as Ellis and Egna 7 suggest," she said. "That means these vibrations can work on any skin, *including* the Kclabs. But we have to... reverse them. They won't require the high octaves that we do. But a *lower* frequency should do it."

"What are you saying?"

"I'm saying that," she paused and paced her words, "I'm saying, sir, that we can use their own weapon against them, and to do that we'll need Ellis's help."

"Are you serious?"

"Yes, sir. Give Ellis a chance to adjust a few of those Mecca-infused chips. Then take them to the Keloid colony and meet the Kclabs on their own turf. Arrest them and tell them their bluff is over. If an overly heightened vibration could kill the Mhondora, then a low vibration can impact a glassy-skinned Kclab."

Kwesi closed his eyes tightly and listened to the fierce beat of his own heart. He rose and faced Ellis and the Wilfin. "We're going to that damn asteroid."

Kwesi furrowed his brow and stared ahead like a madman, barely noticing the dark carpet of space that unrolled in front of him. Hazy images of the dead Mhondora possessed him. He'd betrayed his people. Betrayed the entire Coalition.

Ellis sat next to Kwesi, and that only angered him more. The wretch. Ellis had designed and brought protective gloves and was ensuring they were worn properly when activating the chips.

For a moment, Kwesi had entertained the idea of strapping Ellis to the floor of the spacecraft and making him lie there without food or water for the full seven-and-a-half-hour flight. But the moment he thought of it, he was overcome with shame. He tried instead to focus on the vessel's operating signals and noted that they were preset. Under Ellis's guidance, the Coalition had forged a route for two vessels; the six-passenger craft Kwesi was piloting and a jumbo commuter ship that had enough passenger space to transport the colonists – and Kclab prisoners – to holding areas on Toth.

Kwesi wanted to throttle those Kclab brutes, but it violated Coalition ethics. He tried to calm himself. He exhaled and remembered the Wilfin. That lazy Egna 7 had fallen asleep right before takeoff, and no one felt like lifting an eight-hundred-pound creature into the vessel. Otto was another disappointment. He had shown up at the air strip intoxicated on juniper ale, and Kwesi had refused to let him board. In his disoriented state, Kwesi worried that he would have been a nuisance and disrupt the rescue.

The ship prepared to land and Kwesi tried hard to swallow. He peered out of the window and thought he saw the outline of huge boulders balancing in clouds of gray dust.

"What in the galaxy is this?" he snarled.

Ellis gawked. "Awful!" he said.

Kwesi ignored him. If he could get his dial to work on the asteroid, he'd release a burst of electric currents and handcuff that traitor. Looking around, he knew it wasn't needed. No one would try to escape to this place, a desolate wasteland of rocks and haphazard debris. Kwesi squinted and his eyes sped over half a kilometer of nothing. "Let's go," he said, the first words he'd spoken to Ellis since leaving Toth. The other vessel hadn't landed yet, but Kwesi couldn't wait. "Lileala!" he shouted. "Lileala!"

He began searching for tracks. But the soil was parched, too brittle for footprints. He followed a trail of rock chips and pretended he didn't feel his chest tighten. Then he heard dim echoes and a faint rustle.

"Lileala?" he said. He walked farther, felt the crackling of the ground, and heard the sounds again. "Lileala?" About fifty meters to the left, he spotted the vague silhouette of a woman, draped in a soggy black robe. She was looking up, pointing at something Kwesi couldn't see.

"Lileala!" he shouted again.

The woman turned, as if in a dream, and wailed, "Baba? Baba!!!"

A subtle splash vibrated in Kwesi's ear, and he could see Lileala darting awkwardly across dust. She ran toward him, pressing her heels into the ground, balancing like someone treading a slippery trail. Her head tossed from side to side, avoiding something Kwesi could not see, and her movements were jerky, almost as if she was dodging something on her path. Arms over her head, she appeared to be squeezing through a space so narrow, it put Kwesi in mind of a tangle of tall trees.

Kwesi ran toward her. "Lileala!" he said and scooped her in his arms. She was drenched. On dry land?

"It's you!" he said. "You! Praises to the ancestors! It's really you!"

"I can't believe it. I can't believe... Baba!" She hugged him tightly while Ellis stood to the side, fidgeting with his fingers and staring at the ground. When Lileala finally looked up, Kwesi saw both pain and suspicion in her eyes, and he sensed that she didn't feel comfortable around Ellis.

Ellis looked in her direction, but averted her gaze.

Lileala linked arms with Kwesi. "Baba, the Kclabs, they're not what you think. We're –"

"Relax, Lileala. We know everything and we have a cure of our own." Kwesi pulled her closer to his side. Some of the other colonists had surrounded them, and many were wearing fluffy scarves and sweaters and, for reasons Kwesi couldn't figure, they were soaking wet too.

A man came out from among them and extended a moist hand. "Does this mean we're getting out of here?" he asked.

"This is my Baba," Lileala said to them. "Baba, this is Brian. And yes, we're all going home!" She jumped up and down, then looped both arms around Kwesi again, burying her head in his chest.

"Lileala, we also know something else," Kwesi said. "They caused it. The Kclabs have the cure because they are the ones who caused the disease in the first place."

"They caused it!" Lileala elbowed Brian. "I'm surprised, but not at all shocked. How did they do it? I don't understand."

"We'll talk about that later," Kwesi said. "Right now, we're prepared to capture them and make them pay."

"Capture? But, Baba, we don't battle. Swazembians are peaceful people. Since when would we even consider fighting?"

"Since this – this outrage!" Kwesi's voice was hard.

"So, we're reassessing our tactics? Are we abandoning our code?"

"If we have to." He was firm. "Unfortunately, we've been relying on our orb weapons, and we don't believe they'll work in this atmosphere. So, we brought something better."

Kwesi gestured for Ellis to display the chips. But Ellis was moving his hands like they were old buildings, made of cement and too heavy to raise. When he tried to lift them, they fell back to his sides and his head went with them.

"We have these now," Kwesi said, snatching a couple of chips from Ellis.

"Music chips?"

"No, Mecca chips." Kwesi handed them back to Ellis, while he squeezed his hands into a pair of insulated gloves. "We have a solution, but we'll explain that later too. Right now, we have to get ready for those brutes."

Lileala walked up to Ellis. "I can feel your embarrassment," she said, kindness flowing through her words. "It was you who did this, wasn't it? I sense that you're a Coalition official, but also a traitor. You cooperated with the Kclabs, didn't you?"

Ellis began to shake all over.

"You tried, you and the Kclabs, but you couldn't break me," she said. "This is an awful place, but I found my strength here. So, I'm fine. Everything is fine."

"No, it's not!" Kwesi snapped. "He'll be punished severely for this."

Red streaks of shame flared on Ellis's face.

Tenderly, Lileala raised her hand and placed it on his shoulder. "Punishments aren't the end of the world," she said before looking away.

Kwesi observed his daughter with quiet admiration. There was a strange new wisdom on her countenance mingled with a hint of pride. She brushed her fingers over her scars and through mussed, damp hair. "Excuse us," she said. "We had a rainforest underway."

Kwesi and Ellis turned in every direction but couldn't find a trace of water or trees.

"I guess we all have a lot to explain," Lileala said. "But we have to get out of your way. The Kclabs should be arriving soon."

"Before they get here, we're going to need a larger landing site," Kwesi said. "We have one more ship on the way."

"The same size as yours?" Brian asked.

"No, larger. I took a micro spacecraft. But our allies are in a major vessel."

"There's about seventy meters," Brian said, pointing left. "Over there."

"Thank you," Kwesi said. He directed one of the Sonaguard to stand on the southern periphery and flag Commander Coleman to land on that site. "Tell him to activate his fog barrier to shield his ship, then walk north to find us."

"Right, sir. Got it." The guard left at brisk pace.

"Better get in place quickly," said Brian. "If the Kclabs decide to show up today, it will probably be within the hour."

"I'm staying here beside you, Baba," Lileala said. "If you don't mind, most of us will try to assist, but the others…" She pointed to three colonists who were still scampering about in what Kwesi assumed was their private rainforest. "The others are busy."

Kwesi nodded. "We have it under control."

He watched and waited. Nearly a quarter of a kilometer beyond the rock tower, a gray mist was swelling. The Toth vessel had landed. The crew disembarked and remained in the shadows, shielded by the mist.

Forty-two minutes later, the Kclab vessel began its slow descent, clanging as it forced itself onto the cramped airfield. Lileala saw LaJuped appear like a mystery, as he always did, and dart toward the ship. He'd clearly been hiding from the other colonists.

"Here I am!" he announced. "I'm ready to go!"

He rushed forward and tried to board. But Trieca and Mernestyle, along with another Kclab Lileala didn't recognize, were departing and they shoved him to the side.

"So, is this the one you've been laughing about?" the stranger asked Trieca. She didn't answer. Squinting, she looked over his head at the strange dark fog hovering in the background.

"Yes, Chief Hardy," Mernestyle answered.

LaJuped stepped in front of her. "I don't know who you are," he said to the chief, "but I'm ready."

"Ready for what? Get out of the way," Hardy said. "I'm here to get to the bottom of all that foolish talk from the Rare Girl."

"Who is this?" LaJuped asked Trieca. "I've never seen him."

"Don't worry about it," she said. She tapped Chief Hardy's shoulder. "Yes, this is the one I told you about. He sleeps in our little shed, he and that old woman who helps him. They both report whatever they can dig up on the others."

"Today!" LaJuped called out. "Now that my treatment is over, you promised to drop me off at my homeworld *today*. That was the agreement."

"You didn't hold up your end," Trieca snarled. "You were supposed to let us know everything that was said."

"And I did."

"You didn't tell us how the Rare Girl found out about Golong, did you? All you did was make up some dumb story about visions." Trieca pushed past LaJuped. Then she caught sight of Osiris in his water drenched shirt and gawked. Two more colonists stood beside him, also sopping wet and grinning.

"Make yourself useful," she said to LaJuped. "See if they drained the pond."

LaJuped dashed toward the ship again, but Dlareg and Bertram exited and pushed him out of their way.

"There's a problem, is there?" asked Bertram. "Is something else going on with that Rare Girl nuisance?"

Osiris walked up to Bertram. "Let her be. You can meet with me, today. I don't have any visions, but I have a prediction. You're going to jail."

"What is the meaning of this defiance?" Bertram growled. "And what is that in the background, that, that smoky mist?"

"What mist?" Osiris smirked and, still clutching his cane, swerved his body toward the Toth commuter vessel. "Oh, you must mean that lovely cloak of vapors over there." He turned back and waved as a throng of Coalition members emerged from the fog.

"Swazembians!" Bertram yelled. "Swazembians dare to come here!"

Commander Coleman raced to Kwesi's side and placed one hand on his shoulder. Ten more Coalition members and about a dozen Sonaguard fell in place behind him.

"More than Swazembians," said Coleman, coolly. "Toths and Jemtis, as well."

Another dozen Sonaguards appeared and stood at attention, their uniforms shining like freshly polished silver.

Trieca couldn't peel her eyes away. She stared in between them at Ellis and studied his tired face. She approached and stood before him, Lileala and Kwesi, lifting her hand high enough for a slap.

When she stopped, Lileala immediately realized why. The guards would have confronted her, and a scene like that was beneath her dignity. Lileala studied her dramatic stance. Her bare, lucid neck was unadorned, her long gown crisp. Today, it was stiffer than usual and hung like a crystal bell, held in place by a starch that smelled of potato peel and salt. She looked like Kclab royalty. But when she saw Ellis staring, Lileala could tell her blood was curdling.

"I am Trieca," she said to Kwesi, then looked at Ellis. "And you are the grit of my bowels." She paused to maintain her composure. "Now, what's this all about? Did you come for our patients?"

Mernestyle butt in. "Can't you see that the keloids have withered? That's our doing. But go ahead, take the Rare Girl, take the others. We see you need a lesson, so take them home and the scars will get worse. Just wait."

Kwesi held up a small, round chip that emitted a piercing red light. "Is this what you want us to wait for?" he asked, pausing long enough for Mernestyle to stop rambling. "Is this your point of control?"

Mernestyle gasped and Chief Hardy and Bertram began taking slow steps backwards. Trieca, however, maintained her regal indifference. Haliton stood beside her, seething.

"It's a hoax!" he yelled. "Don't listen."

"You think we'd come all the way here for a hoax?" Kwesi shouted. "Try us, just try us." His arm was still raised, and the bright chip was tucked securely between his index finger and his thumb. But he was talking so fast, he was beginning to gag on the waves of mist wafting toward him, intermingling with the dust. Taking one slow breath at a time, he calmed himself. "This is over." He turned to the crew. "Sonaguard, don't let the Kclabs run. And Toths, return to your ship! For you, this might be a harmful frequency."

"Stop it. Everyone." Trieca was speaking in a mesmerizing tone. "This is not a charade."

A frosty hypnosis descended upon the group, stalling them momentarily in one spot while Trieca reached into a flap on the front of her gown and pulled out a hand-length, tin tube with a button on each side. She sharpened the inflection in her voice. "Prepare for defense. Now!" Ten more Kclabs scrambled out of the spacecraft, including Roloc, his head hung low.

While the Kclabs armed themselves with the devices, Trieca held hers close to her throat, allowing her vocal resonance to slowly build power.

Commander Coleman stuck out his hand, his wrist rigid, palm facing the Kclabs. But his movements were slow, made sluggish by Trieca's peculiar pitch.

"We're not here for a battle, so don't force us," he said, dragging out each word. "Our first plan of action is to talk. Like we're doing now."

The stare Trieca gave Coleman was menacing.

"Do you know how many times we've laughed at you, at your pacts of peace and those damned stupid nap pellet bulbs your Sonaguards carry around?" she cracked. "You're weaklings. We're not like you, here to chat and sniffle. We'll torch you and your spacecrafts, just like we torched Golong."

A noticeable slump made Chief Hardy's shoulders suddenly look like pillows. With a look of bewilderment on his face, he whispered to Trieca.

"Golong? Trieca, how come I didn't know about that? How? When?"

"The unders did it," Trieca answered. "I sent them with Mecca guns to every Golong city. We'll discuss it later."

Still using her power tone, Trieca looked directly at Ellis, lowered the tube, and scoffed. "Did you think we'd stop at chips? That we wouldn't be able to use Mecca for weapons? The chips were just to gain your trust, to make you morons think we were healers." Her head fell back, and her laugh made her entire membraned body jiggle. "And you helped us. Because of you and your amusing betrayal, we learned how to maneuver this serum and manipulate it to an octave that burns and disintegrates matter."

Commander Coleman broke through Trieca's lure and regained full control of his faculties. "If a battle is what you want then that is what you'll get. But tell us one thing. Why torch that planet?"

"It was the only way to hide the attack from your Coalition." Trieca grunted, realizing her vocal trick had now fizzled. "The Mhondora's invisibility spell would only work if the planet was pitch black, darkened with burn. But don't worry, we were merciful. We left one church standing and we herded survivors into cellars. Those cellars are everywhere on Golong, but some kiddies, bless them, were afraid to go down there in the dark. So we left them alone in their homes and instructed them to flee to our outdoor schools at the first hint of fire."

As she spoke, Kwesi furtively positioned the chip in his hand.

"Take one step and you'll regret it," said Trieca. "We'll fire."

"You'll do no such thing," a symphony of voices called out. They were mysterious – a prodigious collective with a depth far greater than Trieca's. Yet they came from one person. Lileala.

Her damp face drying in the sun, Lileala anchored herself in front of the Coalition and spoke out in the impassioned chorus of the Dogon. It poured from her, resounding loudly, conveying the glory of masked dancers rejoicing in villages hidden by the escarpment. All of their collective emotions spouted in a sudden gush that clamored within Lileala's spirit and tumbled through gentle waves of juju magic.

With her body covered in rays of golden light, Lileala raised her arms and summoned the other colonists. Stunned, Brian, Martore and the Wasswa sisters took hesitant steps toward her, and they all joined hands.

She began to hum. A shrill, guttural hum that tickled the air around her and formed faint, concentric circles. Then everything intensified. Like the whistling melodies of the ite irhe clams, Lileala's hums sailed to the west, ballooned above the rubble and skirted beyond the towers of boulders. Soon, Brian, Martore and the sisters joined in, humming as Lileala spoke:

"Breath One: I see the flame and I use it for protection.

"Breath Two: the embers and the ashes will take root.

"Breath Three: Fire am I and as of now, I unleash."

Lileala exhaled, and lassos of light, like spinning golden yarn, swooped around the Kclab weapons and hurled them into the murky pond. Before they could run, the light enveloped them. They screamed, but with each scream, the loops pulsated and tightened and whisked them higher. Whirling and somersaulting, their bodies became trapped inside luminescent ropes that held them thirty meters above the ground. They screeched, pleaded and cursed, but Lileala held on, humming and glowing, unfurling more and more bushels of energy.

Once they were locked tight, she bent over like a broken sapling and gently slipped onto the gravel and dust.

"Lileala!" Kwesi yelled, kneeling down beside her. "Lileala, are you okay?"

But Lileala was in a light coma. She heard Ahonotay encouraging her. She heard Tnomo telling her, *job well done*. And she heard the plaintive calls of ite irhe prodding her to come out of her comatose state and enter a deep slumber.

And so she did. Drained, Lileala fell asleep with the Kclabs suspended in their air prisons.

13

"Peace is our highest principle."
– Oath of the Sonaguard

Kwesi scooped Lileala up from the ground and stood.

"She's okay!" he yelled behind him. Then he walked beneath the luminous hives and carried her to the small passenger spacecraft. A few minutes later, he stepped out and glanced skyward. The captives were still up there, vibrating like living kites.

"Lileala's sound asleep, everyone," he announced. "But don't ask me what happened. Before she left, she told me she was clairvoyant. My best guess is that it has evolved into something far beyond trances and telepathy."

"Are they asleep too?" one of the Sonaguards asked, looking up. "They've gotten awfully quiet. Maybe we can grab the tails of those coils and pull them down."

"Good idea," Chairman Dane said. "Everyone, come on. But unfurl slowly so they don't escape."

"What a sight," Commander Coleman said. "If I hadn't seen this with my own eyes, I wouldn't believe it. But yanking them down should be easy."

"Me!" Trieca yelled. "Come over here and yank me down immediately."

"She's talking," Dane said. "I don't know how they can speak while all squished up like that."

"Get me down from here," Trieca demanded.

Dane gave it a try, but when he touched the tail of the light vortex that held Trieca captive, his hand passed through it.

"What are we thinking?" he said. "It's not tangible."

Immediately, Trieca floated to the ground, landing gently as the cords around her dissolved. She ran for the Kclab ship and Dane chased her on foot and held one of her arms behind her back.

"Just swipe your hands through the faint sparks at the bottom of the funnels," he yelled. "Apparently, that's all we need to do to bring them down." While Trieca kicked and protested, he shouted to Kwesi. "Get ready. More are coming down and I think we're going to need your device."

Kwesi lifted his arm. "All of you with lower volumes of melanin rush back to your ship, please. Remember we agreed, this might be a risk."

The Toths fled, all but Commander Coleman. "I'm activated," he said. "My M-S-T is in a heightened phase."

"Are you sure?" Kwesi whispered. "The agreement was that Toths would help lock prisoners in place in the back of their ship. I'm concerned about your safety. Swazembians won't hear what I'm about to release." Coleman didn't budge. With closed eyes, he entered into a deep phase of M-S-T and his skin darkened. Kwesi waited until the other Toths were at a safe range. Then, he shouted: "Now!"

On command, Sonaguards yanked the Kclabs from their spools of light. When they all had touched the ground, dazed, Kwesi waved the chip and pressed. Haliton's mouth flung open, and his skeletal form twitched. Trieca, who was free from Dane's grip, pulled the flaps of her collar up over the lower half of her face. With everyone's attention on the other Kclabs plummeting from the sky, a flinching Trieca stiffly braved the steaming currents coursing through her body and made a determined beeline for the Kclab ship. Hardy, Mernestyle and the remaining Kclabs ran amok, shrieking and sticking fingers into their ears.

Coleman covered an ear and held his stomach. "Uuuugh! Uuuuugh! No! No!"

Kwesi stopped pressing the chip. "My word, man, I'm sorry. Are you okay?"

Coleman doubled over, barely able to speak.

"Run back to the ship," Kwesi said. "Sonaguard, hurry! Help him back to the ship!"

"I'm staying," he said, feebly. "Press chip. Again."

"Are you crazy?" Kwesi yelled. "Do you want to end up like Mhondora Chinbedza?"

"I can take it. Press!"

"Go," urged Kwesi. "You were wrong. You can't take this. Go!"

Zizi, one of the Swazembian Sonaguards accompanying the mission, ran to his side and tried to assist. "I can't," Coleman said, panting. A mahogany tint drained from his complexion as he lost the ability to maintain M-S-T. He dropped to his knees.

"They're getting away," Kwesi said, feeling beaten. The Kclabs were scurrying toward their vessel, but if he aimed the chip, he risked injuring his closest ally and friend.

"Sonaguards, quick," he shouted. "Fire your pellets."

"They're ineffective here, just like we explained before we left," one of them yelled back.

"See if you can emit a few anyway, just to buy us more time," Kwesi commanded. "Do something!"

"Let me try," Zizi shouted. She stepped as close to the Kclabs as she could and, without another word, tossed a handful of gleaming multi-colored wads. Several landed on Dlareg's forehead and neck, wormed their way downward and burned through his high-collar robe, crackling and smoking as it scorched his skin. He howled and keeled over.

"Now," Zizi yelled. "The rest of you, back away from that ship. I have more of these, hundreds more. I don't want to use them, but I will."

Bertram watched Dlareg whimpering, rolling on the ground

and massaging his chest. "Come on," he barked. "Do what she says."

The Kclabs squealed and pulled the bell-bottomed sleeves of their robes over their faces to shield them from Dlareg's noxious odor. He struggled to his feet, coughing and they fanned their noses, trying their best to avoid him as the crew members herded them across the dust and into the waiting Toth vessel.

Kwesi lingered behind. "Zizi, what did you just do?"

"I'm not sure sir, but it worked, least for now. Once we imprison them, we can come up with another plan."

"Okay," said Kwesi. "And?"

"Sir?"

"Zizi, what was that object?"

"Nothing special, sir. You didn't need me; I'm just an apprentice."

Kwesi said nothing and waited for her to keep talking.

She squirmed under Kwesi's glare. "I was simply trying to make sure they didn't get away. And you know what my suggestion is now? Let's corral the Kclabs into a separate chamber, perhaps an underground enclosure on Toth. In there, no one else will be affected by the frequency. You can take the Mecca-filled chips and turn them down several octaves. I bet they'll tell you anything you need to know."

"Zizi!" Kwesi said, looking her directly in her eyes.

"Yes, Baba."

"Answer me," he commanded.

"There's not much to say, sir. I knew Kclabs had thin skin, more like a membrane, really, and I also understood that they could stand very little physical pain."

"Zizi, I'm well aware of Kclab physiology. But I'm not fully aware of what just transpired."

"Well, sir. That was just some little gizmo I picked up on Toth. Some children threw a gummy wad at me when I was on my way to our last meeting. It burned me. Under the sun, the wound healed. Then the wad almost became a liquid. I don't know how to describe it, but it was electric, almost, like a current. I thought it was odd, so I saved it. After it turned gummy again, I had it examined by some Pineal Crew members and had them make some copies so I could study them further."

"Why wasn't I apprised of these weapons?"

"Weapons? Baba, they're broken music chips. No Wilfin serum, nothing, just plain music chips that were melted by some children on Toth. They play with them that way, sting people with them. It hardly seemed worth mentioning… Until now."

Kwesi was silent a moment. "I'm impressed. Let me take a look at them."

"Them?"

"Yes. The others in your possession. The hundreds?"

"That was a bluff," she said sheepishly. "I only had one pocket full."

"You mean you saved the mission with a clump of music chips?"

"I didn't know if it would work." Zizi remained at attention, awaiting another command. Instead, Kwesi tucked one arm into hers and led her toward the remaining colonists, still frolicking in some imaginary oasis. They seemed so taken by what they were seeing and feeling. It was as if they were tossing pebbles into creeks that weren't there and trying to fill their hands with invisible raindrops. Whatever surrounded them had all their attention, leaving them little time to notice the chaotic arrest of the Kclabs. Kwesi heard one of them yell out a comment about a "rushing waterfall" and flower blossoms that "were flapping about in the breeze." He saw a young boy in the air, apparently climbing something. A tree? He kept watching while the others laughed and skipped over a patch of ground. A mud puddle, perhaps?

"Come on, Zizi. Let's round them up and take them home." Kwesi said.

14

"Beauty is when gratitude makes love to the eyes."
– Lileala Walata Sundiata

A quiet rain fell over the sea and drizzled into the neon mists. Lileala knew it was happening, just as she always did. But it was more than a raw feeling this time. It came as a vision. Vivid sparks flitted across her mind, and she wondered, if she tried hard enough, if she could use trinity breath to slow the rapid sail of colors and, perhaps, diffuse their radiation. But she would practice that much later, after all the welcome home ceremonies had ended.

Six days ago, she returned to Boundary Circle, a bedraggled mess. The frightful sight of her caused Mama Xhosi to panic, and Lileala, though not upset about her appearance, had obliged when the High Host sent three Aspirants to her quarters to fuss with her hair and apply Euc skin creams.

Lileala had agreed to a couple of hours, but after only one she tired and sent them on their way. Rest was her first priority, and she did that in the privacy of her dwelling for three days straight.

Now, she had to calm her nerves and prepare to stand before the masses and speak. In preparation, the Pineal Crew had erected a blazing welcome home banner that arched high above the main stage of The Great Hall. From the banner, palm-sized holograms of Lileala were being transmitted into the hall, appearing and disappearing throughout the crowd.

"Sundiata!" the crowd shouted. "Lileala Sundiata!"

From the quiet of her sitting area, Lileala could hear the shouts rippling along Mampong Avenue and the din of an Earth hymn bellowing in the background:

"We are people of the mighty, mighty people of the sun."

The music rang out loudly bathing the avenue in sound that was so bawdy it broke Lileala's concentration. The song was a catchy melody by her favorite ancestral band, Earth, Wind and Fire.

"That's a lot of commotion," she told her elder Ma. "Don't you think?"

Fanta reacted by wiping a tear from her cheek and embracing her daughter for what seemed like the fifth time in one day. Since her return, Fanta had been hovering over Lileala, rushing back and forth between her own quarters and her daughter's adjoining compartment, bringing hot millet patties, cassava biscuits and fresh fruit.

"You haven't had a decent meal in over a month," she said. "Eat. Eat!"

Lileala reached for a date that had been placed on a small accent table and regarded her elder Ma, pleased that the pride in her smile stood out more than her sloped shoulders.

"But, Ma, you didn't answer," she said. "Don't you think they're overdoing it?"

More pride swelled on Fanta's countenance. "No. Not at all," she said. "Nothing can make up for all that you have endured."

Without another word, Fanta left then hurried back with four gowns, all of them courtesy of Mama Xhosi. Quickly, Lileala covered her face with her hands, hoping her elder Ma wouldn't notice the laughter in her eyes.

"Thank you but I need to be alone now, Ma," she said. "Before I face all of Swazembi, I need to collect my thoughts."

The music continued:

"To your own self find the answer. Mighty people of the sun."

The words rang in Lileala's ear, and she rolled her head

in a circle, stretching her shoulders and neck. It wasn't the tiredness that bothered her, for she'd soon be over that. But what about the Swazembi people? Were they really ready to hear what she had to say?

The word was out that she would be on stage at Point Six. She'd heard from her elder Ma that nearly everyone, along with an entire crew of Sonaguards, was below the Surface, crammed on the main level of the plaza in the upper ramps and aisles of The Great Hall.

They began arriving the night before and, by morning, the hall was at capacity. Collapsible benches and vendor tables that transformed into chairs flowed from the courtyard through the lower walkways of The Outer Ring and in front of the revolving shops and boutiques. Boundary Circle residents were guaranteed first pick of the one hundred and seventeen thousand seats, but Swazembians from Togu Ta City East and the outlying villages and towns in Gwembia were also welcome, even though it meant sitting on straw floor mats, squatting or simply leaning against limestone pillars. Some Boundary Circle compartment owners had even agreed to take in boarders for a night, but since the ban on tourism had not yet been lifted, there was plenty of space in the hotels in The Outer Ring.

"– Sundiata, Lileala Walata Sundiata –" the crowd repeated.

Her name swam in her ears and made her forget what she was writing. Without the quiet and semi-solitude of the barren asteroid, it was actually harder to think. Deciding that maybe a handwritten speech wasn't such a good idea after all, Lileala dropped it, smiling as page after page fluttered to her crystal floor. There was no need to ponder ideas or rehearse lines. She'd speak extemporaneously, nothing prepared. The audience would hear of her experience straight from her heart. She relaxed. Her remarks would be easier than other burdens that lay ahead and much simpler than the announcement she was about to make to Mama Xhosi. She had to let her know that after a forty-one-year wait, Swazembi was to lose another Rare Indigo. No matter how gracefully Lileala delivered the news or how carefully she weighed her words, she figured Mama Xhosi would be crushed. She dreaded telling her, though she had to do it. But how? How would she prepare Mama Xhosi for the inevitable? At that instant, Mama Xhosi appeared on her dial without being summoned. She seemed flustered and Lileala recognized a somberness in her demeanor that hadn't been there earlier. Clearly, Mama Xhosi was dealing with some inner conflict.

"Lileala, you need to know this now," she said, getting right to the point. "You are no longer the Rare Indigo. The Uluri and I have discussed it and we're sure you'll understand. We asked The Nobility to provide you with a different opportunity. Go to the Grace Chapel and you will see."

Lileala hid her shock... and her joy. *What made Mama Xhosi realize she no longer wanted her title?*

"But Mama," she said. "The ceremony is in two hours. Why would I go to the Grace Chapel?"

"You'll report there first," Mama Xhosi explained. "The Nobility and The Uluri will be waiting."

She vanished, and Lileala wanted to shout. What a relief! She checked the time on her dial and began dressing for the upcoming events. Fanta hovered again, and Lileala requested her help clipping a beaded sash over her shoulders and dabbing makeup around her eyes.

Outside her sphere, the crowd was smaller and the noise had waned. Surrounded by four Sonaguards, she exited quickly, glad that many of the revelers apparently had seated themselves around the auditorium stage. The few who remained near her dwelling only got a slight glimpse of the former Rare Indigo, swaddled in luminous fabric and shielded by the guards. She might have made it all the way to the chapel without being interrupted if a trembling voice hadn't trailed behind her, pleading with her to stop.

"Excuse me, please slow down a minute," a woman begged. "Please. I've been waiting a long time."

Lileala peeked between the shoulders of two guards and instructed them to pause. The Indigo Aspirant, Issa, approached, and the expression on her face was humbler than Lileala had ever seen it. "It's okay," Lileala said to the guards. "Let me talk to her."

"Waves of joy," Issa said. "Allow me to welcome you home and share feelings that have been heavy on my heart. When I heard of your journey, I felt nothing but sadness." She held out her hands, then clasped them in front of her waist. "This, I must do. It is tradition, you see. Before moving to Centerfree, my family lived in Mbaria. In the village, we use the hand gesture to show our emotions. This is my way of seeking forgiveness."

"Waves of Grace," Lileala said. "But how did you know it was me? I was hidden by guards?"

Issa blushed and a river of blue brightened her cheeks. "My dearest Indigo," she said. "All Aspirants know a Shimmer when we see one. That part of you can't be hidden. Your glow remains strong."

"Thank you for the compliment," Lileala said. "But now I have to hurry to an event."

Issa still stood in Lileala's way. "Lileala, one last thing. When I shared your pain, I never wished for it to deepen. Never. On the honor of The Grace, I could never delight in such a hardship."

"You're forgiven, but please, now I have to go."

Issa took a step to the side and Lileala had a brief chill that made her wonder if the Centerfree Aspirant was sincere or merely putting on a show. She dismissed it and continued on with the guards, weaving around the outskirts of Great Hall marketplace and arriving at the Grace Chapel just in time for her first event. The minute she walked in, there was applause. All thirteen of The Uluri rose from their seats and Lileala was moved to see Ataba Malik beside them, beaming as if this was his proudest moment. He hugged Lileala and walked to the front of the chapel.

"Our young Indigo has amazed me, amazed us all," he said.

"But I will be brief." He turned toward Lileala. "Your path has taken you places none of us have been, and you have moved beyond your previous status. We're holding this gathering to commend you and give you our blessing as you undertake your new role."

"What new role?" Lileala asked.

"It's not our place to reveal that yet," Ataba Malik said. "That announcement will take place on stage for all of Swazembi to hear. For now, we want to congratulate you personally, young one, and also give you the honor of helping us select your replacement. We don't want to invest time in starting over. We're going to elevate another Aspirant, possibly, Issa Ashanti, the one next in line.

"Have a seat up front and think about it," he added.

"Oh, I don't need to think," Lileala answered. "For my replacement, I choose Yemisi Itefayo. I still recall how kind she was to me when I began my ordeal. She delivered Euc to me and wouldn't leave until I cracked the door to my sphere to let her see I was okay."

Lileala paused and reflected on Issa's apology. Was it real? Or was she angling for a recommendation?

She continued: "Issa was my chief competitor, and if you wish to pass the title to her, then I respect your decision. But I want to suggest that you at least consider Yemisi as well. Please don't focus solely on the physical. There are many Aspirants who are alluring but also have hearts seared with gold."

While Lileala made her request, she noticed Cherry sitting in the farthest pew of the chapel, nodding her head in agreement. Cherry sat alone and Lileala could tell she was trying to be discrete, but her concern was obvious to Lileala. She detected her glances skipping across her forehead and sliding over the glint of Shimmer on her cheeks. She took in a flame breath and sparkled a little more, just for Cherry's sake. She knew that's what everyone was waiting for. That, and to hear her story. She walked over to Cherry and gave her a hug.

"I'm still readjusting," she said. "I'm not even sure I'm used to being back."

"The other surroundings will be the crowd in your mind for a while. Ye, you will not be able to scare them off," Cherry said. "Surely, they will leave when it is time."

"Yes, I know. It's just that everything is happening so fast," Lileala said. She and Cherry embraced once more and strolled out of the chapel.

An hour later, the Sonaguards escorted Lileala through two wide double doors leading up the stairs to the side entrance of the auditorium stage. Mama Xhosi was already there, and in her classic, aloof manner, the Aspirant High Host gave Lileala a brisk pat on the hand and strutted onto the stage. Before thousands of anxious Swazembians, she poured fig wine into a large clay pot of soil and called out the names of seven ancestors.

"Pouring libations is one of our most sacred traditions. Now, we offer it to the Dogon ancestors introduced to us by Lileala Sundiata," she announced. "We will proudly restore the old ways that have been denied us for far too long."

In between Mama Xhosi's words, Lileala heard the repetitive thump of drums. Her heartbeat quickened and she fastened her gaze on the second tier of the hall. Someone was peering out from a peep hole of an aluminum ball that was almost as large as a mini spacecraft. It drifted over an upper breezeway, wavered beneath the ceiling, then descended slowly, looming several meters above the stage. Its flimsy aluminum flaps peeled open, and dozens of drumming dancers leaped out, holding beaded gourds and large, talking drums. Pounding out ferocious beats, they spun across the stage, gyrating in unison. The audience roared:

"– Sundiata Lileala Walata Sundiata Lileala –"

When they heard the drumming and the chants, Swazembians began spilling out of the second level of The Outer Ring globe havens. Some had to jump onto fast-moving automated floors and hurry onto a lift that would get them back to ground level.

The experience was a first for many of the rural folk, particularly the aged ones from Mbaria who had never set foot inside a wall shuttle or eaten a meal in a twirling restaurant.

Lileala stood in the stairwell, imagining what the villagers might say when they returned to their communities awestruck by such oddities. With the drummers still pounding and the crowd's chants growing louder, Lileala's forebears, Fanta and Kwesi, arrived and accompanied their daughter. Fanta's head was wrapped in a bundle of decorative cloth and her eyes had shed their tired appearance. She waited beside Lileala, while Kwesi, draped in a shawl of clashing colors, moved ahead and took center stage.

"The first thing I want you to know is that you don't have to worry about the Kclabs," Kwesi said, then paused while the audience clapped. "It's true that they caused the damage they claimed to be curing. But their security team and overseers are in prisons on Toth, and the Pineal Crew has obtained the secret to their Mecca serum. Questions are still circulating, and I have answered many of them, including a few about my daughter, about the unusual powers she has developed. Today, she's here to speak for herself."

The crowd applauded wildly.

"As you know, my Lileala was handpicked to become the next Rare Indigo. That was a decision made decades ago when she was still emerging as an Aspirant. Well, the Grace of the Ancestors has a way of making its own decisions. I suppose that is exactly what happened in this case. Lileala has decided to renounce the title of Rare Indigo. However, the Aspirant selection process will not start anew. The High Host Xhosi has just revealed to me that one of the seventeen current Aspirants will be named in time for the Eclipse Ceremony.

"Meanwhile, both The Uluri and The Nobility have decided that Lileala will take Baba Chinbedza's place as Mhondora, seer of the highest order. She is the first woman, and the youngest to ever hold such a position."

Cheers and shrieks filled the hall and turned into thunderous chants: "Ma Mhondora! Ma Mhondora!"

Amidst the noise, Kwesi and Fanta left the stage and Lileala placed both hands on her chest, trying to slow her breath and mask the fact that she was overwhelmed.

The next Mhondora?

She strode before the audience, and tried to pretend she wasn't shocked. If she was to be Mhondora, she had to learn to think fast and project confidence and a strong will. The audience was enthralled and nearly everyone was waving optic strips. Lileala moved to the fringe of the stage and stood still, allowing them a full view of her attire.

She wore a veil over her face, a sheath of transparent lilac and green. A kente cloth garment of the same colors hugged her bodice then cascaded into a waterfall of floor-length ruffles.

"This is a fresh beginning for me, and probably one of the most precious moments of my life," she said softly, letting the veil slip off her face and onto her shoulders. Lileala's skin was flawless, without a trace of a blemish. As she looked over the crowd, she went into a full Shimmer to display her passion. "It's wonderful to be back, but also bittersweet. The last time I stood in this hall, I was trembling, crying like a minor-child, worried that my skin was forever marred."

She paused and sighed for emphasis. "How much I had to learn. And if I had known then how tough the days ahead would be, perhaps I wouldn't have taken the steps that led me down that road of horrors. Perhaps I would have stayed here and lived with the disease. Perhaps I would not be standing before you now."

Murmurs rose and fell and Lileala proceeded. "In the colony, I slept in caves. I consumed offensive powders for meals. I was ridiculed and I lived in darkness and deprivation. Yet, I also found truth. I retreated to a place where I couldn't muster my regenerative melanin, a place where I would ache and moan from the sensation of physical discomfort. Not momentary pain. Elongated pain. The kind that extends itself into the long night. And in that retreat, I learned something about our past. The past that our ancestors on Earth survived. And yes, those melanin bearers of Earth, despite what you were taught, are indeed our ancestors."

Lileala stared into the audience. "We've been denied that knowledge for too long, and because of it, our history was nearly erased, just like our melanin-bearing ancestors. For them, a time came when their knowledge sources, binders of papers called books, were denied to them. Critical facts and truths were called theories and then erased.

"So, I stand before you declaring that the ancients of Earth are a part of our heritage, and we have risen to where we are because of their journey. We have much to understand about them. On that galaxy-forsaken asteroid, I realized that we can give to those of the past just as we give to the present and the future. We can reach anyone at any point of their existence. Time is only energy. We use that energy, don't we? In our trinity breath, we Indigos see fire and absorb it for our Shimmer. I demand that the spiritual avenues created by this breath be used to send hope to our ancestors."

She paused again, pacing herself, searching for just the right words. "As the new Mhondora, I will spread the Euc more generously, and I won't rest until all Swazembians of age are taught the flame breath walk, but not just for making the skin shine. It will be redirected to develop skills, and, most importantly, to forge a connection to the past. The ancestors aid us. We are here because of them.

"My challenge as Mhondora, is to encourage all of you to learn the truth. We are the direct descendants of an Earth tribe, the visionary Dogon people, who found an unknown star and learned from the beings who lived there, on Po Tolo. The inhabitants hold the knowledge of our early beginnings. I will continue to communicate with them and share all I learn with you."

She stopped and waited. "As we open our minds to the old, we must open it to the new."

Lileala raised one hand and waved it in front of her. "Look around you, and please, do not be upset," she said. The banner above the stage stopped releasing floating holograms of Lileala and replaced them with a grim looking face of someone whose head was covered with clear membrane instead of skin. As the face drifted through the crowd, people backed out of its way. After a brief pause, there were several shouts.

"A Kclab!"

"A Kclab! I'm sure of it."

"Yes, he is a Kclab." Lileala waited, then raised her hand again in a gesture of silence. "Be patient, please. I want you to get used to this face. This is Roloc. He is a Kclab, but he is not to be feared. While I was in the colony, he was benevolent, and it is because of him that I am making the most outrageous proposal you will hear today.

"Roloc is in a holding cell on Toth with the others. But he is to be treated for a medical condition and released. He will live on Toth, and then he may be allowed to visit Swazembi's Outer Ring. Roloc's integration, and our acceptance of him, will mark the beginning of an experimental Kclaben entry to the Coalition."

The audience was silent.

Lileala went on, "As I prepare for my new life, I hope to study under the former Rare Indigo, the advanced clairvoyant, Ahonotay. I will seek out her counsel and wisdom for guidance as I take my first steps as the Mhondora." Lileala paused and smiled. "Please support me in this new undertaking."

Everyone seated stood up and clapped while Lileala hurried down from the platform, her heart racing, her hands tingling. She had spotted Otto standing near the front of the crowd, waiting for her. With several Sonaguards on each side, she made her way through the crush of people and walked toward him, taking slow, deep breaths.

Otto stared through her, as if she wasn't really there.

"Well, let me break the silence," Lileala said. "How are you?"

"I'm much better now that you're back, Lileala," he said. "I'm sorry I didn't come to meet you after your release. I started to, but under the circumstances, I –"

"Otto, don't explain. I didn't expect you to be there, at least not... I just didn't expect you to go through all that."

"I suppose I was respecting your wishes," he said somberly.

"And adjusting."

"Adjusting?"

"My clairvoyance, my trances, all the changes you couldn't..." She trailed off.

"Yes," Otto blurted. "And adjusting." He glanced at the ground and cleared his throat. "I'm ashamed, though. I guess I just lost it, but I'm better now. Just like you, better."

"We're survivors, you and me."

Otto didn't answer. The Sonaguards were close, forming a chain around the two of them, trying to control the crowd. Lileala assumed they were making him uncomfortable. She watched him, ached with him. He had become so insecure, lost so much confidence. He didn't seem anything like the man she thought she knew so well.

"Otto," she said. "You received my letters?" She gave him an anxious look.

Otto swallowed. "I did and well... that was an overwhelming experience, an awful thing you went through."

"I made out okay."

"Yes, you did. That was quite a speech you just gave. You really are – have become – quite a person." He looked down.

"Thank you."

"I really mean that. It was a brilliant speech."

"We'll talk about it sometime," Lileala said.

"Lileala?" Otto's face was limp, and he was shifting from leg to leg.

"Yes?"

"Are you certain? Are you really certain about your

decision? I mean, do you really want to erase what we have?"

She paused, before correcting him. "Had."

Otto lowered his gaze again and Lileala leaned over to hug him.

"I still love you, but we're too different now, don't you see? I was gone less than six weeks, but it felt like years. I'm not the same person. I can never be that person again."

He said nothing and avoided looking at her. Lileala squeezed him tighter. "I had been changing all along. Before I left, I was hearing whispers, thinking in ways that didn't fit the kind of life I was expected to lead. I was just too cowardly to tell you way back then."

Otto sighed. "Maybe it was my fault too. Maybe I was too much of a coward to accept it."

"We'll talk later, I promise." She turned to walk away, her eyes watery. She didn't want him to see her cry.

"Lileala?" he said again.

"Yes." She wiped her eyes with the backs of her hands and turned to face him.

"Believe and proceed," he said. "That's what you told me, and I'm going to think of you whenever I repeat it."

"Sure, Otto," Lileala said and moved on. She was fighting the urge to change her mind. She glanced at the Sonaguards marching alongside her, barking out orders. Lileala waved to the masses surrounding her. They reminded of her of minor school children in a playfield, scrambling and shouting. The chief guards turned into a tight chain and were doing their best to keep them under control.

"Give her more room," they said. "Please give her more room." They marched along and Lileala daydreamed.

"What's next?" she asked.

"What?" one of the Sonaguards replied.

"Oh, nothing," Lileala said. "Just thinking out loud. Tell me, that lift ahead, in the western corner of the courtyard, it looks empty. Is it?"

"Yes, it certainly is."

"Then, since it's free, I'm wondering if you can walk me there and let me ride to The Sweep station by myself?"

"Certainly, Ma Mhondora." The guard turned to the crowd. "Move back and give her some space."

The people swarmed as they chanted, "Lileala Sundiata! Mama Indigo Mhondora!" But the guards kept them from accompanying her onto the lift. She hurried inside and sped off.

A few moments later, she reached a Sweep platform and leaned into the inviting winds. She relaxed, smiling like it was her first time ever being transported by the brisk currents, her first time hearing that subtle swoosh. She was free now. Her chains had been broken. As the tangle of energy absorbed her, she reached into her sleeve and pulled out a square of molasses that she had tucked inside the cuff. She unwrapped it and swirled it around her tongue, savoring the sweetness. The candy stuck to the roof of her mouth, and she laughed.

"Szewa," she said out loud. "Everything is now."

She sank deeper into the currents and soared toward the Surface.

ACKNOWLEDGMENTS

First and foremost, I thank the friends I like to call "The Three Jans," my besties – Janice Joseph, Janenetta Toles and Janice Hayes Kyser. There were times when your faith and encouragement were the fuel that kept me going.

I also want to give a big shout out to the crew I have adopted as my West Coast family, Geraldine, Madeline, Diane and Paula Edwards. What would I have done without your love and support over the years?

As for inspiration, the thanks go to Melvin Peters (aka "Pete"), the professor who opened my eyes to a wide realm of black writers, and Malik Yakini, the first person to introduce me to the connection between color and sound.

On that note (pun intended) I also acknowledge the Rotary Foundation International for the travel fellowship that exposed me to the wonders of Africa.

Then there's Herminia Alfred, a true friend indeed, my meticulous agent, Nikki Terpilowski of Holloway Literary and my readers, Val Overton, Colette Sewell and Jerome Andre Watson.

Further, I extend a very special from-the-bottom-of-my-heart appreciation to the visionary staff of Angry Robot. You guys are the best! Gemma Creffield and Eleanor Teasdale, thank you for encouraging me to dig deeper. Your insights were the sparks that added clarity to the manuscript.

And finally, I thank the Dogon tribe of Mali for their

steadfast spiritual awareness and an understanding of the cosmos that staggers the imagination. I have never met any of you. However, I'm convinced that your direct forefathers and all of our West African ancestors appointed me to tell this story. I can only hope that I did it justice. Asante Sana!

GLOSSARY

Ataba – Teacher

Aswaka – Sphere shaped condominium towers for the wealthy

Baba – Father

The Bagoe River – A river flowing through Gwembia

Boundary Circle – The underground capital city on Swazembi that does not allow tourists

Centerfree – Swazembi's art district and a residential community for the non-wealthy

The Coalition – A organization representing twenty-two neighboring planets, including Swazembi

The Dogon People – A non-fictional tribe in Mali, West Africa

The Drifts – Mists of electromagnetic colors that drift across the planet's surface

Elder Ma – Mother

Euc – Powders used to protect and nourish the skin

The Grace – Symbolic reference to the graciousness of the ancestral gods/deities of the Swazembi

The Grand Rising – A cluster of shining structures that serve as the dwelling place, special gathering site and knowledge chamber for The Nobility, The Uluri and the Mhondora

Gwembia – A rural region in the province of Otuzuweland with farms, bungalows and an agricultural university

Indigo Aspirant – Female Swazembians who are striving to be named the Rare Indigo or become part of her court

The Inekoteth – Cryptic messages that clairvoyants in a trance can send or receive to and from the ancestors

ite irhe – Giant whistling clams

Jemti – A Coalition world

The Kclabs – A translucent species that develops a cure for a skin disease affecting people of color

Knowledge Chamber & Knowledge Stream – Educational system that provides data and information via an automated voice or words that flow through a stream of air

Mamadou Park – A large park on The Outer Ring filled with gum trees

Mampong Avenue – A lane of sphere communities for upper middle-income residents

Mbaria – A village in Gwembia

Mecca – A healing serum created by the Kclabs

The Mhondora – Swazembi's highest-ranking clairvoyant

Mirth – An alcoholic beverage made from fermented berries

M-S-T – (Mental Self Tan) A tanning process that occurs when the tanner relies on mental strength to hold deep concentration

The Nobility – Rulers of Swazembi

The Outer Ring – Three rings of spinning hotels, dance havens and restaurants in Swazembi's underground

Otuzuweland – A province in Swazembi consisting of towns, villages, farms and rural homesteads

Po Tolo – The star Sirius B that was originally discovered by the Dogon Tribe

Rare Indigo – A regal tourist attraction and symbolic dignitary whose poise and sparkling black skin earn her the status of the most beautiful woman in the galaxy

The Scientific Pineal Crew – Team of scientists that conduct research, build technological devices and explore the ruins of the late Earth

Scuffs – Furry, toothless critters that live in Mamadou park

The Sea of Vapors – A sea of colored mists

Shimmer – A visible glow produced by Swazembian women with blue-black skin

The Sonaguard – The official guards of Swazembi and Toth

The Surface – A tract of land and tourist attraction of floating colors in the Sangha province above Swazembi's underground community

Swazembi – A culturally ambiguous planet believed to have been influenced by Africa

The Sweep – An energy force of swarming winds that transport passengers around Swazembi's resort areas on The Outer Ring

Tawny Dramatic – Term used for Swazembian woman with golden or copper complexions

T.E.T. (Tossing Electronic Tops) – A popular spectator sport on Swazembi and its neighboring planets

Toth – A Coalition world and chief ally of Swazembi

Togu Ta City East – A semi-industrial Otuzuweland border town with manufacturing plants and a trade school

Togu Ta City West – An upscale port city with an intergalactic air base and a transit station on the edge of the Sangha province

Trinity Breath – A special breathing and meditation technique that makes the skin Shimmer

Twilights – Scuffs that grow feathers and fly after exposure to the radiation on the Surface

The Uluri – A clandestine governing body that enforces moral codes of conduct on Swazembi

Unders – Impoverished workers on the Kclab planet

Vandiagara Cliffs – A cliffside village in Otuzuweland

The Wilfins – Bulbous eel-like creatures that are nearly extinct

Wmet – Old communication device